nut plc 08

 P9-CEG-259

The Bee's Kiss

THE BEE'S KISS

Barbara Cleverly

CARROLL & GRAF PUBLISHERS
New York

For my three literary graces:

Juliet Burton   Krystyna Green   Imogen Olsen

Carroll & Graf Publishers
An imprint of Avalon Publishing Group, Inc.
245 W. 17th Street
11th Floor
New York NY 10011-5300
www.carrollandgraf.com

AVALON
publishing group incorporated

First published in the UK by Constable,
an imprint of Constable & Robinson Ltd 2005

First Carroll & Graf edition 2006

ISBN 13: 978-0-78671-736-1
ISBN 10: 0-7867-1736-X

Printed and bound in the United States of America

Chapter One

'I do all my thinking in the car nowadays. And why? Because, whatever I do or say, I can't get away from blasted Audrey!'

A flash of resentment expressed itself in a sharp stab on the accelerator and the red Chrysler two-seater swept smoothly onwards over the Hog's Back and on to London.

'Eight years ago she was innocent, pliable, uninventive but co-operative. And now? Sycophantic, eager to please but having no longer the power of pleasing. She'll have to go! And this time I shan't relent no matter how many damp handkerchiefs she waves before my face. She's completely suffocating me. I should have left her where I found her – second from the right in the chorus of *Florodora*.

'It was a good idea, throwing my luggage in the back and just leaving. I certainly needed to get away, to get away to London . . . to get away from cosy domesticity in the country to the supple hospitality extended by the Ritz. "Your usual suite?" I like that! I like the purring familiar voice, confidential and knowing, so calming in all this storm and stress. But now – what to look forward to? A dreary evening. Cousin Alfred's fiftieth birthday party. A roomful of people I hardly know. A roomful of dull nieces and nephews. But – you never know your luck! That little girl who's just got herself engaged to the appalling Monty – she might be quite promising. Might be distinctly promising! I can remember everything about her except her name. Jennifer? Jasmine? Sure it began with a J . . . Joanna! Got it! Black hair in a fashionable bob, slender figure. Slanting green eyes. Naughty and knowing green eyes perhaps? I'm sure I encountered a look of complicity when we met. And any girl cultivated by that louche lounge lizard Montagu Mathurin is bound to have reached a certain level of initiation into the ways of the world. An initiation acquired in an upper room at the Café Royal, perhaps. What can she see in him? Much too good for him – she's bound to have realized by now. It mightn't be such a bad evening after all!'

Detective Sergeant William Armitage's handsome features contorted briefly in an attempt to stifle a sigh, or was it a yawn? Overtime was always tedious but really, he felt – and resented the feeling – that he was out of place here. He'd rather have been on duty at the dog track. Better still, he could have taken the day off and gone to Wembley for the Cup Final. A northern Derby but worth watching all the same. Still, you had to take what you could get these days. They were cutting down on overtime next week and the old man desperately needed that cataract operation. That didn't come free. Austerity. They were living in times of austerity, they'd been told. The force, just like everyone else, had to tighten its belt. Cut down on unnecessary expenses.

'Huh! Try explaining austerity to some of this lot.'

He ran his eye with disfavour amounting to hatred over the birthday guests assembled in the private dining room of the Ritz. The end of the seemingly interminable speeches had come at last. The old geezer in whose honour they were celebrating fifty years of parasitic idleness risked running into his sixtieth year before his friends and relations had finished queuing up to listen to their own voices telling family jokes and relating embarrassing incidents in the fruitless life of Alfred Joliffe. But now the last cheery lie had been told and welcomed by the receptive audience and they were all knocking back the champagne. And this followed the sherry, the white wine and the red wine with the meal. Eyes were sparkling, laughter louder and shriller, behaviour more exaggerated. It all made his surveillance difficult. It had been a piece of cake while they were all seated at those little tables but now they were wandering about, going to the cloakrooms, stepping outside for a cigar, dancing in the small circle the Ritz flunkeys had cleared in front of the eight-piece band. Armitage wondered if young Robert, stationed outside in the corridor by the lift, had stayed alert.

His eye ranged over the men, about thirty of them in the group, eliminating the elderly, the unfit, the inebriated. That left two – no – three whose movements he should follow closely. Waste of time. None of them looked remotely like a cat burglar. Still, what did a cat burglar look like? Nobody knew. Bloody clever, those lads – never got caught. Briefing him, his inspector had explained that, in the series of break-ins and robberies that had occurred in London hotels in the last few months, the Ritz could well be the next target. Bedrooms had been entered sometimes by means of the fire escape and turned over, while the guests were busy at some sort of knees-up in the building. You could almost think somebody had checked they were occupied elsewhere and then ransacked their rooms but that was to imply that the burglar was one of their number, someone close who knew them and who could watch their movements unobserved. A member of their class. Obvious really. And Armitage had tried to put this idea into his boss's head. But, of course, no one in any position of authority was willing to believe this. Even the victims wouldn't admit the thought. Thieves were lower class, weren't they? Destitutes and relics of the war. '. . . terribly sad, darling, and naturally one understands and sympathizes, but it just has to be stamped out and quickly before one becomes the next insurance claimant.'

There had been one sighting, but so far only one. A guest

at Claridge's last month returning unexpectedly to her room had found a man standing inside. He was wearing evening dress and was very well spoken. A gentleman, she had said. Charming and attractive. He had apologized for mistaking the room, explaining that his own was on the floor below, and had left offering to buy her a drink in the bar to make up for the intrusion. It was some time before she realized that a hundred pounds was missing from her bag.

'And good luck to you, my lad!' thought Armitage mutinously. He was perfectly aware of a fellow feeling for anyone who had the nerve and the skill to pluck a living from these fat birds and yet he knew that if the occasion offered and he found himself feeling the collar of one of the light-fingered sportsmen he had been assigned to track down he would stifle his sympathy, bounce him off down to the clink and take all the credit that was going. 'Felix! Felix, the Cat Burglar! Are you here now? Mingling with the crowd, unremarkable behind a fashionably languid voice and the right evening suit? Stalking your victim and preparing to nip off upstairs and do out a room? Waste of time, mate! *I* could tell you that. The jewel cases are lying open and empty on the dressing tables. It's all down here . . . must be ten thousand quid's worth of sparklers hanging round the undeserving necks of these toffee-nosed tabbies.'

He looked again at the three young men who had caught his attention earlier. They were deep in serious conversation at the other end of the room. They were still sober, they were lithe and looked keen and clever. Were they up to something? It was just possible . . . He didn't want any amateurs fouling up his evening. Better be certain. He strolled around the perimeter of the room and edged within earshot of their table. So oblivious of his presence were they, their earnest debate continued without hesitation: a debate on the new backless, double-breasted waistcoats – could one possibly wear these things? Snooty Felbrigg had been seen in one . . . but, on the other hand,

8

Fruity Featherstonehaugh had been heard to declare them 'flashy'. Armitage was interested enough to linger close by until they delivered their decision – a decided thumbs down.

'Where are you, Felix?' he wondered. 'Not at this table, I think.'

He moved around towards the door, staying on the fringes of the party, confident that the official Ritz security staff uniform he had put on for the occasion would render him invisible. If they noticed him at all, the toffs would be mildly reassured by his presence. But the guests were paying him no more attention than they paid the waiter who served them their *consommé en gelée*. Apart, that is, from two young girls who had been eyeing him for some minutes now, giggling to each other behind their hands. Both were a little the worse for drink. Drink? The worse for *something* anyway.

The sergeant gave them his reproving police stare which usually did the trick. He knew that he was a good-looking man and he came in for his share of female appreciation. It wasn't always unwelcome but he wanted no attention from this pair. Underdressed, in his opinion, for a family do – those wisps of dresses were a plain incitement to crime – and their eyes were too bright. They'd spent quite a long time out of the room – in the ladies' cloakroom perhaps? – and Armitage's suspicious mind conjured up activities more often associated with nightclubs. Not Ciro's, he thought – the Embassy, more like. They said you could get anything at the Embassy. People of this class spent more on an evening's shot of cocaine than he spent on his week's rent. His stare grew more deadly.

The girls walked flirtily in front of him, turned and walked back again, passing more closely. The small evening bag one had been carrying suddenly slipped and fell at his feet. Automatically he bent and picked it up. Clicking his heels smartly, he held it out. '*Excusez-moi, mademoiselle, vous avez laissé tomber ce petit sac.*'

9

Disconcerted, the girl took it from him. 'Ooh, er, thank you,' she mumbled.

'*De rien, mademoiselle. De rien.*'

Wide-eyed and giggling, the girls scurried back to the flock.

He smiled with satisfaction. It never failed. He could always put people on the wrong footing by addressing them in French or German. The English would run a mile rather than deal face to face with a foreigner. He decided that if anyone else approached him he would give them a burst of Russian. He continued to survey the crowd. The three waistcoat fanciers were still at it and presenting no problems. No, if there was to be any suggestion of disorder arising from this group it was more likely to come from the women.

His eye followed the striking redhead he'd marked down earlier. She stood out from the crowd of flappers and gigglers, distinguished by her height – she towered over most of the men – and by her colouring. Her dark red hair was unfashionably long and piled on top of her head. This had the effect of lengthening further her elegant neck, her elegant neck around which hung a very remarkable necklace. Armitage had lost no time in giving it his professional attention. Emeralds, he judged, and the real goods. A family piece, he guessed, recently and fashionably reset. The stones were large, carried in a simple but heavy gold setting. She had chosen to emphasize their colour by wearing a low-cut gown of dark green taffeta which framed them as they lay gleaming against her smooth white throat.

He indulged for a moment or two in salacious thought. He acknowledged that she was, by his standards, quite old – perhaps even forty – but, given a chance to lay aboard, he wouldn't have refused. He didn't think many men would have refused. He watched on as she made her way towards the group of three who had become the focus of his surveillance. Well, at least it simplified things to have all his targets in one shot for a while. He approached the group softly, intrigued to hear their conversation. The woman laughed and flirted and sipped her cocktail prettily. The men vied to exceed each other in gallantry, obviously flattered by her attention. She twirled the stem of her glass and, when one of them noticed it was empty and called to a passing waiter, she asked for 'Another French Rose. And no sugar round the rim!' He had not been keeping count but he was aware that she was drinking steadily though you would never have guessed it from her speech or her behaviour. Yes, she could manage her drink, that one.

Now she was moving on to join that rancid toad Sir Montagu Mathurin at his table. There were stories circulating about him that made the sergeant's flesh crawl and for a split second he was tempted to approach and warn her to move on. But then he pulled himself up. What was he thinking of? The chap was probably her second cousin or something and, anyway, this lady was capable of looking after herself. She greeted Mathurin's rather sulky-looking little girlfriend (fiancée rather, judging by the ring which was visible clear across the room) with much warmth but at once turned the full glow of her charm on the rogue Mathurin. This was decidedly a display of a sexual nature, Armitage reckoned, frowning anxiously as he watched the apparently casual but practised gesture with which she leaned towards him and adjusted his tie. Anybody could see what that meant! Even across the room the sergeant felt the force of it and he swallowed in sympathy. Certainly Mathurin was responding in a predictable way. It was a relief to see that after a few minutes of fascinating Mathurin she had the good manners to draw the fiancée into the conversation. Trouble averted then. The last thing he wanted was the distraction of a pedigree cat fight but all claws seemed to be sheathed. And this was the Ritz after all, not the London Apprentice. And these were ladies not dockers' molls.

A clock chimed midnight and this was greeted with raucous calls for more champagne. The redhead rose to her

11

feet and began to thread her way through the crowd towards the door. She paused, turned and directed a look at someone on the other side of the room. Damn! Armitage looked round but he wasn't quick enough to catch an answering look of complicity from any of the other revellers and wondered cynically which of the assembled men was the chosen one. He wished he had a mate in earshot to take on a bet with him. Whichever bloke rose to his feet and excused himself within the next five minutes, he reckoned was the lucky one. A matronly lady in wine-red brocade staggered to her feet and made her way, listing heavily, towards the door. A pretty girl in a short dress about as concealing as a cobweb noticed her predicament and with a cry of concern hurried after her, steadying her with a hand under an elbow and an encouraging smile. At a look from the maître d'hôtel, a waitress scurried after the pair to check there were no embarrassing scenes in the corridor. A group of chirruping girls followed, flighting their way like finches to the powder room, and Armitage wondered what instinct compelled them to undertake this journey across the room in flocks. Mathurin, deserted for the moment by his fiancée, looked at his watch in anxiety – or was it just boredom? But he stayed in his place. And that was the only excitement. After ten minutes Armitage decided with a sigh of relief that he'd misinterpreted the signals.

At exactly twelve fifteen he was given the nod by the maître d'hôtel and he embarked on the next stage of his surveillance. He was being cleared, as arranged, to make a tour of inspection of the exterior of the hotel. Action at last. A real job to do. His muscles began to tense in anticipation. It would be good to escape from this overheated room and overloud laughter to clear his lungs in the sharp London air. But he only had the designated half-hour. He slipped away and, having given a brief nod to young Robert by the lift, he hurried to pick up his bag of equipment from the staff cloakroom. On a wet dark night like this he needed his police-issue flashlight and some protection for his uniform. He couldn't come dripping back into the party room without raising a few eyebrows even amongst this paralytic mob.

Alert and purposeful once more, Armitage stepped out into the chilly April night.

Chapter Two

Joe Sandilands had just been to a performance of *No, No, Nanette* at the Palace Theatre. He was in the kind of mood that only a third exposure to those tinkling tunes could bring on. It was always a mistake to ask a girl what she wanted to see. And a carefully timed three-second farewell kiss on a face-powdered cheek was no reward for two hours of tedium. Here he was on the doorstep of her family home in Belgrave Square, the rather grand doorstep of a rather grand house. The house of the Second Sea Lord, he understood. The lights in the hall clicked on in response when she rang the bell.

'Oh, I say!' she said in tones of mock surprise. 'Golly! It looks as though Daddy has waited up. He's dying to meet you. Won't you step inside for a nightcap or something?'

Joe explained that he had to dash away to call in at the Yard on his way home and with a hurried promise to ring her the next day he walked as swiftly as manners would permit out of range of a naval engagement. 'Never more, Nanette!' Joe promised himself with relief. 'And never more Elspeth Orr!'

Morosely Joe flagged a passing taxi. Satisfactorily, he did not need to give any directions to the cabby. They most of them now knew him by sight.

'Had a good evening, Super? *No, No, Nanette*, was it?' (Good Lord! He'd been humming out loud!) 'Couldn't be doing with it myself but the wife enjoyed it.'

They spent a happy few minutes agreeing that it wasn't what it was cracked up to be ('enjoyed that *Rose Marie* though') and set off west towards the Victoria Embankment, turned right and drove onwards following the river. Soon the uncompromising bulk of Lot's Road power station loomed through the dusk and this to Joe was truly home. Amongst the clutter surrounding that unattractive edifice there was a small four-storey block of flats converted from the power station offices and now the property of a retired police sergeant and his wife. Not many could understand why Joe should elect to live in this manifestly unfashionable if not to say squalid corner of Chelsea but their wonder turned to understanding when, trusting themselves to the wheezing rope-operated hydraulic lift, they arrived on the top floor and found themselves with one of the finest views of the river in London with its constant procession of river traffic: sailing barges with red-brown sails crowding the timber-yard, lighters, police launches passing up and down, all to the soothing accompaniment of hooters and sirens and, perpetually, the thresh and rustle of passing tugs.

As he stood at his window watching the navigation lights below and loosening his tie, Joe's thoughts were interrupted by a series of clicks announcing an incoming call. Well, at least there'd been one good line in the musical. 'Tea for two' – how did it go? 'We won't let them know, dear, that we own a telephone, dear . . .'

Only one person would ring him at one o'clock in the morning.

Generations of past good living had imparted to his boss, Sir Nevil Macready, a fruity resonance that was unmistakable. 'There you are, Sandilands!' he boomed.

Joe could not deny it. His boss knew he kept no butler. But the important thing with Sir Nevil was ever to retain the initiative. 'Good morning, Sir Nevil,' he said cheerily. 'You're up early! Is there anything I can do?' This was not such a silly question as might appear because Sir Nevil was quite capable of ringing up at any moment of the night or day just for a chat. But this was not one of those occasions

'Got a little problem,' he said.

An invariable opening. It signified nothing. If the entire royal family had been gunned down at a world premiere this would have been 'a little problem'. If he'd lost the address of 'that restaurant where we had lunch the other day' this would, likewise, have been 'a little problem' and one which he would not have hesitated to air with Joe at midnight or even one o'clock. This time however it seemed his little problem was quite a big problem.

'Just up your street. Incident requiring the most careful handling. Possible military – or I should say naval – implications. You're the obvious chap for the job so just drop anything else you may be involved with and handle it. Woman got herself bludgeoned to death at the Ritz. Are you familiar with the Ritz?'

'Reasonably familiar, yes. Are you going to tell me some more about this?'

'Yes. Ever heard of Dame Beatrice Jagow-Joliffe? Ridiculous name! Ever heard of her?'

'Er . . . yes, but I can't think for the moment in what connection.'

'That's the kind of thing you're supposed to know!' said Sir Nevil reprovingly. 'I'll have to help you. One of the founding fathers or perhaps I should say founding mothers of the Women's Royal Naval Service. The Wrens. Alarmingly distinguished but formidable nuisance if you ask me. And evidently somebody must have thought likewise because she's just been murdered. In the Ritz! Can't tell you what a hoo-ha there'll be when the news gets out. Many thought the damn woman was God. Or Florence Nightingale. Or Boadicea or some other heroine of our Rough Island Story, with a wide following – mostly of silly girls – silly old fools too (many of them in the Admiralty), stretching from here to Portsmouth. I spoke to the manager just now and, I can tell you, they're not giving a damn for Dame Beatrice – all they want is no publicity. I told them I was sending my best chap. Discretion guaranteed. Right, Joe? I'm handing this over to you and we'll talk about it in the morning. As luck – or good management – would have it, we've got a chap in place already. A detective sergeant. You can liaise with him. Um . . .'

There was a pause while Sir Nevil, Joe guessed, rustled through his notes. 'You're not obliged, of course, to make any further use of this chap once you've taken his statement. I mean – feel free to pick your own team, what!' A further pause. 'In fact, there seems to be, perhaps I ought to tell you, something of a question mark against his name. May be nothing . . . Anyway, I've arranged for an inspector and some uniformed support for you and I suppose you'd better have a police surgeon . . . oh, and one of those photography fellows you're so keen on. . . . Won't be long before the place is swarming with reporters so I suggest you get dressed and go on down there.'

'I *am* dressed. I'd only just got home.'

'Only just got home! Some people live for pleasure alone! If you were any good at your job you'd get an early night occasionally. Oh, and Joe, what was the name of that young woman . . . Millicent something or other . . . Millicent Westwood?'

By a mighty effort Joe deduced that he was referring to Mathilda. Mathilda Westhorpe was a woman police constable. She'd worked with him on a recent job and had obviously impressed Sir Nevil. She'd impressed Joe too. Sir Nevil was not easily impressed but, almost alone of the higher echelons of Scotland Yard, he was at this time tremendously in favour of the women police and during his recent spell as Commissioner had, whilst trimming their numbers, managed to establish them as a regular arm of the force.

'I mean,' he continued, 'if you're going to find yourself searching through this lady's drawers you ought to have a little female back-up.'

'Searching through her drawers? It may conceivably come to that but I wouldn't think of starting there –'

Impatiently: 'Searching through her things, I mean, and to spell it all out for you since you seem somewhat obtuse

17

at this time of the morning, searching through her effects – jewellery, furs and the like. Female things. This is a scene of crime. It would be the usual thing to do. I'm suggesting you'll need a little female assistance – that's what they're there for after all – to save your blushes. Might as well make proper use of these gels as we seem to have got them. Are you beginning to understand me?'

Tilly Westhorpe had been seconded to Joe's unit and, the more he thought about it, the more he thought her caustic and irreverent common sense would be valuable, to say nothing of her drawer-searching skills. Joe rang her at home, a number in Mayfair. A fashionable area but that was no surprise. Sir Nevil's recruiting methods were aimed, as he put it, at girls 'of a certain position'. At this time of night she wouldn't be able to get to the Ritz in a hurry . . . it probably took her an hour to struggle into the uniform. And there was always the possibility that her parents wouldn't let her out at night by herself.

A carefully enunciating voice answered, a male voice which managed, though remaining impeccably correct, to convey suspicion, disapproval and surprise that a gentleman should be calling at that hour. Miss Mathilda was not at home and, no, he was not at liberty to tell Joe when she was expected to return. Joe left a message that she was to contact him at the Ritz as soon as she was able. The voice took on several more degrees of frost and assured him that the message would be passed at the earliest convenient moment. Joe was left in no possible doubt that this moment might arise round about teatime the next day.

Hastily doing up his tie, grabbing his Gladstone bag and picking up an old police cloak he kept behind the door, he ran down the stairs to the taxi stand on the Embankment.

The Ritz was wearing its usual air of dignified calm. The street lamps under the arcade swung gently to and fro and were reflected from the wet pavement. The foyer lighting

18

was discreet and taxis were standing by; various parties were just breaking up amidst bibulous faces, female laughter and male guffaws, flirtatious farewells. Evidently the news had yet to break but somewhere in that refined interior lay the body of a distinguished public figure, 'bludgeoned to death' as Sir Nevil had put it.

Such was the efficiency with which the Ritz closed ranks, the atmosphere was entirely normal. Staff were at their posts or moving at an unruffled pace. The night receptionist, outwardly calm, was, however, Joe judged, secretly a-quiver, both awed and delighted by his responsibility. Joe advanced on the desk. 'In a manner of speaking,' he said, keeping his voice low, 'I could claim to have an appointment with Dame Beatrice Jagow-Joliffe. Here's my card.'

The Ritz smelled strongly of fitted carpet with a faint overlay of scent and cigars and somewhere in the background – but discreetly a long way in the background – expensive food. The receptionist crooked a finger and summoned a page boy and he led Joe to the gilded cage of a lift. They got out at the fourth floor and stepped into a silent corridor. A figure posted by the fourth door along acknowledged them with a nod and Joe dismissed the page boy, to his grave disappointment. As Joe approached he noticed that the door of Room 4 stood a fraction open and lights were on inside.

Joe guessed that the guard was part of the hotel security staff. The tall, slim figure, the smart black coat and striped trousers were at odds with the severe police face. Joe looked at him and looked again, encountering a jaw dropped in disbelief, disbelief which rapidly turned to happy recognition. It was a face last seen leaving the mud and misery of a French battlefield on a stretcher.

'Just a moment,' Joe said. 'I know you, don't I?'

'Yessir. Detective Sergeant Armitage, sir. With the Met. Was Sergeant Armitage, C Company when we last met.'

'That's right! Cambrai, Bill?'

'Cambrai it was, sir. And if I may say so, sir, you look a

good deal smarter now than you did when I last saw you,' he added, eyeing Joe's dinner-jacketed elegance.

'I could say the same, Bill,' said Joe. 'We were none of us looking too sharp then. But I'm really glad you got out of that all right. We must have a talk and a pint. But in the meantime perhaps you can tell me what's been going on here?'

'Murder, sir, is what's been going on here.'

'Perhaps we should view the body? Take a look at the crime scene?'

Armitage led Joe through into a small lobby. Three closed doors faced them. Joe opened the door on the right and stepped into an opulent Ritz bedroom. The furnishings reflected the taste of the court of Louis XVI as perceived by Waring and Gillow of Tottenham Court Road. The main illumination was supplied by a chandelier; bedside lights were in the manner of Pompeii. The carpet was the best that Wilton had to offer and each of the two bedside tables carried a cargo of carafe, biscuit barrel and ashtray. A voice tube was clipped to the wall. There seemed to be something missing.

'I see no body,' said Joe.

'Next door, sir. Next door,' said Armitage. 'This is the Marie Antoinette suite and it has a separate sitting room. That's the door on the left – there's a private bathroom between the two.'

He stood back as Joe stepped into the sitting room.

The first impression that hit Joe was the unmistakable metallic smell of freshly spilled blood. He realized he must have made an involuntary movement of revulsion as Armitage stepped forward and put an arm under his elbow murmuring, 'Steady, sir. I should have warned you . . .'

'That's all right, Bill. We've seen worse.'

And on the battlefield they had, but this small room with its pastel walls, its gilt, its brocades, seemed to Joe to be frozen in horror and reverberating still with echoes of the murderous violence which had so recently erupted in its calm interior. The eighteenth-century elegance threw into shocking relief the chaotic scene before him. The walls were spattered with a rich tapestry of blood and at the centre of the spray, in front of the marble fireplace, lay a sprawled corpse, its head battered and resting in a pool of thickening blood.

'Definitely dead by the time I got here, sir. First thing I did was check her wrist for a pulse. A gonner. But not long gone. I touched nothing else, of course.'

Joe stood in the doorway looking, absorbing, noting. A Louis XVI sofa remained upright but its companion chair had been overturned. An arrangement of white lilies on a spindle-legged table in a corner, incongruously still upright and intact, was dappled with a surreal maculation. The room's only window, a casement, stood broken and half open, hanging into the room. Shards of glass littered the carpet.

A cough to Joe's right attracted his attention. A boy dressed in the Ritz uniform was standing in the corner as far away from the corpse as possible. Tense and embarrassed, he had been set there by Armitage to guard or perhaps even to restrain a girl who was sitting resentfully in a chair. A pretty girl angrily smoking a cigarette in an ebony holder.

'Ah, yes! Here's someone you ought to meet, sir,' said Armitage with a trace of satisfaction in his voice, waving a hand towards the girl. 'Our prime exhibit and, for want of a better, our prime suspect, as it happens!'

The girl flashed him a scornful look and took a drag through narrowed eyes at her cigarette. She puffed out smoke in the general direction of her guard who coughed again and, obviously uneasy with his role, looked for support or release to Armitage.

'All right, Robert, lad, you can stand down now,' said Armitage, dismissing him.

The girl shrugged her slim shoulders and jumped to her feet. She was wearing an evening dress of some pale grey silky fabric done up fashionably low on the hips with a

21

silver belt. Silently Joe noted the bloodstains on the hem of her skirt just below her left knee.

She glared at Joe. 'Can it possibly take thirty-five minutes to get here from Chelsea?' she asked.

'Good evening, Westhorpe,' said Joe. 'Perhaps you could explain what the devil you're doing here? Not only what you're doing here but how you come to be covered in gore and, as I believe, standing over a recently murdered Dame of the British Empire? I'm sure there's some perfectly logical explanation but I would be glad to hear what it is.'

'Do you know this young person?' said Armitage, disappointed and mistrustful.

'Yes, I do. This is Constable Westhorpe. She's one of us. WPC number 142 – in, er, plain clothes – but I still want to know what she's doing here.'

'Are you taking a statement, sir? Because, if so, I would welcome the opportunity to correct the over-coloured assertions you have just made. I am neither covered in gore, nor am I standing over the body. The stains you have noted were acquired when, on discovering the body of Dame Beatrice, I knelt by her side to check for signs of life. I didn't touch her – she was quite obviously dead.'

Armitage drew in a hissing breath at the girl's challenging tone. 'You should stand to attention, Constable, when you report to the Commander,' he said repressively.

The girl collected herself and, handing her cigarette to Armitage, assumed the rigid policewoman's stance, feet eighteen inches apart, hands behind her back and with what Joe guessed she thought was a demure expression. 'I was having dinner here, sir,' she said. Her affectation of subservience was so overplayed and so unconvincing that even Armitage was prepared to smile.

'In the dining room?'

'Yes, in the dining room. I wouldn't be likely to be having dinner in the lift, would I?'

'That'll do!' said Armitage, scandalized. 'Remember you're under arrest. You're not in cuffs yet but you very soon could be! Just answer the Captain's questions, miss,' he added more gently. He had noticed, as had Joe, that the hem of her dress was quivering, betraying a pair of legs that were nicely shaped but shaking with tension.

'He's not a captain and when he asks me a sensible question I'll answer it. As I say, I was having dinner here in the dining room. I'm the guest of Rupert Joliffe at his uncle Alfred's birthday party. At about midnight I saw Dame Beatrice, who was also of the party, leaving. I wanted to see her. Rupert was so tight by then I don't suppose he's noticed yet that I'm not there.'

'You wanted to see Dame Beatrice? Why?'

'A personal matter,' she said defensively.

'You can't leave it there,' Joe said, 'but that'll do for the present. I shall need to know the nature of the personal matter. But, in the meantime – you saw her leave the dining room?'

'Yes, there was something I wanted to ask her. It was important. I extracted myself from my dinner party. The dancing was under way so it wasn't difficult. I helped old Lady Carstairs to find her way to the ladies' room and then I went to the desk and asked for Dame Beatrice's room number. I had to wait quite a while because the after-theatre crowd had just come rushing in. Then I followed her up the stairs.'

'The stairs? You didn't go in the lift?'

'No. A mass of people had flooded out of the bar and were waiting to take the lift so I ran up the stairs to the fourth floor. This floor. To this room. As I arrived on the landing the lift went down.'

'Did you see who was in the lift?'

'No, sir.'

'Right. Then what happened?'

'The outer door was ajar. I pushed it open and stepped in. I was glad to think I'd caught up with Dame Beatrice.'

'Yes?'

'Well, I had caught up with her. At least somebody else had caught up with her before me. Blood all over the place – as you see. But I was careful, sir! I disturbed nothing. Head bashed in. Fire irons scattered. The window had been broken open and I thought a burglar must have got in. From a fire escape or something because we're sixty feet above ground here.' She pointed to the casement swinging desultorily in the night air. 'I didn't go over and look out. Didn't want to risk obscuring the footprints.' She nodded at the carpet between the window and the body, presumably seeing traces which were so far invisible to Joe.

'Well done, Westhorpe,' Joe said, wishing he had managed to sound less like a schoolmaster. But, then, the girl was evoking this response in him by behaving rather in the manner of a schoolbook heroine. *Dimsie Does Her Best* perhaps?

'Go on, will you?'

'She'd obviously put up quite a struggle. Her hands and arms are injured too. She'd defended herself.'

'She *would* have defended herself,' said Armitage. 'Very forthright lady, Dame Beatrice, I hear. Not one to stand any nonsense.'

Joe observed an affinity between Sir Nevil and Sergeant Armitage. To one, murder was 'a little problem'; to the other a murderous assault was 'a bit of nonsense'.

Tilly Westhorpe resumed her story. 'Having established that she was indeed beyond any help I could immediately offer, I needed to notify the police and the hotel management. There was no one in sight and it seemed to me the quickest, most sensible thing to do would be to go down to reception.'

Sally Sees It Through? With a burst of irritation Joe wondered why the bloody girl couldn't just have stood in the doorway and screamed her head off like any normal female. Or used the voice tube?

She caught his thought. Or his swift glance towards the bedroom perhaps. 'I didn't use the voice tube. You never can be quite sure who's picking up at the other end. Even

24

at the Ritz. Discretion, sir, I thought the situation called for discretion.'

'Yes. A good thought. So you opened the door . . .' He looked up sharply. 'Prints, Westhorpe? Prints?' he reminded her testily.

'As you see, sir, I'm wearing gloves.' With more than a touch of professional satisfaction, Tilly held up two evening-gloved hands of pristine white satin. 'I took care not to touch the body. Alive *or* dead.'

Her eyes flicked sideways to Armitage and at last Joe understood. He reckoned that this calculated display of innocence and foresight was aimed not at himself but at the arresting officer.

'I'd left the door ajar as I found it,' she continued with her story, 'so I pushed it open and went down in the lift to the reception desk. I informed the manager who rang the Yard from the rear office and they said they'd send someone. I must say the manager was calm about it,' she added, wondering. 'This is surely a major incident but if I'd been reporting a broken fingernail he couldn't have been more undemonstrative.'

'It's part of the training. But go on.'

'Then I came straight back up here to stand guard on the body until help arrived. Five minutes later I was joined by . . . er . . .'

'Detective Sergeant Armitage, miss.'

'The sergeant arrived and put me under arrest.'

'A perfectly reasonable thing to do,' said Joe. 'Anyone would have done the same.'

'Oh, yes,' said Tilly. 'Quite proper in the circumstances.'

She turned to Armitage and smiled. The sudden intensification of the glow from her cornflower blue eyes would have lit up Tower Bridge for thirty seconds. Joe remembered that Armitage in France had had a reputation for susceptibility and a quick glance at the sergeant revealed that he was not unaffected. Joe was considerably amused by this. His own previous encounters with Constable Westhorpe had taught him the wisdom of looking the other way when she unsheathed her smile. Lucky for him, he thought, that in all their previous dealings she'd been wearing the thick and calculatedly unalluring serge uniform, its uncompromising skirt almost brushing the tops of her black boots, her pretty face all but quenched under a high-crowned wide-brimmed felt hat and chin strap. The trembling shoulders and the slightly heaving white bosom at present on view were beginning to have an effect on Armitage, Joe decided, and he took off his heavy police cape and held it out.

'Don't get cold, Westhorpe. I'm afraid I can't offer to close the window yet. And all this must be quite a shock,' he said. 'Put this on.'

She opened her mouth to return what would be bound to be classed by Armitage as a saucy remark. 'I'm all right,' she said belligerently, making to shake Joe aside.

Joe eyed her with authority. 'Just put it on,' he said. He was relieved to be interrupted by the shrilling of the whistle in the voice tube.

'See who that is, Bill,' he said. 'Find out what they want.'

'It's reception, sir. There are three police officers below and a gentleman from the *Evening Standard*.'

Joe thought for a moment, finally saying, 'Right, Bill, go on down, will you? Contain the reporter in the manager's office and stand Robert over him. Tell him we'll have something for him in a while. Encourage him to stay. Incommunicado, of course. Tray of Ritz coffee served up every quarter of an hour, you know the sort of thing. I'd like to find out how he got hold of this so soon. Brief the officers and send them up by the stairs. I want the lift sealed off and the whole of the fourth floor. And then I think you'd better stay on down there – watchdog on guard! The Yard will have sent a medico and a photographer. I want them brought up as soon as possible. And sometime in all this we'll have to think about informing the next of kin.'

'Yessir,' said Armitage coming automatically to attention. There was something in his manner that alerted Joe to a potential problem. The hostile and suspicious look he flung at Tilly on receiving his order to take charge downstairs, leaving her alone in the murder room with the Commander, did not go unnoticed by Joe. He sighed. It seemed to be a case of hatred at first sight between these two. When he considered the possible causes of this he was not reassured. Instinctive antipathy, class rivalry – there was no doubting that the two came from vastly different strata of society – and (probably the prime motive for the mistrust) professional jealousy. Intelligent and ambitious, the pair of them. They would each try to outdo the other to gain credit in Joe's eyes. How tiresome! He calculated promptly that there was no way in the world he could work efficiently with two warring officers under his command. One would have to withdraw from the case. He thought for a moment and made his decision.

'Oh, Sergeant, you'd better get hold of one or two of the officers down below and set them to take statements from the party guests. Corral them in the dining room. They won't like it, but stress that it's for their own good – with one of their number killed they would do well to cooperate discreetly. And we'll need a complete list of guests and their room numbers as well as the IDs of everyone who was known to be in the hotel this evening.' He shook his head. 'It's over an hour since she was killed. And this place is a beehive. No, a sieve more like. And, shall we admit it? – any one of the hundreds of people who were milling about in the building this evening could have got up here unnoticed and have slipped away equally unnoticed. Hours of work to be done and all with the extreme of discretion.'

He and Armitage looked at each other steadily, contemplating for a moment the mountain of routine but tricky police work before them.

'Leave it to me, sir,' said Armitage with quiet energy. 'I think I can manage.'

Joe smiled. He knew he could.

*   *   *

When the sergeant and his assistant had left the room, Joe felt free to go and look down at Dame Beatrice. 'Like Boadicea', Sir Nevil had said, he remembered as he stared in surprise and pity. What had he expected? Her reputation and her rank had led him to believe he would be dealing with an elderly tweed-skirted spinster with iron gaze and incipient moustache but the body before him at first sight recalled a pale-faced, languorous and frankly erotic woman seen in a painting by an Austrian painter whose name eluded him. 'Decadent' was the word that came to mind. Her dark red hair, unfashionably long, lay spread, dishevelled and blood-soaked, a fitting frame for the smashed and distorted white mask of outrage and hate it outlined. So must the Queen of the Iceni have looked, he thought, as she snarled defiance at the Roman legions.

She was wearing her evening dress, an ankle-length gown of green taffeta. Joe knelt by the body, noting with a stab of disgust that the bodice had been torn. The seams along each shoulder had been wrenched apart with considerable force and her small white breasts lay exposed. The urge to cover her nakedness was almost overwhelming but Joe steeled himself to observe and note.

To his further embarrassment Constable Westhorpe came and joined him. A well-bred young girl should have kept her distance, pretended to look the other way, even called weakly for smelling salts, he thought resentfully.

'Terrible sight,' he said and would have said more. Would have suggested that she might like to leave this next distressing part of the enquiry to him but she looked down calmly enough at the body.

'Is it Gustav Klimt,' he wondered out loud to bump them over the awkward moment, 'the painter that this lady's appearance calls to mind?' Too late he remembered that a reference to a foreign painter with a reputation for decadence would be bound to be offensive and shocking to the good taste of a young lady of Tilly Westhorpe's background. But, with a bit of luck, she would never have heard of the chap.

The constable considered for a moment. 'Oh, yes, I see it . . . *The Kiss*, you mean? It's the angle of the head, I think. No . . . I'd have said rather Dante Gabriel Rossetti. His darkest nightmare.' She looked stonily down at the battered features and then, caught by an emotion Joe could not fathom, she spoke again as though to herself.

'Evil, evil old devil!' she said passionately. 'Killing's too good for her!'

Chapter Three

Joe let the words lie between them for a moment, puzzled and apprehensive.

'Would this be a good moment to explain just how familiar you were with this lady, Westhorpe? And what exactly was the nature of your personal reason for coming up here to see her? Sir Nevil has asked for you to be associated with this enquiry but if there's the slightest suggestion of an interest other than professional, you'll be asked to withdraw.'

Calmly she took her eyes off the corpse and transferred her gaze to Joe. Direct and searching, it had the effect of making him feel himself to be the one undergoing questioning. 'We were never introduced. As far as I know she was perfectly unaware of me. The party tonight is the first occasion on which I have ever seen her. But sir! Surely you cannot be unconscious of her reputation? In the circles in which I move, I can assure you, Commander, Dame Beatrice is not venerated . . .'

She was just getting into her swing and Joe was eager to hear more when something prompted her to cut short her attack on the character of the deceased. 'But this is hardly the place to swap gossip, I think. And one shouldn't speak ill of the dead, and all that . . . Oh, for goodness sake! What am I saying? You *ought* to be aware, sir, and, in the circumstances, there will be few enough to tell you . . . The woman was a monster! Dissolute, degenerate, debased . . .'

'Run out of d's, Westhorpe?' said Joe, taken aback and

trying to take the sting out of her remarks, almost sacrilegious, he felt, when delivered with such vehemence over the cooling body. 'What about, er, Dame . . .? Darling of the navy . . .? Doyenne of London society?'

'I'm trying to be helpful, sir,' she said repressively. 'You are not obliged to give any weight to my information but if you enquire in the right quarters you will hear other evaluations of Dame Beatrice's character and habits than those you will read in next week's obituaries. But for now, there's work to be done – work in which you will find me perceptive and efficient.'

She didn't quite click her heels but Joe almost expected to hear it.

'Very well. We'll leave it. But I'm not satisfied with your explanation and will come back to it. I shall need to know precisely what brought you to this room at such an unlikely hour to see someone you say you were not acquainted with. Now, we need to establish without further delay who is her next of kin.'

'I could just tell you but perhaps you'd rather read the details from her diary which is in the bedroom. She lives in Surrey with her mother. Not married, of course.'

At a nod from Joe, Westhorpe went into the bedroom, emerging with a small black notebook. 'Here we are . . . Mrs Augustus Jagow-Joliffe, King's Hanger, near Godalming. There's a telephone number. Dame Beatrice has a flat of her own, I think . . . yes . . . here's the address – it's in Fitzroy Gardens.'

She handed the book to Joe and he put it in his pocket.

'Where would you like me to start, sir? Shall I make a sketch of the crime scene?'

'Hold on, Westhorpe. That's a job for whichever inspector they've supplied us with. You can make a start on her personal effects. An inventory, if you like.'

Westhorpe just managed not to roll her eyes in disbelief. 'Very well. I'll start in the bedroom as that's where most of the effects are and leave the field clear for the attentions of a superior officer.'

Joe opened his bag and took out a notebook and a pencil. 'Here, use this.' He stood in the doorway watching as she set about making her inspection. He had expected her to make at once for the wardrobe or the chest of drawers but she stood by him, surveying the room.

'First of all, the bed's been turned down so a member of the hotel staff has been in the room this evening though it will probably have been well before the time we're interested in. They usually come in about nine o'clock . . . though I did see a maid pushing one of those little chariots they have with bed linen and towels and so on down the corridor when I got up here the first time.' She looked thoughtful.

'Indeed? Was she coming towards the room or going away?'

'Hard to tell. She was right at the other end. Going away, I'd say. When I came out again, there was no sign of her. If she'd been there I would have sent her down with a message.'

She opened the notebook at a clean page and prepared to write. 'I'll start with what she's got on, shall I? Evening dress. I'll leave the interesting condition of same to others. No gloves, you see, sir. They're over there on that table. Neatly folded, worn but unstained. First thing a woman does when she gets back to her room is take off her gloves and kick off her shoes. But she still had her shoes on – did you notice? Could have been expecting someone? Perhaps her evening wasn't over? She hadn't started to draw a bath.'

'Just list the items, please, Westhorpe.'

'She's put her gloves down with her evening bag.' Without compunction, Westhorpe picked up the delicate, bead-sewn satiny confection and checked the inside. 'Lanvin. Contents just what you'd expect for an evening out. Female things!' She held it under Joe's nose. 'Small amount of cash . . . oh, and a couple of keys. Door keys.'

Joe took them and slipped them into an envelope. Westhorpe noted this.

He followed her through to the bedroom. 'Wardrobe first, I think.' She swung the doors back and began her list, commenting on the items she saw. 'Not much here. I assume she had only booked in for two nights.'

'Why do you say "only two nights"?' He had already ascertained as much from reception.

'It's a two-day wardrobe. Her travelling suit – of good tweed with a matching blouse which presumably she was wearing when she came up this morning . . . and a spare blouse for the journey back. Two day dresses . . . both by Captain Molyneux . . . yes, she *would* wear Molyneux. Two hats, one chestnut felt, one black grosgrain with a brim. A fur jacket. One pair of walking brogues and a pair of lighter shoes in kid. That's it.'

She moved to the dressing table. 'One ivory-backed hairbrush and a leather trousse for toiletry items. Hair pins. Packet of "quelques fleurs" powder leaves.'

Joe's interest sparked as she finally moved to the drawers, the searching of which was the reason for her being here, getting under his feet, he reminded himself. She took off the police cape and put it down carefully at the bottom of the bed. 'Do you mind, sir? It's really rather hot in here. Central heating. Wonderful, isn't it? And, after all, the reason for wearing protective covering seems to have evaporated. Now . . . two camisole sets, one lawn, one . . . ooh!' To his surprise, she shook out and held up to his embarrassed gaze a slippery-looking undergarment in magenta.

'Silk,' she commented. 'The real thing, not crêpe de Chine.' And, examining the label, 'From a very exclusive shop – Ma Folie – in Wigmore Street.' She folded it deftly and replaced it in the top drawer.

'Westhorpe, you don't need to demonstrate the lady's wardrobe,' said Joe uncomfortably.

With a slight smile of triumph she continued her list, calling out the items as she wrote. 'Three pairs of silk stockings, two still in packets. Two slips of oyster satin, six lawn handkerchiefs.'

Irritated that his attention was being distracted by laundry lists of peripheral importance to his enquiry, Joe was edging quietly back towards the murder room when she stopped him with an excited call. 'Oh, *this* is interesting!' She was extracting a small black leather box bearing heraldic gold insignia from the bottom of the underwear drawer. 'You ought to see this, sir!'

'What is it?'

'Well, it's not her secret store of cachous!'

Intrigued by his constable's reaction and the knowledge it revealed, Joe watched, fascinated as she opened the box and showed him the contents.

'Ha! A Dutch cap! And from a very recherché and vastly expensive establishment. The Gräfenberg Clinic. Nothing but the best for Dame Beatrice, you'd say!'

She wrote up the entry in her notebook even adding, Joe noticed, the serial number on the bottom of the box. 'Ah!' she said.

'Yes, Westhorpe?'

Tilly smiled in a knowing way. 'There are two such clinics, one in Harley Street, the other in Berlin. This is from the Berlin branch. Very discreet! Someone of Dame Beatrice's notoriety would never, of course, be seen crossing the London threshold of such a place, let alone Dr Stopes' clinic in Whitfield Street. Far too near home.'

Joe was finding Westhorpe's asides and insights informative – as, indeed, she had promised – and for the moment he held in check his urge to call her to heel and remind her of her lowly professional position. All the same, he was uncomfortable with the role she was assuming for herself and he was relieved when a tap on the door announced the arrival of – he hoped – an inspector. He went to the door, finding, to his annoyance, that Westhorpe had joined him and was hovering at his elbow still holding the box.

At the sight of them, the man standing outside looked up instinctively to check the number on the door. A middle-aged man with an eager expression underlined by a flamboyant moustache, he was wearing a trench coat over a brown tweed suit. In one hand he held a bowler hat and in the other a large black leather bag. He was trying very hard not to laugh.

'You have the right room,' said Joe curtly.

'Good evening, sir. Oh, er, I say,' he said, swallowing a smile. 'Awfully sorry, sir . . . no one thought to warn me that this was a black tie occasion . . . miss.' He nodded politely at Westhorpe.

'Even the corpse is in evening dress, you'll find, Cottingham. Join the party. You're very welcome. I must introduce you to Constable Westhorpe who is seconded to our unit. She's, um, working under cover. At Sir Nevil's suggestion. Westhorpe, this is Inspector Ralph Cottingham. Ex-Guards officer so no doubt you'll feel free to be rude to him too.'

The inspector smiled uncertainly at Westhorpe and seemed relieved when Joe sent her back into the bedroom and led him through to the scene of the murder.

'Notebook, Cottingham?'

'Got everything you might need in here, sir,' said Ralph. 'When I heard you were working the case I thought I'd better bring along the old "Murder Bag". Always keep it ready. Some of the top blokes don't bother but, like you, I'm a keen disciple of Sir Bernard.'

Joe nodded his approval. He knew the bag would contain everything he needed: fingerprint kit, evidence bags, tweezers.

'Got your rubber gloves, Cottingham?'

'Sir! Julia doesn't let me leave home without them. Never know what you're going to fish out of the Thames or the sewer!' He looked around him at the ravished grandeur. 'Nasty. But it beats working in an alley behind the Ten Bells which is where I was last week. Sketch of the crime scene first, sir, before I glove up?'

Joe had worked on one or two cases with Cottingham and knew him to be both clever and diligent. Nothing escaped his sharp brown eye and he had a neat drawing hand combined with an accurate sense of proportion. 'Start with the body, will you, Ralph? The pathologist should be here at any moment and it will be good to give him a clear run.'

'Sir!' said Cottingham, already filling in the boundaries of the room on a sheet of squared paper.

'Oh, and you'll have observed the pieces of broken glass from the window . . . Plot as many as seems possible, will you? Size of shards and position. A pattern may emerge. As with the blood spatter. Get that down too.'

'Someone I ought to know, sir?' said Cottingham without a break in his sketching.

'Sorry. This was Dame Beatrice Jagow-Joliffe. She was attending a party below, returned to her room just after midnight and was discovered, as you observe, about half an hour later by Constable Westhorpe.'

Cottingham paused in his work and looked up questioningly at Joe. 'Looks like a burglary that went wrong. Is that what we're thinking, sir? She disturbed a burglar. Anything missing?'

On cue, Westhorpe emerged from the bedroom, a red leather jewel case in her hand. She opened it and diamonds flashed from the black velvet interior. 'This was under the mattress, sir. A diamond necklace. Under the mattress! The second place any thief would look! Why on earth can't people use the hotel safe? He didn't stay long enough to search properly. Just snatched the emeralds and ran.'

'The emeralds?' both men said in unison.

Westhorpe walked over to the corpse. 'At the party she was wearing the Joliffe emeralds. Family do – of course she *would* be wearing them. Not round her neck any more and not in her room. And look, sir . . .' Peering closely, she pointed with a finger. 'An abrasion, bruise, cut, something there. Someone's pulled at the necklace. Roughly, you'd say, and made off again back the way he came through the window. It *was* a burglary, evidently!'

36

'Thank you for your observations, Westhorpe. Note it down. Have you checked the bathroom?'

With a lingering glance back over her shoulder at the crime scene, Tilly returned to her duties and they heard the banging of cupboard doors as she resumed her steady routine search.

Released after a suitable interval by the vigilant Armitage below, Joe guessed, the next to arrive was the pathologist and, again, this was a man Joe had worked with before, perhaps the best the Home Office could supply. Joe began to see a pattern of selection at work. The top brass had obviously been busy on the telephone for the last hour in an effort to assemble this particular grouping of talent, and the gravity and delicacy of the task ahead were being alarmingly underlined. There was more riding on the quick solution to this mystery than the sensibilities of the Ritz hotel, he realized.

'Good to see you again, Dr Parry!' Joe greeted the portly man who bustled in, wheezing from his ascent of four flights of stairs.

'And you, Commander! Buggers wouldn't let me use the lift! Your orders? Curse you then! Now, what have you got to show me that's so urgent it couldn't wait until dawn?'

Joe led him to the body. 'Died just after midnight. A police witness before and after you might say. The victim was under observation by my sergeant the whole evening and I expect he can tell you what she ate, how many glasses of champagne she drank, who she talked to . . . everything but how she died.'

'Well, that's obvious,' said the pathologist. 'Hardly need to open my bag but I'll go through the motions. Better get this one right, I think!' He knelt and studied the body. 'All observations are subject to further elaboration and adjustment following a complete PM, you understand, but I'll give you my first impressions if that's a help.'

Joe nodded.

'I'll just take the temperature to confirm time of death,' he warned.

Joe and Cottingham discreetly looked the other way while he did this.

'She's been murdered. By a series of blows about the head delivered with some force or passion – five or six – by a blunt instrument. We'll probably discover her skull's smashed. The profile of one of the wounds – look, this one here across the left cheek – is so clear you can tell it was a long thin implement. Can anyone see a bloodstained poker about the place by any chance?'

'Fire dogs in the hearth, sir,' said the inspector. 'Thrown about but there's shovel, brush and tongs present. No poker. None observable so unless it's wedged under the corpse it left with the killer.'

'Not under the body,' said the doctor, easing it over.

Joe glanced at the window. 'How very odd,' he said.

The pathologist checked his thermometer. 'Almost two degrees temperature loss so that confirms what you're telling me.' He turned his attention from the body to the bloodstains spattering the walls, carpet and furniture. 'You know, judging by the intensity of the flow, I'd say that the first and most violent blow was struck right here on the rug in front of the fireplace. Someone lost his temper, helped himself to the poker and hit her. Scalp bleeds freely, you know. I'm looking at that spurt of gore there . . . reaches as far as that chair. Turn it back on to its feet and you'll see what I mean.'

'Got it, sir,' said Cottingham quietly.

'Even odder,' said Joe.

Parry pointed to further bloodstains. 'Then she reeled away . . . fought him off . . . and did a sort of *danse macabre* around the room until the *coup de grâce* was delivered and she collapsed where we see her now. It could have been noisy, Sandilands. Someone might have heard her screaming. There's bruising on her hands and lower arms where she's fended off the blows so she must have remained conscious for a while.'

'Her clothing appears to be disarranged, Parry,' said Joe. 'Any views at this stage?'

'Shan't be able to tell you if she's been subjected to an attack of a sexual nature until I've examined the body at the hospital but . . . oh, I don't know . . . time of the essence and all that . . .' Joe went to inspect Cottingham's drawing while the pathologist probed more deeply into their problem. 'This is a bit queer,' Parry said finally. 'It *looks* as though she's been interfered with. . . dress torn, breasts – you'd almost say on display, wouldn't you? – but down below everything appears to be shipshape and Bristol fashion. She's got on one of those all-in-ones . . . what do they call 'ems?'

'Camiknickers,' supplied Westhorpe from the doorway.

'Thank you, miss,' said Parry, looking from Joe to Westhorpe in astonishment.

'It's Constable, sir,' said Westhorpe and she retreated back into the bathroom.

'Indeed! Yes, well, these garments are all in one piece and button up the front. Camiknickers, as the young lady says. Make a girl practically impregnable,' he smiled, 'and I use the word advisedly. And all the buttons are done up. But, as I say, I'll have more for you later.'

The doctor stood and replaced his equipment in his bag. He stood for a moment looking thoughtfully down at the body. 'What a waste! Spectacular-looking woman! Was she someone?'

Joe made a further introduction, giving Dame Beatrice the dignity he felt she was due even in death.

Dr Parry whistled. 'Oh, I see. That explains the clipped tones and the urgency on the telephone. Well, good luck with it, Commander! . . . Inspector . . . I'll send a couple of my chaps up in, shall we say, twenty minutes to take the body away. There's a back staircase they can use, I understand. Won't be the first time a famous face has been spirited off the premises of a grand hotel.'

*   *   *

39

A police photographer arrived and subjected Dame Beatrice to a last indignity, speedily and efficiently recording the scene as he knew the Commander liked it done. The hotel manager paid a visit to the corpse and, in deference perhaps to the status of his guest, escorted the coffin, forging ahead of it like a Thames tug as it was discreetly conveyed down the back stairs. Joe wondered whether the hotel kept a spare coffin permanently on hand or whether the obliging Dr Parry had provided.

'One last task for tonight, Cottingham, before I send you to your bed – would you go down and have a word with the reporter they're detaining? You may give him the outline of the crime but not, of course, the victim's name yet . . . next of kin to be informed and all that . . . and then I want you to find out how he was alerted. His source may also be a witness. Don't stand any nonsense. Get the truth. I need a name.'

'I think I know the gentleman,' said Cottingham confidently. 'And if it's who I think it is, I also know how to get the info out of him. No need to enquire further, sir. Would there be anything else, Commander?'

'Yes. The cat-burgling fraternity. Find out what we've got. Get hold of any informers and encourage them to tell what they know. Not my preserve, the rooftops of London – so find me someone who knows his way about. Someone with knowledge . . . oh – and someone with a head for heights who can lend us a hand tomorrow.'

'Got you, sir!'

Joe glanced at his watch. 'Good Lord! Three o'clock! Leave one of your chaps on duty here and go home and get some sleep. Apologize to Julia for me, will you, and give her my regards. See me in my office . . . shall we say at noon tomorrow? I'll phone the family in Surrey from the lobby and motor down myself to see them tomorrow afternoon.'

Constable Westhorpe had joined them in the sitting room, standing in the at-ease position by the door. But there was nothing at ease about her eyes, Joe thought. No sign of fatigue, flushed cheeks – overexcited if anything. Her glance flicked from one to the other attending to every word.

The inspector bustled off leaving Joe alone with Westhorpe. He turned to her and said, 'Very well, er, Tilly, I'm sure you've formed an opinion as to what went on in this room tonight. You were, I suppose I could say, closest to the murder in time. What really happened here? Share your views with me.'

She looked surprised but pleased to have been asked and did not need to pause to order her thoughts. 'She was killed by whoever got in through that window, sir. There are marks on the lock made from the outside – you can see them from here – and that can only have been done by someone standing on the roof. You'll have noticed there's a sort of ledge running around the building at this floor level. Very convenient. He stood there and tried to lever the window open. Couldn't manage – good strong frames and locks – so he broke the glass with the sharp end of his tool – I think they call it a jemmy, sir – put a hand through, opened the lock and got in. Perhaps Dame Beatrice was in the bathroom or the bedroom and she came out and confronted him.'

'She didn't run to the door to raise the alarm? Wouldn't that have been the most natural thing to do?'

'For most women. Not for Dame Beatrice. As the pathologist said – I was listening at the door – she was facing the man when he hit her with the poker. The blows landed here and here . . .' Westhorpe demonstrated.

'Poker? Why not use the jemmy he must have been holding in his hand?'

For a moment Tilly was disconcerted. 'I've never seen a jemmy, sir . . . perhaps a poker makes a more efficient murder weapon? But as we have neither jemmy nor poker to hand yet, who can say?' She frowned and went on, 'Dame Beatrice was no ordinary victim. She wouldn't have been prepared to just hand over her jewels – especially not those emeralds. She was ready to stand her ground and fight. Perhaps the intruder was afraid for his own life!' she said with sudden insight. 'Perhaps it was *she* who snatched up the poker and rounded on *him* . . . He took it from her and hit her to stop her raising the alarm.'

'Mmm . . . yes . . . Look, could you walk out of the bedroom and retrace Dame Beatrice's steps? That's it. Now you catch sight of me. Dash to the hearth and pick up an imaginary poker – use the tongs – and go for me.'

Tilly walked through the space which short hours ago had witnessed the outburst of deadly violence, miming the victim's surprise on catching sight of the intruder, snatching up the tongs and rushing at him. They met on the hearthrug at the spot where the first jet of blood marked the overturned chair and carpet. Joe wrested the shovel easily from Tilly's hand, mortified to see that she was trembling. She had turned pale and he forbore even in mime to smack her across the head with the implement. He was feeling it himself: the eddies of evil which still surged about the room. They were standing on the blood-soaked rug where the Dame had fought for her life and, defeated, had breathed her last, a defiant sneer on her face. And if *he*, battle-hardened survivor of many worse scenes of carnage, was affected by the atmosphere what must be the strain on this young, inexperienced girl?

Guiltily, Joe put down the tongs and patted her shoulder. 'That's enough for tonight, I think, Tilly. And, yes, it's a distinct possibility, your scenario.'

She had apparently not noticed, as he had, that the first blow had been struck while the attacker had his back to the door, the Dame facing him, her back to the window. Could they have circled round each other like adversaries in some grotesque parody of a gladiatorial combat? A combat which would end with the death of one of them?

'Sir? Are you all right, sir?'

Tilly's over-excitement was beginning to annoy him. He was reminded of his sister's awful little spaniel: bright-eyed, quivering with its need for attention and under his feet whichever way he turned. 'Thank you, Tilly. And now – it's extremely late even for a fashionable young lady from Mayfair and I want you to go home in a taxi and have a well-earned sleep. You've rendered valuable assistance and insight tonight in circumstances which must be personally distressing to you. I don't lose sight of that and, believe me, I'm very grateful.'

Her expression had become cold and watchful. 'And? Sir?' she prompted when, embarrassed, he ran out of polite phrases.

'And I would like you to take a day off to recover yourself from this ordeal before resuming whatever are your usual duties. I am, as I say, most grateful and will inform Sir Nevil that you made an invaluable contribution to the enquiry tonight.'

The blue glare stopped the words in his throat and her reply was at once soft but oddly menacing: 'My usual duties, as you call them, take me this week to Hyde Park where I am on Public Order patrol. If you should wish to engage my further attention in the matter of Dame Beatrice you will find me there between dawn and dusk dealing with roisterers, runaways, drunks and prostitutes.'

'Thank you, Westhorpe,' said Joe, unbalanced once again by the girl's forthright expression. 'I hope it won't be necessary to tear you from your valued work.'

As she turned with a curt nod to leave, he called after her. 'One thing before you leave . . . you were going to tell me why you came up to see Dame Beatrice . . .'

She paused with her hand on the door knob. 'I was going to seek her assistance in a project of mine,' she said mysteriously. 'I was going to ask her advice on joining the navy. I was hoping to become a Wren, sir,' she said and smiled with satisfaction on seeing his surprise.

Chapter Four

'You, Westhorpe? A Wren?' Joe couldn't disguise his astonishment. 'But surely you were aware . . . they were disbanded after the war?'

'I am perfectly well aware that the Wrens are no longer officially in being as one of His Majesty's auxiliary services, of course,' she said stiffly. 'Perhaps you didn't know that the association continues in an informal way? Dame Beatrice was gathering about her an elite and useful group of girls like me, a group whose abilities will be valued in the event of a future war. The armed services appear to know how to make intelligent use of their recruits. Goodnight, sir. Shall I send up . . . Armstrong, was it?'

'Armitage. Thank you, Tilly. Yes. Please do that.'

She left, dragging Joe's thoughts after her. He was left feeling uneasy with his decision to retain the services of Armitage at the expense of Tilly and began to rehearse his explanation to Sir Nevil. There was no obligation to justify himself – after all, it would have been most irregular (unprecedented even) to make use of a woman constable in the way Tilly had apparently assumed she would be used. He recognized and admired her intelligence and strength and, unusually for a man in his profession, did not feel threatened by her presence. He was aware of a general hostility from the other men in the force to the employment of women but, while he could understand and allow for this, he could not share it. His own mother and older sister Lydia were cut from the same cloth. He had grown up in a family where females were regarded

44

as, at the very least, the equal of males. Delightfully different, occasionally intimidating, but always competent and reassuring, was Joe's experience. His mother had for years managed the family estates in the Borders following his father's crippling accident while Lydia, he knew, helped to run a suffragist group which had splintered from Emmeline Pankhurst's. Married to a wealthy, indulgent, charming but lazy man with a grand house in Surrey, she led a life which suited her exactly. While raising her two children and running a hospitable household with an indoor staff of twenty and an outdoor staff so numerous Joe had never counted them, Lydia found time to involve herself with the advancement of women, with prison reform, the welfare of retired pit ponies and other good causes. Quaker blood, Joe thought. It led to Quaker conscience and a belief in the redeeming nature of hard work. Could be a curse.

'Still here, sir?' Armitage's brisk voice cut through his increasingly rambling thoughts. 'Why don't you go off home and leave me to clear up the bits and pieces?'

'Thanks, Bill, but we're almost done for now. Look, I'll be telling my boss that I want you moved from whatever you were doing to join me in this case. It would be good to be working together again.'

Armitage allowed a flash of eagerness to light up his stern features for a moment and then he replied soberly, 'I'd consider it an honour. And a pleasure, Captain.'

They smiled at each other with mutual regard.

'Before we both head off into the night, Bill, one last thing. You were very quickly on the scene . . . on patrol outside, I understand? Did you notice anything untoward? Crash of breaking glass too much to hope for, I suppose?'

'I've been going over and over it, sir.' Armitage almost ground his teeth with frustration. 'Didn't hear a thing. I could have been round the other side of the building and it's a windy old night, sir. Sorry I missed it. I circled the building using my flashlight at intervals. I gave the ledge outside a good dowsing. It runs all the way round and I'd marked it as a useful platform for anyone wishing to gain unlawful entry.' He paused for a moment. 'I saw nothing. Not even a stray moggie. Disappointing that. I was . . . hard to explain . . . keyed up the whole evening. Sure something was about to happen.'

Joe nodded.

'And I'd persuaded myself that if there was going to be trouble it would come from outside.' Armitage succinctly filled Joe in on his observations of the company in the party room. 'I'd ruled out that lot as pretty useless. Couldn't see any man jack of 'em staggering further than the nearest taxi.'

'You say no one left the room immediately after Dame Beatrice except for old Lady What's-er-name and Westhorpe?'

'That's right, sir. Of course, I'd no idea at the time she was a lady policeman. She was just a pretty girl in a rather revealing silver frock to me. It must have been about ten past midnight when she went out. That would have been five minutes after the Dame. I went out on patrol at twelve fifteen and got back inside about twelve fifty by which time there was quite a stir-about in the manager's office and I was sent straight up here with Robert to keep the lid on, sir.'

'So thirty minutes, near enough, separate your last sighting of Dame Beatrice and Tilly's finding her body?'

'Yessir. I beg your pardon, sir, but . . .' Armitage was uncharacteristically hesitant.

'Go on, Bill.'

'Well, I've learned in this business to trust no one. And I did come upon the young lady bold as brass standing over the corpse . . . no real idea of why she should have been in the room at that hour . . . nothing she was prepared to confide in me, anyhow. I checked up on her movements downstairs.' His tone was of defiance rather than pride.

'Quite right. And?' Joe was serious but encouraging.

'Well, I thought it was a bit off, her taking nearly half an hour to get up here, so I asked about that. She was observed rendering assistance to the old lady who was feeling a little unsteady and that took up some of the time. She finally turned the old dear over to the care of an attendant whom I have interviewed, sir, then she went up to the reception desk where she joined a queue for some minutes to find out the number of this room – as she said, a large theatre crowd had just come in. Then she went up by the stairs. The lift boy has no recollection of a young lady in a silver dress taking the lift but he can't swear to anything much as every lift load was a full one around that time. It would have taken her inside ten minutes to get up here and locate the room. I've just timed it, sir. Though she is a rather . . . um . . . athletically built young lady. She could have sprinted up.'

'You'd really like to pin this one on Miss Westhorpe, wouldn't you, Bill?' said Joe, amused.

Armitage flushed. 'I can't deny the thought has its attractions, sir.' He grinned suddenly. 'And wouldn't *you* give a lot to hear her exchanges with the judge! Can't say I haven't tried to work out how she could have done it but . . .'

'But you keep coming back to the picture of Tilly Westhorpe in spotless gloves and gown (apart from the hemline) snooping around the crime scene?'

Armitage sighed and nodded. 'We're looking for someone covered in blood, sir, with an emerald necklace, a jemmy and a bloodstained poker concealed about his person.' He grinned. 'Constable Westhorpe's get-up didn't even conceal Constable Westhorpe!'

'No indeed. As you say – an athletically built young lady! But how likely is it that it was the murderer who got in through the window?'

'*Somebody* broke in and he didn't come to change a light bulb! I've looked at that window. Those marks were made from the outside. The glass shattered inwards. Look at the way the shards have fallen. Could you fake that?' He shook his head impatiently. 'Do you think we're playing at detectives, sir?' he burst out in some anxiety. 'Over-egging the pudding? Poncing about being clever when all we should be saying is it's a burglary gone wrong? I must say, common sense says that's what it is.'

'I'd like to come to that conclusion,' said Joe, 'but there is something distinctly odd about this set-up and I think you've seen it too. Constable Westhorpe certainly has. I've heard from her. Now *you* stop poncing about and tell me clearly what are your impressions.'

'It's the violence I don't like, sir. Cat burglars don't kill. We all know that. If our lad had got in in the hope of lifting the odd necklace left lying about while its owner was in the bath and he'd been disturbed, he'd have legged it back the way he came or even, if he had the nerve, said, "Excuse me, madam, wrong room!" and strolled out of the door. It's been done.'

'Westhorpe thinks the Dame caught him at it and went for him with the poker.'

'Could have something there,' said Armitage grudgingly. 'But he could still have run. I must say, face to face with a poker-wielding, six-foot redhead, I'd scarper. And, anyway, one blow would have incapacitated her, wouldn't it? Why go on and on? Did you count the wounds? Four or five, I'd have said. Sort of damage you get in a domestic altercation, sir. No, there's more to it than just a burglary.' Armitage sniffed the air. 'It's gone now but it was still lingering when I got up here to find the body. Can't explain it scientifically, sir, but . . . well . . . you remember in the trenches how you could smell . . . I mean really *smell* fear?'

Joe nodded.

'The air in here was thick with – not fear, no – the opposite, violence and anger . . . yes, anger. It was a red smell, sir. As though there'd been a blazing row. I think the killer got in through the window but it wasn't an opportunistic, random visit in the line of burglary. It was surely someone who knew and hated her, you'd say.'

'Her emeralds were stolen but he hadn't searched the

48

room professionally,' Joe commented. 'Westhorpe found a diamond necklace secreted in a rather obvious place.'

'He took the emeralds because they were easy to snatch to make it look like a burglary.'

'And disordered the clothes to add the extra dimension of rape, to exercise the coppers' minds?'

'Ripping the dress to make it look like a sex crime? Bloody amateur! Who does he think he's fooling?'

'Obviously the chap has never seen the victim of a rape other than in his own imagination, I agree, Bill. And there was something about the gesture . . . so unnecessary . . . that makes the skin crawl.'

'It's all linked up with the personal aspect, sir. Whoever killed her knew her, hated her, wanted her dead and wanted her corpse to lie exposed to view. There was an element of display there that you couldn't miss. You and I, sir, we were being manipulated by this sadistic bastard, being involved by him, being invited to leer at her in her degradation.'

Joe looked curiously at the sergeant, intrigued by his vehemence.

'You'll think I'm getting carried away,' said Armitage, reading his thoughts, 'but I saw the lady, don't forget – I know *I* never shall – only minutes before this happened. She was full of life, having a good time, flirty, sexy, irresistible. She was taking Monty Mathurin's eye all right and, I have to say, he wasn't the only man in the room calculating his chances. Myself included,' he finished defiantly. 'Zero,' he added with an apologetic grin.

'Mathurin was at the party?'

'He was. And there's another I wouldn't mind pinning it on!'

'Nasty bit of work, Mathurin, if all I hear is halfway correct,' said Joe, 'but I doubt he fits this frame. He'd have trouble catching a 42 bus – there's no way he could have undertaken a climb of this nature.' Joe sighed. 'I think at this stage we'd better arrive at a portrait of the killer. Firstly, he would have to be young and extraordinarily agile – that's not an easy climb on a dark, wet night. Probably wore gloves – Cottingham's dusted the window area for prints and there's no sign of anything we can use.'

'Let's say under forty, fit and probably known to the victim. That's Mathurin out of it on two counts. I'd say our man knew her well – family, friend, work colleague, lover or ex-lover, sir? Don't know anything about the lady's private life, do we?'

'Ah, well, thanks to Westhorpe's drawer-searching expertise we have a clue there.'

Armitage listened with a gleeful expression as Joe told him about the device found in the underwear drawer. 'And you're saying the little minx appeared familiar with such a contraption?' he wanted to know. 'Well, bugger me!'

Joe registered that his sergeant's thoughts were dwelling on Westhorpe and not the Dame. Again he seemed to have touched the animosity running between these two.

'You don't have a high opinion of the constable, I think, Bill?'

'I'm not unusual in that, sir! Most of the men on the force resent the women. Jobs are hard enough to come by. There's good men starving on the streets, unable to support their families. Hard to see why she's not at home, married and producing little 'uns for the next lot, some would say.'

'Are you among them, these critics?'

'Not all the way. I'm one of those who can see they have their uses but this particular one – well, I'd like to know what she thinks she's doing, with all her advantages; hobnobbing with riff-raff on the streets and taking orders from the likes of us.'

'Mmm . . . not sure Westhorpe takes orders from anyone in spite of her lowly rank, even when she's mouthing, "three bags full, sir".'

'Water off a duck's back, sir. I'd noticed. It's the class. It's that look in the eye that says, "I'll listen to what you have to say and if it makes sense, then I'll probably agree to do what you suggest, but never make the mistake, my man, of assuming your stripes give you any influence over me!"'

To Joe's surprise, Armitage's supple voice had taken on the carefully enunciated archness of Mayfair and he remembered that Bill had shown considerable talent for picking up accents and languages.

'You won't be dismayed, then, if I tell you I've asked her to return to her regular duties?'

'She's off the case?'

Joe was puzzled by his sergeant's reaction. He had expected relief, gratification, vindication – perhaps, even a flash of triumph. He hadn't expected surprise and disappointment. Good Lord! Could it be that those blue eyes, icy though they were, had found a target?

'Pity that! I was looking forward to teaching that little madam how the world works.'

Joe eyed him steadily. 'You know, Armitage, I think Westhorpe could have taught *us* a few things.'

After an intensive ten minutes of checking and comparing notes, issuing orders and taking a last look at the scene, Joe finally called it a day. 'Look, it's late, Sarge.' He stifled a yawn. 'I'm going downstairs to the office to put through the dreaded call to the lady's mother in Surrey. I'm driving there tomorrow afternoon and I'd like you to come along. It'll be another long day, I'm afraid, Bill, and I'm not sure what your domestic arrangements are . . . a wife to placate, perhaps?'

'Single, sir. I've managed to stay single. I'm living with my old father down the East End.' He grinned. 'The old feller would worry if I *didn't* stay out late some evenings.'

'That's fine then. Look, can you lock up here and liaise with the hotel staff? And there's a night duty copper from the Vine Street station on his way and he'll need briefing.'

'I can manage, sir!'

Chapter Five

Armitage left by the staff entrance. Looking doubtfully at the rain-wet street and the dangling lights swinging in the wind, he stood for a moment fastening his police cape tightly about his shoulders. He patted his pockets and checked his belongings then pulled a fashionably rakish peaked service cap on to his head and adjusted the neb to the angle he favoured. He'd begged it from a mate who served with the Thames Police and those boys knew about weatherproofing. He glanced up and down Piccadilly, all senses still alert. The night's events had given his nerves a shaking and he had too many thoughts chasing each other through his head to allow him to slope quietly off back to the rat hole he called home and get a few hours' sleep.

He wondered what impression he'd made on the Commander. And what a turn of fate that he, of all people, should be in charge of the case! Best officer Armitage had come across in the four years of fighting, but that was ten years ago near enough and Armitage was too experienced to think you could rely on past goodwill. *He* never did. What had Sandilands said? 'We must have a pint and a chat sometime.' Oh, yer! Friendly enough but meaningless. Just a polite formula. Armitage's lips curled in derision. What did he expect his response to be? 'Delighted! Your club or mine?' He shrugged his shoulders. Take the Commander for a jar to his own local, the Dog and Duck? That'd show him how the other nine tenths live!

With a cynical smile, he set off east down the almost deserted but still brightly lit street. Nearly all the revellers had gone home or into the smoky dark depths of some nightclub. He passed a couple in fancy dress, wandering drunk and disoriented, hand in hand, shivering and giggling. Armitage approached them, putting on a copper's voice, firm but jocular. ''Allo, 'allo! Captain Hook and Miss Tinkerbell, is it? May I direct you to the nearest taxi stand before the lady's wings get wet?' He pointed and pushed them in the right direction and went on his way.

He managed to keep the rhythm of his stride when he first became aware that he was being followed. He did not look back. He slowed to exchange a few words with a street washer. Boots and oilskin apron shining under a streetlight, the workman was directing his powerful jet at the pavement, washing the day's and night's accumulated filth into the gutter. He grinned a toothless grin at the sergeant and was pleased to turn off his hose to share a companionable moment.

'Wild old night, Sarge!'

'Still – no May flowers without your April showers.'

'Did you hear who'd won the cup, then?'

'Some bloody northern team,' Armitage grinned.

'Bolton Wanderers!'

'Sod it! I had a bob on Man. City.'

'Didn't we all? Working late, sir?'

'No rest for the wicked.'

The reassuring platitudes flowed, bonding two fellow workers through the small hours.

Turning to raise a hand in final salute, Armitage took the opportunity to scan the deserted street behind him. Not quite deserted. Three weary ladies of the night were gathered together in a disgruntled group under a lamp on the pavement across the road, screaming abuse at the street washer whose renewed efforts were persuading them to move on down Piccadilly. In the dark alcoves fronting a gents' outfitters two or three pairs of legs protruded: down-and-outs who hadn't quite made it all the way to the Green Park railings for the night. The sergeant was a cautious but confident man and he was puzzled. Who was

53

out there? No street thief would take on a policeman even at night. Particularly not a swaggering six-footer like Armitage. He thought for a moment then smiled and walked more carefully on his way eastwards.

In a spirit of mischief he stood for an annoyingly long time shining his torch on to the display of books in Hatchard's window. He walked on for some yards down the well-lit middle of the road to allow his pursuer a clear look at him, then quickly nipped down Swallow Street, passing the Vine Street nick and coming out into the graceful curve of Regent Street, now deserted. He crossed at once and plunged into the narrow streets of Soho. Glasshouse Street. Brewer Street. The tail was still in place. Armitage grinned. He was enjoying this. Just what he needed. He used all his tricks to get a sight of his follower. He knew these alleyways like the back of his hand. So, apparently, did his shadow. He wondered for a moment whether he was imagining it. But the sensitive spot on his spine was still sending warnings. God! His leg was killing him! Couldn't keep this up for much longer. It was time to face him out. He turned and looked over his shoulder then walked down the middle of the road towards Golden Square.

He reached his goal – an all-night coffee stall which seemed to be doing good business. Three gents in silk top hats and opera cloaks were talking loudly, sipping fragrant coffee from china mugs. A taxi driver rolled in for a couple of saveloys and a pint mug of tea. A medical student asked for an Oxo and a ham sandwich. Two lean men whose faces he thought he recognized faded rapidly into the shadows at the sight of the police cape.

Armitage approached the counter and looked up into the sweaty, beaming face of the proprietor.

'Mug of your best java, Zeek, and a couple of those saveloys – they smell good. Keeping busy, I see.'

'Musn't grumble. It'll get busier when the nightclubs turn out. There yer go, Sarge. Mustard with that?

'No, ta. Do right well as it is. I'll park me owd bum on that there bench to enjoy 'em.'

He sat down at a rudimentary table thoughtfully and illegally provided on the pavement by the management for revellers too unsteady to hold their mugs after a night on the town. He waited, his back to the stall, a smile on his face.

There it was, the upper-class baritone he'd been expecting.

'I'll have the same as the sergeant, thanks.'

Joe put his mug down next to Armitage's.

'Shove over a bit! Cigarette first or are we straight into the sausages?'

'Sausages first, I think, before they start to congeal.' He noticed with satisfaction that Joe was breathing heavily. 'Too many hours at the desk, is it, sir?' he asked innocently.

'Far too many! God! You're a hard man to keep up with! Good practice, though! I haven't done that since I was on the beat.'

'You haven't lost the knack, sir. I was well into Soho before I twigged.'

'Really? Didn't think I was *that* good! I must confess I lost you in Bridle Lane. I just guessed you'd fetch up here.'

The two men grinned, open enjoyment outweighing the embarrassment of discovering each other indulging in an activity more suited to a recruit.

'You're more at home here than I am, I think,' said Joe.

'London man?'

'Born and bred.'

'And congratulations on making sergeant, by the way. You can't have wasted any time?'

'Five years. No, you're right, sir. That's as fast as it gets in the force. Unless . . .' he added with a sly but obvious sideways look at Joe.

'I'll save you saying it,' Joe interrupted, good-humouredly. 'Someone once told me I must have had a rocket up my arse to get to my present elevated rank so quickly! True. And the rocket had a name on it! A few years back when I was pounding the beat in the ordinary way – and believe me, Armitage, I've done all the basics! . . . ex-officers weren't spared the training – I had a bit of luck.' He added slowly, 'Though it didn't seem like luck at the time. And it was an odd time. Police unions, police strikes considerably more than a possibility, a good deal of disenchantment in the force . . .'

'I remember that,' said Armitage. 'Before I joined. I wouldn't have considered it if it hadn't all turned around.'

'Not surprised to hear it. Enormous amount of unfairness and injustice and what happened? To my horror, a delegation of the rank and file – my fellow bobbies – waited on me and asked me if I would not only join but spearhead the police union's protest! Pretty unpromising situation for a bright young chap like me, on the threshold of my new career! Overnight I had the reputation of being a firebrand, a dangerous man . . .' Joe dropped his voice and added theatrically, 'an agitator.'

The word, though lightly offered, made Armitage shudder. 'Bad situation, sir! Promising police career looking a bit blue round the edges? Sacking offence, isn't it? Union business . . . can get you into trouble.'

'Certainly did then,' said Joe. 'And it wasn't as though I hadn't been warned . . . the chap before me who'd complained on behalf of the men – Thomas Thiel, that was his name, ex-Guards officer – had just been dismissed. Sir Edward Henry, the outgoing Commissioner, had got rid of him for fomenting trouble in the ranks. And here I was being invited to put my neck on the same block.'

'But you did it anyway,' said Armitage with a smile and a nod. 'Always did lead from the front!'

'Well,' said Joe, 'it didn't feel much like leadership at the time. Someone behind me kicked my arse and I picked up the cudgels. There I was, agitating away if you care to put it like that, and my name came to the notice of the man at the top, the new Commissioner of Police. I was put up to represent the men in an informal interview with this chap.'

Joe paused and smiled a grim smile. 'He was General Sir Nevil Macready.'

Armitage's face stiffened. 'Blimey! That old war horse.' He took a bite of his saveloy and chewed thoughtfully.

'None other. From the siege of Ladysmith to the Easter uprisings, he was used to getting his own way. He was violently against police strikes and had already squashed one in 1918. And now this Big Gun was trained on me! I was summoned to see him in his office. You can imagine how I felt as I entered. But the first thing I saw – and, I must say, for a moment it put me off my stroke – was a poster pinned up on the wall behind his desk. It was one of ours. It said "Macready Must Go!" Bloody cheek! But I liked that. I thought that perhaps, after all, this was a man who was, like us, agitating away too. He didn't approve of police strikes (not keen myself, as it happens), he did see that there were grievances, did see that the police were a bumbling and incompetent body wandering round the streets of London with a lantern in one hand and a bell in the other.'

'Past seven o'clock and all's well?'

'That's the sort of thing. Anyway, soldier to soldier – he'd taken the trouble to find out all about me – we put our cards on the table. He listened to all I had to tell him about the front-line copper's problems and was able to assure me that many of them were already receiving his attention. And, with Sir Nevil, I was to find that this was not just a way of putting an inconvenient matter in cold storage. He's a man of his word and a man of fast reactions and in no time after that meeting he'd weeded out the injustices of the fines system and the sick pay which were the main bones of contention. He organized a meeting with Lloyd George for several of us union officials at Number Ten and we squeezed out even more concessions.' Joe grinned. 'We negotiated a pay rise, war bonuses and widows' pensions. We even got Thiel reinstated!

'He had a thousand and one projects on the move, all improving, all practical. Everything from redesigning the officers' dress uniform to modernizing, motorizing and re-equipping the whole force.'

'I think that's where I came in,' said Armitage. 'When it all started to look more like a career I might enjoy. But – you, sir? Constable to Commander in one easy move? Bit bold, wasn't it? Must have raised a few eyebrows, if not to say hackles?'

'It did! But it wasn't quite that obvious. It was one of several new appointments and it took a couple of years for me to work through. Sir Nevil – and others – had noticed that policing requirements had changed as a result of the war. Men trained to kill and use their resources to stay alive were suddenly unleashed on the world again. Clever, ruthless, experienced men . . .'

'You could be describing us, sir.'

'I am.'

'But – "Commander" – that sounds a bit naval. Was that intentional?'

'Probably was. It gets me the entrée into whatever corner of society needs to have a torch shone on it. The aristocracy have treated the police – on the rare occasions when they've had to have dealings with them at all – as their servants. But a *Commander* arriving at your front door has to be shown a bit more respect! Sir Nevil invented the title for the benefit of a free-wheeling new division responsible to him and nominally under my leadership. He still runs it on the quiet, though he retired as Commissioner some time ago.'

Joe broke off and gave his sergeant a steady look. He was not unaware that the information was flowing one way. Armitage was remaining politely inscrutable.

'So, Armitage. I thought you ought to know what you've got yourself into.'

For answer Armitage fished around in an inside poacher's pocket in his cape and produced a small silver brandy flask. He uncorked it and handed it to Joe.

'Sippers, Sergeant?' asked Joe, raising the flask.

'Gulpers, sir!'

*   *   *

Both pleased and disturbed by his encounter, Joe worked his way back towards Piccadilly Circus. A gathering rumble in the night air reminded him how late – or was it how early? – was the hour. The country carts were lumbering down Piccadilly, jogging along on their way to Smithfield, Covent Garden and Billingsgate. When the market bells rang at five o'clock a new London day would begin. He crossed the street, dodging a flower-laden cart heady with the scent of wallflowers and bright with tulips, and picked up a cruising taxi-cab for home. His mind was racing, trying to order the many things he would have to do in a few hours' time. He peered blearily through the cab window at the now milky sky as they turned on to the Embankment and he wondered if they would get to Chelsea before daybreak. Perhaps he should ask the cabby to loiter on Westminster Bridge so that he could enjoy the moment when the sun rose up from the grey waters of the Thames and brought back life to the capital; the brief moment before the houses and factories started puthering out their wreathing layers of yellow-grey smoke. Nocturne in black and grey perhaps? Variations in black and gold?

A river police launch shot the bridge like a swimming rat, its three-man crew alert and looking out into the oily depths of the river, the sinister grappling iron projecting from the stern announcing their grim purpose. Joe shivered. The sun would rise too late to bring warmth to some poor, cold, hopeless bugger. He was faintly embarrassed that he'd been about to linger, fancifully trying to decide whether the misty grey scene would have been more effectively rendered by Monet or Whistler. Some other day, he decided. And he wasn't quite in tune with Wordsworth this morning either.

He yawned. Another thing he must do was put through a call to Records before the meeting. He wanted to ask them to look out a file for him. The name on the file would be Sergeant W. Armitage. He wondered whether Sir Nevil's question mark was the same as his own.

Chapter Six

'Sir! I've been detailed to lend a hand this morning. Constable Sweetman. Attached to Vine Street.'

The eager young policeman in his impeccable uniform was, Joe judged, in his probationary year.

'Good morning, Sweetman. You have your instructions from Inspector Cottingham?'

'Yessir. He'll be here in a moment. I think we're both early, sir.'

'You're aware that I may require you to demonstrate your particular skill?'

'That's what I understand, sir.' He grinned and added, 'Won't be the first time.'

'Good. Then we just have to wait until my assistant, Sergeant Armitage, gets here.' Joe checked his watch. He was five minutes early.

'I think they're just arriving, sir.'

Cottingham strode up looking disconcertingly dapper. Starched collar and bowler hat, spats and smart black cashmere overcoat, he'd dressed for a working day in the West End. Bill Armitage, on the other hand, to Joe's satisfaction looked more blurred around the edges than he did himself, though the sergeant had obviously taken pains to make himself presentable. His light tweed suit topped off with a sample of the nob's version of the proletarian flat cap favoured by the royal princes was giving out signals complex enough to hold the attention for a good five minutes. Joe thought his choice was perfectly in tune with the bright spring day and with the task in hand.

They greeted each other with slightly twisted smiles and wry pleasantries, agreeing to get on with the job at once. The four men set out to retrace Armitage's tour of inspection the night before, circling the building until they reached the façade on the eastern side. They all looked up, eyes following the ledge below the mansard roof and focusing on the one window which had been boarded up. For a moment there was silence as they examined the challenging climb.

'Fire escape as far as the third floor,' said Joe, 'but then it gets a bit tricky. It's a fingers and toes job up the next floor and then there's the ledge overhang to negotiate before he can inch his way along to the broken window. Not pleasant but it has to be done. Heaven knows what clues, what evidence he might have left behind. Well, you know . . . button, thread of fabric . . . identity card?'

'Found a pair of false teeth at the scene once!' said Cottingham jovially. 'Clamped around a beef and horse-radish sandwich, they were.'

Armitage handed his cap to young Sweetman and began to take off his jacket. His usual swagger was absent, Joe noticed, as he said, 'Leave this to me, sir.' He clenched and unclenched his large hands and the knuckles were white with tension as he scanned the façade.

'Stand down, Sergeant,' said Cottingham. 'No need for that! Constable Sweetman is here for a purpose. Not just a pretty face – the lad has hidden talents, I'm told. Rock climber at weekends! You may divest yourself of your helmet and tunic before commencing, Roy, if you wish.'

The constable grinned and cast an assessing eye over the climb. 'It'll be a doddle, sir. Shall I start now? Is anyone going to time this?'

Cottingham took out a stop watch and moved off with his officer to the foot of the iron ladder of the fire escape. When they were out of earshot Joe said quietly, 'Very bold of you in the circumstances, I think, Sergeant, to volunteer for a climb like that?'

He paused, waiting for a response. Armitage looked truculently at his feet.

'The leg, Bill? Anything you want to tell me about the leg?'

Armitage's face stiffened with resentment. 'Following me down the street last night, was it, sir?'

Joe was unapologetic. 'Yes. Couldn't help noticing you were favouring your left leg . . . when you thought no one was looking. War wound, I take it?'

'It comes and goes, sir.'

'For example it comes when you think you are unobserved and goes when you're up for a medical?' Joe enquired with an interested smile.

Armitage's eyes glinted and his chin came up in defiance. 'All right, so you can get me sacked for disability . . .'

'And deception.' Joe was not prepared to let this go. 'I remember every recruit has to make a statement about his physical condition as well as prove it in the medical examination. And the three months' training is no cakewalk. I'm surprised that you managed to pull the wool over so many eyes for so long, Armitage.'

'So am I,' he admitted. 'And I can tell you it was bloody painful! But there were some good fellers who knew when to look the other way. Five years ago, the force was desperate for a certain calibre of recruit and in all other ways I fitted the bill. I've had no complaints. My record is a good one, you'll find when you've time to check it. Perhaps you already have, sir?'

Joe was silent for a moment, wondering exactly what he had uncovered and what action he should take.

'There's a telephone in reception. One call should do it, Captain.' The voice was icy and resigned.

The use of his old army rank was the only appeal the man would allow himself, though it was potent in itself, Joe recognized. He was too proud to allude to the many favours he'd done Joe over the months they'd fought together; it was bad form for survivors of the war to mention their experiences even to those who'd shared them. For men of his generation, four years of life – if you could call it that – were edited out of conversation. But not out of memory. Joe remembered the cups of weak tea proffered with a smile and an encouraging quip, the last drops of the sergeant's rum ration swirling muddily in the bottom of his dixie. 'Sippers? Naw! Go, on – finish it! You're the barmy bugger who's going over the wire. I'll keep the next ration safe. Be here when you get back, sir.'

And the life-saving shot of raw spirit was, indeed, there waiting for him but much more. Still fifty yards short of the trench and a grey dawn breaking, he'd been spotted. Rifle bullets cracked around him as he wriggled on elbows and belly, following the intermittent shelter of a tuck in the land. A bullet through his shoulder, exhausted and drained of any will to go on, Captain Sandilands had slumped on to his face on the earth waiting for death.

'Fucking sniper!' Bill's voice growled suddenly in his ear. 'Overdone it this time, though! We got a flash of him when he started having a go. Lads have got him in their sights. Listen! That'll make him keep his bloody head down – if it's still on his shoulders! I think we could break for it now. You okay?' And strong hands had hauled and pushed and rolled him the rest of the way back to shelter.

'Perhaps I'm one of those fellers who know when to look the other way? It's a skill I learned from a past master of the art in India,' said Joe.

They watched in companionable silence as the constable swarmed fearlessly up the fire escape. 'Tell me, Bill, did you ever stop counting those minutes?' Joe asked quietly.

Armitage responded at once to the allusion. Perhaps it had been in his mind also. 'Funny thing that. The counting had become so engrained I missed it when it all came to a stop. It kept me going. We all had to find our own ways of getting through.'

Joe was remembering the iron gleam in the sergeant's eye as he fired a captured enemy machine gun at a row of

German infantry emerging from their trench only yards away. They'd been sitting ducks for the raking gun. When, finally, the pitiless racket stopped and no more figures came on towards them through the smoke Joe had touched Armitage's shoulder briefly with a stiff, 'Well done, Sarge!' He'd realized with a shock that Armitage had been counting throughout. 'Twenty-five!' he'd said with satisfaction. 'Every bugger I get, I reckon as another minute off this bloody war. So that's near half an hour saved, Captain!'

Joe had known many men go through the war without ever firing their rifle. Some, no more than boys, he'd seen close their eyes before firing. Some had loosed off everything they had at the horizon. But not Armitage. He had placed every shot deliberately and counted every hit.

Joe's thoughts were interrupted by a triumphant crowing from Constable Sweetman who took time off from his climb to point to his left and stick a thumb in the air, indicating he'd spotted something of interest. He finished his climb, mimed jemmying and then smashing the window, and began the descent. This was done more slowly, with an eye open for evidence. When he reached a piece of roof invisible to those standing below he moved sideways from his course and, pausing, took a white handkerchief from his pocket. Using this, he carefully picked up an object and examined it uncertainly. Coming to a decision, he adjusted the handkerchief and took the thing firmly between his teeth before continuing his descent.

'Good Lord, Sweetman!' said Cottingham, impressed, handing back his helmet. 'It only took you four and a half minutes to get up there. Well done! What athletic ability! Nothing like it since Douglas Fairbanks swarmed up the rigging in *The Black Pirate*.'

With a flourish, Sweetman removed the object he'd retrieved from between his clenched teeth and gingerly held it out. ''Cept this should be a dagger, sir, or a cutlass, maybe! Murder weapon! Would this be the murder weapon, sir? It'd rolled under a lead flashing. Hard to spot! But at least the rain's not got at it. Look here, sir. And

64

here. Them's hairs . . . red 'uns. And that there's not tomato ketchup neither.'

They all looked with curiosity at the fireside poker.

'No, indeed,' said Cottingham. 'And, again, well spotted!' He took a brown paper evidence envelope from his murder bag and wrapped it loosely around the poker. 'I'll get this straight down to the lab, sir. It may have prints on it.'

The meeting broke up in great good humour with much self-congratulation and with a renewed appetite for the next stage of the case. Sweetman made his way back to Vine Street to impress and entertain his mates with an account of his exploits while Cottingham hailed a taxi for Scotland Yard where he intended to spend the day, as he put it, 'working on the forensics'.

Joe was left facing an Armitage still apparently ill at ease and subdued by the uncovering of his deception. 'Shouldn't think they'll find much more than the chamber-maid's dabs on that,' he said finally with a dismissive shrug. 'Let's not be forgetting our friend was wearing gloves. Hardly likely to have said, " 'Ere, hang on a minute, madam, whilst I divest myself of these gloves prior to seizing this 'ere poker and bashing you about the 'ead with it," now is he?'

'Doesn't sound reasonable to me either,' said Joe. 'And I expect we're in for a disappointment. Oh, and, Sergeant, I'm afraid you must prepare yourself for a further setback.' He sighed and smiled a rueful smile. 'I reported by tele-phone to the boss this morning and . . .' He hesitated, wondering how to go on. 'And for reasons I can't readily understand – yet – I am directed once more – and very firmly directed, I have to say – to make use of the services of Constable Westhorpe.'

'No!' Armitage was gratifyingly thunderstruck.

' 'Fraid so. She is to accompany us this afternoon to Surrey to investigate Dame Beatrice's home and family. There may well be female insights she can offer us, I'm told. But the first of our problems will be locating the wretched girl. I telephoned her home to make suitable arrangements at nine this morning only to be told by her father that Mathilda had already left the house in her uniform, reporting for duty in Hyde Park.' He waved an arm vaguely to the west. 'So she's out there somewhere in six hundred acres of woodland, lake and garden.'

Armitage's expression hardened but he commented lightly enough, 'And they do a good job, these women, I understand . . . fishing little boys out of the Serpentine, protecting laundry maids taking a short cut between the wilder parts of Bayswater and the Knightsbridge hotels, reuniting straying toddlers with their nannies.'

'The weaker members of the park-going community must be comforted by their presence,' said Joe firmly.

'Yers, and I've heard as how they've protected many an unworldly politician from the terrifying advances of ladies of a certain profession,' drawled Armitage with undisguised sarcasm. 'Did you hear, sir, about the Assistant Commissioner last December . . .' He looked about him. 'Must have been somewhere round here . . . Caught in flagrante with a Miss Thelma de Lava. I know the two lads who made the arrest. Takes courage to pick up the boss! Stout chaps!'

'Would you say stout chaps? I'd say pig-headed prudes,' said Joe mildly. 'Anyway – the gentleman in question was the *ex*-Assistant Commissioner. And why the hell shouldn't he treat himself to an early Christmas present?

'Look, I suggest we start our search at the police station. They should be aware of her route. It's up near the new bird sanctuary just past the Rangers' Lodge. Hang on, though – let's not forget it's a Sunday.'

'Right, sir. And that means there'll be half London in the park and most of those'll be milling about at Speakers' Corner up by the Marble Arch.'

'And you're thinking that's where she'll have been deployed? Makes sense, don't you think so?'

'I'd rather *not* think so!' Armitage's face clouded. 'It's not a place I'd deploy a woman in uniform. Not today.

Word is, things are likely to get a bit lively in the parks over this next bit. It's this bloody strike that's getting everyone het up. People are violently in favour or the reverse. And that's where you're likely to get clashes. Trouble. And there's the usual pack of no-goods who can smell it across the city. They're not interested in debate – all they want is a barney. They'll turn up in their hobnails with their white scarves and their bull terriers just to see what's going on. And if nothing's going on – well, they'll soon fix that!' He added thoughtfully, 'A woman in uniform is just their idea of an easy target. Shall we start searching at the Arch, sir?'

Joe responded to the concern in the sergeant's voice. 'Very well, Bill. Look, to save time, we'll get a taxi to take us down Piccadilly and up Park Lane. We'll check through the crowds there and work our way through the half-mile of wilderness across to the police station.'

'Good to have a plan to work to, sir!' said Armitage with a grin and Joe imagined rather than saw the salute.

'If all goes well, we might even have time for a cuppa in the Ring Tea House,' he said cheerfully. 'Come on!'

When it could make no further headway against the strolling, laughing crowds, the taxi dropped them off to make their way over the turfed stretch of ground facing the Arch, the grassy area already thick with orators, street corner preachers and their audiences. Speakers' Corner. You could always tell when the country was in a ferment, Joe thought, by counting the numbers of men and women standing on soapboxes, shouting, and by the size of the crowds prepared to stand and shout back at them. He turned a professional law-man's calculating eye on the speakers as they threaded their way through. The passionate rhetoric and hot dark eye of a striking coal miner almost stayed his step and this was undoubtedly where the thickest crowd was congregating. A sympathetic crowd, judging by the absence of heckling and the trickle of applause when the man paused for breath, they were responding, as was Joe, to his starveling good looks, his white skin blue-traceried below the surface with ancient coal dust scars and stretched over bones which seemed about to break through the thin confines of flesh at chin and wrist.

Not to be wondered at, Joe thought with a rush of pity, when the man's pay had been reduced by a quarter and his working week extended by ten hours. A fine reward the working man had been offered for four years of sacrifice.

'Here, duck, 'ave a sixpence for a sandwich and a cup of tea,' said a matronly figure. 'You'll feel better with summat 'ot in yer belly.'

The miner accepted the gift with grace and the surprising flash of a smile.

'Not a penny off the pay!' he shouted, encouraged.

'Not a minute on the day!' they responded, with music hall timing.

'Don't give 'em owt for nowt!' growled an East Ender in heavy mimicry of the Yorkshireman's accent.

'Silly buggers,' commented Armitage. 'We'll see if they still think the same when their milk supplies aren't getting through.'

No discernible trouble yet though. No pit-bulls with their owners in tow. Probably still in the pub. No sign of a lady policeman either. In her dark blue serge, Mathilda would have been very obvious amongst the women who, it seemed, had decided that enough was enough – winter was finally over and they were welcoming the spring. Cotton dresses had appeared in honour of the bright April sunshine, though shoulders were still prudently covered by cardigans and even shawls.

Further on they dodged an ear-splitting harangue from a member of the fascist movement. He was shouting and gesticulating in an effort to outdo the man next door, a communist, judging by the red sash he wore around his chest. Joe noticed that Armitage's step had slowed perceptibly as they passed the Bolshevik and he thought he might have lost the sergeant to the entertainment had they not been on a mission. Spotting a couple of uniformed bobbies patrolling, arms behind their backs, Armitage showed his warrant card and consulted them. He reported to Joe that they understood the women police to have been diverted to the Serpentine area. 'Sunny day like this, the nippers are likely to go a bit mad and get themselves into trouble diving into the water.'

Keeping each other in sight, Joe and Armitage made their way through the crowds until, emerging on the other side, both men stopped to take a deep breath and stare at the open green spaces about them.

'The lungs of London, they call them, sir,' said Armitage with something very like the modest pride of ownership. 'And what with Kensington Palace on one side and Buckingham Palace on the other, London's lucky to have it still. You'd have thought it would have been pinched for the palaces long ago.'

'Don't think they haven't tried!' said Joe. 'George the Second's wife – Caroline, I think she was? – once had the nerve to ask the Prime Minister what it would cost to enclose the whole of the three big London parks for the exclusive use of the Court. Wise old Walpole replied, "Madam, it would cost you three crowns: those of England, Ireland and Scotland." She didn't pursue the idea.'

Armitage grinned, enjoying hearing the old story repeated.

'There's the Serpentine.' Joe pointed to the gleam of the lake ahead of them, glimpsed through the thickening trees. Stately elms and groves of silver birch sported fresh green foliage as yet undarkened by soot. Joe suddenly grasped Armitage's arm and pointed. 'Look, Bill, do you see it? There!'

Armitage was puzzled.

'A wood-wren!' said Joe. 'I'll swear that was a wood-wren.'

'Looked like a sparrer to me, sir,' said Armitage repressively.

'Listen. What can you hear?' Joe persevered.

'Nothing . . . silence . . . No, I can hear traffic in the distance . . . kids screaming down by the lake . . . birds . . .'

'Birds!' Joe shook his head and grinned. 'There speaks a city boy. There's a blackbird, and that's a mistle thrush, a . . .' Abruptly Joe's pleasure in his surroundings faded. 'And . . . someone calling for help. Listen! Did you hear it? I'm sure I heard –'

'Over there – behind that scrub.'

They both began to run towards the sounds of distress. A female voice wailing and then a second voice, female this one also but louder and peremptory and calling for help, drew them on.

Joe was beginning to outdistance Armitage when he spotted a large man, running from the scrub towards the main carriageway leading to the exit. He was red-faced and lumbering along slowly, hindered by a considerable beer-belly and a preoccupation with the fastening of his trousers which appeared to be gaping open. Head down, he was too concerned to outrun the figure chasing after him to catch sight of Joe as he pounded forward to intercept him. Tilly Westhorpe, face like an avenging Fury, elbows pumping and heels flying, was hurtling with the speed of a miler, closing rapidly on her quarry.

God! What would the girl do if she caught up with this barrel of lard, Joe wondered? Six strides later he found out. With a whoop of triumph, she launched herself at the man's ankles and brought him crashing to the ground. Before he could struggle to his feet, she had plonked her nine stone frame firmly on top of his head. Taking a whistle from her breast pocket, she was about to emit a blast when she noticed the arrival of the cavalry. She seemed pleased to see Joe.

He sat down without ceremony on the man's flailing feet. 'Good morning, Westhorpe. Are you going to tell me who we're sitting on? Who's your friend?'

'Fiend, more like!' she panted. 'Been trying to catch him for weeks, sir. Rapist of the worst kind. Normally attacks females after dark, those stupid or desperate enough to come out here at night, but the supply of idiots has dried up lately and he's taken to daytime attacks.'

A foul cursing made its way upwards through several layers of serge skirt. Westhorpe bounced briskly, banging the man's head on the ground. 'No swearing!' she said. 'Lady present!'

'Er, I think you could get up now, Westhorpe. Don't want to afford the reprobate a further frisson of an arousing nature, do we? Too much excitement for one day, perhaps?'

Armitage had arrived and was taking in the strange scene, mouth sagging slightly. 'Ah, Sergeant! Your handcuffs, please,' said Tilly. 'And then, if you wouldn't mind – there's a poor girl in the bushes over there who will be needing our attention. It's all right,' she added, seeing Armitage blanch, 'I think I disturbed him before worse occurred. And perhaps you could do the honours here, Commander? Female constables do not have the authority to make an arrest.'

Knee in the man's back, Joe cuffed him. He informed him that he had been arrested by a Scotland Yard Commander and was on his way to the Hyde Park police station to be formally charged. The imposing arrival of two plain clothes detectives on the scene appeared to take the wind out of his sails and, abashed, he began to whine explanatory, man-to-man excuses. '. . . only a bit o' fun . . . just a skylark . . . you know how it is, sir . . . but who can tell what these silly cows'll say . . .' His whine turned to a howl as the sharp edge of a police boot caught him across the shin.

'Westhorpe!'

'Sorry, sir, but you didn't seem to be about to oblige.'

Armitage joined them. He was carrying in his arms a slight, sobbing bundle. Thin white arms were clasped around his neck. Stick-like white legs protruded from a short black skirt, ending in red socks, and one black patent-leather shoe dangled from a toe. Joe saw the expres-

71

sion of concern on Westhorpe's face before she could compose herself to look at the victim.

'Says her name's Vesta, miss,' said Armitage.

'Vesta,' said Westhorpe gently. Joe noticed that she took off her police hat to talk to the girl to avoid frightening her further. 'Hello, Vesta. I'm with the police and these gentlemen are detectives. You're safe with us. Vesta, are you feeling strong enough to identify this person as the man who attacked you just now? Don't worry, it's just a formality,' she added, 'and he can't do you any more harm.'

A tear-stained face looked up from Armitage's tweed waistcoat and glowered through a thick fringe at the prisoner. A small, accusing finger pointed.

Her shriek startled Joe. 'That's 'im! That's the whoreson, great pile o' pig-shit! I know 'im! It's my dad's cousin 'Erbert. Just let 'im wait till I tell my mam! She'll fillet 'im! She'll 'ave 'is cockles off and feed 'em to our cat! An' where's my other shoe got to?'

Joe and Armitage exchanged long looks.

'Shall I propose that we drop this little lot firmly into the lap of whatever lucky inspector is on duty over there in the station this bright a.m.?' suggested Joe.

Chapter Seven

Two hours later Joe was easing his Morris Oxford Cabriolet down Upper Brook Street looking out for Tilly's home. With an embarrassing grinding of gears he spotted it and slowed down. Armitage winced. Joe could not be certain whether it was his boss's driving skills that so irritated the sergeant or the aristocratic appearance of the spacious Georgian house in front of which they had just rolled to a halt.

'This looks like it,' said Joe, heaving on the handbrake. 'Hop out, will you, Bill, and sit in the back. I'll go and let them know we're here.'

'I think they'll have heard you, sir.'

The front door opened to reveal Tilly Westhorpe remonstrating with an elderly man. The silver-haired, straight-backed figure, of perceptibly military bearing, seemed to be losing an argument with the uniformed Tilly. She gave him a swift kiss on the cheek and stepped eagerly down the short path to the car. Joe opened the rear door and handed her over the running board and into the back seat.

This was not a social occasion and etiquette was unclear but, dash it all, what were good manners but an expressed consideration for others? On impulse, Joe turned and walked up to the house, swept off his hat and bowed his head briefly with a disarming smile. 'Sir, I cannot drive off with a chap's daughter without introducing myself. Commander Joseph Sandilands. We spoke on the telephone this morning. I've been advised by Sir Nevil to make use of Mathilda's special skills in a particularly distressing case –'

'Don't concern yourself, Sandilands,' came the swift interruption. 'No need to explain. I've already spoken to Nevil about this. Frederick Westhorpe. How do you do?'

They shook hands.

'Tilly's told me a good deal about you, Commander.' The shrewd blue eyes sparkled with humour for a moment. 'The girl seems to have acquired a grudging respect for you. And, believe me – that's unusual for her.' Catching Joe's surprise, he added, 'And for heaven's sake don't tell her I've said that! Can't say I approve of what Tilly gets up to but she tells me it's "worthwhile, socially desirable and personally fulfilling". I just pray it's one of her passing enthusiasms. But that's today's young ladies for you! Refuse to listen to their elders and betters. Will she listen to you?'

Joe grinned. 'Barely, sir. I have to bark a bit, I'm afraid.'

He moved aside to make way for a footman bearing a hamper.

'Hope you don't mind?' said Westhorpe, nodding at the offering. 'I try to look after her. Thought you might be glad of supplies if you're off into the wilds of Surrey.' A shadow fell on the bluff features. 'Take care of her, Sandilands. As far as she'll let you, of course! She's very precious . . . and she's all I've got . . . now.'

A toot on the horn and Tilly's cross face and an impatient wave put an end to the conversation.

The constable and the sergeant were settled in the back seat, the hamper wedged firmly between them. Each was studiously ignoring the other. Tilly sat rigidly, taking on just the degree of frozen composure to signal that her proximity to the sergeant was imposed and displeasing. Armitage looked fixedly through his window, whistling a tune under his breath. Joe thought he made out a snatch of 'Ain't We Got Fun.'

'Lovely house, Westhorpe,' he commented politely.

'Ah, yes. Jolly expensive to keep up though,' she replied coolly.

Joe sighed. He was not going to have his investigation compromised by a display of entrenched hostility but he decided against offending the intelligence of either one by delivering a pep talk on the necessity of pulling together. No, he decided it would be more productive to attempt practical methods of achieving some sort of fusion. And he'd already begun by installing them together in the back though he was aware that each had expected to sit in the front next to him.

Joe fought his way through the Sunday afternoon strollers and chugging omnibuses, south-west over the river, through Putney and Kingston and on to the Portsmouth road. The rows of neat villas petered out. Single, grander villas took up the tale and these too gave way to hedgerows, fields and church spires glimpsed across meadows. Soot-blackened trunks of elm trees lining the route were replaced by the unsullied boles of beeches trooping down green hillsides to gather in stands by the edge of the road. Gentle hills rose up before them, offshoots of the North Downs, and river valleys beckoned and wandered off enticingly into a blue distance.

Though Nature still had the upper hand here, Man was fast encroaching. Chimney stacks projecting above concealing trees and shy glimpses of impressive façades revealed that houses had recently been built. New money was moving out of London into hunting country and acquiring for its owners the trappings of gentility. The more discerning nouveaux riches were engaging architects of talent who knew how to make good use of local materials and how to position a house perfectly in its site, surrounding it with gardens designed to help its stone, brick and oak timbering to flow naturally into the countryside.

When Joe was confident he could identify buildings or an architectural style, he pointed them out with comments for the benefit of his silent passengers. He had slowed to 10 mph, talking enthusiastically of the romantic vernacular sweeps of tile-hung walls to be seen if they would just look to their left, when an exasperated sigh cut through his eulogy.

'Please don't feel you have to be so *interesting*, sir!' said Tilly.

'Ah! Time for a sandwich, I think,' said Joe good-humouredly and pulled off the road into the shade of a small spinney. He got out and settled himself against a fallen tree. 'I think you two can wait on me. What's in the hamper, Westhorpe?'

'Oh, sorry about that, sir. Couldn't stop him. There'll be the usual . . . ginger beer, a flask of coffee, cold roast chicken, smoked salmon sandwiches . . .'

'Quails' eggs?' asked Armitage brightly in what Joe had come to recognize as his 'posh' voice. 'I'm *so* hoping there'll be quails' eggs!'

'It's not the season for them,' said Tilly, closing down the conversation.

Joe grinned. There was no season for quails' eggs and he wondered how the pair had scored themselves on that opening round.

Joe eyed the tempting spread laid out in front of him on a picnic rug, hungry but hesitating as to how to start. Armitage came to a decision. He reached out and lifted a dish of tiny blue-shelled eggs and offered them to Tilly. In a voice so controlled he managed to speak with only the slightest emphasis he asked, '*Plover's* egg, Constable? Will you start with a *plover's* egg?'

Tilly looked at the sergeant with any attention for the first time that day and smiled her kilowatt smile. 'How too, too marvellous! I'd simply adore one!'

If it wasn't quite a truce, it was at least a slackening of hostilities, Joe reckoned, and set himself to chatter through the improvised luncheon party, insisting that each contributed to the conversation, an exercise which tested even his supple skills. In the end he decided that this was not a game for three adults but rather for one grown-up faced with two strange and hostile children. He changed tack and embarked on the one subject he knew would get a positive response from both.

'We're about half an hour short of our destination, I think,' he said in his professional voice. 'Not sure what to expect. But it's bound to be awkward.' He sighed. 'Worst part of the job . . . breaking the news of a death . . . hearing the first reactions. But, unpleasant though it may be, you can pick up some useful information at such times. Stay alert, both of you. Just remember that we're looking for someone close to the victim who had a motive for bashing her head in. And I hardly need to tell you that the people closest are most often to be found in one's home.'

'I can help you there, sir,' said Westhorpe. 'I did a little telephoning before you arrived and I've scraped together some information about the family. The Dame's mother is Alicia Jagow-Joliffe. A widow, wealthy on her own account, I understand. Well known before the war for her efforts on behalf of women's suffrage. She must be in her sixties but don't expect a capped and mittened old lady. Like daughter, like mother. She has a son living with her, Beatrice's brother . . . Orlando . . . I'm afraid.'

'Anything known? Romantic poet by any chance?'

'No. Seems to be a romantic artist. Spends a lot of time up in town paying court to the likes of Augustus John, buying rounds for the scroungers in the Fitzroy Tavern and paying the bill at the Café Royal. That sort of artist.'

'I'm supposed to infer – dilettante . . . *flâneur*? Has he had time to get married, this boulevardier?'

'I believe not. Though he does have an . . . er . . . attachment. Not always the *same* attachment. The current one's called Melisande . . . Melusine . . . something like that. She's his model. One of his models.'

'How too bohemian for words!' drawled Armitage.

For once, Tilly Westhorpe seemed to be in accord. Disapproval was evident in her voice as she pressed on: 'Orlando is in his late thirties but he's had time to provide himself with several offspring. No one's quite certain how many. They all had different mothers and the mothers

77

have all legged it, I understand. The present incumbent of his affections has taken the whole brood under her wing. And that's the extent of the family. You will enjoy the house, sir. Though not grand, it's reckoned to be of some historic and architectural interest.'

'Makes a change from the widow in Wapping whose daughter got her head bashed in last week,' commented Armitage in a neutral voice. 'I had to tell her her oldest girl had snuffed it down by the docks where she had her beat. With six other kids in a single room I think they were all glad of the extra space on the mouldering mattress.'

'Well, I think we'd better break up this jolly *déjeuner sur l'herbe*,' said Joe, 'and move on. I said we'd arrive at about three so we're on schedule.'

'Would you like *me* to drive, sir?' said Westhorpe and Armitage in chorus.

Joe held his hands up in mock dismay and surrender. 'Oh, all right! You've suffered enough, with no more than the occasional hissing intake of breath as a commentary on my driving skills, so I'll surrender the wheel to . . . eeny, meeny, miney, Westhorpe. And I promise you can drive us back all the way to London Town, Bill.'

Even Armitage seemed content to be in the hands of Westhorpe who moved off smoothly and worked her way up through the gears, proceeding, on reaching a clear stretch of road, to put her foot down and try for the 70 mph Joe had assured them his otherwise unspectacular car was capable of.

'Er, we don't want to get there too early, Tilly,' was all he would allow himself for comment.

To his surprise, Armitage leaned forward and engaged Westhorpe in conversation. Not very elevating conversation in Joe's estimation but both seemed to find it absorbing enough: 'What sort of car do you drive yourself, then, Constable?'

'Oh, just a little thing. A two-seater sports car. A Bullnose MG. A red one.'

'Very nice too! '

'Oh, underneath the pretty bodywork, you'll find much the same chassis and engine as you've got in this Oxford.'

'Ah! I thought you climbed behind the wheel with a lot of confidence.'

'Easy to drive but one could always do with a bit more power.'

'I'd have thought it was lively enough . . . gold medal in the London–Land's End trial, wasn't it?'

'Well, yes. I can get it to 60 mph from a standing start in twenty seconds so I suppose you're right. And yourself, Sergeant? What do you drive?'

'Anything I can get my hands on! I haven't got a car of my own – not possible on a sergeant's pay – but I trained in high speed driving and did six months in the Flying Squad.'

'So you were a thief-taker?' Tilly was impressed.

'Yes. Not as exciting as it might sound though,' said Armitage modestly. 'Too many hours cooped up under cover with a squad of sweating coppers parked outside a bank, waiting for something to happen. And then, as often as not, we'd find the villains had a faster set of wheels.' He shook his head regretfully. 'With so many motor bandits operating these days, someone up there in the hierarchy –' he glanced at Joe to check that he was listening – 'is going to have to bite the bullet and put in for something a little more lively than the old Crossley RFC tenders. Perhaps when they've re-equipped with Bentleys I'll reapply.'

'Now you're talking! They say the new model will be able to do over 100 mph.'

Well, it was a start. Joe groaned in boredom, closed his eyes and tuned out.

Westhorpe slowed down as they approached their destination. They looked with varying degrees of appreciation and envy at the house coming into view about a quarter of a mile from the road. It was attractive; it was unpretentious. It was distorted as, over five hundred years, the timber frame had settled into the soft heart of the land. Through years of faithfully applied ochre lime wash, the silhouette had blurred to a point where the house seemed to belong to the earth. The many-faceted lead panes of the oak-mullioned windows gave back a reflected sparkle as they picked up the rays of the afternoon sun.

Distantly, two enormous pear trees of incalculable age and white with blossom like ships in full sail formed a background to the house, peering over the mossed confusion of the steep-tiled roof with its soaring cluster of chimney stacks. It was a house Joe would have counted himself blessed to possess.

The approach was by a narrow carriage drive running between two imposing gate piers. Westhorpe saw them first. 'Look, sir! I think that's a welcoming party forming up. Or are they preparing to repel boarders? Not, apparently, mourning the dear departed exactly.'

Joe caught sight of two small figures – no more than children – who had been loitering at the base of the stone piers and were now furiously climbing upwards. Joe could guess what they were up to. Every county magazine featured photographs of bright young things at country house parties posing on top of gate piers pretending to be stone lions or Egyptian deities.

Joe smiled. 'Approach slowly, Westhorpe, and pause in the gateway. Pay no attention to what I say. Hand me that leather-backed notebook from the glove locker, would you?'

The car came to a halt and Joe stepped out, book in hand. Placing himself in the centre of the driveway, eyes flicking from the distant house and back to his book, he began to pretend to read for the benefit of his passengers: '"The original structure is that of a modest West Surrey brick-built farmhouse of the sixteenth century. To this has been added a centre block in rough imitation of the style of Sir Christopher Wren: rosy Home Counties brickwork, solid, substantial white-painted sash windows . . . Skilful additions made probably in the early years of this century, somewhat in the manner of Charles Voysey . . ." There – the wing to your right. Observe, Constable. Voysey? Would you say Voysey? I'd have said rather – Lutyens.

' "All is well until we come to the gate piers where a regrettable piece of naughtiness breaks out. Classical in style and combining practicality with grace, though the architect's vision and – we have to say – taste desert him when it comes to the statuary atop each pier." Note the statuary, Sergeant.' Joe waved a dismissive hand.

The statuary, which had hitherto remained commendably motionless, now began to twitch.

' "Diana on the left, holding her bow, and, on the right, her target, Actaeon. Perhaps that was the intent? More Grotesque than Grecian will be the judgement of the discerning visitor." '

Diana on the left uttered a strangled gurgle and allowed her bow to droop. Actaeon on the right uttered a hissing, 'I say!'

'Drive on, Constable. I think we've seen enough here!'

The butler flung the door wide a carefully calculated five seconds after Joe's double knock. Joe greeted him by name: 'Reid? We spoke earlier on the telephone. Commander Sandilands.' He presented his card which received a careful scrutiny.

'Mrs Joliffe is expecting you, Commander. I will let her know you have arrived, sir.' He nodded to a footman who took Joe's hat and Armitage's cap. With a shake of her head, Westhorpe indicated that she would retain her hat and they followed the butler along to a small south-facing drawing room. French doors were open on to a lawn set for croquet. A fire burned cheerfully in the grate under a carved oak mantelpiece. The room was furnished with a mixture of elegant pieces of traditional English design – Joe briefly noticed a particularly good set of Hepplewhite chairs – and some objects of more recent Arts and Crafts style. Oak tables, Turkey carpets and old pewter had settled down companionably side by side with modern hangings and silver ornaments. Joe thought the blend seemed right in this very English house in the shelter of the North Downs.

The tall, slender woman who turned to greet them on hearing their names announced, however, was straight out of a London drawing room. Dark red hair, short-cropped and turning to grey, strong features and haughty gaze gave Joe a disconcerting impression of the daughter he had only known in death.

She was pale but calm as she rustled forward in a black silk tea gown to acknowledge them. She briefly took Joe's hand and nodded in an unfocused way to the other two. The slight hesitation in her greeting alerted Joe. The appearance of the odd threesome before her created problems. She was instinctively preparing to speak to Joe while dismissing the inferior officers to some suitably distant back quarter of the house but Joe swiftly introduced Armitage as 'my colleague' and Westhorpe hurried forward, hand outstretched. 'We met at Lady Murchison's ball three years ago, Mrs Jagow-Joliffe, though you won't know me in my uniform, I'm sure. Mathilda Westhorpe. My father, General Westhorpe, sends his warm regards and, of course, his condolences.'

'Well, you'd better all sit down and I'll have tea brought,' she said. Her clear voice just failed to be musical. Deep and resonant but with a slight edge of sharpness, it fell on Joe's ear with the disturbing quality of an ancient bell developing a hairline crack. 'You will take tea? China? Will you drink Lapsang Souchong?'

Armitage and Westhorpe nodded dubiously and Joe, sensing their reluctance, said cheerfully, 'I'd much prefer Indian if that's available. Acquired something of a taste for it when I was in Bengal.'

'Certainly. Bring a pot of kitchen tea as well for the Commander, will you, Reid?'

Westhorpe earned her month's pay in an hour that afternoon, Joe reckoned. Supremely at ease, she was everywhere, oiling the social wheels: 'Do let me pour, Mrs Jagow-Joliffe. May I pass you a scone? What delicious honey! Off the estate? How delightful! Plum cake? William, I'm sure I can tempt you to a slice of plum cake?'

After a moment's adjustment to the phenomenon of a girl of her own class appearing in the highly dubious guise of a police officer, Mrs Joliffe allowed herself to be seduced by Tilly's impeccable manners, cheerful competence and – not least – by her smooth undertaking of the tea-table chores. After their improvised lunch, the take-up of the sweet things on offer was a minimal token though the excellent strong tea was welcome. Joe noticed that, with silent understanding, Tilly refilled Bill's cup from the Indian pot.

The pleasantries exchanged, Joe turned to the formalities. He expressed his sorrow at her loss and, under close questioning, filled in the details of Dame Beatrice's death. The old lady was grief-stricken but controlled, and he guessed that a quietly burning anger was glowing just beneath the surface and giving her the strength to get through the difficult interview.

'So, you're implying that my daughter was murdered and by someone who was known to her and not, as you first said on the telephone last night, by a burglar?'

'I have an open mind at the present time, madam, whilst we explore every avenue. But, for various reasons, yes, we are inclined to think that such a frenzied attack is most likely to have been carried out by someone who knew her and had reason to resent her.'

'But the family emeralds were stolen, you say? Have you *any* idea of their value, Commander? They were worth a very great deal of money. Motive enough to kill someone who has caught you in the act, I'd have thought?'

'Indeed, madam, and I assure you I do not lose sight of that. Meanwhile, exploring all avenues, as I'm sure you would wish me to do, will you tell me if, amongst Dame

Beatrice's friends and family, there is anyone who bore a grudge against her? A grudge amounting to hatred?'

Mrs Jagow-Joliffe favoured him with a wintry smile. 'Where to begin, Commander! I loved my daughter dearly but I have never been blind to the fact that she was the subject of much envy, much criticism. Many disapproved of the progress she made in throwing off the shackles of femininity. But I am prepared to cut your investigation short and put this nightmare behind us as soon as possible. A few hours before her death, Bea was involved in a blazing row with someone close to her. My daughter could be very insensitive . . . no, I'll say it . . . vindictive and quarrelsome. I knew one day she'd go too far.'

She rang the bell, lost in thought. When the butler appeared, she spoke again. 'Reid, take the Commander to Miss Blount's rooms, would you? Audrey Blount. You'll find Audrey Blount is the person you're looking for. You may take her straight back to London with you if you wish.'

Chapter Eight

'Audrey pursued my daughter to London yesterday afternoon, following a violent quarrel.'

'A *violent* quarrel?'

'I don't think blows were exchanged, if that's what you're trying to ask. Not on this occasion, at any rate. Screaming and crying out, a little wrist-slapping and hair-pulling perhaps. It has happened before but there was something about my daughter's determination to flee the field this time that made me think that finally she meant business. I heard her shouting at Audrey, telling her to pack her bags and that she didn't expect to see her in residence when she returned.'

'Did Dame Beatrice say when she was coming back?'

'No. She had an engagement or two – Alfred's party . . . a meeting with some of the Admiralty top brass . . . you'll have to consult her diary. You probably already have. She has a place in London and after her little self-indulgence at the Ritz she would have planned to go on there, I'm sure. I was not always privy to her personal arrangements. She came and went as she pleased, Commander.'

'And Audrey left shortly after Dame Beatrice? How long after?'

'About an hour. She spent some time sulking in her room and then came out with a small suitcase and shot off in the old Ford.'

'She didn't tell you where she was going?'

'Audrey and I do not converse.'

'And when did Miss Blount return?'

'I know the car was back here when I rose at seven this morning.'

'And can you tell me what was the nature of the relationship between Dame Beatrice and Miss Blount?' asked Joe in puzzlement.

'You must ask her,' said the old lady frostily. 'Officially she was a paid companion. She would have wound my daughter's knitting wool, had Bea been the slightest bit interested in knitting. You must have encountered the breed in London drawing rooms, Commander – ladies' companions? They sit about quenched and dusty in corners trying not to draw attention, hovering somewhere between Company and Domestic Staff. Bea did not make friends easily and, once made, they were soon lost. She found it suited her to pay someone to bear the brunt of her ill temper. And, when you've had your fill of Audrey, you may ask Reid to escort you to my son's wing of the house. He may be able to shed more light on his sister's relationships and acquaintances, though they were not close. In particular there is an Irishman, a naval person, I understand, with whom she was involved.'

'Involved?' Joe questioned.

'In a professional capacity but also on a personal level,' she enlarged. 'He was her lover.'

Three pairs of eyes flicked to her face but no questions were put so she continued. 'Orlando, my son, hates the man so he'll probably make out a convincing case for your clapping Petty Officer Donovan in chains when you get back to London. A course I too would recommend. The world would be happier without the creature's loathsome presence.'

Joe noted down the names of the two suspects handed to him with such cold relish.

'And your son, madam? He is your only remaining child?'

She nodded. 'How often Fate makes the wrong choice,' she whispered.

Choosing to ignore this, Joe asked, 'Was he older or younger than Beatrice?'

'Younger. He has four ruffianly children – all of them illegitimate – and you'll find them about the place somewhere.'

'I think they have already found us, Mrs Jagow-Joliffe,' Joe smiled.

'Then take care. They will most probably pursue you with some villainous scheme. They continually seek entertainment and distraction and any visitor is liable to find himself the butt of their humour and the target of their practical jokes. My son has failed to instil any sense of decorum, duty or good behaviour in his offspring and they run wild like savages about the estate. About the house too – open a cupboard and one is likely to spring out. The eldest, having had fourteen years of anarchic existence, is the one of whom you should be most wary. She is the ringleader.'

'Ah! Diana, I think,' murmured Joe.

'The child's name is Dorcas.'

Joe listened for any note of affection or humour or indulgence in her tone but could hear none.

'But Orlando's qualities as a parent are of minor importance in the scale of things . . .' She hesitated, appearing reluctant to go on. 'There is something you should know about my son, perhaps, Commander. Difficult to confide in strangers but I would rather you heard it from me. I understand that you are . . . were . . . a soldier? Much decorated? A war hero in fact? Am I right?'

Her questions puzzled Joe. She did not sound warm or admiring; he would have said – bitter. 'Not *much* decorated. And "hero"? I wouldn't use the word. I did what was necessary and survived. That's all. I survived,' he murmured uncertainly.

'A becoming modesty. But you're a military man and as such you will find you have nothing in common with my son and may, indeed, find that communicating with him is difficult if not impossible.' She paused, took a deep breath and spoke again into the expectant silence. 'Orlando did not have a good war. In fact he did not have a war at all. He was a conscientious objector.'

Joe wondered if she had noticed the slight pursing of Armitage's lips. 'Any sane man objected to the war,' said Joe, pacifically.

'Nonsense! Any *man* will answer when his country calls!' she said stiffly. 'It was of some consolation that my *daughter* responded to the challenge. She, at least, knew where her duty lay and the family was thereby not disgraced. But I do him too much credit – Orlando was not even a conscientious objector. I know that many men of principle showed great courage in revealing themselves as such . . . but Orlando left the country before hostilities were declared and spent the war years in a clinic in Switzerland. A lung complaint, he will tell you. He recovered sufficiently to return home after the war ended. I wish you to bear this history in mind when you speak to him. He resents military persons and, by extension, the police. He will do his best to throw difficulties your way.'

With a curt nod they were dismissed and entrusted to Reid.

'Blount and Donovan – two suspects!' whispered Armitage to Tilly as they followed a few paces behind the butler. 'Worth coming for!'

'Two? I make it three,' said Tilly.

'Three?'

'Imagine having Beatrice for an older sister,' she said. 'I'm just surprised that Orlando stayed his hand for so long.'

'And what's wrong with those nippers that they haven't bumped off Granny yet?' Armitage grinned. 'If they were as evil and resourceful as they're cracked up to be, she'd have been cat's meat long ago.'

'I thought of a dozen ways of doing away with her while we were taking tea!' Westhorpe chortled.

'Don't laugh yet,' said Armitage sternly. 'The old bag may

well have done for *us*! That tea! Poisonous or what? Tasted like Derbac nit-soap!' He shuddered at the memory.

Joe listened to the conversation, reflecting that there was nothing like a common enemy to make the most disparate forces form an alliance.

Reid paused at a door of the easterly, more modern, wing of the ground floor and he tapped lightly twice.

'Bugger off, Reid!' came the clear injunction. 'Tell the old baggage I won't see her.'

'It's the police, Miss Blount.' Reid's calm was unshaken. 'Officers from Scotland Yard would like to speak to you.'

'Officers? How many officers?'

'Three, Miss Blount.'

'Good God! A posse?'

The door opened six inches and a tear-smudged face inspected them.

'You'd better come in, then.'

The door was flung open and they stepped inside. Reid disappeared with an apologetic smile and Joe took charge. 'We're sorry to intrude, Miss Blount, at such a stressful time –'

'No need for all that, officer,' Audrey interrupted. 'Just tell me who you are. Make yourselves at home. Smoke if you want to.'

Audrey Blount was not what Joe had been expecting. This was not the mousy, amenable creature trailing about with a Pekinese under one arm and her embroidery under the other that he had looked for. She was quite short but strongly built, a rather charming figure, Joe thought, and with a certain presence. Blonde hair stylishly cut in an Eton crop framed a pretty, if puffy, china-doll face with slightly protuberant green eyes. Large and watchful green eyes. The pulpy red mouth was set in an unalluring, rebellious pout.

'I'm Commander Joseph Sandilands and I'm in charge of

the enquiry into the murder of Dame Beatrice.' He showed his warrant card.

'It *was* murder, then? Poor old cow! Can't say she didn't deserve it though,' was Audrey's display of grief. Her cat's eyes swept Joe with, he thought, surprise and approval. 'Well! Standards seem to have gone up a bit in the force. Who's this?'

Joe noted with amusement that her eyes had slid over his shoulder and fixed with flattering attention on Bill. He wasn't surprised; he'd seen this before. Bloody Armitage! What was it in the fellow that women gravitated towards? The finely cut features, the broad-shouldered, slim-hipped frame were no disadvantage but there was more to it than that. Where Joe felt obliged, in the presence of the fair sex, to show his better profile, smile a lot and prattle cheerfully to attract attention, Armitage could just stand there silent and lugubrious and they'd flock round him like wasps in a mulberry tree in summer. Until he encountered Westhorpe of course. The thought cheered Joe.

'Detective Sergeant Armitage, ma'am,' said Bill stiffly.

'Nice suit you're wearing, Sergeant.'

She looked with round-eyed disbelief at Westhorpe who now stepped forward. 'Oops! Can't say the same for you, dear. Why do they make you wear that god-awful get-up while they pose about in Savile Row suits? At least take your hat off!'

Uncertainly, Westhorpe took off her hat. 'Constable Westhorpe, Miss Blount. Uniformed branch assisting the CID on this occasion.'

Audrey was studying Westhorpe with more than usual interest. Finally she said, 'What's that mean – "on this occasion"? Do you mean to say you're *personally* involved in some way, dear? Were you one of . . . Did you know Beatrice?'

'Constable Westhorpe discovered the body,' said Joe, firmly taking back the threads of the conversation, 'so I suppose you could say that.'

'Ah. I see. So you were actually in the hotel when she died? You were in her room? You saw her body?'

Westhorpe was growing uncomfortable under the scrutiny and looked to Joe for help.

'You can leave the questioning to us, Miss Blount. Shall we all sit down?'

He looked around. They were in a small sitting room, an open door of which gave a glimpse of a further bedroom. An empty suitcase lay open on top of the bed. A dressing table, its top crowded with bottles and jars, was surmounted by a large mirror flamboyantly lit by a row of electric light bulbs. Audrey fetched a chair from the bedroom and positioned it alongside two others in the sitting room and with a gesture invited them to sit in a row. She settled on a sofa opposite, awaiting their questions. Joe had a sudden illusion they were occupying the front seats in the stalls.

'You were Dame Beatrice's companion, I understand? This must have entailed an intimate knowledge of her life?' Joe began.

'Of her domestic life, yes. I was not encouraged to take an interest in her professional life. I was paid to be here when she got back from London, to listen to her complaints and rantings, to run her bath, to massage the bits of her that needed massaging and tell her she was wonderful. You know the sort of thing . . . most people would call it being a "wife", Commander. I expect yours would recognize the job requirements.'

'When did your employment commence?'

'About half an hour after we met. She came backstage after a performance – the last night as luck would have it – of a revival of *Florodora* at the Gaiety – oh, it must be eight years ago. At the time I was glad to be offered any employment. Though I've regretted it every day since then.'

She jumped to her feet and went into the bedroom, returning with a framed photograph. 'There we are – the chorines. That's me second from the right. We were all five foot four and weighed 130 pounds. And we could all sing and dance, of course. The six girls in the original production all married millionaires, they say . . . I know for a fact that three of this line-up,' she pointed to the photograph, 'did very well for themselves. This one, Phoebe, my special friend, married a lord.' She sighed. 'Should have waited. Something would have come along.'

Joe looked with interest at the smiling line of chorus girls arm in arm with their six matching, top-hatted escorts. All young, innocent and lovely. The opening line of the musical floated into his mind. *Tell me pretty maiden, are there any more at home like you?* He remembered the girls' reply delivered in a teasing Mayfair accent. Phoebe and, next to her, Audrey. Indistinguishable one from the other. Eight years ago. He briefly wondered what Phoebe was doing now.

'And what are you intending to do in the immediate future, Miss Blount?'

She sighed and bit her lip, her confidence ebbing away at the stark question. 'I'm leaving this place tomorrow. I'm going back to London. I've a sister in Wimbledon. I can stay with her for a bit. Not that she will want to put me up for long. I don't get on with the fool she married. I'm too old for the stage now, though I've kept fit – I can still dance – and I still have my figure. I shall have to look for work in a shop . . . do a bit of waitressing . . . Nippy in a Joe Lyons? How about that? They say the tips aren't bad. Who knows?'

'I'd be obliged if you would leave a forwarding address at which we may contact you if necessary.'

Audrey nodded and gave the information to Armitage who noted it down.

'And now, will you tell us what happened yesterday? Perhaps you could start with the quarrel it is reported that you had with your employer?'

'I can't recall what it was all about now,' she said doubtfully. 'I mean, what triggered it. What it was about was we couldn't stand any more of each other's company. I'd had enough of her bad temper and her vicious tongue. She wanted to get rid of me. "Whining, demanding and dreary," she said. Told me to pack and clear off. I think she meant it this time. She delivered her ultimatum and swept off up to London in her Chrysler.'

'And what were your feelings on hearing this?'

'I was popping with rage. I expect there are witnesses in the house who'll delight in telling you I stormed about swearing and yelling and breaking things. I'm not denying it. I did. And then when I calmed down a bit I decided I'd get the old Ford out and go to London myself. She gave me use of it when she got the new car . . . I say – do you suppose I'll still be allowed to . . .? Oh, never mind! I followed her. I knew where she'd gone. While she was booking into a suite at the Ritz, I was being chucked out on the street. Eight years, Commander! Eight years of persecution with nothing to show for it and too late to start my life up again. I decided to kill her.'

Joe stirred uneasily. 'And *did* you kill her?'

He was taken aback by a blast of astonishment. 'Eh? What is all this? Course I didn't! How can you ask that? Wasn't it *you* who told her mother it was a *burglar* that got her?'

'We're keeping an open mind on that at the moment. It's very likely that she was indeed attacked by an intruder gaining access through a window – but continue, please. Tell us what happened after you got up to London.'

'It wasn't difficult to get into the Ritz and track her down.' She looked slyly at Joe and went on with something like pride in her tone, 'I can still act a bit, you know! Easy to get past people if you use the right accent. I got her room number and hung about wondering what to do while she was at the party downstairs. And then I saw one of the chambermaids was going about turning down the sheets in the rooms, freshening the flowers and checking things while the guests were living it up down below. They have these little trolleys piled up with towels and linen and they push them about the corridors. I watched when one of them hung up her uniform and parked her trolley and scarpered. It only took me a minute or two to slip on the gear – shapeless overall and fancy cap – and waddle about as though my feet were killing me. Nobody notices the hired help. Everybody looked through me. You can go anywhere!'

She gave a dry laugh. 'Even her bloody ladyship didn't recognize me! She came hurrying back to her room . . . it must have been about ten past twelve . . . I was getting a bit fed up by then, temper cooled, feet beginning to ache for real and wondering what on earth I thought I was doing in this farcical get-up when madam comes rocketing along the corridor from the lift, peeling off her gloves. She saw me lurking about near her door and yelled at me. "You there! I hope you're not expecting to gain admittance to my room at this late hour. What has happened to the schedule? I shall have a word with the manager. Go away! And don't think of disturbing me."

'She paused at the door to her suite and kept looking back at the lift. Waiting. Expecting someone to follow her, I thought. Well, by that time I'd lost all enthusiasm for topping her anyway. Never had thought through *how* I would do it and seeing her suddenly again like that, on her high horse, well . . . she was a big, strong woman, Commander! You'd have needed to take a crowbar to her to make any impression. And if my attempt was about to be witnessed by some drunken sot she'd managed to lure up from the ballroom . . . well . . . I thought, "Blow this for a game of soldiers!" She went in and shut the door and I grabbed my trolley and meandered off down the corridor, feeling silly. I hung about a bit, just out of curiosity. I wouldn't have minded casting an eye over her date for the evening!'

'And while you were lurking along the corridor, did you hear any sound from the Dame's suite?'

Audrey thought carefully. 'Not a sound. No one came up. No one went down. Nothing.' She laughed. 'I'd love to be able to say I saw So-and-So or What's-His-Name nip-

94

ping in but my memory's a total blank on that one. But give me time to think, will you? There may be details that didn't register as important at the time that come back to me now I know what you're looking for. Tell me, Commander – how did she die?'

'A poker. Not a crowbar but a solid Ritz poker,' said Joe. 'About five blows to the skull.'

'Did she suffer? Oh, daft question! Of course she must have suffered.' Audrey's eyes were glazed with tears and she fumbled in her sleeve for a handkerchief.

'She defended herself bravely. I think she died more in rage than in pain,' said Joe.

Audrey nodded. 'Sounds like Bea.'

'Perhaps a good moment to establish something of the nature of the Dame's relationships,' said Joe. 'I'm sure there must be much you can tell us about whom she was close to and so on.'

Audrey looked from one to the other uncertainly. 'Look, it's a bit delicate. Her love life was chaotic as I'm sure you've guessed and there are . . . um . . . certain . . . things . . . you really ought to know about her if you're to get a clear picture of her. But, I say, I don't really think I could . . .' She faltered, blushed and then came to a decision. 'Would you mind very much if I talked to the lady policeman? Miss Westhorpe, did you say? I feel I could talk more easily to a woman. Would you mind, miss?'

'I think that would be a good idea,' said Westhorpe helpfully. 'Sir – there's a door to the garden and I notice a particularly fine example of a Dutch garden out there. If you and the sergeant would like to take a stroll while I talk to Miss Blount, I think everyone's sensibilities would be served.'

Amused and intrigued, Joe nodded his acceptance of the scheme. He got to his feet and handed Audrey a card. 'This is where you may contact me, Miss Blount. At any time. Should you recall something of relevance to the enquiry.' He nodded to Armitage and they walked together through the french window into the garden.

'Perhaps Sir Nevil knows what he's doing,' said Armitage. 'I begin to see some real advantages in employing these women. Save our blushes, like you said, sir. Wonder what on earth she's telling her? Er . . . is there any guarantee that the constable will understand what she's hearing?'

'I hardly know the constable but I think I can guarantee that if anything she is told is unclear she will insist on a clarification,' said Joe. 'Let's go and admire those tulips in the sunken garden. Then if we follow the flower walk and take a turn around the monticule over there I'd guess by then they should have finished.'

'Unless the Dame's catalogue of excesses is longer than we have any suspicions of,' said Armitage, raising a salacious eyebrow.

'Perhaps Audrey thinks she's auditioning for the part of Leporello? Reciting a list of Donna Bea's indiscretions?'

'Perhaps, sir. Not really fond of the opera, myself,' sniffed Armitage. 'All that murder and mayhem . . . get enough of that on the job, I'd say. Give me a good musical any day. Now what you ought to go and see is that *Lady Be Good*. Opened last week at the Empire. Usual silly story but the dancing's good. Fred and Adèle Astaire.' He started to hum 'Fascinating Rhythm' under his breath, turning back repeatedly to look over his shoulder. Strung up, Joe thought. Bill had never been happy with inactivity.

Joe noticed that his sergeant's attention was continually drifting back from the soldierly ranks of bright tulips to the two pretty heads, one fair, one dark, leaning close together, side by side on the sofa. They strolled on and had discovered the Japanese water garden, the thatched summer house on stilts over a pond and the sunken rose garden before the watchful Armitage announced, 'There she is, sir. That's the constable waving to us at the window.'

The fifteen minutes' tête-à-tête had quenched Westhorpe. Pale and thoughtful, she made no attempt to relay her conversation. 'I've rung for Reid to take us on to our next interview. Orlando lives over there in the oldest part of the house, the west wing. Here comes Reid now . . . Later, sir! Later!'

Reid emerged into the sunshine, head on one side, smiling slightly. 'If you would come this way, gentlemen. Miss. We can cross the lawn and enter Mr Orlando's quarters at the rear.'

Before they could start off, a small figure detached itself from the woodwork of the open verandah which linked the new wing with the central part of the house and stood firmly blocking their way.

'Thank you, Reid. You may dismiss. I shall conduct our guests to the west wing.'

'Certainly, Miss Dorcas,' said Reid gravely. 'That is very considerate. Will there be anything further?'

The girl gave him a dazzling smile. 'Well, if you could sneak some of that fruit cake along for later, that would be good. We've got nothing to offer these people otherwise.' She looked up at Joe and added, confidingly, 'Mel can't cook. Well, apart from stews. She's quite good at stews.'

'I'll see what I can do, Miss Dorcas.' Reid bowed his head and left them with their new guide.

Joe looked with surprise and concern at the child. In appearance she was little different from any of the waifs you saw by the roadside playing hopscotch in the dust. Her feet were bare and dirty, her ragged dress trailed about somewhere between her knees and ankles and her thin shoulders were concealed under a much-darned brown woolly cardigan. But her face, Joe thought, was quite exceptional. It was thin and brown but lit by the intelligence of two large dark eyes. Joe knew he had seen something very similar and quite recently. She turned her head to look at Armitage and Westhorpe with the intensity of a child examining exotic creatures at the zoo and he had it. Her profile, neat nose and almond eye framed by an abundance of glossy black hair, could have inspired a painter of ancient Crete. Armitage and Westhorpe shuffled their feet uncomfortably and looked back for assistance from the retreating Reid but Joe held the child's gaze. 'It's very thoughtful of you to undertake escort duties,' he said lightly but formally, 'and we look forward to meeting your brothers and sisters.'

'You've already seen my brother, Peter,' she said.

'Ah. Actaeon, I believe.'

'No, actually, you got that wrong. Diana never shot Actaeon, you know. She threw a bucket of water over him when she caught him sneaking a look at her in the bath and he turned into a stag.'

'Yes, of course, you're right. And the poor fellow was chased and torn to pieces by his own hounds.'

'He died calling out their names,' said Dorcas with relish. 'Imagine what that must be like! To know your friends are ripping your flesh to bits and you shout out their names . . . "Stop – it's me! Theron! Tigris! Don't you know me?" And they don't know him and they tear his throat out and eat his liver!'

'Er . . . sir?' said Armitage uncertainly.

'Ah, yes, much as I'd like to wander with Dorcas through the murkier groves of mythology we have work to do. I'm Commander Joe Sandilands. Here's my card.'

She looked at it carefully and pushed it up the sleeve of her cardigan.

'I expect you know why we're here? This is my detective sergeant, Bill Armitage.'

'He's very handsome,' said Dorcas seriously.

'I was sure you would think so. He's also very clever. And this is Constable Mathilda Westhorpe.'

'Is she your mistress?'

'No. She's my constable. We work together.'

'Orlando has mistresses and they work together but he's never married any of them. What do you think of that?'

'Speaking as a man who is himself unmarried, I can only say, "Sensible chap." He'll probably do the right thing when he's made his selection,' said Joe, rapidly losing the thread of the conversation. 'And now, miss, if you wouldn't mind taking us to him . . .?'

'Right. This way. Granny keeps us confined to the oldest part of the house, you'll find. Not that I mind all that much because it's the most interesting part. In fact, I shall go on living over there even when Orlando plucks up courage enough to claim what is legally his and takes over the whole house.'

Joe stopped and waved a hand at the building. 'You mean all this is . . .?'

'Oh yes. Orlando's father left it to him. When he died ten years ago. Grandmother ought to have moved out to the Dower House down by the river over there – or anywhere else she wanted to go – she's very rich, you know. She could live wherever she wanted. But she won't give it up. And my father won't make her – he's rather a weed where Granny's concerned. Most people are. I know she was trying to leave it to Aunt Bea along with all her money when she dies. It's in her will. I've seen it.' She hesitated and then said without a trace of guilt, 'Better, I think, if you don't tell Granny I've seen it. She'd have a fit! She left it on her desk while she spoke to the lawyer on the telephone in the hall and I went in and read it. Orlando is to get nothing. What do you think of that?'

'I don't have opinions on everything,' said Joe, annoyed. 'I'm here to listen and ask questions and find out what everyone else is thinking.'

'Men! Why are they all so devious?' commented Dorcas.

Chapter Nine

'So your father's a weed, then, is he, miss?' said Armitage, taking up a position alongside the child. 'Not a very polite thing to say?'

'It's his own description . . . Bill . . . And it's true. Orlando's very gentle and easy-going, sunny-natured, hates to offend anyone, charming. Makes you sick. I hope you're not going to be rude to him . . . give him the third degree or anything like that . . . because I won't allow it!'

'We can be pretty charming ourselves, miss. Thumb-screws are a bit old hat these days, you know.'

'That's good. I just thought I should warn you.'

'Now let me understand this,' said Armitage cheerfully, 'you're fourteen, right? So born in 1912, two years before the war broke out. And according to Grandmama, Orlando spent the war years in Switzerland. Did you go with him?'

'No, Bill. He left me and my oldest brother, who was just a baby, here with Granny. Our mothers – we didn't have the same one – went away. We don't remember them.'

'Sounds like a bleak situation?'

'It could have been if we hadn't had Grandnanny Tilling. She had been Aunt Bea and Orlando's nanny when they were little and she came back from the village to look after us. She stayed on when my father got back from Switzer-land and didn't leave until she retired again last year. She wasn't just a nanny – she had been a governess once and she taught us to read and write and all that.'

'And do you go to school in the village?' Armitage wanted to know.

'Oh, no. We tried to go once but the other children fired lumps of turnip at us with catapults. Peter got into a fight with a gang of village boys and broke his arm. Grandnanny Tilling came to the school and made a complaint but they went on calling us "gippos" and "conshies".'

'Little monkeys! Need their hides tanning!' said Armitage, glowing with sympathy.

'Oh, we didn't mind. We could read better than the teachers anyway. They were as glad to get rid of us as we were to leave,' said Dorcas philosophically. 'I've got all the education I need – well, most of it – from the books in the library. At least Granny lets me use it whenever I like. She never goes in there. Are you married, Bill?'

'Oh, Lord!' thought Joe. 'Here we go! Is there no limit to the sergeant's powers of attraction?'

'No, miss. Never found anyone who could pass the test.'

'Pass the test?' Dorcas chortled. 'Sounds like the start of a fairy story! What does your intended have to do? Answer a riddle? Run a hundred yards faster than you? Break out of a set of handcuffs in ten seconds?'

'I don't set the tests, miss! A policeman's wife must be able to prove to the police authorities that she is of good character. She has to provide three testimonials from reputable members of society to that effect.'

'How perfectly dreadful! Would you seriously like to marry someone that proper, Bill? I think you would lead a very dull life!'

'Policemen are supposed to lead dull lives.'

'I don't think the Commander has led a dull life,' said Dorcas with a swift sideways look at Joe. 'How did he come by that dramatic scar on his face? Was he raked by a lion's claw, snatching some poor dusky maiden from the jaws of death?'

'No. It was a tiger, miss,' lied Armitage. 'Though I believe the maiden was dusky.'

*   *   *

They had arrived at the part of the house which Joe had identified as the core of the building, the original Surrey farmhouse. As they stood by the back door, Dorcas confirmed this. 'Jacobean,' she said. 'It's very homely, you'll see, and it suits the way we live. It would never do for Granny though.' She grinned. 'Too many spiders! Too much dust! She sends maids in once a week to "do the mucking out" as she calls it but she never comes here herself.'

They followed her through the generous oak door into a room which must once have been the hall of the farmhouse. Ancient beams mellowed to a rich brown held up the low ceiling and Armitage cast a wary eye on the height, judging that he would, by a fraction of an inch, be able to walk unbowed through the room. A stone floor was scattered with brightly coloured pegged rugs, a hand-painted dresser held a collection of blue china, a gouty old sofa was covered with drapes of, Joe guessed, Provençal origin. The room appeared to serve several functions, one of them dining room. A long table and benches occupied half the room and stood within a ladle's reach of the pot sitting on a trivet over a slow-burning fire in the hearth.

Joe looked into the pot and sniffed. He reached for a spoon sitting by the pot and moved the glutinous brown contents around a little. 'Just caught it! Is no one watching this?' he asked, looking around the empty room.

'It's a stew. It watches itself,' said Dorcas defensively. 'Mel calls it a "daube".'

Joe took a fork from the table and poked at one of the unrecognizable lumps that his stirrings had brought to the surface. 'Well, whatever it is, it's ready. Any longer and it'll be reduced to a stringy mush or stick to the bottom and burn. You've got two choices: you can take it off now and reheat it for supper or you can add about half a pint more liquid, stir it and keep a closer eye on it.' He sniffed again. 'Have you got any herbs?'

'In the garden. How do you know about stews?'

Joe grinned. 'When I was your age, I spent the summers

out on the hill with my father, shooting things for the pot. I can tell you exactly how long it takes to cook a haunch of venison, a saddle of rabbit or even a hedgehog. Believe me – you *can* overdo it.'

Westhorpe cleared her throat and looked at her watch. Joe took a folded kitchen cloth and lowered the pot to an iron stand in the hearth. 'Well, that'll have to do for culinary conversation. Tell me, child, where is everyone?'

'They *were* here half an hour ago, expecting to see you. You talk so much, you're overrunning. I expect they've gone out into the garden. Father's finishing a painting. It's how he earns his living. Mostly portraits but some landscapes too.'

Armitage looked around the lines of paintings hanging higgledy-piggledy in every available space on the walls. Most of them were dangling on strings from nails hammered into the beams. All were modern. Cubism, Joe noted, seemed to have broken out.

'Any of this lot by your pa, miss?' Armitage asked in a tone of studied lack of interest. Joe smiled. He knew that tone. Armitage would welcome another reason to despise Orlando and being the originator of any one of these modernist pieces would do.

'Oh, no. Orlando doesn't display his own work. He picked up most of these when we went to France. We took the caravan and went all the way down to the south coast. To Martigues and Toulon and Cassis. He met lots of other painters down there. They're all very friendly and jolly. Some are skint like us but some have begun to do well and actually make some money. Orlando swapped some pictures. Others he bought when he could raise the cash. That one's mine,' she said, pointing to what Joe thought was probably the best of the display which were, on the whole, rather too free and modern for his taste. 'It was a present from the artist.'

He looked more closely. A small girl in a white dress was standing on a Mediterranean beach, dark hair springing against a vivid blue sky, clutching a large shell and looking with intense enquiry at the painter. It didn't take Joe long to recognize the subject as Dorcas but he was puzzled as to the identity of the painter and walked over to peer at the scrawled signature. P. Ruiz Picasso.

'Pablo did it,' supplied Dorcas. 'Pablo Picasso. Orlando thinks he's rather good. Do you like it?'

'It's wonderful! And how lucky you were to have caught him in a classical mood! You could well have ended up . . .' He trailed off, fearing his next comment might give offence or reveal his artistic prejudices.

'. . . like this stew?' she said happily. 'Bits and pieces all over the place!'

'Cubed!'

They grinned at each other and Westhorpe again looked at her watch.

As they made their way back out into the garden Joe was aware of a surprising moment of communication between the sergeant and the constable. Tilly reached out and touched Bill's shoulder. He leaned his head towards her and she whispered something which made him smile broadly and, with a darting look at his boss, nod in agreement.

Joe could interpret clearly the message: 'Time the Commander was married and had children of his own, perhaps?' Well, if ever the day came, he would make a much better job of it than the oaf Orlando, he thought resentfully. This bright little madam should be receiving a decent education which was obviously what she craved instead of being allowed to run around like a street urchin. But then, if the child's awkward eagerness to communicate with anyone outside her narrow world – even a policeman – were to result in a rapprochement between his assistants, he could welcome that. He lengthened his stride and engaged Dorcas in conversation, leaving Bill and Tilly space to do what he knew the lower ranks most enjoy – sending up the governor.

He didn't need to glance back over his shoulder to check the success of his scheme. After a long stare, Dorcas remarked, 'She must be *his* mistress then. They seem to like each other.'

'Oh, I don't imagine so,' something impelled him to say. 'They only met yesterday.'

Dorcas gave him what he could have sworn was a pitying look.

Orlando and the rest of the tribe had gathered round his easel in a distant part of the grounds. A pregnant girl in a long skirt and a shawl, a scarf knotted casually around her head, was pouring out lemonade from a large jug and handing a glass to the artist. Two boys were laughing and wrestling in the grass and a small girl was whacking them both with a hazel switch. Joe paused to take in the idyllic scene and decided, with a flash of irritation and amusement, that it was surely posed, so perfect an image of English country life did it present. A green-painted gypsy caravan was parked in a stretch of wild, unmown orchard which linked the tended grounds of the house and the beechwood beyond, flowing seamlessly between them. A froth of waist-high Queen Anne's lace under the apple trees merged in the distance with a mist of bluebells and the breeze wafting towards them from the wood was heavy with the almond scent of may blossom. Joe stood entranced.

'England, 'ome an' beauty!' Armitage growled in his ear. 'So this is what we were fighting for! Wondered if I'd ever see it. Was it worth four years of our lives to pay for it? *Some* people paid with their lives, at any rate, I seem to remember,' he muttered.

Years of Flanders mud in a monochrome landscape followed by years in a city which he saw as black and grey, soot and fog, had left Joe with an unquenchable thirst for the healing greens of field and hedgerow. He didn't want this moment of delight smudged by Bill's prejudices, however justifiable. 'Yes, it was,' he replied simply. 'And I'd do it again if I had to.'

He ignored the sergeant's look of disbelief.

They strolled on towards the artist. Aware of their

105

approach, he remained facing his easel, all his attention on his work. As they drew near he raised his brush from the canvas and took a step back. 'I can never quite get it,' he said. 'Every year I try to recreate the blue of those bluebells in the distance but it's unseizable! Damn frustrating! Do you paint?'

'No, I don't,' said Joe. 'Though I enjoy paintings.'

He looked over Orlando's shoulder, prepared to say something polite and non-committal. It was always diffi-cult to find the right formula to avoid giving offence when faced with the efforts of enthusiastic amateurs. These days there were no more rules, it seemed to him. The fast-changing fashion for Cubism, Fauvism, Dadaism, Surreal-ism had left the public – and Joe – gasping and uncertain how to interpret what they were seeing – a situation ripe for painters to exploit. All too easy to retreat behind a gently knowing, 'Oh, but I wonder if you can have under-stood? Surely you're au fait with Ordurism? But it's the latest thing! When I was last in Montmartre . . .'

Joe tried to keep up. He went to galleries and viewings, he learned the vocabulary of the latest trends. He stood by open-mouthed at his sister's side as she, a quivering flame of concupiscence, spent a very great deal of her husband's money in the Cork Street galleries.

He looked at Orlando's painting and tried to imagine the comments of the two elderly uncles who had taken on the task of civilizing the rough young Scot when he was sent to them after his father's death. In the long vacations of those sunny Edwardian years before the war Joe had spent hours in their company, trailing through museums and grand houses, occasionally going to the opera, the theatre and – his greatest delight – the music hall, and these hours spent in their company had marked his tastes indelibly. But he was always conscious that Harold and Samuel had been Victorian at heart, formed and bound by the traditions of an iron generation. Joe felt himself chal-lenged and excited by the cultural yeast he was aware of

106

on all sides, bubbling its way up through the lumpen acceptances of an earlier age.

The polite, pre-prepared phrases remained unspoken. 'I like that,' he said. 'I like that very much indeed.' His eye ran over the free-flowing lines, the bright bursts of colour running into the mysterious dark depths of the woodland. 'It's the essence of England. It's what I'll close my eyes and see on my death-bed.'

Orlando turned and looked at him, his attention finally caught. 'Then there's something lacking,' he said uncertainly. 'I hadn't thought of it in paradisal terms . . .' He selected a fine brush from the jar at his feet and loaded it with paint. In the few quick strokes of an expert draughtsman, he had transformed the picture, Joe thought, watching, enchanted.

Now, a figure was to be seen under the eaves of the wood, running out, mouth open in horror, one hand pointing back into the dim depths.

'That's better,' said Orlando. 'No such thing as paradise. Especially not within twenty miles of King's Hanger. There's always a lurking serpent in this place. A Lucifer? Some frightfulness in the woods? That's more to your taste, I expect, Mr Policeman?'

'At the risk of a further sneer, I'll be honest and say – yes, in fact, it is. You've turned, in a few strokes, a good painting into something quite exceptional.' He hesitated. 'Tell me – was this particular picture commissioned?' he enquired, trying not to betray his fascination. 'Does it have a home to go to?'

'Yes, it does. The Countess of Deben is quite a collector of bucolic images. The English countryside through the seasons is her interest. Though the harbinger of doom I've just painted in will unsettle her – I shall have to turn it into a scarecrow.'

'A pity! Can't you deck him out in a few leaves and an enigmatic smile and he can be the Green Man, emerging from his winter sleep, rude and rammish, and all ready to leap upon the Maiden of Spring. There she is! I see her lurking behind the apple tree.'

Orlando smiled, put away his brush and wiped his hands on his pinny. He pushed his over-long, springy reddish hair off his face. A good face, Joe thought, and not the weak-featured, placatory mask he had been expecting. Intelligent hazel eyes, long-lashed and upswept, unusual in a man, accounted for his success with women no doubt. He was of medium height, probably an inch or so shorter than his sister had been, lean and wiry. He had the brown and creased skin of a man who spent much of the year out of doors and this impression was underlined by his clothes. Stained brown corduroy trousers, a linen shirt which had once been white and of good quality, and a red kerchief knotted, gypsy-fashion about his neck made a clear statement. And nothing about the man was suggesting ill health.

'Lemonade? Will you have lemonade?' Orlando offered.

'Gladly,' said Joe and the girl he assumed to be 'something beginning with M' began to pour and hand out glasses.

'Thank you, Miss, er . . .' he said and introduced himself and his officers.

'Mel,' she said. 'Short for Melisande. Muse and bottle-washer. I'll leave you to it. If you want to speak to me you'll find me in the caravan. Help yourselves if you want more lemonade. There *was* some fruit cake a minute ago but the kids have scoffed it,' she said cheerfully and wandered off.

They settled cross-legged in the grass, Westhorpe perching uncomfortably on a fallen log. Dorcas, with a few rude words and harsh phrases, herded the rest of the children together and swept them off into the orchard.

'Condolences I don't need if you were thinking of offering them, Commander,' Orlando began bluntly. 'I'm shocked by my sister's death, of course, but you should understand that I was never fond of her and she resented and, I do believe, hated me. Nevertheless, I'm unhappy that she should have met such an untimely, dreadful and unnecessary end. She had much to achieve in her life still and I am aware that the country is poorer for her passing. Battered to death by a burglar, I understand? A terrible way to go!'

'She went down fighting at least, sir,' said Armitage. 'A spirited lady.'

'Ah. Yes. That would be the way of it with Bea. She was always a splendid fighter,' said Orlando easily.

'Will you tell us, Mr Jagow-Joliffe, where you were last evening? Were you at home? The sergeant will take notes.'

'No. I wasn't at home. As a matter of fact, I was in London. At the Ritz. Family party on. Uncle's birthday. We'd both been invited. Naturally, I didn't travel up to Town with Bea – we avoided each other's company. I took the train and then a taxi. Still got the ticket stubs if you want to see them.' His smile was innocent, open and totally disarming.

Joe shot a look at Armitage and Westhorpe who silently shook their heads.

'Would you like to reconsider your answer?' Joe asked mildly. 'Since we have it on good authority that you were not present at the celebrations in the small dining room of the Ritz.'

'Hey? What the hell's going on?' said Orlando in sudden alarm. 'What does it matter where I was? What's this "authority" you speak of?'

'Two police witnesses, sir.'

'Police? In the Ritz? What would they be doing in the Ritz? And what possible business can it be of yours whether I was there or at the North Pole? Why aren't you off chasing the burglar responsible instead of wasting your time down here?'

'There is serious doubt that she was killed by an intruder. We have reason to believe that it is more likely that she was killed by one of her own circle of family and

109

friends. We are establishing the precise whereabouts of all these people at the relevant time.'

Armitage leaned forward. 'I was on duty at the Ritz party throughout the evening, sir, and I have to say I didn't clap eyes on *you* all evening.'

Orlando held up his hands in surrender. 'Good God! There were rumours that something had happened to the force since the war but this is impressive! Very well. But keep your voices down, will you?' He lowered his own voice and continued after a furtive glance at the caravan. 'I *was* in London. I *did* go up by train but you're right – I didn't go anywhere near the awful shindig at the Ritz. I don't actually possess a dinner jacket any more and wouldn't have been let in without one. I used the invitation as a cover for a dash to London. I stayed overnight with a friend.'

'A male friend?' asked Armitage.

'Yes, a male friend . . . and a female friend . . . lots of friends in fact. I spent a drunken evening with some other artists. We started in the Fitzroy Tavern, went on to the Mont Olympe restaurant in Charlotte Street and then a nightclub. After that I don't remember much. I know I woke up next morning in a strange room and in the bed of a woman I'll swear I've never met before and don't want to see ever again. Still . . . no one looks their best at five in the morning which is when I crept out and made my way back to the station. I had to wait ages for a train and I was back here by lunchtime. I say . . . you don't need to tell Mel any of this, do you? Not something she'd want to hear in her present condition. She'd be furious. She's got the devil of a temper. Goes with her red hair, I suppose. I always paint her as half woman, half tigress! Tawny, you know. She coincided with an urge I had last year to paint in Fauvist shades. Last time she caught me out she set my canvases on fire. Next time it'll be me that goes up in flames, she's promised me that.'

'Can you give us the names and addresses of people who can confirm this account, sir?' Joe asked.

'Certainly not! Would *you* involve your friends in such a murky matter? Wouldn't name any of them even if I could remember who they were. And, anyway, they were all as tipsy as I was and they'll be sleeping it off till next Wednesday.'

Seeing a steely look in Joe's eye he added, 'Well, you might try Freddie Cooper. I started the evening with him so he may have some glimmerings and the room where I fetched up was halfway down Fitzroy Street. Blue door. I noted it particularly in the firm intention of avoiding it in the future.'

'Is there anyone at all who will remember seeing you in the course of the evening – someone sober . . . a maître d'hôtel . . . a waiter? The time you should concentrate on is from midnight until one o'clock.'

Orlando sighed. 'The maître d'hôtel at the Mont Olympe may well have noticed me.' He spent a moment peeling paint from under his fingernails. 'We had a whip round to pay the bill and I – as usual, I'm afraid – made a rather larger contribution than most. I say, it's damned embarrassing to be talking about money like this, don't you fellows understand? But just for once I may have done myself a favour. I left a large tip. Doesn't often happen but I'd just sold two paintings. Rather well. Someone will remember the tip.'

'And when did you leave the restaurant, sir?'

'Oh, yes. That would have been before midnight because we were going on to a nightclub to meet some of the dancers from the Russian ballet after the performance. Lydia Lopokova was meant to be there but she never put in an appearance. Look, Commander, I'm getting pretty fed up with all this. It really is none of your business. I'm a gentleman – you're some sort of a gentleman, I observe – why can't you take my word for it? I had absolutely nothing to do with my sister's murder.'

'We must insist, I'm afraid,' said Joe patiently. 'From midnight until one o'clock, if you wouldn't mind? That's the time we're interested in.'

111

'Oh, all right then,' he grumbled. 'Anything to get rid of you. Well . . .' he said, suddenly brightening, 'you may not find anyone who can vouch for my presence or, more likely,' he grinned, 'you may find that *everyone* vouches for my presence! Policemen tend not to be very popular with this crowd and they won't hesitate to lead you up the garden path, running rings around you and tying you in knots until you fall over your own flat feet – but what if someone could corroborate my impression of the events of the evening? Wouldn't that be more useful to you than a chummy alibi?'

'Go on,' said Joe, uncommitted.

'Well, two of the male dancers came in – we were at the Cheval Bleu by then – did I say that? And though they must have been well-nigh exhausted after their evening they cleared the floor and did a turn or two. One had red tights on.'

Armitage glowered, licked the end of his pencil and noted down the tights.

'Any further impressions lingering from this jolly jamboree, sir?' he said. 'Just to get you through safely to the other side of one o'clock?'

'Yes, but I'm not sure I can reveal them in the presence of a lady.'

'Constable Westhorpe has nerves of steel. I guarantee that she will not faint at any revelation you may care to make,' said Joe.

Orlando looked at Tilly with awakening interest. 'Oh? Right. Well, there's a young Hungarian . . . or is he Bulgarian? . . . chap out and about at the moment. Writer of some sort, I believe. All the rage. He's been taken up by some of the fashionable set. Trouble is he's got too big for his boots and everyone decided it was time he was taken down a peg or two. He got roaring drunk and – resenting the attention being paid to the dancers and not liking Russians much either – he decided to steal their thunder. He stalked into the middle of the floor and started stripping.'

'I'm sorry, sir?' Armitage's pencil lifted from the page. 'Stripping what?'

'Himself of course. Good-looking chap, as all agree, and I must say he did it with panache. Well, everyone gathered round – they were all there, the Slade gang, the Café Royal mob – shouting encouragement and then . . . it was one of those incredible crowd movements, you know, all acting together, without a word said . . . he stood there taking a bow, naked apart from his socks, and everyone, to a man or woman, went absolutely silent and turned their backs on him. Choreographed, you'd say! Then Tonia Fawcett, I think it was . . . yes . . . Tonia strolled over, put a hand on his shoulder and said confidingly in that devastating drawl of hers, "Darling, just put them back on again, would you?"'

Orlando was twitching with excitement as the memories sharpened. 'There you are! Impossible to make up a scene like that. Bound to be lots of people who remember it. You'll just have to ask around.'

He closed his eyes to aid the effort of remembering.

'Oh! One sock was blue, the other black!' he finished on a note of triumphant recall.

Armitage solemnly wrote it down.

Chapter Ten

'Tell me how the death of your sister is going to affect your life, will you?' Joe asked.

'Just as well you put me through the process of establishing my else-whereabouts before you asked a question like that, Commander,' said Orlando lightly. 'Or I might well have incriminated myself. Oh, it's all a matter of record. One phone call to a lawyer will establish the facts so I may as well impress you with my openness and honesty.' He took out from a baggy pocket an evil-looking old pipe and a pouch of tobacco and looked at them consideringly. 'Won't offer you a smoke. I expect nothing rougher than the best Virginian passes your metropolitan lips.'

There followed that seemingly interminable pause when a pipe-smoker half closes his eyes and puffs away, oblivious of his audience. Or, all too aware of his audience, collects his thoughts and gains himself some time in the most annoying way. 'My rich old parent,' he went on, apparently satisfied at last with the pungent eddies he was creating, 'who, by the way, looks like living until she's a hundred, had willed her worldly goods exclusively to my sister. What she'll do now, I really have no idea. A suspicious mind might well think she's bound to leave her money to her only remaining offspring – me. But that would be a mind unacquainted with my mama. She's just as likely – no, *more* likely – to leave it to a good cause. Or even a bad cause. If I had money to bet on the outcome I would guess that some women's organization – the suffragettes, the Wrens – will suddenly find themselves awash with cash when she finally pulls up the anchor.'

'And the house and estate?'

'Is mine. It was all left to me in its entirety by my father. Though without the funds to maintain it, I'm afraid I shall have to sell up. Over her head if need be. So, a year from now, Commander, you will see me starting off once again for the South of France. Mel loves life over there . . . the warmth, the wine, the company . . . She learned to cook daubes and pasta . . . But this time I shall be taking my family on the Blue Train and we'll stay in a hotel while we search for a small farmhouse in sight of the sea. I'd decided to do this, no matter what. So Bea's death, you could say, has not affected my plans in the slightest.'

'Does your mother not have other relations to whom she could leave her wealth?' Westhorpe asked.

Orlando showed no surprise at being suddenly addressed by the junior and female member of the police squad. 'I've been trying to think,' he said, all interest. 'Hard to establish because her family doesn't live in this country, you know . . . You *didn't* know? Ah. Well, she's German. Educated in England so no trace of accent. Grandfather was an ambassador and they were stationed over here for years. She hardly returned to her homeland after she married my father.'

'Oh, I see!' said Joe with sudden insight. 'Jagow. Your mother's maiden name – not *Jago* and Cornish as I had supposed but *Jagow*.' He pronounced it in the German way.

Orlando nodded. 'That's right. Add a "von", von Jagow, and you've got it. But after her marriage everything about my mother became more English than the English, including her name though she maintained her family contacts. Beatrice was encouraged to spend the summer holidays in the ancestral schloss. She spoke the lingo perfectly – that was one of the many qualities that made her indispensable to the Wrens. I went over there with her one year. Not a success! My hearty German cousins beat me to a pulp and

115

it was suggested it might be a good idea if I didn't return. I wonder where those cousins are now? Probably didn't survive the war. They were the sort who would have marched at the double straight into the front line. I'm sure my mother will do her best now to find out exactly which of her tribe are still flourishing. Her personal fortune all came from Germany so I suppose it would not be unfair if it were to return there.' He shrugged.

Joe found himself admiring the man's candour though there was a quality about his dispassionate account of his mother that made Joe uneasy. He wondered briefly what Sigmund Freud would have made of this can of worms.

'She never forgave me, you know,' Orlando went on, 'for developing a lung complaint. My father – it was three years before he died – was seriously concerned. So was I. He shipped me off to Switzerland and then the war broke out. Halfway through I was just about cured and well on the way to a reasonable state of health but I decided to stay put. I would never have enlisted. I could never take a life. What would be the use of putting a rifle in my hands and telling me to shoot? I couldn't! Not even if I had one of my awful German cousins in my sights! I would have declared myself a conscientious objector and they would have stuck me away in some prison or jam factory for the duration. No use to anyone. And a considerable embarrassment to my family.'

'How did you spend your time in Switzerland?' Joe asked to change the subject. He knew Armitage's views on conscientious objectors and wished to avoid an outbreak of verbal hostilities.

'I discovered painting,' said Orlando with a vivid smile of enthusiasm. His eyes darted back to his unfinished picture and his attention was lost.

Joe got to his feet. 'If you don't mind, sir, I'll just have a word with the young lady . . . Melisande? . . . a matter of confirming your departure and arrival times, and then we'll be off.' He looked at Armitage and Westhorpe who had risen with him. 'Not much room in a caravan, I think.

116

Perhaps you two would like to take a turn under the apple trees? Get a few pure lungfuls of country air before we go back?'

He watched for the automatic expression of displeasure at the suggestion and was surprised to see none. They both nodded and set off into the orchard examining Armitage's notebook and murmuring to each other.

Joe approached the open door of the caravan. All was silent. Had she fallen asleep? Hesitantly, he called, 'Hello. It's Sandilands. I'm here at the front door. Do excuse me.'

'Come in, officer. That didn't take long! Look, I could come out to you but I expect you want to see the inside of a caravan? Everybody does!' Her voice was light and attractive with the hint of a country accent he could not place.

He climbed the wooden ladder and entered the small gloomy space. Mel was lying with her feet up on a divan running the length of the caravan. Pots and pans hung from hooks in the ceiling and piles of artist's materials cluttered the floor, vying for space with baskets over-flowing with clothes and blankets. Joe looked around uncertainly.

'It's not usually as tidy as this,' said Mel. 'You should have seen it when we all went to France. You can sit here.' She swung her legs to the floor and patted the space next to her on the divan.

'How absolutely charming and romantic,' said Joe, find-ing his conversational gear with a crunch. 'The children must adore having a hidey-hole like this in the grounds.'

'Are you mad? The place is a midden! Best thing that could happen is for someone to set fire to it. All that linseed oil and turpentine, rags and suchlike lying about – it's a death trap. Do you smoke?'

'Only cigars and only after dinner,' said Joe carefully.

'Good. Wouldn't want to see the Law blow itself up.

They'd pinch *me* for it. I've got previous! Now, what do you want to know? Inspector, isn't it?'

'Commander. Sandilands. CID. We're checking the movements of all members of Dame Beatrice's family at the time of her death yesterday. We've heard from her brother and would now like to hear your confirmation.'

'Whatever he said, I'll go along with that,' she said with a shrug.

'Not acceptable, I fear,' said Joe, smiling with difficulty. 'What time did he set off for London yesterday? Let's start there, shall we?'

'Sometime in the afternoon. I was having my afternoon nap. Before I went to sleep he was there. When I woke up he wasn't. He caught the 3.40, I expect. He got back this morning late – about midday. He looked the worse for wear and stank of booze.'

'He attended a very boozy party, I understand,' said Joe.

She took off the scarf she wore around her head and shook out her rich russet hair, running her fingers through the length of it. 'I'd like to have short hair but he makes me wear it long. All his models have had long hair. I'm just surprised he hasn't told me to dye it black – he's got this fascination for gypsies. You only have to look at his kids to see that! The minute he hears there's an encampment within hiking distance – he's off! He can actually talk their language, you know.' She cast a sideways, speculative look at Joe. 'Can't think why you need to come all the way down here to find out what Orlando was up to last night, but as a matter of fact I'm glad to hear he really was in London.' Joe waited for her to go on. 'There's a bunch of Romanies just set up camp near Dunsfold, I hear. He could have walked there, had a sing-song round the campfire or whatever he does and got back in the time. You have witnesses who saw him there, then, at the party?'

Joe was aware of the insecurity behind her question. 'I believe there are people in London who can vouch for his presence there,' he said carefully. 'The champagne flowed well after midnight.'

'Champagne at the Ritz, eh? Funny . . . when I took up with him I thought he was just a penniless painter but, you know, he owns all this. Did you know?'

'I understand his sister was proving quite an obstacle to his enjoying his inheritance?'

'Obstacle! She and that harpy of a mother of hers were trying to do him out of it! Everything! They'd hired lawyers . . . Orlando couldn't afford to retaliate. And he won't have it out with her no matter how I try to push him forward. He's such a jelly-baby! "Think of the kids!" I keep telling him. "Don't they deserve a better life?" Can you imagine a mother hating her own son like that?' Unconsciously she placed a protective hand over her swollen belly. 'You'd do anything, wouldn't you, to make sure your own child was all right? She's not human!'

Joe had a feeling that Orlando's fifth child was going to make a welcome appearance and have its share of maternal affection. 'Your first child?' he asked.

She nodded, a passing expression of, as far as he could ascertain in the gloom, panic twisting her face. He realized that she was much younger than he had at first thought. Young and quietly terrified when she looked into the abyss of uncertainty before her. Unmarried, about to produce the fifth in a chain of bastards, her presence in this idyllic place tolerated as long as her colouring continued to satisfy the painter's artistic compulsions, she must feel the ground could give way under the next footstep. Joe was filled with a stab of anger for Orlando, the undependable centre of this growing web of needy dependants. 'Must be quite terrifying,' he said tactfully, to draw her out, 'the thought of giving birth. Have you anyone who could . . .? I mean, how on earth will you manage? I'm sorry, I should not have asked the question. It's none of my business.'

She smiled and patted his hand. 'In my state, believe me, sympathy is very welcome . . . from any quarter. And all the more valued if it's coming from a policeman. Can't say

I've ever met one before but you're not well known for your understanding.'

'That's the first thing we have to be,' said Joe. 'Though I usually find the people I talk to try to avoid being understood. But, tell me, can you count on Orlando's mother for help when you need it? I mean, when the time arrives?'

'Oh, no!' she said decisively. 'Yet another little illegitimate baby to do her discredit. She won't lift a finger. My family all cut me off years ago – they don't know where I am or what I'm doing. There's a woman in the village – Grandnanny Tilling, the kids call her – and she's promised to come up and help when I send word. And then there's Yallop to do the fetching and carrying. Good old Yallop! He'll always help Orlando.'

'Yallop?'

'Groom, chauffeur. Soldier. He was a rough-riding sergeant in the King's Dragoon Guards. He's taught all the kids to ride. They wouldn't get far in a county gymkhana but they can all stay glued to a horse, with or without a saddle. He's very tough and you'd think he would have no time at all for a man like Orlando but he's always there when he needs him.'

She rummaged in a drawer and took out a folding photograph frame containing three sepia prints. 'Here it is – the Orlando gallery,' she said, smiling. 'That's Yallop, on the left.'

Joe held it to the light and was just able to make out the two figures on horseback. He saw a slender young man, the pre-Switzerland Orlando, he guessed, and a heavier, middle-aged figure with an easy seat in the saddle who must be Yallop. Before passing the frame back he glanced quickly at the other two photographs. In the centre, Orlando posed with two children at his feet and two on his knees and, in the right-hand frame, in an Alpine setting, a man clad in heavy tweeds and leather helmet dangled on a rope from an overhanging cliff.

'Can this be Orlando?' he asked.

Mel grinned. 'So he tells me. He learned to do mountain climbing when he was in Switzerland. Says it's what cured his disease. All that sharp air cutting through your lungs!' She shuddered. 'I suppose it *would* cure you if it didn't kill you first. He says that when he showed this photo to that sister of his she laughed and said it was a cheat – it couldn't be Orlando in the photograph because climbing called for courage and her little brother didn't have the nerve to take his feet off the ground. She was a cow, Commander! Whoever this burglar chap was, I hope he gets away with it. And the emeralds as well. If you do ever catch him you can pin a medal on him from me.'

Joe was drawing the interview to a close and was fleetingly aware that she was not eager to see him move away. For a second her hand reached out to him, without quite making contact, the hand of a woman drowning in her own sea of insecurity, before being snatched back. 'It's been nice to talk to you, Commander,' she said and added, disarmingly, 'We don't get all that much company down here.'

He took a card from his pocket. 'Here are my details and the telephone number of my office at the Yard,' he said. 'If there's anything you want to communicate, please do give me a call.' On impulse, he took out a pen and wrote a number on the back of the card. 'Look. My sister Lydia lives not far from here . . . just this side of Godalming . . . She's a capable, resourceful lady with two little daughters of her own. If you should feel the need of a sensible woman's advice or help, ring this number.'

Mel took the card, looked at it and put it away in the drawer with the photographs. 'Thank you very much, Commander,' she said seriously. 'I may well do that but only to tell her what a very nice brother she has.'

Joe collected up his assistants and after a further short conversation with Orlando and a long look at his painting set off back towards the house. He had vaguely looked for

Dorcas to see them off the premises but it was Reid who was watching out for them.

'I will inform Mrs Joliffe that you are ready to leave, sir. If you will come through to the hall?'

He handed them their hats and left them standing at the foot of the rather grand staircase. The late afternoon sun had left the façade and slanting shadows were beginning to creep over the chequered marble floor. A handsome grandfather clock whirred, clicked and cleared its throat before launching into its tuneful strike and, as the last note died away, they were joined by Mrs Joliffe. She rustled in with the discreet swish of silk, a Whistler symphony of grey and white and black.

'Reid, you may return to your duties. I will see our guests out.' She looked around in an exaggerated way, her eyebrow twitching with austere humour. 'I see you have taken no prisoners, Commander? Has no one confessed?'

'I've heard several confessions, madam, all surprising, but none of them to murder,' said Joe politely.

A door to one of the upper rooms banged loudly and all turned their faces to look upwards. A figure in red was drifting along the landing, one hand trailing on the banister. Mrs Joliffe's hand flew to her throat and she gasped, 'Bea! Bea?'

The figure came slowly on, now descending the sweeping staircase. The old lady's shock turned in a second to savage anger and her voice rang out, cold and peremptory. 'Come down at once!'

A barely recognizable Dorcas continued, unflinching, her stately progress, holding up the trailing hem of the dress in one hand. Joe peered through the gathering shadows. Yes, it could only be Dorcas but a Dorcas transformed. The red dress of some floating fabric reached to her ankles though she had attempted to hitch it up with pins at the shoulders. Her face was made up with darkened eyes and bright red lips. She was biting her lower lip with the effort of concentrating on her hazardous descent.

122

Joe's jaw sagged. Armitage, standing behind him, breathed, 'Coo er! Well, I never! What a little corker!'

Mrs Joliffe was the first to recover. 'Well, the question *is*,' came her withering comment, '*can* Dorcas wear *tomato*?'

Reaching the bottom of the stairs, Dorcas gave her grandmother a wide berth, holding out a hand to each of them in turn. In a formal voice she said goodbye and that she looked forward to seeing them again. They all murmured politely in kind and, with a nod to Mrs Joliffe, stepped out, closing the door behind them.

On leaving, Joe had looked back at the tiny, vivid and ridiculous figure of Dorcas and caught her swift, frightened glance over her shoulder at her grandmother. 'Walk on, the two of you, will you? I'll join you at the car in a moment.'

He bent his head and shamelessly listened at the door. Even the thick oak was not equal to the task of muffling the angry voice.

'What *do* you think you're about, you stupid little creature? No – don't bother to explain. It is plain enough! Trying to attract the attention of the sergeant, were you? Are we now to expect you to parade yourself before every handsome young man who calls here? And stealing clothes to do it? How like your gypsy mother! How can you think you could ever fit into *anything* of Bea's? You look unnatural and debased – go and wash your face!' And, working up to a pitch of rage, 'If it's colour you want, I'll give you colour!'

The resounding slap spurred Joe to fling the door open and stride back into the hall. 'Ladies! I do beg your pardon,' he said cheerfully. 'I fear I left my notebook in the drawing room. No!' He held up a hand. 'Please carry on. Don't let me disturb you. I'll get it. I know exactly where I left it.'

He hurried into the drawing room, pulled his notebook from his pocket and returned, waving it with a smile of triumph. Mrs Joliffe was standing frozen and unbelieving, speechless with embarrassment. Dorcas was drooping, tears beginning to flow, one hand hiding a spreading red mark on her left cheek. Gently, Joe pulled her damp hand away and with formality kissed the dirty little fingers.

'You look like a red, red rose that's newly sprung in June,' he said. 'And my sergeant thinks you're a "little corker" – whatever that is! Now, just be careful where you go pointing your arrows, Diana. I don't want to be called back to arrest you.'

When he spoke the last sentence, his eyes locked with the defiant gaze of her grandmother and held it until she looked away.

Chapter Eleven

They had reached the end of the drive before either of his companions spoke.

'Ugly scene back there, sir?' said Armitage, negotiating the tight turn between the gateposts.

'Not pretty,' said Joe heavily. 'Sadly, I fear Orlando has it right – there *is* something evil lurking about that lovely house.'

'It's Granny,' said Armitage decisively. 'She's right in the middle of it all, I'll bet. Pity they can't just paint her out of the picture.'

'Imagine what the atmosphere was like when Beatrice was alive and kicking!' Westhorpe found her voice. 'The two of them together! Must have been unbearable. They really made poor Audrey's life hell on earth.' She paused tantalizingly for a moment. 'I expect you're both dying to hear what she had to say?'

'Do tell,' encouraged Armitage.

Westhorpe cleared her throat and composed herself. 'I take it you both understand what is meant by the term "lesbian"?'

The car appeared to hit a rut but the sergeant quickly had it under control.

'Well, she was one. A lesbian. According to Audrey who, you must agree, was supremely well placed to judge.'

They nodded.

'But that's not all and here, I'm afraid, my knowledge of the correct sexual terminology threatens to let me down

125

and I have to rely on my readings of Havelock Ellis which are –'

'Get on with it, Westhorpe!' said Joe. 'Four letter words will do if they're all that come to mind.'

'Very well. According to Audrey, who, having a theatrical background, is unsurprised by these things – and I interpret what she had to say, you understand – her vocabulary is decidedly –'

'Westhorpe!'

Westhorpe cleared her throat. 'The Dame was a psychosexual hermaphrodite.'

'Come again, Constable?' Armitage was mystified.

'She alternated between heterosexual activities and a subordinated but significant tendency towards sexual inversion.'

'Sir – what's she on about?' Armitage appealed to Joe.

'I think she's established that the Dame batted for both sides,' said Joe, bemused.

'Is that what they say?' Tilly took up the tale again. 'Well, anyway, she had male lovers, she had female lovers.'

Armitage was stunned. 'What? At the same time?'

'Ah. That much I can't say. Consecutively – certainly; simultaneously or orgiastically – who knows? Audrey didn't go in for titillating details of that nature. She was very direct.'

'All the same,' said Armitage, understanding dawning in his voice, 'I can see why Miss Blount shied away from taking the lid off all this in front of a mixed audience. Good Lord! Dirty old devil! Well, who'd have thought it! I mean, I quite fancied her myself. The Dame, I mean.'

'Many men did,' said Westhorpe coldly.

'But she looked so . . . so . . . female . . . I mean . . .' Armitage was still struggling to reassess the Dame's allure.

'Well, of course she did,' snapped Westhorpe. 'I don't believe women of this persuasion choose to go about looking calculatedly unattractive. If you were imagining a monocle-wearing Burlington Bertie from Bow, Sergeant, you would be way off beam. That's all very well in the music hall but I'll bet when Ella Shields has taken her last curtain call she puts out her cigar, unscrews her monocle and climbs into something short and silky to go home to her husband. I don't believe transvestitism,' she stumbled over the word, 'should be confused with inversion.'

'No indeed,' said Joe, trying to keep a straight face. He was playing with the outlandish picture of a crop-haired female in ginger plus-fours in the tattooed arms of a chief petty officer. 'But tell us, Westhorpe, was any mention made of her male lovers?'

'Her principal male lover was what Audrey called "her bit of rough stuff". An ex-naval man. The Donovan that her mother handed to us on a plate. Good-looking and plausible, according to Audrey, and he seemed to exert a strong influence over Beatrice. Though it could well have been the other way round, don't you think? They were, at all events, closely associated in dubious goings-on in London. She's no idea what was involved.'

'A naval man?' mused Armitage. 'One accustomed to climbing rigging, I wonder? With a good head for heights?'

'I don't believe rigging features strongly in the modern ship,' said Tilly. 'All that went out with Trafalgar, surely? But it's a thought. He's definitely worth investigating, sir, wouldn't you say?'

'Certainly would. I've got him booked in at the Yard for tomorrow morning at nine o'clock sharp,' said Joe. 'He's the blighter, according to Inspector Cottingham, who informed the press of last night's occurrence. Audrey wouldn't, perhaps, be aware that this gentleman is now working as a night porter at the Ritz?'

Armitage turned to Tilly with a broad smile. '*That's* why he's a Commander, miss!' he said.

'Tell me, Tilly,' said Joe, 'you mentioned your readings just now of the works of Dr Henry Havelock Ellis. I'm intrigued! His books are available legally only to the medical profession – and the odd policeman who has a professional need for clarification and enlightenment on a murky subject. I had a particularly distressing case two years ago where information of this nature was vital to my understanding of the crimes committed. I had the devil of a job to get my hands on the books. How come you managed it?'

He turned to see Tilly blushing. 'Nothing underhand, I assure you, sir. I haven't broken any law! My uncle, my father's brother, died last year. He was a doctor and left an extensive library. I offered to catalogue it and prepare it for sale. It contained a collection of Dr Ellis's works.'

'Ah. *Sexual Inversion? Erotic Rights of Women?*'

'Those, among others, featured in the collection, sir. I have to say, they have provided a useful theoretical framework to the practical aspects of my work. In my duties at the railway stations and public parks, I witness and, indeed, have to deal with displays of aberrant human behaviour which would be inexplicable without some guidance.'

Armitage grunted. 'I could have written a book by the time I was fourteen! And all researched within ten yards of Queen Adelaide Court off the Mile End Road. Mind – we didn't go in for any of that trans-what's-it and inversion stuff you're talking about!'

Joe smiled. 'Those chapters'll be reserved for the nobs, I expect,' he said. If they'd been alone he would have reminded the sergeant of the additional research done in France. There was no doubt that having a woman aboard, however bright and effective she was, changed the atmosphere. He was immediately ashamed of the thought.

'I'll need time to sort through this lucky dip,' he said cheerfully. 'I'm going to close my eyes and ponder it. Look – let me know when we're getting into town, will you, Bill, and you can drop me off at Hyde Park Corner. I'm going to my club and I can walk from there. And why don't you continue up Park Lane and deliver Tilly safely home, then drive to the Yard and leave the car there? I can take a cab in the morning. And I'd like to see you both in my office at . . . shall we say midday? You are both clear about what you have to do tomorrow?'

'Yessir.'

'Yes, sir.'

Joe pulled his hat down over his eyes and nodded off.

It was twilight when he stepped from the car and watched it draw away to the north. When it was out of sight he turned his back on Piccadilly and St James's which would have led him to his club and started out in the opposite direction. After five minutes' brisk walk down Knights-bridge he turned off to his left and entered a small square of neat Victorian houses, secluded from the road by banks of thick greenery. The lamps had just been lit and Joe walked quietly along, avoiding the pools of light they created. He reached the house he was looking for and paused in a patch of thick gloom on the pavement oppo-site, watching.

A casual observer would have assumed that a party of some kind was breaking up early. Taxis were drawing up, a chauffeur-driven Rolls-Royce purred away from the kerb. A couple, chattering excitedly, climbed into their parked Dodge and set off in fits and starts. A weeping lady being comforted by two escorts was handed, unseeing, into a taxi. Strange guest-list! Joe counted eight people. Some were in an emotional condition, distraught or openly in tears, some were exclaiming and gesticulating. Joe waited until the last motor car had pulled away then he crossed the road and walked quietly up the secluded drive and tugged at the bell-pull.

The door was opened at once by a maid in ribboned cap. Joe stepped inside and handed her his hat. 'No need to announce me, Alice,' he said, making for the drawing room.

A dimly lit and heavily curtained room greeted him. A fire was sinking in the hearth, discreet electric lamps illum-

inated a polished table, chairs had been carelessly abandoned. There was a lingering scent of cigar smoke on the
air but no trace of food or drink. Head in hands, a dark-
haired woman sat at the head of the table. Her low-cut,
sleeveless dark red gown revealed a magnificent if unfashionable bosom and white shoulders. She raised her head,
sighed, took off her earrings and unpinned her glossy
black hair which fell to her shoulders. The simple gesture
had the effect of changing her appearance from that of a
tone-deaf duchess who'd just endured the whole of the
Ring cycle to that of a tired girl in dressing-up clothes.

'Mrs Freemantle! An exhausting evening?'

Joe's question was greeted with a groan. 'Not as
exhausting as it's going to get!' she said with foreboding.
'What's this? A police raid? Not sure I can cope with a
police raid just now, Commander. That was a particularly
draining session. I gave my all.'

'Sorry to hear that, Minerva. Seems to have invigorated
your audience though. I passed them on my way in. Don't
worry! I skulked behind a laurel bush. No one noticed me.
Wouldn't want a police presence to put the punters off!'

'Very considerate of you, I'm sure. And now, if you
wouldn't mind, show a little more consideration will you,
love, and shove off! I'm knackered.'

Joe grinned and went to open a cupboard by the fireplace. He found a bottle of eighteen-year-old Macallan and
two glasses and poured out generous measures. He added
a few drops of iced water from a pitcher on the table to one
of the glasses and handed it to Mrs Freemantle. She sipped
her drink delicately, her eyes on Joe over the top of her
glass. He drank his whisky quickly and put the glass on
the mantelpiece. In a proprietorial way he bent and poked
at the fire, damping it down for the night, and carefully
placed the fireguard in position. He walked around the
room turning off the lights one by one and lastly flung
back the heavy brocade curtains.

'That's enough for tonight, Maisie, love.'

He took her in his arms and stroked her hair. 'Time you

were upstairs in bed, safely in the arms of the law! We'll talk in the morning.'

Joe poured a cup of tea from the six o'clock tray discreetly delivered to the door by Alice and went to hand it to Maisie. Bathed, shaved and dressed, he was already into his day and eager to get on but he was reluctant to leave without the comforting and intimate routine of exchange of gossip and friendly insult. He stirred her awake and waved the fragrant cup under her nose. As she shook herself into consciousness he remarked, 'It's April, Maisie. Damned nearly the end of April.'

'So?' she said, mystified.

'Four years since we met in Simla!'

'Good Lord! Only four years? You sure? Seems more like ten. Can't say I've ever bothered with anniversaries. You're too damned romantic . . . can get quite annoying. Did the paper come?'

'Here it is. Full of details of the royal birth. To the Duke and Duchess of York, a daughter. Little Lady Elizabeth. Fourth lady in the kingdom and all that. You'd think that with a general strike looming they could come up with something a bit more serious on the front pages.'

'Oh, I don't know. What's more serious than new life? Makes a nice change to think about birth instead of death . . . for me at any rate. Give it 'ere.'

'Tell me about your evening, Maisie. Seemed pretty successful from where I was standing. Emotion swirling thickly around, you'd say!'

'It was good. Better for some than others, of course. It always is. Never held a seance yet where all the punters got through. Just as well. The new bugs would often rather just watch and listen and not participate. They like to get my measure and hear the exchanges with the old hands. When they're confident, they'll try for a contact. There were three approaches last night. Out of eight guests around the table – that's not bad.'

Maisie, he knew, preferred to speak only glancingly of her work as a medium. She could never be certain that Joe believed in what she did. Nor could Joe. A profound sceptic, he had had his firm beliefs shaken to their foundations by Maisie's powers one night in Simla. Working under her professional name of Minerva Freemantle, she had been coerced by Joe into helping him to pursue a murder enquiry. They had fallen, since their return from India, into a routine of discussing her occupation as the remarkably successful and profitable business that it was. Profitable, certainly, but Maisie was convinced that her work had therapeutic value. If someone desperately needed her help to make contact with a loved one who had passed over – and eight years after the war there were still many of these – the help would be given and free of charge if the client could not afford to pay. Her many well-heeled and grateful callers made up for any losses. She owned her own smart house in its discreet square in an increasingly fashionable area and had, as long as Joe had known her, been financially independent. Emotionally independent also, he recognized with some relief. He sometimes wondered if she filed Joe Sandilands under the heading of emotional charity case. She was difficult to read. He accepted the comfort and support their relationship offered but it was not a connection which could ever be made public and both acknowledged this.

'But if it comes to swirling emotion, mate, how about you? How did your evening with the Sea Lord's daughter go?'

'Elspeth Orr? Champion bore!' Joe grinned. 'Won't do, Maisie. Won't do.'

Maisie made clock eyes and held out her cup for a refill. 'You're too bloody choosy! How old are you now? Thirty-two? Three? Certainly time you were settling down. You should be thinking of moving out of that crazy flat of yours on the river and buying a nice little villa in Hampstead.'

She smiled to see the look of horror on his face. 'What?

Not tempted by the idea of a neat little house . . . up there on the hill? Somewhere to walk the Labrador of an evening?'

'No indeed! But I'll tell you, Maisie – I *have* found the house of my dreams. Yesterday. In Surrey of all places,' he said conversationally to distract her from her favourite topic of settling his future.

She listened, absorbed by his account of King's Hanger and its assorted inhabitants. She exclaimed with indignation as he told her of the treatment meted out by Mrs Joliffe to her grandchildren. 'Some women don't know when they're lucky! Undeserving bitch! Two boys and two girls and one on the way? She should be thrilled. What's the matter with her?'

'Lord knows! She seems quite determined to make life unpleasant for those children. I had a bad feeling about the whole set-up. There's more than unkindness in her attitude . . . it's . . . vindictive. As though she's holding them responsible for some injury or slight . . . punishing them. The children are as poor as church mice. They run around barefoot . . . No toys . . . the only books they have are the leather-bound tomes in Granny's library and they're about a hundred years old . . . Tell you what, Maisie!' said Joe, struck by a sudden thought. 'When you next pop into Harrods – could you get some things for me?'

Maisie groaned. 'Should I be making a list? Go on.'

'Well, you could start with . . . yes . . . that's it! A red dress! Something to fit a skinny twelve-year-old. She's actually fourteen but you'd never guess. And a book. Let's think . . . Something the oldest can read to the rest. For fun. How about *The Wind in the Willows*? Oh, and,' he gave a wicked smile, 'a copy of *The Constant Nymph* and I'll put a note in saying "This is *not* the way to live your life."'

He stopped, catching Maisie's indulgent and quizzical expression.

'You're a great softie, Joe Sandilands!'

*   *   *

133

Bill Armitage, a short pigeon's flight away across London, stirred and swam up to wakefulness, hanging on to an entrancing and dangerous dream of a black-bobbed head, sleek as a seal, an elegant straight nose and mocking blue eyes. He clutched at a foam of silver chiffon which melted through his fingers and as the image faded he became aware of the sound that had awakened him and he groaned in frustration and disgust. In an unaccustomed flash of bad temper, he jerked his heel backwards, hitting his companion viciously on the kneecap. A shriek of pain split his skull.

'What the bloody 'ell do you think you're up to, Bill Armitage? You meant that to 'urt! What's got into you? What 'ave I done to deserve a kicking at six in the bloody morning? Eh? Answer me, you great lummox!'

Armitage rolled out of bed and went to stand at the foot, tugging down the hem of his athletic vest and wondering where he'd left his drawers. Wishing he could present a more impressive figure to underline his comment, 'You snore and you sweat and you stink of fish,' he said. 'And your name's Edith. That's what.'

'God's sake! What's got into you? I'm human and my old man works at Billingsgate! What do you expect? And you wake me up with a kick at six to complain about my dad's taste in Christian names? You knew I was called Edith before you started calling round 'ere. I'm not good enough for you any more, am I? That's what this is all about! Seen it coming for some time. Well, bugger off! And don't come back 'ere. Frank's on the other shift next week anyway and if 'e caught you 'ere all your police clout and your posh ways wouldn't stop 'im rearranging your face! Push off! *William!*'

The angry face took on a narrow-eyed, vindictive sneer. 'Just you wait! 'E'll get his own back on *you!*'

'Good. That Frank should get his own back again is exactly what I have in mind. He's very welcome.'

'Clever sod! I'll report you to your inspector. That's what I'll do. I'll go down the nick this morning and tell them what you've been up to! Policemen's supposed to 'ave standards.'

'I wouldn't advise such a course of action, Edith. Listen – tell you a story . . . last week one of our lads was reported for having it off with some trollop in the park. It was broad daylight and he was wearing – well, half wearing – his uniform at the time. A crowd gathered. Certain amount of public disorder broke out. Bets being placed . . . underage ruffians shouting encouragement . . . you can imagine the scene. What do you think happened? A mild reprimand. On that scale my governor will buy me a jar of ale when he's sent you off with a flea in your ear. Not a good idea to snitch on the police, Edith. We look after our own.'

She rallied and then attempted a last defiance, her pretty face twisted into ugliness by petulance. 'Well, they might be interested in hearing what you get up to on Tuesday nights, my lad! Ha! Didn't know I knew that, did you? I thought you might've got yourself a fresh piece on the side and I followed you. I saw where you went and asked about a bit. Very surprising! Nobody likes your kind! Things like that can get you into a lot of trouble. Someone might end up with a red face if 'is bosses found out. Very red! Now – what's 'is name? That officer you're so fond of? Sandilands! That's it! I'll go down the Yard and have a word with *him*!'

Her scornful laughter was cut short as Armitage leaned across the bed. With a quick flick of his strong wrists he flung off the sheet and stared stonily down at her as she wriggled helplessly, clutching at her shell-pink celanese shift. His voice was soft, polite and totally chilling. 'Don't try sounding off like that, Edith. It would be the last unwelcome noise you ever made.'

Choking back his rage and disgust, Armitage scrambled into his clothes and made for the Russian Steam Baths in Brick Lane to wash away the night's sourness. They'd be open by now. When he was thoroughly cleansed he would go home and change into something suitable for his morning's assignment. He'd go through the motions, carry out Sandilands' instructions to the letter and a fat lot of use it would be. Armitage knew where the case was going.

He grimaced as he remembered a chequered schooling in a drab Victorian building a few streets away from here. His best mate who sat on his form was a special kid. Clever was an understatement. Especially when it came to arithmetic. He could always figure out the answer in a flash. In his head. He didn't need to work it out on his slate. One day he'd sung out the answer to a problem before the teacher had even finished chalking it on the board. The teacher had swung round, purple with rage, and accused Dickie of cheating. He'd called him out to the front for ten whacks with the ruler. Armitage had protested. 'But sir! That's not fair! *Where* would he get the answer? None of us knows it!'

And he had joined Dickie at the front for ten cuts for insolence. Armitage clenched his fists. The pain still burned. But it had taught him a valuable lesson that the teacher had no suspicion of. Never appear to get ahead of the boss. Walk a pace behind, looking over his shoulder. Let him think he's making the running and tell him how clever he is when he gets there in the end. It might take longer but at least you'll come out of it smelling of roses.

He wondered whether to broach the subject of his Tuesday night activities with Sandilands. Better to hear an explanation from his own mouth probably. Up-front, honest, nothing to hide. That's the tone that worked with the Commander. Sandilands was clever – worldly even, he would have said. Nothing much would surprise *him*. Yes, he'd bring it up before he was challenged. No need to chuck old Edith in the Thames. Not yet.

Chapter Twelve

Joe left his taxi at Westminster Bridge and continued on foot along the river, shouldering his way through the crowds of workers beginning to flood across the bridges from the rail and underground stations. In they came, a stream of black bowler hats and overcoats, moving like iron filings inexorably drawn to the magnet of the city. He approached New Scotland Yard from the Embankment, ducking through the high wrought-iron gate left permanently wide open, day and night, to welcome members of the public. He paused, in a ritual that had developed over the seven years he had been presenting himself at the building, to cast an offended eye on the streaky-bacon stone and red brick layers of Norman Shaw's Scottish Baronial confection before hurrying up three flights of stairs to his office overlooking Horseguards and the crowding tree tops of St James's Park.

A figure lurking by his door stepped forward with a cry of welcome. Inspector Cottingham, Joe reckoned, must have the most sensitive moustache ends in the business. They quivered at the slightest emotion and at this moment they were vibrating with excitement. His assistant had obviously been lying in wait for Joe in the corridor and he followed him unceremoniously into his office, juggling two bulging cardboard folders from arm to arm. 'Glad to see you in early, all bright-eyed and bushy-tailed, sir,' he said jovially, standing to attention on the other side of Joe's gleaming walnut desk.

'Sit down, Ralph. Put your stuff here,' said Joe, clearing

a space. 'Good Lord, man! It's only seven thirty. Cup of tea?' He pressed a buzzer on his desk and a young officer appeared at the door.

'Usual, sir? Times two?'

'Thanks, Charlie. Mugs'll do.'

'Good day in Surrey, sir?' Cottingham's query was polite, expecting no more than a brief response.

'Excellent. One or two people I need to follow up on. One's booked in for nine this morning – the Donovan you tracked down. Will you sit in on the interview?'

'Delighted, sir. And while we've got him down there we can get his prints.'

'Ah! You've got something back from Forensics to match them with? Already?'

Cottingham's moustache was now demonstrating puzzlement. 'Yes. Already. Look, sir . . . is there anything you want to tell me about this case? Or are you just going to leave me with my shirt tail flapping in the breeze and say nothing?'

'What's your problem, Ralph?'

'Well, I never thought you'd hear me say it but – speed and efficiency! I ask for something and the reply is, not the usual, "You're joking, of course? Not before Tuesday fortnight at the earliest . . ." No, it's more like, "Certainly. At once. Anything more we can do?" Really, sir, if the king had been assassinated, it couldn't be slicker!'

Joe chortled. 'Tell me more.'

'And all this at the weekend. And overnight. You know what that entails. People brought in specially. The best people. Home Office involvement. And all that means overtime. Heavy expenditure! The top brass are telling us to cut down dramatically but here they are signing a blank cheque, it seems, to push this one through. What's going on? Do I put it down to the Sandilands magic?'

'Sorry, Ralph. Whatever else – not that! I'm as puzzled as you are. I can only guess that the urgency is created by the two words "Wren" and "Ritz". Dame Beatrice was quite a character, I'm beginning to see. Friends in high places;

friends in low places. And a good deal of mystery surrounding her. I've honestly no idea who's up there pulling strings but, like you, I become suspicious when doors fall open before you've knocked. I think, Ralph,' Joe looked consideringly at the anxious face across the desk, 'when we're offered a Trojan horse, we'd do well to take a good look at its undercarriage! Until someone decides to take us into his confidence all we can do is play along. But at least we can stay alert and watch each other's back!'

Cottingham nodded and got straight down to business. He opened a file. 'First things first. Autopsy. Findings exactly as initial examination at the scene indicated. Skull cracked. Probably on the second blow. Profile of the wounds matches the profile of the poker found on the roof. Killer right-handed. No other findings to take us by surprise. Definitely wasn't raped. Definitely wasn't virgo intacta.' He handed the report to Joe.

'The murder weapon. The poker which formed part of the set of fire irons, sir. Condition as new. Since central heating was installed not many guests call for an open fire. And the management discourages it – fire hazard and all that – but they keep them there in the hearth for the look of it and because people expect to see them there. Microscope analysis reveals blood and hairs attached to the business end. The hairs match the Dame's and analysis of the blood gives us a Blood Group III. Rather unusual. Only twelve per cent of the population are Group III and this too matches that of the Dame. So far, so good.'

He paused tantalizingly. 'Fingerprints. The boys have done a good job. Must have worked through the night. At least three sets have been photographed and recorded. All from the handle end. Two sets are small, probably ladies' and probably the prints of chambermaids. The third set . . .'

Joe sat forward, fighting down the urge to hurry him on.

'Large. A man's prints, sir. Thumb and two partial fingers clear as day. Oh, and you'll see they managed to lift a fingerprint, index finger, right hand, off the victim's neck.'

'Off her neck, Cottingham? Can they *do* that?'

'They can indeed. When it's bloodstained. Interestingly, this one was right on the pulse spot where you'd put a finger to check for signs of life.'

'Unusual behaviour for your average panicking burglar, isn't it?'

'Exactly, sir. But it is the technique men are trained in when they join the services or the police force. It's an automatic reaction.'

'Westhorpe says she didn't touch the body and Bill checked her pulse at the wrist.' Joe looked pensively at the photographs in front of him. 'Do we have the owner or owners – could be more than one subject – of these prints on record, Ralph?'

''Fraid not, sir.' Cottingham sighed. 'The Criminal Record Office have ransacked their card indexes and come up with nothing. Our boy has kept his nose clean until now. We'll just have to come up with a suspect first and match him to what we've got. Still, it's better than nothing.'

'And we know that our bloke must have left the murder room somewhat bloodstained,' Joe mused. 'He could have cleaned up in the bathroom and then cleaned the bathroom but he'd have still been at his housework when Westhorpe arrived, surely?'

'Or he'd have run straight into Constable Westhorpe in the corridor,' said Cottingham finishing for him. 'But he didn't. So did he leave by the window, dropping the poker as he went?'

'Having put his gloves back on again?' objected Joe. 'Doesn't add up. We know he was wearing gloves when he got in through the window. Why in hell did he take them off to grasp a poker and take a whack at the Dame? Then, having conveniently left his dabs on the murder weapon, he gloves up again, exits, and leaves the thing where we were bound to find it on the roof?'

'Someone's playing games with us, sir.'

'And don't forget Sergeant Armitage was patrolling outside. He'd have to be blind and deaf to avoid seeing a bloke covered in blood clutching a jemmy and an emerald necklace shimmying down the drainpipes. Bill's one of the most alert men I've ever served with. I honestly think no one would have got up the building, shattered a strong Ritz window and climbed down without him being aware. You know, Ralph, I incline to the suspicion that the killing wasn't done at all by someone coming through that window . . . Leaving nothing out for the moment, of course, but let's just think about this. Could all that glass smashing have been a distraction? Have you got the plan you drew up at the scene?'

Joe noticed that Cottingham already had it in his hand. His inspector betrayed by a quick smile of satisfaction that he had got there before the boss.

'The pane was smashed from the outside – no doubt of that – but it could have been done by opening the window and standing inside the room to do it. And you'd expect to find the shards of glass,' he pointed with a pencil, 'here, right below the window in this sort of pattern.' He paused. 'And we did. But I took the opportunity of returning to the scene yesterday before cleaning took place. I got the temporary boarding removed and with daylight streaming through the window –' his moustache bristled with triumph barely held in check – 'I found quite another pattern, sir, which I have drawn up here.'

He produced a larger scale plan of the window area. 'Shards, as I say, here right where you'd look for them but also marks, scrape marks across the nap of the Wilton carpet, *here* near the south wall. And also splinters of glass so small we didn't see them on the night of the murder.'

'So someone stood here at the window, swung it open and smashed it from inside. Someone bright enough and cool enough to sweep the shards into exactly the place you'd look for them.'

Cottingham nodded. 'And there's more. I took samples

141

of the bigger pieces and sent them to the lab for micro-scope analysis. Well, you never know . . . just in case . . .'
He pushed another sheet across the desk. 'One of them had tiny fibres of cotton attached, sir. Ivory, Egyptian. Matches exactly the Ritz bathroom towels. Our lad had muffled the sound of breaking glass.'

Joe smiled. 'What a performance! But at least Bill will be pleased to hear there may be, after all, nothing wrong with his hearing . . .. Oh, thanks, Charlie!'

They curled their fists around the china mugs and thoughtfully sipped the strong Assam brew.

'Right, then. We're looking for someone large, a man most probably, who was admitted to the Dame's room – and therefore, we assume, was known to her – had a violent quarrel with her and killed her, apparently with some passion. Then he calmly and – does the word "pro-fessionally" intrude here, Ralph? – fakes up the burglar-through-the-window business and gets away, somehow managing to avoid being seen by Westhorpe on her way up.'

'That's about it, sir.'

'And if a certain level of climbing ability is no longer required of our suspect, it looks as if Orlando could be joined in the gallery by a few more suspects. That Monty Mathurin, Cottingham – he's moved up a few places. We'll go and call on him.'

'I'm not aware of an – Orlando, did you say, sir?'

'Ah, yes. Beatrice's brother. Interesting man . . .' And Joe reported his findings in Surrey to an intrigued Cottingham.

'Orlando, though he has the strongest motive for bumping off his sister, would appear to have a watertight alibi. An alibi which Sergeant Armitage is checking this morning.'

Cottingham nodded his approval. Sandilands had a reputation for meticulous checking. He never took anyone or any statement at face value. Everything by the book. Steady police teamwork. He knew his boss would now spend an hour looking carefully through the reports delivered to his desk. But Sandilands was no plodding automaton. Cottingham had seen the man get to the heart of a problem in minutes but Joe's flashes of inspiration were always backed up by days of evidence-collecting, interrogation and sound use of forensic science. Cottingham smiled. He wondered if Joe was aware of his nickname amongst the lower ranks. Padlock Holmes. It seemed to suit his style. And it was a style that suited Ralph Cottingham. He glanced about him at the opulence of the furniture, the good carpet, the personal telephone, the view over Horseguards, and was cheerfully envious. He sighed. One day, perhaps *he* might have a bit of luck?

Sandilands was talking again. 'Ralph, when we've finished with this Irishman I'd like you to go straight back to the Ritz. Check the duty rosters. Any witnesses who were about in the corridors at the crucial time. If our bloke emerged from the murder room I'll guarantee he didn't use the lift. Check anyway! Again! But then, if he used the stairs, he would have encountered Westhorpe as you say. The third possibility . . .'

'He had a room of his own at the hotel? On the same floor, likely as not? He could have ducked through a doorway before Westhorpe surfaced. We did a preliminary check on Saturday night – there's a list in the file – but now we know more I'll be asking different questions.'

'Draw up a short list of everyone who'd booked accommodation on the fourth floor or above on that night, will you?' Joe grinned. 'It's all moving, Ralph!'

They met at one minute to nine before the door to one of the basement interview rooms. Peering through the small spyhole in the door they saw that their guest was already installed on the hard chair allocated to interviewees. A young detective constable was standing in the at-ease position opposite, avoiding eye contact with his charge.

Joe looked with interest at the Dame's alleged lover. A

143

tall, rangy man in his mid-thirties, he was sitting in a relaxed manner, one long leg thrown casually over the other and smoking a cigarette. Curly bronze-coloured hair, well-barbered and combed (nothing less than perfection would be accepted by the Ritz management), framed a lean brown face. An intelligent face, Joe decided, watching the grey eyes narrow against the smoke as he took another draw on his cigarette. Joe looked at his mouth. This neglected part of the human face, he always reckoned, could give away clues to character that the eyes were capable of disguising. Narrow lips but well-shaped. A mouth whose strength was outlined by deep lines running down on either side. Lines that could indicate humour and a readiness to laugh. Handsome? Yes, as reported. Attractive to women? He would expect so. Perhaps at some stage he would be lucky enough to be favoured with a judgement on the matter from Westhorpe. For a passing moment Joe wished that she were by his side.

'Good-looking chap, sir,' whispered Cottingham, echoing his thoughts. 'No one's idea of a villain, I'm sure.'

'The best-looking bloke I've ever set eyes on stuck a knife in the throat of a young child and damn nearly shot *me*,' said Joe wryly. 'Shall we go in and get the measure of this Adonis?'

Donovan stood politely when they entered, looking them firmly in the eye as names and ranks were announced. 'The inspector and I have already met,' he murmured, acknowledging Cottingham with a warm smile.

They seated themselves and Cottingham produced a notebook and fountain pen.

'Your name, please?' asked Joe. 'And your address and occupation. For the record.'

'It hasn't changed since the inspector last enquired on Saturday night. I still answer to the name of Thomas Donovan. I still may be reached at the Ritz where I have a room and I work there in the position of night porter, occasionally desk clerk. I also man the telephones.' His voice was a pleasant baritone with only a trace of a soft-ening Irish accent. His smile, quizzical and deprecating, took the edge off any possible sharpness in the response. He added, confidingly, 'Dogsbody, you're thinking, of course, and so it is, but when I'm trying to impress I'm apt to say Assistant Manager.'

Joe fought down an instinctive reaction to answer in the light, conspiratorial tone that the man was trying to elicit. 'Thank you. Yes, we have the Ritz statement on your employment. With records of your duties on the night in question. Tell me, Mr Donovan, why are you so favoured as to be allocated a room in the hotel?'

'Ah, that'll be due to the unsocial hours I have to work and the extra duties. If I'm there on the spot they feel free to call on me whenever they have a staffing problem. Day or night. It suits them. It suits me fine. Being an unmarried man with no ties.'

'And the number and floor of your room?'

Cottingham's pen was poised for his answer.

'Oh, it's number 12 on the top floor. Not the finest accommodation – under the leads you might say – but it does well enough.'

Joe was aware that Cottingham, next to him, had become perfectly still like a spaniel on the point.

'Tell us where you were, will you, between midnight and one o'clock on Saturday night.'

'I was on duty in the back office, on call. There was no call until the emergency occurred. That would have been at about twelve forty when the manager came in to alert me to the situation. He telephoned Scotland Yard from my office, it being more discreet than the front desk, and told me to stay alert and cover for him while he dealt with the police and the disposal of the unfortunate deceased.'

Joe let the impersonal words echo for a moment then, his voice hardening, said, 'Tell me, Donovan, was the deceased fortunate enough to be acquainted with you?'

'I was able to arrange Dame Beatrice's accommodation

145

when she stayed with us. She liked to return to the same suite.'

'She had a flat up in Bloomsbury, I believe. Why did she need to stay at the hotel?'

'She was a busy lady. Hard-working. Many calls on her time. She was rich. She needed and could afford to be cosseted from time to time. When she met her important military and naval contacts, she liked to be picked up from the Ritz. Handy for the Admiralty. It suited her well.'

'Were there any other services you performed for Dame Beatrice?' Joe asked bluntly.

Donovan lit another cigarette, taking his time. Not needing a pause for thought, Joe was sure; the man had already carefully rehearsed his script. He was teasing them, trying to trigger a heavy police response so that his triumph when he launched his no doubt impeccable alibi would be all the more satisfying.

'Oh, yes. Busy ladies can be very lonely, Commander. I don't know if you were acquainted with her?' He gave Joe a slow and insolent appraisal. 'No? Dame Beatrice was . . . emotional and sensitive. She appreciated the occasional presence of a warm-blooded man. A discreet man.'

'A man whose room was conveniently located on the floor above her suite?'

'Yes, of course. There is a flight of stairs . . . as I suppose you've noticed . . . not for the use of staff in normal circumstances, you understand, but I have never been challenged.'

'And were you booked in to attend the Dame on the evening in question?'

Cottingham had stopped breathing.

'I was to go to her room when my shift ended.'

'And what time was your shift scheduled to end?'

'At six o'clock.'

'What? Six o'clock? In the morning?' Cottingham could not hide his astonishment.

'It was usual,' said Donovan with a half-smile. 'Dame Beatrice's energy and . . . libido, if I may use a technical

146

term? . . . were apt to peak in the early hours. Neatly coinciding with the masculine urges, as I'm sure I don't need to explain to two men of the world.'

'Good Lord!' said Cottingham faintly.

'So we have you in the back office from midnight onwards, ticking off the hours until it should be six,' said Joe. 'Can anyone vouch for your presence there?'

Donovan looked thoughtful for a moment. 'You could speak to Jim Jordan. The boot-boy. Poor Jim finds it diffi-cult to stay awake through his nightly duties – the lad's only fourteen. He often brings his boots into my office and works on them there. I keep him awake with stories and merry banter. He likes the company. He was there from eleven when he came on duty until the manager burst in with his news at twelve forty. Jim will be able to confirm that I was there on the ground floor at the time in which you are interested.'

'And your first act on hearing the news of the murder of your lover was to pick up the telephone and alert the press?' said Joe coldly.

Donovan shrugged his shoulders. 'We all need what cash we can come by these days. They pay well. And I wouldn't flatter myself by calling her my lover . . .'

'Very well then – client,' said Joe sharply. 'How about that? Is that the term a gigolo would use?'

He was pleased to see a flush of anger begin to light up the controlled features.

'We will of course check on the facts you have given us this morning, Mr Donovan. And perhaps, before leaving, you would allow the constable to take a sample of your fingerprints.'

'For purposes of elimination, naturally,' said Donovan.

'Naturally.'

As he reached the door, Joe spoke again. 'Donovan? . . . Irish, I believe? Which part of Ireland do you hail from, I wonder?'

'County Antrim.'

147

'Ah? As did Sir Roger Casement? The county would seem to produce its share of . . . handsome men.'

Joe seemed to have at last got under the man's skin. He turned from the door and spoke quietly, his lilting accent now unrestrained: 'You'll be referring to the notorious traitor, Casement? Executed by the British? Yes, I understand him to have been born in Antrim. Now tell me – was not William Wallace born a Scot and Guy Fawkes an Englishman – like your honours? We all have to share our native soil with rogues and villains and misunderstood heroes, don't we now? Well, gentlemen, if there is nothing further I can do for you, I will return to my duties.'

'You let him go off? Just like that?' Cottingham was squeaking with distress. Realizing he was on the point of insubordination he collected himself and hurried on, 'Sir, was that wise? Weren't there many more questions we had to put to the bastard?'

'Hundreds,' Joe replied calmly. 'But until I've done a bit more research into the character and career of Mr Donovan I'm going to let him run loose. Look, Ralph, when you've finished at the Ritz, make a few enquiries at the Admiralty, will you? Check this bloke's record with the navy. We'll need to know what rank he reached and why he left . . . how did his path cross that of the Dame . . . what were his specialities . . . you know the sort of thing. I'll give you a number to ring and the name of a contact.'

'Won't be necessary, sir. I have my own.'

Joe smiled grimly. 'The next time I see Mr Donovan, we're going to be armed with incontrovertible evidence of his villainy and *we'll* be booking *him* into a room! In Pentonville!'

Joe was still working his way through the reports in his office when the telephone rang.

'Commander Sandilands? Glad to catch you at your

148

desk for once!' said Sir Nevil. Without preamble and without his usual bonhomie, he hurried on: 'Now then, our Wren at the Ritz. Decisions to be made, conclusions to be arrived at. Look, why don't you pop along to my rooms, shall we say in five minutes? Join me in a cup of coffee.' There was the slightest of pauses. Was he conferring with someone? Receiving an order? 'Oh, and it might be helpful if you brought your files on the case with you. Your complete files, Commander.' Another pause and then, decisively, 'I'm saying – clear the case off your desk. If you have any officers out in the field on duties related to the enquiry, then call them in at once.'

Joe guessed from the unnatural and strained phrasing that Sir Nevil was not alone in his office. The abrupt use of his rank and surname at the outset was signal enough to Joe that the conversation was being overheard. He would pick up the hint and reply in kind: formally and loudly. He managed to keep his voice level as he replied. 'Of course, Sir Nevil. I'll be right along. Oh, look – could we make that in fifteen minutes? I'm in the middle of a briefing here – a briefing which I shall now have to turn around.'

He put the phone down, grim-faced. Joe knew how to interpret this summons. He was being instructed to bury Dame Beatrice.

For a moment the soldier's automatic reaction to a command had kicked in. His shoulders had squared on hearing the General's clipped voice and he could have done nothing other than respond as he had. 'Yessir. Yessir. Three bags full, sir!' was still the formula. But instinct was warring with training. He'd played for time simply to give himself a chance to think. Dizzily, he stood at his desk gripping the smooth rolled edge but staring into a void before him.

He got his bearings.

He grabbed his briefcase and set it open on the desk. He reckoned he had ten minutes. Swiftly he cast a calculating eye over the Beatrice files and made his selection. Into the case went Cottingham's scrawled interview notes on

149

Donovan, the Dame's diary and Westhorpe's handwritten inventory. He carefully detached the paper-clipped flimsy copies of Cottingham's typed-up reports, blessing the man for his thoroughness. He emptied the pile of photographs of the corpse and the murder room and selected two for his personal collection. Looking critically at what was left of the evidence files, he thought they looked substantial enough – an impressive coverage for the thirty-five hours that had elapsed since the murder. On a fresh sheet of foolscap he wrote out a quick summary of the depleted contents. He took the trouble to change pens halfway through and squeeze in a supposed omission in pencil. Deciding it looked convincing, he pinned it at the top. He packed the files back into the two cardboard folders in which Cottingham had carried them.

One last thing to do. He lifted the receiver and asked to be put through to the Fingerprint Section. He identified himself and requested the Head of Department. 'Larry? Listen. In a bit of a rush here . . . Yes! As you say! . . . You'll be getting a sample via Cottingham. Subject: Thomas Donovan. Process these as soon as you can and send the results by special messenger to my home address. You've got it? Good. Buy you a pint next week!'

He locked his briefcase, pushed it under the desk then tucked the files under his arm and set off upstairs.

Chapter Thirteen

Was there evasion behind the clever eyes? Joe thought so as he listened to Sir Nevil's voice booming at him over the broad desk. '. . . grateful as usual, Joe, for the speed and quality of your attack. Good team effort, I hear? And one which enables us to tie up the ends remarkably quickly. Let me know the names of officers who've impressed you, will you, my boy? No need to interview anyone else in connection with this sorry business. Did you have anyone else on your list?'

The question was casually put.

Joe replied carefully, reciting a selection of names, some of which he hadn't the slightest intention of following up. He was watching for a reaction to the candidates on offer. No response to the names of family members, he decided, but he could have sworn he detected the slightest narrowing of the lips when he listed an admiral and a senior member of the Wrens. So that was it. Someone else was aware of the Dame's colourful forays into bohemian life. If the lurid details got out, it would do nothing but damage to a revered service. Enemies of the state, and they seemed to be ever-increasing and coming from all sides of the political spectrum, might well use such a scandal to attack the country in its most sensitive part – its pride.

Sir Nevil spoke decisively: 'Don't bother. No need at all to disturb these people. Let it rest.' His tone softened as he went on, 'Look, Joe, there can be no possible question that the CID has pulled out all the stops to account for the death of a highly esteemed lady. The funeral is set for next

Thursday at St Martin's. The top military brass will all be there in support. I believe her mother wishes to keep the ceremony simple and short. In fact she has asked that no uniforms be worn. It'll be homburgs rather than tricornes on parade. Quite proper in the circumstances – she did not, after all, die on active service. We're preparing an announcement for the press to coincide with the release of ceremony details. We've been lucky – what with the royal birth and the impending strike, they haven't needed to search about for headlines this week!'

He looked Joe straight in the eye. 'They are to be told that she was killed while bravely attempting to repel a burglar who subsequently made off with an item of jewellery. Commander Sandilands of the Yard will be reported to be hot on his trail. Just the sort of lurid story the sensation-seeking public will smack its lips over. What do you say, Joe?'

Pitching perfectly the degree of bitterness in his tone, Joe said, 'I notice you do not seek to know what I *think*, sir. I will say that I understand. I'll leave you with the case notes and should it ever be thought appropriate to pursue it further, I hope the reports will be of use.' He dropped his voice for emphasis. 'I think you'll find them well worth reading, sir.'

Sir Nevil's eyes clouded with uncustomary indecision.

Joe decided he knew his boss well enough to risk an off-the-record remark. Again he spoke quietly, though they were alone in the room. 'We jumped the gun, sir?'

Sir Nevil gave a fleeting smile. 'You have it right, my boy!' he growled. 'You've no idea from how many directions I've been prodded since the powers in this land woke up to what had transpired.' He whistled under his moustache. 'Damned lucky you kept the lid on it! If you'd spilled all to that reporter on Saturday night, we'd both be for the high jump. Still – that's what we pay you for – discretion. Can't discuss it with you, of course, but the Foreign Office, the Home Office, Room 40, the wraiths at MI5 and the Special Branch thugs – they've all been holding a knife to my throat. No idea what's been going on . . . couldn't tell you if I had.'

Joe replied lightly. 'Probably all so busy watching each other they didn't notice the Plod had made off with the case from under their noses.'

'Must say, I can't be doing with all this cloak-and-dagger stuff.' Sir Nevil's candid old soldier's face suddenly looked tired. 'It's all the go, I know, this shadow-boxing, but I prefer a target out there in front of me, in plain daylight and preferably in range. Old school, what! Time I was dead, I think!'

He added, in a brisker tone, 'Look, Joe, now you've got this report off your hands, why don't you take a few days' leave? You'll need to make an appearance for the funeral – that would be appreciated, I know – but why don't you take the rest of the week off? Come back on Monday? And why don't you give similar instructions to your staff, the ones who've been involved with all this? Tell them to go off to the country or the seaside – reward for zeal and effort – you can think of something, I'm sure.'

'Put myself out of the way – is that what you mean, sir?'

'Of course that's what I mean! Your ugly mug is not unfamiliar to the lads of the press. All too recognizable! Don't want them hounding you with their magnesium flashes or whatever those infernal devices are. Not suggesting you flee to Paris or Scotland – just lie low for a bit, eh? Them's orders!'

'I have a sister conveniently in Surrey. She's always saying she doesn't see enough of me . . .'

'Capital! Capital! Leave your telephone number down there with my secretary, will you, Joe? And I don't, I suppose, need to say how much I . . . er . . . appreciate your co-operation?'

His smile faded as Joe closed the door behind him and he remained seated, bushy white eyebrows knitting together in unwelcome thought. His hand reached for the buzzer on his desk and his secretary entered.

'Miss Holland, one or two memoranda to shoot off, if you wouldn't mind.'

'Of course, Sir Nevil.' She sat down and her shorthand pad appeared miraculously on her lap, a sharpened pencil poised for the first word.

He glanced with slight irritation at the slim, upright figure over the desk. She was always a few seconds ahead of him and he found it disconcerting. 'How did she *do* that?' he wondered. Whenever she entered or left the room he had the clear impression that she had saluted. Must be the training. He recollected that Miss Holland was an ex-Wren. When the service had been disbanded after the war many of these girls, hand-picked for their intelligence and capacity for hard work, had been snapped up by husbands and one or two by men like Sir Nevil who appreciated their skills and their discretion.

The 'new shore service' as it was billed had been founded in 1917, late in the war, under Dame Katharine Furse, ex-VAD who'd already put in three years of service in France. She and a committee of formidably effective and experienced women had to cope with a flood of seven thousand girls who flocked to the white ensign to enlist. It was a wonder they'd had time to kit the recruits out in a uniform before it was all over and they found themselves turned loose with a week's pay. But in the short year of their existence, the Wrens had impressed and won over the men of the navy from the lowest rating to the highest admiral.

Sir Nevil had witnessed a quite extraordinary scene a year after the war's end in July 1919. He had attended the Great Peace March through London and, standing in Hyde Park at the finale, he had watched Dame Katharine herself leading the Wrens' contingent. Stepping proudly in impeccable formation, the girls in blue entered the park and, as they drew level with the Achilles statue, they were greeted by an unrehearsed burst of applause from the admirals who had been leading the main contingent. Sir Nevil's frosty old eye had moistened. He thought it a graceful tribute to the Wrens' devotion.

If the highest authorities in the land were prepared to lean on him and pull out all the stops to prevent the good name of the service being besmirched by this . . . this . . . rotten apple – well, so be it! Should he have taken Joe into his confidence? No. Better to play by the rules. Anyway, the chap was sharp enough to have worked it out for himself. And tactful enough not to have made a song and dance about it. What had he said in a meaning way? '. . . find the files well worth reading . . .' Sir Nevil groaned. If Sandilands had done his work thoroughly, he didn't doubt it. Contents more than likely to stand your hair on end! Good thing he'd asked for the files. Would be dynamite in the wrong hands.

A slight cough from the other side of the desk reclaimed his attention to the job in hand.

'I'll address and deliver this myself, Miss Holland. Just type, "Top Secret", would you? To keep everybody happy. They like that sort of nonsense. And say, under today's date and time: "Action taken in accordance with suggestions made this day. Closing case. No problems envisaged." That's all on that one. Oh, before we move on – there's a little florist . . . on Jermyn Street, I think it is . . . I want you to order me a wreath for Thursday.'

'Ophelia's are generally reckoned to be the best, I think, sir.'

'If you say so, Miss Holland. And . . . lilies? Do you think lilies? *Lilies that fester smell far worse than weeds,*' he quoted to himself. 'Very appropriate.'

Too late, he realized that out of habit he'd spoken the line from Shakespeare's sonnet out loud.

'*For sweetest things turn sourest by their deeds,*' Miss Holland said happily. 'That was the *preceding* line so – two points to me, I think!'

They regularly batted quotations at each other over the desk; the game was their only intimacy. But, sensing his dismay on this occasion, she added smoothly, 'But I take your point and will insist on absolute freshness, Sir Nevil. And the modern lily has excellent keeping qualities, I do believe.'

When Miss Holland had made her phantom salute, turned on her heel and left to return to her typewriter, Sir Nevil took a deep breath and opened the files.

Joe slammed into his office disturbed and angry. He was surprised to find a file sitting precisely in the middle of his desk. Surely he hadn't missed one in his hasty clearance? A pencilled note attached to the top sheet answered his question:

From Constable Smithson, Documentation Section.
Sorry to have found you out, Commander.
You requested this file yesterday a.m. I experienced some difficulty in location of item which had been removed from dept. without authorization. A further persistent check half an hour ago revealed said file back on shelf. Please note sir that file should be returned a.s.a.p.

Joe smiled and resolved to compliment Constable Smithson on his persistence. The contents had probably ceased to be of any further relevance, following his interview with Sir Nevil, but his curiosity pushed him to open it anyway.

'Right, Armitage, my lad,' he said under his breath, 'let's see what's so special about you that there's a waiting list to read your file!'

He leafed his way through the details of Bill's acceptance into the force and his subsequent training assessments (outstanding). Joe noted no reference to his disability. His commanding officer's yearly reports were glowing. Joe recognized the signs. His CO appeared to have nurtured the young constable's career, putting him through a series of increasingly demanding and varied assignments. A pattern was emerging. Bill was being groomed for a high position in the force.

The file ended abruptly with an entry on Armitage's success in closing the Wapping Steps murder case. There was no written reference yet to the death at the Ritz. 'A question mark by his name,' Sir Nevil had said vaguely. Joe couldn't see one. Had the damaging remarks been removed? Patiently, Joe started again at the beginning, trying to view the material through Sir Nevil's eyes. At the very front of the file was glued the statutory form summarizing the subject's character and achievements. One comment held his attention. Bill's fluency in foreign languages, acquired during his war service and a year's wandering around Europe immediately following his demob, was commented on, predictably, with favour. This would have distinguished him from the other recruits and been regarded as an indicator of his ability. But a footnote dated September 1925 took this further.

Bill was reported to be taking lessons in the Russian language. With a Russian native. Place and times of meetings were attached, it added helpfully. Joe searched the file, even upending it and shaking it, but the advertised surveillance sheets were missing.

So that was it. Bolshevism. The bogeyman of the British. More feared than the Fascisti at the other end of the spectrum, the Bolsheviks had replaced Anarchists as everyone's *bête noire*. If Bill did indeed have red tendencies he would find his promotion blocked, his movements vetted, his whole career in jeopardy. The man could not be unaware of the arrest only six months ago of the whole executive of the Communist Party of Great Britain. The twelve top members had been unceremoniously bagged by the Branch and put on trial immediately.

Joe had gone along to the Old Bailey to witness the proceedings. All were brought up before Sir Archibald Bodkin and found guilty of some pretty serious charges including incitement to mutiny. All were found guilty. The five ringleaders who had previous convictions were sent down for twelve months, the other seven, with unexpected leniency, Joe thought, were offered the choice of six months in Pentonville or their freedom against a guarantee of good behaviour. To everyone's surprise the men had conferred for a few seconds in the dock and unanimously agreed to accept the jail sentence. An impressive show. Joe, and others more influential than he no doubt, had been impressed and – yes – alarmed. Bodkin's generous gesture, his warning shot across the bows, had misfired.

Men of integrity, men with a fire in their belly, men ready to take a term in one of HM's prisons to flaunt their dedication to a cause – these were men who would be respected by a romantic like Joe but feared by the state.

Joe looked again at the few words scribbled on Bill's sheet. Words that could ruin a man's prospects. He sighed. He hoped he hadn't added two and two and made five.

On closing it, he was struck by the unusual slimness of the file. He'd established that the surveillance sheets were missing. But there was more. Where was the usual clutter? Where were the loose paper-clipped sheets of commendation, requests for leave, sickness reports? Where also was the all-important war record? If this had been lost, Joe could have dictated a replacement, for the time of his involvement with Bill, at least. It would have begun with the words: 'This man is, in the estimation of his commanding officer, the very best the country has to offer. He is one hundred per cent loyal, fearless, energetic, intelligent and resourceful.' It could have gone on with illustrations for pages.

Joe was left holding the bones of the sergeant's file. The flesh had gone somewhere else. He scribbled a note to Charlie to fetch him from the finance department any stipendiary documents and overtime schedules held on the sergeant. He didn't think interest would have stretched as far as this lowly section. He might strike lucky.

A smart rap on the door interrupted his thoughts and he hurriedly placed the file in a drawer and called, 'Come in!'

'Not interrupting anything, sir, I see!' said Armitage, cheekily surveying the suspiciously empty surface of Joe's desk. 'There's two of us. I've got the constable with me.' Joe pressed the buzzer. 'Charlie – two more mugs, please.'

They settled themselves purposefully opposite Joe and each took out a notebook. Joe wondered whether to break the news that the case was on the point of being closed down, the hounds called off, and decided to hear them out.

'We gave up and returned to base when we'd collected the eighth corroborative statement, sir. We started with the name he gave us and we were passed on from one to another – names and addresses. "You really ought to speak to old so and so. He's bound to remember . . ." That sort of thing. Went like a breeze! I spoke to the gentlemen and the constable interviewed the ladies, seeing as how some of them . . . *all* of them,' he corrected at a look from Tilly, 'were in a state of *déshabillé*.'

'This class of person keeps late hours with a correspondingly late rising,' said Tilly crisply.

Joe could feel for the poor inhabitants of bohemian Bloomsbury being faced with this wide-awake pair before they'd properly surfaced. 'And could you get any sense out of this dissolute mob?'

'Oh, yes,' said Armitage confidently. 'Too befuddled still to make anything up. Some of them were where they shouldn't ought to have been, if you follow, and very eager to trade an honest testimony for a touch of police discretion. Tap the side of your nose and wink –' he demonstrated the technique and Joe winced – 'and they'll eat out of your hand. Never fails!'

'And the upshot was . . .?'

'A majority confirmation that Orlando was where he said he was. Just as he predicted, sir, some swore he wasn't there at the Cheval Bleu nightclub, others were equally

159

confident that he was.' He paused and pretended to refer to his notebook. 'But all those who were at the club tell the same story. It must have made a great impression because they all agree on the details down to the red tights and the mismatched socks. One black, one blue it was, sir.' He grinned. 'Looks as though Orlando's in the clear. As far as we're concerned, that is!'

Joe nodded. 'Westhorpe? Any jarring notes?'

'The same responses, sir. Oh, and to fill in the remainder of Mr Jagow-Joliffe's night of adventure, we managed to find the blue door he referred to – the house from which he fled to the station to return home.'

'Yes? And is he lucky enough to have the lady's corroboration of his unscheduled overnight stay?'

'Two, in fact, sir!'

'Two? Two nights?'

'No. Two ladies. On the same night. The night in question. They remembered him clearly. They had some hard things to say on the subject of Mr Jagow-Joliffe.' She cleared her throat. 'It would appear that he failed properly to establish the precise terms of his welcome and by shooting off before cock-crow next morning, he left behind him the distinct impression that he had . . . would the expression be "welshed on the deal", sir?'

'Ah! The ladies were expecting some more tangible souvenir of their encounter than a trace of Bay Rum on the pillow?'

'Exactly!'

'You'd better have this, sir,' said Armitage, handing over a sheet of paper. 'List of the names and home addresses of all the contacts we spoke to. And brief notes on what they said. Just for the record.'

Joe took the sheet and decided the moment had come to bite the bullet and tell them what instructions he had received from his head of department. Looking at the eager faces before him, he knew his task would not be an easy one. Carefully he outlined his interview with Sir Nevil and waited for their response. For a moment they sat in silence, eyes downcast. Then they exchanged a brief look. Neither, for a change, seemed to want to speak first.

Finally, Armitage said in a level voice, 'Sorry to hear that, sir. Goes against the grain being cut off like that right in the middle of something. I thought we were getting somewhere.'

'That, I suspect, is the nub of it, Bill. Someone doesn't want us to get any further. And we are not encouraged to wonder why or who.'

'Don't need to wonder, do we? Obvious really. We ought to have expected it as soon as we found the Dame was a bit dodgy. The Admiralty put pressure on Special Branch via Room 40 – though they're not supposed to – the Branch duly report directly to the Commissioner himself. He picks up the phone and asks Sir Nevil what the devil he thinks he's doing allowing one of his best blokes to poke about inside this anthill. Upshot – you get pulled off the case and now we'll never get to interview old Monty Mathurin. Pity that . . . I was looking forward to it.'

Joe grinned with relief. 'Very philosophical approach, Bill, and I'm sure you have it right. Westhorpe?'

Westhorpe would not be prepared to take lightly her dismissal from a case where she had shone and her abilities had been acknowledged. But training and good manners carried her over her disappointment. 'A pity, I agree. But there are larger issues even than the Dame's killing. I can see some good people might be embarrassed by the findings we were making – so lightly, I now have to think. And the official story is very credible. The burglary turning to violence, I mean. It really has always seemed to me to be the most likely explanation. You could say they've just made us take a short cut but we've arrived at the right destination.'

Some of the assurance faded from her voice as she added, 'I have enjoyed working with you, though so briefly, sir. And with the sergeant.'

'And may I return the compliment? said Joe sadly. 'Who

knows? Perhaps we may find ourselves working together again should someone find himself stabbed at the Strand . . . garrotted at the Garrick . . .'

'Clubbed at Claridge's?' suggested Westhorpe. 'I could help with that!'

Joe smiled. 'So – it only remains for me to pass on Sir Nevil's instruction to take a few days' paid leave. You are required to fade into the background. Disappear. Can you manage that?'

'I've got an aunt runs a boarding house in Southend,' said Armitage dubiously. 'She's not too full at this time of year.'

'No one sends me away from the capital,' said Westhorpe firmly. 'Of all the cheek! I shall get Daddy to have a word with Sir Nevil.'

Joe couldn't be quite certain that she was teasing him. 'Two further matters to clear up before you make yourselves scarce. Individual things – I'd like to see you one at a time, if you wouldn't mind. Won't take long. Tilly, go and sit in the corridor for a moment, will you, while I speak to Bill and then I'd like a word with you.'

In some surprise, Tilly withdrew, leaving Joe facing his sergeant.

'Your career, Bill . . . there's something I want to discuss with you.'

Before he could go further, Armitage had adopted a defensive posture. 'There aren't any problems, are there, sir?' His voice had an edge of anxiety. 'I suppose you've had a look at my record? It's clear, isn't it? Have they got me for the leg?'

'Is there something else that's troubling you, Bill? Something you fear may be on file against you?'

'As a matter of fact, there is. Been meaning to bring it up but there never seemed to be a right time. I'll come straight out with it and perhaps you can advise me what to do . . . Every Tuesday evening after work I go to a flat in Bordeaux Court, that's off Dean Street. It's a neighbourhood favoured by immigrant families, sir.'

162

'Know it well.'

'There's a Russian émigré lives there. He does a bit of waiting at tables and teaches Russian in his spare time. At least he did until trade dropped off after last year's hue and cry after reds under the beds.' Armitage's head went up in defiance. 'Nobody was asking *me* but I thought that whole thing was a load of bollocks. A set-up, sir. I learn Russian. The language – nothing to do with politics. Always been keen on languages. This chap's a good teacher. Inspiring. And I count him my friend.'

'I appreciate your honesty,' said Joe. 'And, on a personal level, I can sympathize with what you say – but have a care, man! These are strange times. The country's like a champion boxer who's damn nearly been knocked down in the final round and knows he may have to pick himself up in time to fight another challenge to his title before he's recovered. There are some who think the gauntlet's already been thrown down.'

'And some who think the real enemy's closer to home. The unions, the strike they're threatening next week. Could lead to panic and witch hunts . . . people denouncing their neighbours. Could be nasty. Civil War all over again? With the divide along class lines this time? We never did have our French-style revolution over here,' said Armitage gloomily.

'Have you seen the news from Parliament this week? "Rigorous measures" are being proposed to counter red tendencies in HM forces. Apparently, the loyalty of the army and navy are thought to be in danger of being undermined by what MPs are calling "the cunning and devilish ways of the communists". They'll be looking at the police next . . . indeed, I believe we are already under scrutiny. And I don't much like the intemperate tub-thumping they're having printed in the newspapers. Just take a look at today's *Mirror*, Bill! Stirring stuff!'

He passed his copy over the desk. 'I don't often dole out advice,' said Joe, 'but – leave it, Bill. Leave it over. Don't give them anything. Spend your Tuesday nights at the dogs or at the pictures. It wouldn't be a good idea to bring down the attention of the Branch on you.'

He watched Armitage's face closely as he mentioned the Special Branch. The political police force bridged the gap between the Met and the Intelligence Service and, surely, if anyone was taking an unhealthy interest in the sergeant, it was the Branch.

What he saw in the handsome face was not alarm or suspicion but, surprisingly, concern. Bill grinned and shook his head. 'And I've never given *you* advice, Captain, but just this once, I'll say: let this case go. I know what you're like. The words bloody-minded ferret come to mind. Leave it, sir!'

They smiled at each other and shook hands.

'Show Westhorpe in, will you?'

With Armitage's advice still sounding, unheeded, in his ears, Joe broke into a charming smile and asked briskly, 'Tilly. Do you happen by any chance to be free this evening?'

Guardedly she replied, 'Yes, as a matter of fact, I shall be free – in the changed circumstances, sir.'

'Jolly good! Right then. Why don't you slip into your glad rags and I'll take you out to a supper dance? We'll go and cut a rug or two at the Embassy, shall we?'

Chapter Fourteen

Joe was pinned to his chair by the sudden flare of astonishment she turned on him. But, in a second, this gave way to amusement and she replied flirtatiously with a good deal of fluttering of eyelashes, 'Oh, but sir! This is so sudden!'

Then, knowingly, 'Who are we trailing? Monty?'

'The very same! I'm no longer officially allowed to chat to the fellow so we'll have to work our way around it.'

'Can you be sure he'll be at the Embassy tonight?'

'No. Not certain. Inspector Cottingham has established that nightclubs are where he generally spends his evenings and this one is his favourite but . . .'

Her eyes flicked to the telephone. 'Can you get an outside line on that?'

'Yes, of course.'

'May I?'

She took a notebook from her bag and leafed through it then picked up the receiver and in a starched voice asked the operator to connect her with a number she read out. A few moments later, Joe was surprised to hear her asking in a breathless, little girl's voice, 'Oh, hello? Jenkins? Joanna here. Look, I've gone and forgotten where Monty asked me to meet him tonight. Drat! This is a terribly crackly line! Can you hear me? What have you got in his diary? Was it Ciro's? No? . . . Oh, silly me! Yes, of course! Thank you, Jenkins. You are a poppet!'

Joe had left his desk to stand by Tilly as she made her phone call, alarmed but intrigued by her boldness. He leaned towards the earpiece but was not able to make out the words to which she was responding with wide-eyed mischief.

She set down the telephone and turned to him. 'Got it! The Kit-Cat Club tonight at eight.'

'Well, of course! The Kit-Cat! Where else?' Joe slapped his forehead with the heel of his palm in a stagey way but he couldn't disguise a spurt of real excitement. 'We should have guessed. Mathurin's not known for missing out on something special, is he?'

'Special? What's special?'

'You're telling me you hadn't heard? And you one of the brightest young things about London? There's to be an appearance every day for a week – this week! – by Paul Whiteman and his band. Shove over Jack Hylton and your creaking orchestra and make way for a touch of American glamour!'

'Paul Whiteman? Are you sure?'

'Yes. He's touring England. They've been playing at the Tivoli cinema but just for a short time they've been lured away to the Kit-Cat.'

'Ah. Not difficult to guess why,' said Tilly knowingly. 'They have very well-placed admirers, the sort who expect cocktails and dancing laid on when they hear their favourite band perform. The Mountbattens and, they say, even the Prince of Wales . . . Ooh, sir! Do you think he'll be there?'

'I should think it very likely. Put your best frock on just in case!'

Tilly was struck by a depressing thought. 'There'll be crowds there. We'll never get in. And don't you need to be a member? I think you do, you know.'

'You do and I am. A sort of honorary member. And for the same reason, we'll get past the doorman however crowded they are.' He smiled to see her puzzled face. 'I raided the Kit-Cat soon after it opened. Just routine, to establish our authority, you understand. Gave them a clean sheet. Since when the management is always careful to

166

extend a warm welcome. Oh, don't worry – I shan't arrive with cuffs clanking in my back pocket.'

She smiled back nervously. 'I say, sir, this is a very surprising side of you. I mean, I didn't take you for a jazz fiend. Um . . . can you dance?'

Without warning, Joe advanced a step, caught her in a tight embrace and swung her into a showy quickstep around the room, growling the tune of 'You Took Advantage Of Me' in her ear. She responded without hesitation, moving with him as nimbly as her heavy uniform would allow. The impromptu dance came to a sudden end as Tilly knocked over the hat-stand by the door, got the giggles, missed her step and crunched down hard on Joe's foot with her police boot.

They sat down again, each slightly embarrassed, and Tilly was the first to recover her poise and her breath. 'I'll be wearing the lightest of dancing shoes this evening, I promise. I must say, I'm looking forward to it very much but . . .'

'You're concerned that we might be contravening instructions?'

'Something like that.'

'Then stop worrying. We're both off duty.'

'But you were told not to do any more interviews and to wrap up the case, you say. Why are you – excuse me for being so inquisitive, I can't help it! – pursuing the enquiry?'

Joe considered the question for a moment. 'I can't leave the Dame adrift. I can't bury her without knowing who put her in her coffin and why. It's always like that with murder cases. The moment I look into the dead face I'm claimed by it.'

She was silent, waiting for more, understanding that this was perhaps the first time he'd given words to the thought.

'Like the Ancient Mariner with his wretched albatross, an unavenged corpse hangs around my neck and I go about bothering people until I know the truth. I shan't be able to cut her loose until I know. It's not necessary for heads to roll or even for justice to be done (though that would be good) – just as long as someone cares enough to unravel the tangle and say to her memory: "I know what happened. I know who did this."'

Tilly nodded. 'Very well. I'll help you to bother some more people. Mathurin will be there with his fiancée. At least he'll start the evening with her. Her name's Joanna and I know her quite well. Good family. Filthy rich. We came out in the same year. Not a bosom pal but we're friendly enough to meet casually and share a table perhaps. Then I could lure her to the ladies' room and leave you to talk man to man with Monty. What about that?'

'Sounds perfect to me!'

'But how will you get him to talk about anything we want to hear? You can't exactly get out your notebook between numbers and ask his precise whereabouts on the night of his cousin's murder. He's not a fool, though people would like to believe he is.'

'Don't worry. I'll think of something. Shall I pick you up at eight? Explain to your father, will you? I wouldn't like him to have any misgivings.'

'I'll make sure he doesn't misconstrue the situation, Commander. Or should I call you Joe now we're walking out?'

'Everything all right, sir?' enquired Charlie, righting the disturbed furniture as he entered to take away the tea tray. 'Bit of a racket in here?'

'Perfectly all right. Some of these young women police can be remarkably clumsy. Have you noticed the size of their feet? Don't seem to know where to put them. No – leave those mugs, will you? Take the rest of the things away but leave the mugs. And here's a file to go back to its home. Oh, and, officially, I'm out for the rest of the day to anyone except Inspector Cottingham.'

He reached for the telephone.

'Larry? Look, I'm sorry to bother you again. Tell me – is the department still . . . um . . . expediting work on the Jagow-Joliffe case? No counter order as yet? Excellent! I'll be bringing you a little extra.'

It couldn't possibly be the same girl, Joe decided, as he sat next to Tilly in the taxi. A short, spangled red dress and matching shoes, a black velvet wrap clutched around her scented shoulders, huge eyes and red mouth and a general air of lively anticipation made him wonder. No, not the same girl. But, whoever she was, they made a handsome pair, he thought, not unaware that he always looked his best in evening dress. He nervously adjusted his white tie.

The Haymarket was bustling with motor cars and taxis and all seemed to be heading for the Kit-Cat. One hand lightly on his arm, Tilly watched with an assumed lack of interest but with bated breath as Joe presented his credentials at the door and was hurried through with a warm smile and a wink.

The assault on the senses was overwhelming. Joe stood for a moment, enjoying the loud laughter and bold glances, the whirl of colour against the austere black and white background of the men's evening dress, the musky hot blend of female sweat overlaid by expensive perfume. And all were moving joyfully to the creamy sounds of a jazz band. They were whisked through the milling guests by a maître d'hôtel who led them out on to the gallery where diners were gathering, drinking cocktails at small tables overlooking the huge dance floor below. The sounds of 'Whispering', always the band's opening number, spiralled up from the stage, lifting Joe's spirits further. With a rush of pleasure he slipped an arm around Tilly's slender waist and she raised an excited face to his.

'Oh, Joe! We're not too late. Isn't this wonderful!'

She reached up and kissed his cheek, murmuring, 'They're right next to us.'

'I never like to leave things to chance,' he murmured back, slipping a folded white banknote into the maître d'hôtel's discreet hand.

'*Un moment, monsieur.*' Their guide spoke to a couple seated at one of the best tables at the edge of the balcony with a good view of the nine-piece band and the dance floor. With many a gesture he was enquiring whether he might impose on them to share their table with two other guests . . . so crowded this evening, you understand . . .

Before a refusal could be risked, Tilly had rushed forward with an excited shriek. 'Joanna! Well, good heavens! Fancy seeing *you* here! How wonderful! But I hear you're engaged now?'

'Oh, Tilly! Do come and sit with us and I'll introduce you . . .'

She seemed all too delighted to have company at her table. Perhaps tête-à-têtes with Monty were beginning to lose their charm?

Joe had to fight back a laugh to hear the innocent little girl's voice identical to the one Tilly had used on the telephone. Joanna was a knockout. She was slim and dark-haired like Tilly with a short nose and full, pouting lips. Her green, heavy-lidded eyes moved slowly and speculatively over Joe. He felt uneasy with her appraisal and fought down an urge to run a finger around his collar. With a sudden smile, she released him from scrutiny and began to perform the introductions.

'My fiancé, Sir Montagu Mathurin . . .'

'My friend, Commander Sandilands . . .'

Too late, Tilly heard her faux pas. Surprisingly, it was Mathurin who unwittingly rescued the situation. 'Naval man, eh? Might have guessed! Put your head too close to the boom, hey, what?' he laughed, looking at Joe's scarred forehead.

'Sorry, Joe! I shouldn't have announced your rank just like that.' She smiled sweetly at the other two. 'You know what these war heroes are like! They do so hate to be reminded of it.'

Sir Montagu didn't appear to Joe to have the slightest knowledge of war heroes or the war. His dissolute good looks were marred by a fleshiness acquired during a life of moneyed indolence. His thick black hair was swept off his forehead and plastered to his scalp with brilliantine. The dark eyes were bright and, set in a less bloated face, would have been handsome.

'Just call me Joe.'

'Monty. How d'ye do? Have some champagne?'

Joe caught the eye of the maître d'hôtel, who was discreetly lingering in anticipation of his request. 'Have the waiter bring us another bottle. One of your best, Emil,' said Joe with largesse, in the knowledge that it would in some mysterious way be charged to the house.

They settled to an easy and meaningless conversation. After the right interval, Joe politely asked Joanna to dance and Mathurin held out his arm to Tilly, executing, Joe noticed, a surprisingly skilled and energetic black bottom. Joe was amused to see that Tilly was playing her role with mischief and was quite obviously setting out to charm Mathurin.

Two foxtrots and another bottle of champagne later, Tilly caught Joanna's eye and, giggling together, they began to make their way towards the powder room. Joe undid a button of his waistcoat and leaned confidentially towards Mathurin. His eyes flicked to the girls who were weaving unsteadily, arm-in-arm, across the floor.

'God! They're young!' he said with a sigh. 'Much too young for a pair of dissolute old hulks like us. Why do we get entangled?'

'Are you mad?' grinned Monty. 'No such thing as *too* young when it comes to fillies, I'd say.'

'Ah yes, of course. Your reputation in that quarter goes before you, old man!' He gave what he thought was a convincing leer. Mathurin would have been very surprised to learn that Joe's information had come that afternoon from a disgusted perusal of a file held on him at the Yard.

At that moment the girls stood aside, wondering whether to curtsy and deciding it would be inappropriate, as a tall and elegant woman passed them, returning from the dance floor. Joe's eyes fixed on her and trailed her as she swayed past their table in a cloud of Gardenia. He surreptitiously twisted his head, the better to appreciate her lean but sensuous figure in its low-backed, clinging gown of some golden stuff.

He turned back to Mathurin, face blank, having apparently forgotten what they'd been talking about. Then, recollecting himself, he picked up the thread. 'As I say . . . no rudeness intended, old boy. We all have our preferences . . . Man of the world, what? I must say I can't share your enthusiasms though. I've sailed the seven seas, I know seventy ports inside out. Could tell you stories that'd curl even your hair. And, in the end, you know, it's experience you look for. Experience and maturity.' He gave a world-weary sigh. 'No new chapter to be written for *me* in the *ars erotica* but at least I can try to avoid going back constantly to page one, chapter one. So irritating these little English girls!' He'd heard much the same nonsense trotted out by Edgar Troop, drinking companion and brothel-keeper in Simla. 'Just as well, I suppose *you'd* say? Wouldn't do for everyone to go sticking his rod into the same over-fished pool!'

'Look, is all this leading somewhere?' asked Mathurin, his porcine features gleaming with cunning. 'This is a nightclub, not a confessional.'

Joe grinned and leaned towards his target. 'No fooling you! I see I'd better come clean! As a matter of fact, I *do* have a confession to make. It was not by chance that we were shown to your table . . .'

Mathurin waved a negligent hand. 'Thought I saw a folded note join the others in the flunkey's over-stuffed back pocket,' he said casually.

'I wanted to meet you. I wanted to ask a favour. It's a rather delicate business . . .' He hesitated.

'You're talking to the soul of discretion,' said Monty,

encouragingly. 'A favour, eh? I often do people favours. You'd be surprised to hear . . . but then, as I say – clams are garrulous in comparison with me! But when I do people favours, I find they generally like to repay me.' His gaze wandered off towards the disappearing girls and, Joe was sure, lingered lasciviously on Tilly. 'Perhaps you would be in a position to repay me in kind?' He smirked, happy with his subtlety.

Joe's right fist clenched and, for a moment, he balanced the satisfaction of punching it into Mathurin's face and hearing the snap of breaking cartilage against the distress such a scene would cause to the Kit-Cat, to say nothing of Scotland Yard. He flexed his hand and reached for the champagne bottle. 'It would always be my intention to make an appropriate repayment,' he said.

Mathurin's interest was caught. 'Then go ahead, old man. Just ask. But if it's an introduction to the lovely Countess,' he indicated the woman in gold, who'd joined a group on the balcony, 'you can forget it!' He gave a deprecating bark of laughter. 'Some mountains even *I* can't climb!'

Joe did not laugh with him. 'No. I have in mind an introduction it *is* within your powers to make. I work, as you've probably guessed, at the Admiralty and I've seen there and admired from a distance a certain lady whom I am rather anxious to get alongside. A lively and popular red-headed lady who, I have it on good authority, is a cousin of yours . . .'

There was a stunned silence.

'Good Lord! Beatrice? You're saying you've been lusting after Beatrice? Oh, good God! How dreadful!'

'Something wrong with that? I had heard . . .'

'You can bet there's something wrong with that, you buffoon! Is this a joke? Where the hell have you been for the last two days?'

Joe replied stiffly. 'If it's any of your business – three floors down under the Admiralty building is where I've been, in the cryptography room. Just surfaced this evening in time for a shave and a shower,' he improvised.

Mathurin relaxed. 'Ah. Then you wouldn't have heard. Prepare yourself for a shock, man.' He said quietly, 'Bea got herself murdered. Saturday night. In the Ritz. She's dead.'

Joe contorted his face into a series of expressions passing from disbelief through shock to dismay, making matching sounds to accompany the display. Mathurin seemed to be enjoying having such a receptive audience and he launched into a sprightly account of the whole evening spent at his old relative's party.

'. . . so I think *I* must be the last person she spoke to before she left the room on the stroke of midnight to go to her death,' he said dramatically. 'She disturbed a burglar in her room is what everybody's saying because it wasn't long after that we found ourselves surrounded by swarms of bluebottles. She'd just disappeared when the band started up again. I didn't do any more dancing – after a quickstep, a foxtrot or two and a rumba, I blew a gasket and Joanna must have found someone else to dance with. Halfway through "Umcha, umcha, da, da, da" someone stopped the band and everyone was told to return to their seats. Officers of the Yard circulated amongst us taking notes. They even grilled the band! Joanna escaped all that – she'd nipped off home before it all got going. "Female problems" she calls it but she only seems to suffer when she's bored, I notice. Can't say I blame her. Family party . . . not the jolliest scene for a young girl. Finally someone came out with it. Then they let us go. Rum do! One minute she's sparkling away – I'd have guessed on her way to some assignation or other – few dances later, she's a gonner!'

Joe could only mutter incoherent condolences.

'Sorry, old chap – you've missed this boat! But, hang on a minute . . . if it's maturity and experience that stokes the old boiler, I'm sure my aunt Cécile . . . she's French, you know . . . would . . .'

He droned on and Joe prayed for Tilly's swift return.

Half an hour later, and just as the menus were being offered, Tilly was struck by a headache so debilitating it called for an instant return home. Sunk in the seclusion of the back seat of a taxi they looked at each other and laughed with relief.

'Sorry, sir! I couldn't bear to sit and watch Monty socking back the oysters.'

'Damn it! No ear-nibbling smoochy last dance for me!' grumbled Joe.

'And we never did manage to hear the band play us out with "Three O'Clock In The Morning"! Do you really mind?'

'No. Their licence runs out at two. I'd have had to arrest the management. Glad to have missed it,' said Joe. 'Sing it for you if you like?'

Joe recounted his talk with Mathurin, ending with, '. . . so if you hear on your social grapevine that a certain police commander is a degenerate who's run off to Antibes with Mathurin's frisky old aunt, you are to squash the rumour at once!'

'If I can do that without compromising my own reputation, I certainly will, sir. But it looks as though Monty's in the clear. I got Joanna to tell me all about that evening – no difficulty – she was spilling over with enthusiasm for the intrigue, and all she had to say confirms Mathurin's story. Just one little extra detail I found quite intriguing.'

'Go on, Westhorpe.'

'Well, do you remember Sergeant Armitage was convinced that the Dame signalled to someone across the room before she left to go upstairs?'

'Yes, I do.'

'Joanna knows who it was!'

Chapter Fifteen

Their taxi was turning into Park Lane and Joe was suddenly aware that time and opportunity were slipping away from him, the case already beyond his control. He leaned forward. 'Slow down, cabby, will you?'

It wasn't the first time the driver had received the command. He grinned and obligingly began to hug the kerb, moving along at ten miles an hour.

'Good idea, sir. We're nearly home. You could come in if you like but I wouldn't advise it. My father always waits up. He's got a little list of men he perhaps won't set the dogs on just yet and you've been added to it. In fact you've moved up to a jolly high position. He tells me he "likes the cut of your jib" or something. Thought I'd better warn you.'

'I'm on quite a few lists,' said Joe lightly. 'I've got very slick at smooth take-offs down driveways. I particularly favour the laurel-lined ones.'

Tilly reached for his hand and squeezed it. 'Goodness, you're easy company, Joe,' she said softly.

'It was Joanna,' she went on hurriedly.

'Joanna? What was Joanna?' Joe's senses were still reeling from the sudden show of warmth and – could he have been mistaken? – affection.

'The recipient of the Dame's signal was Joanna herself.'

'Eh? But why on earth . . .?'

'My friend may *look* as though she's sculpted out of the same stuff as a sugar mouse but don't be deceived!'

'I expect hobnobbing with Monty would open a girl's eyes to the world?'

'Well, Joanna's not averse to a little hobnobbing from time to time but not with Monty.'

'What do you mean?'

'She told me she's been keeping him dangling. No hanky-panky before marriage. She's quite cold, you know, tough and rather businesslike. Monty may not look much of a catch to you but, believe me, he's not despised in the matrimonial stakes. He's got a title and expectations of something even grander when his grandfather dies. And the old boy is rumoured to be on the rocks and breaking up fast. Monty's got connections on the Joliffe side as well and there's money there.'

'He'll be needing it! The cad's got expensive and dangerous tastes.'

'Yes. I got a feeling that all may not be quite as it seems with the Mathurin finances . . . I was offered a close look at her engagement ring. It was big but old-fashioned. I'd say he'd pinched it from his granny not offered Joanna her choice of the sparklers on display at Asprey's.'

Joe wondered for a moment how he was going to manage without Westhorpe's female insights and her unique access to the powder rooms of London.

'But Joanna's tale backs up Audrey's version of Dame Bea's proclivities, sir. She was prepared to have quite a laugh about it. She wouldn't have shared the confidence with most girls but she knows what I do and assumes I'm not about to have a fit of the vapours at the revelation. During the party Beatrice joined them and made herself very agreeable to Joanna. She must have seen something in the girl that Joanna is not admitting (to me at any rate) is there because she made a louche suggestion. She invited Joanna to come up to her room. Right there in front of Monty! Joanna can't be certain that he didn't overhear but he made no comment.'

'So the Dame flung her a last come-on, vampish look from the door and disappeared. No wonder Armitage missed it. He was scanning the blokes for a reaction! Explains why she left her door unlocked if not open, perhaps even called an excited, "Do come in!" to her killer,' said Joe with a shudder.

'But who came through the door? Cousin Monty seeing red and prepared to wield a poker to avenge his fiancée's honour? I can't see it, sir. Even if he could have got away unseen from the party.'

'Not for honour. I don't believe Monty would wield so much as a fish-knife for honour. Oh, Lord! We're here! All lights on, I see. A moment, cabby . . . Look, Tilly, no notes, remember! This was an entirely unofficial evening. But most enjoyable . . .'

He would have said more but she turned to him and put a finger firmly over his lips. 'I had a wonderful time! Goodnight, Joe.' A swift kiss on his left cheek and she was gone.

He sat on, wrapped in disturbing thoughts and wishing he hadn't drunk so much champagne.

'Where to now, sir?

The cabby's tactful question stirred him to say decisively, 'Scotland Yard. The Derby Street entrance.'

'Young lady nicked your watch in that last clinch, did she, sir?'

Joe laughed. 'No. Not my watch.' As though to double-check, he ostentatiously consulted his wristwatch. Well after eleven. What the hell did he think he could achieve at this late hour, boiling his brains over a stillborn case? He thought there might be waiting on his desk a delivery of notes from Cottingham who'd been sent off with a day's steady police work under his belt before the axe had fallen. Joe was feeling too agitated to go straight home and he didn't have the effrontery to face Maisie's sharp tongue and knowing comments in his evening dress with lipstick on his left cheek and reeking of champagne and cigars. An hour's clandestine work would steady his jumping thoughts. Scotland Yard never slept. Lights were on from top to bottom of the building when he left the taxi. The uniformed man at the entrance saluted him and waved him through. As he passed the reception desk on his way to the stairs, he was hailed urgently by the duty sergeant.

'Sir! Commander Sandilands! This is a piece of luck! We've been trying to get hold of you. Something's come up. All too literally, sir! There's a couple of river police here won't go away until they've seen you.'

Joe approached the desk in puzzlement and the sergeant opened the office door behind him calling, 'Alf! George! Got him! He's all yours.'

Alf and George slammed down mugs of cocoa, bustled out of the office and stood, giving him a slow police stare. They were wearing their river slickers and naval-style peaked caps and very purposeful they looked. The leader glanced uncertainly from Joe back to the duty officer, who swallowed a grin and said, 'Yes. This is who you've been waiting to interview. Commander Sandilands.'

'Off duty,' Joe muttered, aware that he looked as though he'd just strolled off-stage from his bit-part in a society farce at the Lyric. 'Sandilands it is. Tell me what I can do for you.'

'What you can do for us is identify a corpse, sir. It's down at the sub-station by Waterloo Bridge. It's a fresh one – only been in the water an hour at the most. A suicide.'

'I'd like to help, of course,' said Joe, stifling his irritation. 'But suicides are not my department. Can't you just go through your usual channels?'

The last thing he wanted was to be lured away to that stinking hole down by the bridge. The river police, the only arm of the service the people of London had ever really taken to their hearts, were a force Joe could admire too but he wanted nothing to do with them this evening. As well as coming down hard on theft, piracy and smuggling in the docks they managed also to patrol the sinister reaches of the Thames which were favoured as the last resting place of unfortunates driven to take their own lives. Sometimes the three-man crews were so quickly on the spot in their swift river launches that bodies were netted and fished out before they'd breathed their last, and in that cold, stone, carbolic-scented little room by the arches they would squeeze and pummel the victim laid out on the canvas truckle bed until, willing or not, the dank river water spewed out of the lungs to be replaced with the breath of life.

'Regular channels no use, sir. It's you we have to see. Just to take a look at the body before it goes off to the morgue. Won't take you a minute and it will save us hours.'

'Why me?' Joe shivered. The evening's euphoria had evaporated, leaving him full of cold foreboding.

'No identification to be found, sir. No documents, no labels on clothing, nothing at all. Except for one item in her pocket.'

'*Her* pocket?'

'Deceased is a young female, sir.'

He fumbled under his cape and held up a small white object.

'We were lucky we got there before the printer's ink ran. You can just make it out.' He read from the card: '"Commander Joseph Sandilands, New Scotland Yard, London. Whitehall 1212."

'It's your calling card, sir.'

Chapter Sixteen

For a moment, Joe's face and limbs froze. When finally he found his voice it rapped out with military precision: 'Waterloo Bridge. We'll never get a taxi at this time of night. Half a mile from here? We can run it in five minutes.'

He was sprinting out of the door before the river police had pulled themselves together. They pounded after him, boots thumping, capes flying.

As the door swung to behind them, the duty sergeant caught the eye of a passing constable who'd loitered to witness the strange scene. ''Struth! That got him moving! D'you see his face when the penny dropped? Wonder how many girls the old fart's given his card to lately?'

'Sounds like a case of unrequited affection to me,' commented the bobby sentimentally. 'Probably got some poor girl up the stick.'

Joe pounded along the Embankment, evening shoes giving him a perilous grip on the wet pavings. He looked ahead through the half-grown trees lining the river to the shimmering line of pale yellow lamps studding the bridge along its great length. Cleopatra's Needle. More than halfway there. He tore off his tie and cracked open his collar. He pushed on, glad to hear his escort panting and cursing close behind.

Three young females. He'd given his card to three and that only yesterday. With dread he listed them. 'Audrey,

Melisande . . . And her baby . . .' His heart gave a lurch which threatened to cut off his breathing as he added, 'Little Dorcas.'

He could have asked the sergeant one simple question which would have reduced the choice to one: blonde, auburn or black hair? He knew very well why he'd not asked. One answer from the list would have been more than he could bear and he could not risk showing emotion right there at the reception desk.

It must be Dorcas, he decided. Driven to distraction by her grandmother's cruelty she'd run away to London, swelling the numbers of waifs and strays who fetched up on the cold streets of the capital in their thousands. He'd been kind to her. Armitage had paid her flattering attention. Perhaps she'd been trying to contact one of them? He ran on. Without a word spoken, they all stopped and, hands on knees, gasping for breath, they tried to gain a measure of control before they entered the dismal little rescue room. The older of the two officers flung him a wounded look. 'It's all right, sir. She's not going anywhere, whoever she is. Five minutes is neither here nor there for the deceased.'

'It's a bloody eternity for me,' said Joe with passion.

A tug hooted mournfully, echoing his words. A sickening stench of decay belched from the ooze below. It was low tide and several yards of stinking mud fringed the sinister black slide of the river.

'Let's get on with it, shall we?'

They exchanged looks, nodded and went inside.

A third river officer was sitting over his tea, a brimming ashtray on the floor at his feet, filling in the crossword on the back of the *Evening Standard*. He shot to attention as they entered. In the centre of the room on a still-dripping truckle bed lay a white-shrouded figure. The cocktail of carbolic and Wimsol bleach was almost a relief after the river smells. As Joe advanced to lift the sheet he started in horror to hear a voice behind him intoning:

'One more unfortunate,
Weary of breath,
Rashly importunate,
Gone to her death!
Take her up tenderly,
Lift her with care,
Fashioned so slenderly,
Young and so fair!'

Joe turned and addressed the sergeant angrily. 'Who or what in hell is that?'

The sergeant's voice was a placatory whisper. 'Witness, sir. He was on the bridge when she jumped.'

A bear-like figure shambled forward into the light shed by the solitary electric bulb and presented himself.

'He's a down-and-out, sir. Harmless. We know him well. Came forward with information and we asked him to stay in case a statement was required. Name of Arthur.'

Joe turned to the man. 'Arthur? Thank you for staying. And thank you for your sentiments. Now, gentlemen, shall we?'

The constable moved reverently to turn the sheet back. Joe stared.

'Young female,' the elderly sergeant had said. And, in death, wiped clean of coquettish artifice, her doll's face framed by a mop of curling blonde hair, Audrey had shed the years along with her life.

'Known to you, sir?' the sergeant enquired gently.

'Yes. Audrey Blount. Miss Audrey Blount. I can give you her address. Two addresses in fact. She has a sister in Wimbledon, I understand. I interviewed her yesterday . . . was it yesterday? . . . Sunday, anyway. It was Sunday. You can have her taken to the morgue now. I'll arrange for a police autopsy. Not usual, I know, but there are special circumstances. I'll see that her next of kin are informed. Look, can you be certain it was suicide?'

'Better have a word with old Arthur, sir. He's very clear on what took place, you'll find.'

'I'd like to do that.' He cast an eye around the crowded and unpleasant room. 'But not here. I could do with some fresh air. How about you, Arthur? Shall we go up on to the bridge and you can tell me all about it?'

'Here, take this spare cape, sir,' said the sergeant. 'Can get a bit nippy up there and there's a mist rising.'

Joe approached the body and quietly spoke over it a further verse of Thomas Hood's lugubrious poem. He'd always hated it but here, in these ghastly surroundings, it flooded back into his mind with awful appositeness.

> *'Touch her not scornfully,*
> *Think of her mournfully,*
> *Gently and humanly,*
> *Not of the stains of her . . .'*

His voice faltered for a moment and the deep baritone behind him finished for him:

> *'All that remains of her*
> *Now is pure womanly.'*

Joe dashed a hand at his eyes. The sergeant passed him a crisp handkerchief. 'Here. It's the carbolic, sir. Fumes can get to you if you're not used to it.'

'If we go along to the very centre, I think you'll find the air is fresher there . . . I'm sorry – I don't know your rank?' said Arthur in a tone which would have sounded at home in a London club.

'Commander Sandilands. CID.'

'Indeed? How do you do? My name is Arthur as you have heard. Sometimes I'm known, in a jesting way, as King Arthur and this –' he waved expansively at the great length of the bridge – 'is my kingdom.'

'I had understood that gentlemen of the road were discouraged from taking up residence on His Other Majesty's bridges,' said Joe, responding in kind to the thespian flavour of his companion's language.

'Indeed. But I am happy to say I am tolerated here. This beautiful bridge – and being a man who appreciates the spare, the classically correct, the understated, I concur with Canova that it is the loveliest in London – is much frequented by tourists. Tourists have money to spend and even to give away and I find them very generous, particularly our American cousins. Very large-hearted. But they despise – and are embarrassed to find themselves despising – beggars. So, I entertain them to earn a copper or two. I tell them the history of the bridge; I identify the buildings to north and south from the dome of St Paul's to the tower of Big Ben and I accompany my perorations with appropriate verses.'

'I had marked your facility for poetic effusions,' said Joe. 'Look, can we stop all this nonsense, cut the cackle and get down to business?'

Arthur smiled. 'You may be able to converse in the blunt transatlantic mode of recent fashion but I'm not sure I can change my style for a police interview. Though I will try.'

'What were you in a previous existence? A schoolmaster? A butler?'

A flash of some emotion lit the old man's eyes as he replied swiftly, 'I employed both in my time. No matter.'

He quickened his pace and Joe plodded on, glad of the protection of the police cape as a chill breeze sprang up on nearing the middle. Arthur pointed to the central recess jutting out from the level bed of the nine-arched bridge, on the north-east side facing St Paul's. Behind them, to the left, the lights of the Savoy Hotel shone out their seductive promise of warmth and comfort, a shimmering mirage when, yards away, under Joe's feet, separated from them by a low balustrade, coiled the black river that had taken Audrey's life. Joe hated crossing rivers. They were alive. They had a character, snake-like and sinister, which repelled him. He gripped the granite handrail tightly as they looked over. It eased his vertigo but could not dispel it. As they stood looking down with fascination Big Ben boomed out the twelve strokes of midnight.

'That's where she was standing.'

'And where were you?'

'There in the next recess. I was bedding down for the night.' Arthur produced two penny coins from the depths of his hairy overcoat and held them in front of Joe's face. 'They can't move you on if you've got visible means of support and twopence will pay for a night's lodging. I always keep twopence handy.'

'Very well. Let's go to your recess then you can tell me what happened. Try to keep it short and clear, will you, Arthur? It's been a long night already and it's only just midnight.'

'So I observe, Commander. Time first. You'll need to establish the time,' he began briskly. 'Accuracy guaranteed by Big Ben over there. The lady came along this side of the bridge about two minutes before a quarter to nine sounded. I approached her and she was kind enough to give me a sixpence from her bag. Yes, she had a bag. It was not found with her body. They rarely are. They get washed away and picked up by mudlarks who do not turn them in. Pretty girl, in a good humour, I'd have said. I thought she might have been on her way to an assignation. She had that look of suppressed excitement about her.'

'She didn't strike you as a potential suicide?'

'No. I would have taken strenuous steps to divert her from her intent, had I suspected that.'

Joe thought an intervention by Arthur might just well have tipped the balance. 'And then?'

'She stopped in the central bay and loitered. She looked at the river. She looked up and down the bridge. I assumed she was waiting for someone. As she stood there the nine strokes of the three-quarter hour sounded.'

'Tell me what the conditions were? Light? Visibility? Were there people about?'

'The gloomiest moment of the day. Exactly halfway

between sunset at eight thirty and lighting-up time half an hour later. There was hardly anyone about. It's a very still time. A couple passed. They crossed to the other side when they saw me. A few taxis went by. The eight forty-five omnibus clanged past on time. I began to bed down so I couldn't see her any longer but I could hear.

'A minute or two after she arrived, she greeted someone and held a brief conversation. A few minutes later, before the hour struck at any rate, I heard a shriek though at the time I thought it was a ship's hooter and then there was a splash. I got up and looked about me and the bay was empty. The lights were not yet switched on and I could see only a few yards in the poor light. I assumed that she'd met her intended and gone onwards to the Embankment.

'Just after half past nine o'clock I was disturbed by the river police and I volunteered to go with them to offer my observations. I expect they are also seeking the testimony of the last person to speak to her. The one she appeared to recognize. He passed the time of day with me before he approached her.'

'Good Lord!' said Joe. 'Do you know what you're saying?'

'I do. I hope I express myself with clarity.'

'Who was this man? Can you give me a description?'

'Nothing easier, Commander!' The old eyes twinkled with mischief. 'It was a policeman.'

Chapter Seventeen

Joe fought down his surprise and irritation. He thought he would get the best out of Arthur if he showed a little patience and allowed the man to enjoy his moment in the limelight.

'A policeman you say you know by sight?'

'Of course. It was the beat bobby. Charming young chap. Always stops for a word. He's Constable Horace Smedley and he bears the number 2382 on his collar.'

'And you gave this information to the river police?'

'Yes. Observe!' He pointed to the southern end of the bridge. 'They are acting on it at last. Do you see the red flashing light? They are signalling to Constable Smedley that there is an emergency. As soon as he sees it he will enter the mysterious confines of the blue box atop of which it glows and pick up the telephone therein. He is being summoned to return at once to the sub-station.'

Joe was annoyed to have police procedure explained to him by a down-and-out but he pressed on, keeping his tone polite. 'Where may we find you if we need to refer to you again for a testimony, Arthur? Are you always to be found here?'

'In the daytime hours, yes. At night, if trade has been good, I make my way to a Rowton House. It costs one and sixpence a night or six and sixpence for a week for decent, if plain, accommodation and the opportunity to take a bath.'

Joe was familiar with the excellent hostels for the out-of-pocket dotted around London. 'And which one do you favour?' he asked, thinking he could guess the answer.

'The Bond Street branch, of course,' said Arthur with a smile.

'Well, here's a retainer,' said Joe, fishing two ten shilling notes out of his inner pocket. 'I would be most obliged if you would make yourself available to the force by residing in Bond Street for the next fortnight.'

'It will be my pleasure, Commander,' said Arthur.

Constable Smedley, Officer 2382, presented himself, breathless, at the sub-station minutes after Joe got back there himself. Intrigued and articulate, he was eager to answer Joe's questions, and, Joe guessed, to enliven what had been a dull beat.

'So you passed the time of day with Arthur and moved on down the bridge? Tell me about the lady you observed in the central bay.'

Smedley gave a succinct police-approved, training-manual description of Audrey.

'Tell me why you approached her.'

'Always do, sir. Lonely lady. She was looking a bit lost. Always the danger of jumpers from this bridge, sir. It's a favourite. Whichever side they pick, they go down looking at the best view in the city. And the balustrade's low. Suicides fell off – sorry! no pun intended, sir – while it was being repaired but they're back now the scaffolding's been removed. I can always spot 'em!'

'And you took this lady for a potential suicide, did you?'

The constable considered this. 'Well, obviously I got it wrong . . . but no . . . she can't have struck me as such because I let her be and passed on. She greeted me with a smile and some words . . . "Oh, there you are" or something like that as though she was expecting to see someone she knew. Then, realizing her mistake, she fumbled about a bit in her pocket and took out a calling card and looked

189

at it. Checking the details. Even looked at her watch. A bit of pantomime, I thought. Establishing her bona fides on the bridge. For a suicide she was a damn good actress, sir.'

'Oh, yes, that's exactly what she was. And it was in her pocket, not her bag?'

'Yes, sir. Sort of, at the ready. She did have a bag over her arm.'

'No bag has yet been found.'

'Wouldn't expect it. They normally throw their bags over first and then jump.'

'Good Lord! But, tell me, who else did you see on the bridge as you proceeded on your beat?'

'No one, sir. I was aware of figures passing along on the other side but nothing out of the ordinary. The eight forty-five omnibus went by. It doesn't stop on the bridge, sir. It was just about dark and a mist coming up. No lighting for another few minutes. If you didn't want to be observed throwing yourself off, it was the best time to choose.'

He looked at Joe thoughtfully for a moment, wondering whether to speak out. This Commander, or whatever he was, might look like a music hall turn but he was quiet-spoken, interested and asked the right questions. Smedley chanced it. 'And a good time to choose if you wanted to *help* someone off, sir.'

Minutes later Joe was gratefully climbing aboard a tram he'd managed to flag down. It was clanking its way back along the Embankment, returning to the depot, and Joe seemed to be the only passenger. The lonely conductor launched into a cheerful conversation. 'I won't tell if you won't, Constable,' he said, using Armitage's tap to the side of the nose to indicate conspiracy.

Joe thought he understood the jibe. He grinned and looked down at his borrowed slicker and the spare peaked cap he'd been kindly handed by the sergeant with the promise that he'd 'be needing it in five minutes'.

''Sawright, mate,' he said. 'Don't 'ave ter plod this next bit. Special dooties. Give us a ticket to the Yard, will you? And don't spare the 'orses!'

In a spirit of mischief, Joe waited until the stroke of one before ringing Sir Nevil.

'Sandilands here. Got a little problem, sir.'

'Sandilands? Joe? What the hell! You're supposed to be off duty!' The voice was irritated but not sleepy.

'I *am* off duty. I've spent the evening at the Kit-Cat and now I'm sitting here in my dinner jacket, full to the gunwales with Pol Roger '21. You'd say:

> *"Gilbert the filbert, the nut with a K,*
> *The Pride of Piccadilly, the blasé roué,"*

if you could see me.'

'You're tipsy! You're ringing me at this unearthly hour to tell me you're tipsy? *Where* are you?'

'At the Yard. In my office. Just finishing a report for you.'

'What are you doing at the Yard? You were told –'

'I came to pick up my motor car. I shall need it tomorrow when I set off for Surrey as per orders. Someone was watching out for me and when I arrived I was shanghaied by the river police who escorted me to their awful lair by Waterloo Bridge to identify a drowned person. It turned out to be Audrey Blount.'

There was a silence at the other end while Sir Nevil rummaged through this mixed bag of information.

'Audrey was –' Joe began helpfully.

'I know who Audrey was. I'm familiar with the file. Get a grip if you can and tell me what happened.'

Joe filled in the details, encouraged by an occasional 'And then?' or 'Tut, tut.'

As he finished, Sir Nevil said heavily, 'Sad story. But, you know, Father Thames accounts for more murderers each year than the public hangman.'

191

'Murderers, sir?'

'Oh yes. It's remorse and fear that push them over the edge. Now . . . let me tell you how this sorry business will be construed by the powers-that-be over the road and over our heads . . . It'll go something like this: Audrey quarrelled with her employer, pursued her to London, as she admitted to you, with the object of killing her and did, indeed, in a fit of rage, achieve her aim. She faked up signs of a robbery and, still harbouring a grievance against her employer, she defiled the corpse in a somewhat unimaginative manner. Very tasteless and amateur attempt! In character, I would have thought. She was seen in the vicinity by a police witness no less. Disguised as a maid, she could have secreted her discarded bloodstained overall in the dirty linen on the trolley and trundled her way, unregarded, out of the hotel.'

He sighed and with affected tetchiness added: 'Do you expect me to do *all* your work for you?'

Caught up in the flow of his reasoning, he rattled on: 'Shortly after, pursued by CID and fearing arrest or simply the victim of conscience, she flees to London and does what hundreds of guilty people have done before her. Leaps off a bridge. Neat, Joe. Neat. This closes the case with a bang. A distressing domestic incident but no more than that. No need now to go on searching the rooftops of London for homicidal burglars. Hotel guests all over the capital may sleep easy in their beds. All round good solution, I'm sure you'll agree. Have your notes sent to my office, will you? . . . Oh, and, Joe, do take care if you're driving your car back across London in your state. You sound a bit wobbly to me and some of those traffic police are sharp lads . . . 1921, eh? Excellent year! Excellent! Goodnight, Joe.'

The connection was cut before Joe could protest or question.

Joe was thoughtful. Earlier in the day, Sir Nevil had been

accepting but disapproving of the pressure put on them to close the case. Now Joe would have said he was eager to connive in the official clampdown. Something was going on that he was not being told about. He sighed. What to do? Give in and go along with the theories being cooked up?

Beatrice and Audrey. He had looked into two dead faces in the space of two days. He felt the weight of two albatrosses around his neck and sighed.

He was on his own. He could call on help from no one. Tilly and Bill had been discharged from the case and were heaven knows where by now. Cottingham would have to be informed by note that he was to do no further work. Cottingham. Perhaps not quite on his own, yet. There was an envelope lying on his desk addressed to him in Ralph's hand.

Inside was a sheet dated and headed 'Informal (underlined) notes for the attentn. of Comm. Sandilands.' Below this were further confirmatory notes of times and locations of various guests around the hotel on the night of the murder. A follow-up interview with the lift operator revealed nothing new. The inspector had even swabbed the interior of the lift but failed to find bloodstains. The maids' trolleys were equally clear of blood traces – Sir Nevil would not be pleased! – and the hotel laundry turned up nothing but the usual assortment of human effluvia. 'Nose bleed in Room 318 duly verified,' Cottingham had added carefully.

Joe turned at last to Donovan's alibi. Just as he had told them, the boot-boy had conveniently spent the vital hour with him in his office. Cottingham had put a note in the margin: 'Give me ten minutes and an extra fiver on expenses and I could break this. Something tells me the rogue Donovan would have a spare alibi up his sleeve, however. Shall I pursue it?'

He went on: 'Work pattern. Employment not as implied by D. Very much a part-time job. Manager reveals his real work is with the Marconi Company. On leaving navy, he joined this wireless firm. Many did when guns fell silent. The manager of the Marconi Co. confirms that D. works for them in their electronics research department. Does the expression "thermionic valve" mean anything to you, sir? They say this is a full-time 9–5 job but the subject insists on taking time off at irregular intervals. He has a dependent relative who needs his support. (Ho! Ho!) The firm goes along with this because he's apparently invaluable. A whizz with the wires or air waves or whatever they use nowadays. If he's moonlighting at the Ritz he's a busy boy! But he probably still puts in fewer hours than us, wouldn't you say?'

Joe looked wearily at his watch. Half past one. He could have been doing a smoochy tango with Tilly. Joe suppressed the thought and read on.

On a separate sheet were notes hastily handwritten in pencil. The heading this time was 'At the Admiralty'. The information had, Cottingham declared, come from a fellow Old Harrovian who owed him a favour. 'Nothing questionable about this,' he had put in the margin and, keel-hauling his maritime metaphors, 'all guaranteed above-board and Bristol fashion!'

'All the info my friend was prepared to pass on is in the public domain. It's just that the public wouldn't have a clue where to look. He wished us luck with the case – Dame B. had many admirers in the Senior Service where they appreciate a spirited lady. Pleased to reveal all he could about D. Not popular! Seems to have jumped ship before he was made to walk the plank.' Joe groaned and vowed to do something very naval to Cottingham if he didn't get a move on.

'Rose to the rank of Chief Petty Officer – that would be "staff sergeant" in our terms, I think. Talented wireless operator and very intelligent.' It was Ralph's next piece of naval gossip that caught Joe's flagging attention.

Donovan had been posted to Room 40 at the Admiralty. In the war, the Royal Navy Code-Breaking Unit had employed a large number of highly qualified civilian men

and women alongside naval personnel. Wireless special-
ists, cryptographers and linguists. It was thanks to their
skills that Admiral Jellicoe's Grand Fleet had had the edge
on the German navy, presenting itself, unaccountably
battle-ready, hours before the High Seas Fleet had left port
on more than one occasion. If Donovan had worked for
Naval Intelligence he was not a man to be underestimated.
Joe was forming a further hypothesis based on this evidence and wondered if it had occurred to Ralph.

No longer 'Room 40', the Government Code and Cypher
School, as it now was, had moved with its director
Admiral Hugh Sinclair down to Broadway nearer Whitehall. Joe was aware that GC&CS used the resources of the
Metropolitan Police intercept station run by Harold Ken-
worthy, an employee of Marconi . . . Set up by the Direct-
orate of Intelligence, the station operated from the attic of
Scotland Yard. What had Nevil said? '. . . the people over
our heads . . .' Joe had assumed that he meant superior in
authority but perhaps the reference had been a more literal
one?

Joe looked up nervously at the ceiling. Were they up
there now? And who were they listening in to? The Met
intercept unit, he knew, was currently monitoring the proposed miners' strike. They had uncovered devastating
evidence of Soviet involvement and mischief-making. Two
million pounds of funds were being provided by the Bolsheviks to foment industrial action and support the miners
for the duration of the strike.

Joe's head was beginning to spin. What was the thread
that led from a wartime Room 40 to the interceptors in the
attic and what did that have to do with a Wren bludgeoned to death? On the next sheet the writing became
ever less restrained, possibly the effect of the contents of
the glass whose dark brown ring decorated the page. Joe
didn't need to sniff to detect naval rum.

Three sheets in the wind – Oh Lord! The condition was
catching! – Cottingham had added excitedly: 'Wonder if
you're aware of where the Dame spent the war years *before*

195

she joined the Wrens?' In block capitals he had scrawled, 'ROOM 40. My contact tells me the Dame was valued for her quick wits and perfect knowledge of German – an ideal combination for cracking codes and interpreting signals. No wonder she was much admired! She was thought to be intime with the boss – "C" no less – Rear Admiral Hugh "Quex" Sinclair, Head of NI, SIS, GC&CS and all the rest of the alphabet soup.'

Joe remembered that the stylish and able Admiral's nickname was 'Quex' from the title of a West End play, *The Gay Lord Quex, the wickedest man in London*. He had a reputation for high living and had reputedly moved the headquarters of Naval Intelligence to the Strand so as to be near his favourite restaurant, the Savoy Grill.

'It's entirely possible that the Dame met Donovan here in Room 40!' Cottingham had added. 'Dame B. was highly regarded in naval circles for the undaunted way in which she set about reconstituting a women's service although it was officially disbanded in 1918. She has collected about her, with the navy's knowledge and approval – though without financial support or official recognition – a corps of girls whose aim is to carry on the traditions of the service. A sort of mob of Vestal Virgins, if you like, who tend the flame until such time as it shall be needed. They're top drawer, apparently. Daughters of very high-placed officers, that sort of thing. Some of the chaps sympathize with Bea's view that the navy has not fought its last engagement and next time they must be fully prepared. Not sure who they see as the enemy but the most likely candidate must surely be the Russians?

'They considered her a pretty stylish lady. Very much ones for nicknames, sailors! They've called this embryonic service of busy young girls "the Hive" of which the Dame was – naturally – Queen Bea.'

It occurred to Joe that they had been so taken up with the forensic aspects of the case, he'd not done what he usually did early in an enquiry. He'd not drawn up a detailed portrait of the murder victim. He remembered that the Dame's diary revealed a dinner date with an admiral. He'd taken time to send out a signal cancelling on her behalf and breaking the news of her death, but perhaps the engagement itself had been significant? With frustration he acknowledged that he would never discover its significance now an embargo had been placed on his interviewing.

Feeling that the time had come to get to know Beatrice more intimately he picked up his briefcase, put away Cottingham's notes and checked the contents of a small envelope. He took out the door keys Tilly had found in the Dame's bag.

'Time to pay you a dawn call, Queen Bea,' he said.

Chapter Eighteen

'Not early risers.'

Tilly had dismissed the inhabitants of bohemian Blooms-bury with a disapproving sniff. Joe hoped she'd got it right. He didn't want to be observed stealing into the Dame's flat at five in the morning. Too embarrassing if someone noticed him and alerted the beat bobby. He'd taken the precaution of putting on protective colouring in the form of a shabby brown corduroy suit, much scorned by his sister, a shirt, tie-less and open at the neck, and a wide-brimmed black felt hat which he tugged down over one eye. He looked at himself critically in the mirror and grinned. He thought he looked rather dashing. And, with his dark features etched by lack of sleep, he'd probably pass a dozen similar on their way back from a night spent on the tiles or behind some blue door or other.

He left his car in Russell Square Gardens behind the British Museum and made his way unhurriedly past the building sites into Montague Street and turned into Fitzroy Gardens. He was not a tourist, he reminded himself; he was not here to enjoy the greenery in the central garden or the Portland stone Georgian architecture. He made his way straight to a house at one end of the graceful crescent, noting the side access and wondering if he would choose the right one of the two keys to gain entrance through the imposing front door. A passing milk float clanked by, jugs rattling, and the milkman greeted him cheerfully as he ran up the four front steps.

Tilly had mentioned the Dame's 'flat' but Joe noticed

there was only one doorbell. The door opened smoothly, answering to the larger of the two keys, and he walked into a wide, uncluttered hallway. He paused uncertainly, his cover story ready against a challenging occupant. No one hurried forward indignantly to ask him what the hell he thought he was doing there. Again, there were no signs of multiple occupancy. No doorways were boarded up, there were no handwritten signs with arrows pointing to the upper floors, no table spilling over with post to be collected by other inhabitants. Joe concluded that the Dame must own the whole of the house. He stood and listened. The house had the dead sound of a completely empty space.

Boldly, he called out, 'Beatrice! Are you there?'

Receiving no response, he opened the door to the drawing room.

What had he expected? Emerald green walls, disordered divans piled high with purple cushions, post-Impressionist daubs, an attempt to recreate the Bakst decor for Scheherazade? Yes, he silently admitted that he had expected something of the sort. He had thought that the Dame, having chosen to live in Bloomsbury, would be playing up to the artistic, insouciant style its inhabitants were renowned for. The room surprised him. Modern but restrained, it was obviously decorated by an amateur with a strong personal style.

The walls were a pale string-colour, the wood floor covered in Persian rugs in browns and amber, the large sofa was of black leather. He ran his hands covetously over a piece that might once have been called a chaise longue but this was a sleek, steel-framed extended chair of German design. There was a good supply of small tables, set beside matching chairs of a blond wood inlaid with a pleasing pattern. Joe was interested enough to turn one over to see the manufacturer's name. Austrian, but available from Heal's in the nearby Tottenham Court Road. Over the fireplace hung a large and lovely seascape, the other walls carried pictures in a medley of styles: a French landscape, a study of horses that might – but surely couldn't? – have been by Stubbs, two golden watercolours of an Eastern scene by Chinery and a small Augustus John portrait. They had nothing in common except the owner's taste, he decided, and again wished that he had met Beatrice in the living flesh. Unusually, there were no family portraits or photographs, nothing of a personal nature.

He counted the seating places and reckoned that the Dame could entertain eight or ten people if she wished. And entertain in some style. She could have invited the First Sea Lord, his lady wife and his lady wife's maiden aunt for cocktails and they would have been charmed. All was correct and elegant, apart from one object he'd spotted on the mantelpiece – a modern bronze of Europa riding half naked and garlanded on the back of her bull. But it was a work of art and only erotic if you had eyes to see, he thought, and were nosy enough to pick it up and view it from an unusual angle. He paused to handle respectfully a chrome and white table lighter and its matching cigarette box. Removing the lid he sniffed the contents. Turkish at one end and Virginian at the other. Nothing more sinister was going to be on offer in this proper setting.

Shrugging off his fascination for the decorative contents of the room, Joe left to survey the rest of the house. He would return to carry out the correct procedure for checking the contents minutely when he'd got his bearings. The rest of the ground floor was less interesting. The dining room was furnished but looked as though it had never been used, the kitchen and pantry were soulless and bare of contents. A refrigerator, he noticed, held bottles of champagne and hock but that was all. Upstairs was a bathroom, simply appointed but with the luxury of a shower, and two furnished bedrooms. The larger of the two, at the front of the house overlooking the public garden, was level with the tops of the plane trees and decorated in green and white. Obviously the Dame's bedroom: the wardrobes were full of her clothes, the dressing table held cosmetic items and a flacon of her perfume which seemed to be Tabac Blond. He admired the square bottle with its pale gold disc and exuberant gold fringe tied carelessly around the neck and lifted the glass stopper. A dark, challenging scent of forest, fern and leather intrigued him. The woman who would wear this he could imagine taking the wheel of an open-topped sports car, perhaps pausing to pull on, but not fasten, a leather flying helmet before she put her foot to the floor. For a moment he pictured himself in the passenger seat with the Petit Littoral zipping past in the background. He put the genie of imagination back in the bottle with the stopper and made for what he took to be the guest bedroom at the rear of the house.

At last he had found a jarring note. The disordered divan – it was here! Large, low, plump and covered in a silk of a rich exotic colour which he thought might be mulberry, it was all he understood to be bohemian. Cushions, tasselled, striped, silken, spilled over on to the floor. There was no other furniture apart from a black and gold lacquer screen which cut off one corner of the room. Joe automatically checked behind it, finding nothing but an embroidered Chinese robe and a discarded silk stocking. On the wall behind the bed was a striking painting. He recognized the style. Modigliani. A stick-like girl who ought to have been deeply unattractive managed somehow with swooning eyes and horizontal abandoned pose to convey a feeling of eroticism. He found the decor stagey, the theatricality underlined by two oversized fan-shaped wall lights. The atmosphere was oppressive, the room airless and scented with something which, worryingly, he could not identify.

He walked to the single window and pulled apart the heavy gold draperies. The fresh green of the wild garden below accentuated the tawdriness of the scene behind him and he opened the window to let in some spring-scented air. Leaning out, he saw that the back garden was bounded by a mews building and a high wall with a door in it. Very adequate rear access, his professional self told him. Comings and goings not effected through the front door could be kept a secret from the neighbours.

He closed up again and looked around him. Was this where she conducted her rendezvous with Donovan when not at the Ritz? The floor appeared to have been recently swept; he could not fault the standard of housekeeping in this or any of the rooms. Without much hope of success, he took out his torch and hunted about on hands and knees on the floor looking for traces of a masculine presence. Something white between the floorboards drew his attention. Using a pair of tweezers borrowed from the Dame's dressing table, he pulled out, to his disappointment, nothing more than a squashed cigarette end from between two floorboards. No lipstick on the end. It seemed to have started life as a Senior Service. Joe could imagine Donovan's taunting smile. The Commander on his knees carefully examining one of his discarded fag-ends – this was a moment he would have enjoyed.

Surprisingly the other rooms of the house were empty. A few stored pieces of furniture under sheets were all that rewarded his search. What was going on? Had the Dame bought this house as no more than a property investment? If she had, he could only congratulate her on her foresight. But he had a feeling it was more than a financial manoeuvre. It was a setting, a shell, though a lovely shell. The drawing room made a public statement about her; the rear bedroom was where she really expressed herself.

He shook himself and prepared to search thoroughly. He disliked this part of the job and would, in normal circumstances, have assigned it to a sergeant. He was carried through it by the strict and still automatic procedure acquired in his training.

He was baffled. The place was virtually clean. He thought he'd struck gold when he found a black-stained oak cabinet containing files. A rummage through them revealed handwritten notes on cryptography, some of them on Admiralty paper. No secrets here, he assumed. Documents of value would never have been allowed to leave Room 40. Perhaps she was practising at home? A manual on the Spanish language seemed to have been well thumbed as did an Ancient Greek primer. A bookshelf held copies of popular modern novels, all read, and a selection of classics, not read. There were no romances, there was no poetry. The writing desk was a disappointment; though well stocked with cards and writing paper, there was no incoming post. Not a single letter.

He concluded that wherever she lived her life, it was not here. He wondered briefly what signs of his existence, if he were run over and killed, would be found in Maisie's neat home. A whisky bottle? He locked the front door behind him with the uncomfortable feeling that the lady had answered none of his questions but had teasingly set a few more of her own.

If Beatrice was not to be found here, then where was she? Cottingham had early in the process checked her car and found nothing. The only remaining location, and he sighed as he contemplated the task, was her own rooms at King's Hanger. Audrey's death, he was convinced, flowed from that of her employer and would only be accounted for when he understood why the Dame had died. Whatever the authorities were saying – and he could perfectly well understand their protective stance – his instincts told him that she had been killed in an uncontrollable fit of hatred. And the behaviour and character that could engender such a deadly emotion normally left traces: correspondence, journals, family albums, gossip. Joe was confident that he would pick up something rewarding between the layers of Beatrice's life if only he were allowed access to it.

His mind flew to King's Hanger, evaluating his chances of invading the house. How in hell was he to talk his way past the old lady? An encounter with Grendel's mother would have filled him with less dismay. With a wry smile, he suddenly saw his way through the problem. Could he possibly? It would take a lot of cheek and determination. He thought he had enough of both.

He decided that he'd earned himself a good breakfast.

He'd make for the nearest Lyon's Corner House and have his first proper meal in two days. They'd be frying the bacon by now. He'd have two eggs, tomatoes and mushrooms, fried bread, the lot. Then he'd go back to his flat and put his head down for a few hours. He was supposed to be on leave after all.

'It's a crying shame, that's what it is!'

'Let's just get on with it, shall we, Mrs Weston?'

'But all these dresses? All this underwear? And look at these good coats! There's folk in the village with nothing to their backs as could do with something like this. I can understand the old girl wanting to get rid of her papers and books and suchlike – I mean, what use are they to anybody? Just a sad reminder, really. But it's *not* right that *everything* should go on the bonfire! I call that real uncaring.'

'Ours not to reason why. The orders are quite clear.'

'In my last position, housekeeper to the Bentleys, when Miss Louise died, all her things were divided up amongst the female staff. I got her Kashmir shawl. This is a very peculiar household if you ask me, Mr Reid, and if I had anywhere else I could find a position within five miles of my old ma, I'd be off like a shot!'

'You have a good position here, Mrs Weston. Be thankful for it.' Reid turned to two young boys who were standing by. 'Jacky! Fred! Clear those files off that shelf . . . Put them into that box . . . Yes, those as well . . . Take them straight down to the boiler room. Papers go in the furnace. Clothes go on the bonfire in the vegetable garden. Come on! Step lively, lads!'

A figure in the shadows on the landing stood watching silently as Jacky and Fred thumped downstairs carrying between them the boxed residue of the life of Dame Beatrice.

'Following her to the flames,' came the sly thought.

Chapter Nineteen

Joe awoke to the shrilling of the telephone, unsure for a moment why a beam of afternoon sun appeared to be giving him the third degree.

'Yes?' he growled.

'Is that Commander Sandilands?' asked a male voice he vaguely recognized.

'No. It isn't. This is his man. The Commander is away in Surrey for a few days and is incommunicado. He has particularly asked me not to reveal his number to the gentlemen of the press.'

'Balls, Commander!' said the voice cheerfully. 'You put that phone down and you'll regret it!'

Joe groaned. 'Cyril! Cyril, the slander-monger. Is the *Standard* still paying you good money for trotting out that tedious tittle-tattle? Haven't seen your name on the Society pages for a while.'

'Ah! You *do* read them then?'

'Only the bits I find sticking to my fish and chips. I'd like to help you, old man, but, as I haven't jilted any duchesses this week or fallen face first into my brown Windsor at the Waldorf, I'm afraid I wouldn't be of any interest to you. Bugger off!'

'No! Hang on! I'm not on Society any more. They've transferred me – promoted me – to current affairs. And I don't want a favour. I'm offering one. Just for once I think I can do something for *you*, Commander. Why don't we meet for a drink?'

'How many good reasons do you want?'

'Oh, come on! I thought we could go somewhere quiet and drink a farewell toast to a Wren –'

'Oh, for God's sake! Not still barking up that tree, are you? It's been cut down, man! Look – where are you? Fleet Street? Make it the Cock Tavern . . . upstairs in one of their little booths. That should be quiet enough.'

'No. Won't do. Too many nosy journalists about and I'd have thought a stylish lady deserved a more salubrious setting for a send-off. I have in mind the Savoy. The American Bar. You can treat me to one of Harry's cocktails. Six o'clock it is then!'

He rang off before Joe could argue.

Cyril Tate had been an odd choice for Society columnist. Joe wasn't surprised to hear that he'd been moved sideways, having privately considered the man too astute, too talented and too middle-aged to be wasting his time trailing around after debutantes. When his copy escaped the editor's blue pencil, it was lightly ironic and certainly lacked the deferential tone the readers of such nonsense expected. He was valued, Joe supposed, by his paper for the quality of his writing but also for his talent with a camera. Readers were increasingly demanding photographic illustrations of their news items and papers like the *Standard* found that their sales increased in direct proportion to the square footage of photographs they printed. Armed with his Ermanox 858 press camera, he could stalk his prey up close and then write the reports to support the photographs. Only one pay-packet. Only one intrusive presence at the scene. Economical and practical.

A confident-looking man in trim middle age and wearing a slightly battered dinner-jacket was standing at the bar when Joe arrived, laughing with the barman. The room was almost empty of drinkers at this early hour and had the air of quiet readiness of an establishment about to launch into something it does well. Everything was in place, shining and smart. Silver shakers stood in a row; the lemons were sliced, the ice was cracked. In a corner, a pianist lifted the lid of a baby grand piano and began to riffle over the keys.

'Harry's working on a cocktail for you, Commander,' Cyril greeted him cheerfully.

'It's called The Corpse Reviver,' said Harry Craddock. 'Very powerful concoction.'

'Trying to put me out of a job?' said Joe.

Harry smiled. 'Not necessarily. Four of these taken in swift succession will *un*revive any corpse.' He listed the ingredients.

Joe shook his head in disbelief. 'Thanks all the same but I'll stick to something simple. What about you, Cyril?'

Cyril was prepared. 'The Bee's Kiss,' he said. 'I'll toast the Queen Bea with an appropriate potation.'

Harry deftly measured light and dark rum into a cocktail shaker, adding honey, heavy cream and ice. He shook it lustily and poured the golden foam into a cocktail glass which he presented, with a flourish, to Cyril.

Joe eyed it doubtfully. 'Spoon? Are you having a spoon with that?'

Cyril took a sip and licked his lips. 'Delicious! Looks so innocent, doesn't it? Honeyed, frothing, inviting? But beware – there's a sting in there! Too much of this and you're on your back and feeling ill. Have one?'

'No thanks. I don't drink rum these days. I'll have a White Lady.'

'Ah, yes. Army, weren't you? I expect it would put you off.' His sharp eyes crinkled with humour. 'Not a problem for me. Ex-Royal Flying Corps – they tried to keep us well clear of intoxicating spirits!'

They took their drinks to a secluded table.

'Right, Cyril,' said Joe, 'that's enough of the heavy symbolism. Get to the point, will you? I'm a busy man.'

'Are you though?' The tone was annoyingly arch. 'You confirmed on the telephone information that had been put my way by an official source. You're off the case. You've been left sitting twiddling your thumbs – just like you left me at the Ritz the other night.' He gave Joe a forgiving smile.

'Ah! That was you?'

'None other. And I mean – none other. Everyone's been discouraged from taking an interest but I'm not so easy to put off.'

'And you have contacts.'

Cyril didn't reply. Joe wouldn't have expected it. Journalists were skunks but they all had honour when it came to refusing to name their sources. He was surprised when Cyril said, 'The Irishman. I'd say – watch him, Commander . . . if you were still allowed to watch him. He's the link between my two areas of expertise, you might say.'

'Not sure I follow you, Cyril.'

'Well, covering this crime story, as I was – my headline was going to be "Mysterious Death of Wren at Ritz" – it occurred to me that I was particularly well placed to have *insights*, what with my society background an' all.'

'Do you have them often, these insights, and are you prepared to share them with me?'

'You know about the Hive?' Cyril's voice had become businesslike and low.

'I know it exists. Nothing more. Peripheral to my enquiries?'

Cyril shook his head. 'I don't believe so. Listen! These girls that buzz about getting ready to save the country, sharpening their stings ready for the Russian bear . . . know who teaches them their skills? Down at the Admiralty building, there's a room that's been set aside for their use and one of their instructors is our friend Donovan.'

'Skills? What sort of skills?'

'Wireless training – intercepts, code-breaking, signalling. The sort of stuff the girls were good at in the war.' He paused and sipped again at his cocktail. 'It just occurred to my suspicious mind to wonder whether the bloke might have extended his brief somewhat.'

208

'I am aware of the man's extra-curricular relationship with the Dame,' said Joe carefully.

'Well, push the thought a bit further. Good-looking bloke. Heart-breaker perhaps? What do you say to *him* being the honey in this nasty little cocktail?'

'Girls apt to develop a crush on the teacher, you mean?'

Cyril sighed. 'This is more than the plot of a girls' school story, Commander. Frolicksome larks among the Wrens . . . I'm talking about sinister manipulation.' He reached out and touched Joe's arm to underline his earnestness. 'Sinister enough to lead to death.'

'Death? Whose death?' asked Joe uncertainly.

'Ah, well. This is where the lighter side of my job gives me that insight I mentioned. Not sure anyone else has made the connection. There's only about six girls in this group. They're crème de la crème – intended to form the core of any future organization. What would you say if I told you that two of them had killed themselves? Over the last two years. Committed suicide. Coincidence? Two out of six? I don't think it could be. Hushed up, of course. *I* only took notice because they were both on my socially-interesting list and now, when I come across a third death connected with this little set-up, I begin to smell a rat – and perhaps a good story.'

'Are they sure it was suicide?' Joe asked awkwardly, uncomfortable to be professionally on the back foot in this discussion.

'No doubt. There were valid reasons, farewell notes and all that. One jumped off a cliff in the middle of a family picnic, the other took an overdose of something no one suspected she had access to. They've been replaced with fresh recruits, of course. But it makes you think. You'd no idea, had you?'

'Cyril, the Dame only died three days ago. I'd have got there.'

'Never will now though, will you? You'll read the official

story of her death in tomorrow's paper. The line we were handed is that her companion –'

'Don't tell me! I practically dictated it,' said Joe. 'And don't dismiss it. It's certainly possible.'

'Plausible at best.' Cyril gave him a knowing look. 'So you're off the case and sent to Surrey?'

'I've a few days' leave lined up.'

A waiter approached and Cyril ordered fresh cocktails. When the man had moved out of earshot he said carefully, 'And it mightn't be a bad idea to be out of the capital over this next bit.'

'The strike, you mean? It'll affect the whole country. Even deepest Surrey.'

'Not talking about whether the trains are running or the milk's delivered to your doorstep – I'm talking politically.'

Joe was silent, afraid he knew where this was leading.

'Word is you were something of a hot-head not so long back, Commander. Union man? If all this turns nasty, people will go about looking for bogeymen. Lists are being drawn up so that if heads have to roll the chopping will be done in an orderly way . . . with *military* precision,' he said with emphasis.

'How would *you* know all this, Cyril? Home Secretary your cousin or something?'

'I'll just say I have a fellow pen-pusher on a grander sheet than mine who's well connected. He occasionally gets hold of stories that he'd never be allowed to print in his august journal. But if another less hidebound paper with a forward-looking owner who's not so impressed by the British Establishment breaks it first, he can then follow suit the next day – once it's in the public domain. That's how it works these days – regulated revelation, you might call it. But the upshot is – and I say this because you've done me a good turn in the past –' Joe couldn't for the life of him remember what it was – 'check your slate's clean. Keep your head down until this has blown over. Someone's got his eye on you.'

Alarmed, Joe decided he'd heard enough of Cyril's ravings and prepared to leave. 'Cyril, I actually think that's good advice and I shall heed it,' he said easily. 'And thanks for the tip about the girls. Now how do I pay you for this? In cocktails?'

'Thank you very much, Commander, but there is one more thing if you wouldn't mind?'

He walked over to the bar, picked up something he'd left concealed behind it and returned to the table. 'Just for my records . . . to use next time you clear up a case. "Debonair detective, Joseph Sandilands, in his favourite watering-hole."'

The flare of the magnesium flash caught Joe wide-eyed and resentful, cocktail in hand. An anxious waiter dashed forward, soda siphon at the ready.

Chapter Twenty

Joe strolled down the Strand, both intrigued and disconcerted by Cyril's flourish. His recipe for good relations with pressmen was a measure of co-operation blended with a strong dash of scepticism and a twist of humour and, on the whole, it seemed to go down well. While resenting their ever more powerful presence in public life, he acknowledged that they did an essential job with some skill and he managed to stay on fair terms with the ones he encountered. And, occasionally, as now, he would be rewarded with a nugget of information. But it was the warning that troubled him.

Sir Nevil had growled the same message and he'd decided to ignore it. Dangerous perhaps. You could get too familiar with the same old sniper who never changed his position. But when you heard enemy fire coming at you from a fresh direction – time to get your head down. And what about Bill? He was more exposed in the firing line than was Joe. He'd tried to warn him, without giving away the details of the plundered file, but Bill had just shrugged it off. He'd said something half-hearted about visiting an aunt in Southend but Joe hadn't believed a word of it.

Tuesday evening. Joe looked at his watch. Seven. On impulse he struck off to his right and made his way up the Charing Cross Road and just before he got to Oxford Street, he plunged west into Soho.

He always felt he was invading these streets. Once off the broad avenues, they became narrow and crooked. Here and there were glimpses of the remains of centuries-old rookeries, tumbledown houses that had been overstuffed with people, throbbing with crime and stinking of poverty. Now, thankfully, almost all had been demolished to make way for workers' houses though these themselves were fast degenerating into slums. In spite of the chill of apprehension and the sharpening of his senses which always accompanied him when he walked along these alleys, Joe knew that life and limb and the wallet in his pocket were in far less danger here in Soho than they were on Oxford Street.

Through these few acres flowed a motley population of uncounted thousands from dozens of different countries. You could even occasionally hear a native cockney voice. Joe was amused to hear one hail him as he strode towards Dean Street:

'Corns and bunions, your honour? Try a dab of my special tincture!' The hawker waved a bottle filled with vivid green liquid. 'Nothing goes into this but pure herbs and the sweat of my brow . . . oh, go on, sir! Man in your job – he'd need a bit of relief for his feet.'

How the hell had he known? Joe crossed the road to avoid the stench of decaying horse-flesh from a cat's meat man's barrow and found himself running the gauntlet of pair after pair of dark eyes and importunate hands that stole out from darkened doorways as he passed. 'Silk dresses, sir? The best in town!' Samples of their work fluttered from poles over shop fronts, relieving with their vivid Eastern colours the sooty façades.

Now what accent was that? And how on earth did you ever keep track of the movement of the races within this small world? One week the shops were all French with *primeurs*, pâtés and pastries. The next they might be Italian, Jewish, Russian . . . His copper's eye took in a chalked sign on a door as he passed and he automatically noted the number. One cross meant opium was available, two offered cocaine as well. So – the Levant was moving north?

But he was looking for a Russian enclave. Bordeaux Court off Dean Street, Bill had said.

A shop front announcing 'Imperial Vodka' told him he must be getting close. He listened to a band of children who were plunging about the streets, kicking at empty cans, orange peel and something that could just have been a dead cat. The chatter and squeals were in a mixture of cockney and Russian. These back streets, he knew, had given birth to Bolshevism. In 1903. Over twenty years ago. Lenin, Trotsky and Karl Marx had all lived here. But he was looking for an unknown Russian.

Bill's teacher was somewhere about but if he were to stop someone and ask where he could find a Russian waiter who also taught the language, he'd be given a dozen different names, all wrong, or a dusty answer. The rozzers were not welcomed in these streets and if a passing quack could recognize him for what he was, he'd get nowhere, or worse – sent around in circles.

He looked at his watch. Nearly seven thirty. He'd come on a wild-goose chase. With some vaguely chivalrous urge to protect and warn the sergeant, who probably knew better than he did how to take care of himself, he'd be wasting a good hour. He admitted that what he really wanted was to share his news about the deaths in the Hive: potentially explosive information which deserved to be evaluated by two professionals and not left to the cocktail-fuelled imaginings of a journalist.

He stood at the entrance to Bordeaux Court and looked down the alleyway. It was dirty, untidy and seething with activity. A mother leaned out of a first-floor window and called her children inside . . . in Russian. This was the place but which room above which shop? Joe studied the lie of the land. A cul-de-sac. If Bill were going to turn up for his evening lesson as usual, he'd do it at a regular hour which would be after his working day and allowing time for his tea and a wash and brush-up. He should be here within the next half-hour, Joe calculated. Unless, of course, he had indeed gone to visit his auntie. He'd have to approach from Dean Street, past the lamp-post where two little girls were swinging about on ropes, squealing with excitement.

A sudden scent of minestrone and the thought of Bill tucking into his tea reminded Joe that he'd eaten nothing since his breakfast at the Lyon's Corner House. The delicious Italian aroma was coming from a tiny frontage in the street facing the head of the court. Joe went in. The room was so small he feared he had invaded a private home but the presence of a smiling waiter in a white apron reassured him. He asked for the table in the window, delighted to have at once an observation post and an opportunity to order a dish of their soup and a glass of red wine.

The kitchen appeared to be below the dining room and its chimney, a piece of metal piping, rose through the floorboards and conducted the spicy vapours outside into the street. Joe's dish of minestrone and hunk of peasant bread came creaking up in a small lift through another hole in the floor.

He was so delighted with the experience, he almost missed Bill.

Whoops and shrieks from the street drew his attention. The footballing boys had gathered in welcome around the tall figure of Armitage as he entered the court.

Joe got to his feet, preparing to dash outside and hail the sergeant, but he hesitated, watching the scene develop, apprehensive and puzzled. A ball had been produced and the sergeant was making his way, dribbling with the skill of a professional down the alleyway. This was obviously a weekly occurrence. Bill scored a goal by hitting the lamp-post squarely in the middle then they all moved into a circle and performed feats of sleight of foot that amazed Joe. Bill did another solo turn, weaving nimbly around the bollards that closed off the alley, the ball never more than an inch from his feet. After ten minutes of this Armitage called goodbye and walked away down the alley, fending off the raucous pleas to do it all over again.

215

Joe didn't bother to watch where the sergeant went. It hardly mattered now.

Hastily, he paid for his soup, pronouncing it the equal of anything he'd had at Pagani's, left a large tip and walked, deep in thought, back to the taxi rank on Oxford Street.

Time he was in Surrey.

Chapter Twenty-One

Lydia Benton hurried to greet her brother with a warm hug when he came down to breakfast on Thursday.

'Goodness, Joe! It's like hugging a hat-stand! However did you get so skinny? Come and have some porridge. And tell me you'll stay a week! It'll take that long at least to put some flesh back on your bones. Now . . . talk to me quickly. I reckon we have ten minutes before the girls come down from the nursery and Marcus gets back in from the stables. So – tell me what you're planning.'

Joe outlined his intentions and Lydia listened, shaking her head with disapproval.

'But are they expecting you?'

'I certainly hope not! Something will have gone very wrong with my plans if they are.'

'You ought at least to telephone them first and ask if it's convenient to motor over. You can't go about the county barging into people's houses unannounced. This isn't Chelsea, you know! Try the smoked haddock.'

'I've no intention of giving warning. That's the whole point. The family will all be at St Martin's for the funeral. And if they're expecting to see me there, they'll be disappointed. I've asked Ralph Cottingham to go in my stead to represent the Met. I've had a hunting accident. I've been in a coma for two days and you've been worried about me, Lydia.'

'I don't know these Joliffe people but this is a small county and we're bound to have friends or acquaintances in common. It's quite bad enough having a little brother who's a CID officer but if he also invades my neighbours' houses when they're known to be away from home – well! – *my* calling list will drop off pretty sharply!'

Lydia made a decision. 'I'm coming with you. A respectable older sister standing by you on the doorstep will lend you a bit of protective cover. You can say I'd promised to call on this Orlando's whatever-she-is. Mel? And we'll be very surprised to hear that the family is up in London . . . "Great heavens!" we'll exclaim. "Was it really Thursday, the funeral? Could have sworn it was tomorrow . . ." No. It's not going to work, is it? You'll just have to get a warrant.'

'Can't be done, I'm afraid. Officially the case is closed.'

'Well, that's it then. Give up the idea. If they've got a halfway decent butler, he'll send you packing. And phone the police.'

'They have an excellent butler but he has a weak spot.'

'What are you talking about?' Lydia sighed with irritation and poured out more coffee.

'Reid the butler struck me as being rather fond of Orlando's eldest. A ruffian called Dorcas. She's older than your two, wild and unpredictable but a taking little thing. I think she can wind Reid around her little finger. She's my entrée. I'll bet you anything she won't have gone to the funeral.' Joe shuddered. 'They wouldn't want to let her anywhere near douce St Martin's.'

'And you can count on this child for a welcome, can you?'

'Oh, yes, I think so. She's rather in favour of us. Would have stood a better chance if I'd had my handsome sergeant with me though. But I shall come bearing gifts. Gifts in rather a spiffing box from Harrods. If I fetch up at the front door delivering this for Miss Dorcas I can't see Reid sending me away.'

'What have you got in the box?' Lydia was curious to know.

'A few things Maisie got together for me. Books mainly.'

'Maisie?' Lydia leapt on the name. 'Maisie Freeman? You're still seeing something of that music hall artiste you brought back from India with you?'

'Like a leopard in a cage?' Joe tried to hide his irritation with a smile. 'Maisie had a first class cabin and was gracious enough to let me share it with her. She's doing very well – you don't ask but I'll tell you anyway – building up an illustrious clientele and investing her money in property.'

'You know my views on Maisie! She's a serious distraction. If you didn't have her in the background you'd find yourself a nice girl and marry her. But, Joe, assuming you manage to bribe your way into the house, what are you proposing to do then?'

'Not sure of my method yet but my object is to get from the doormat into the Dame's rooms. I want to see her records, her correspondence, her diaries, her files. I want to shake up her life until something falls out. I think I know why someone needed to kill her. I think I even know who – but I want to get my hands on the evidence.'

Joe paused between the remembered gate piers to admire the scene. Dorcas on a pony was trotting down the drive accompanied by a grey-haired, straight-backed figure with a soldierly seat in the saddle, riding a large black horse. At the sight of his car, Dorcas squealed and shouted to her companion. They both dismounted and came on towards him.

'Joe! I was hoping you'd come back! Joe, this is Yallop. Yallop, this is the policeman I told you about.'

Joe got out of the car and shook the gnarled hand offered to him. In his early sixties possibly, Yallop was a striking man. His thick hair, now almost white, must once have been black. The eyebrows were still dark, emphasizing the large eyes, which were wary and calculating. He placed his left hand, Joe noticed, protectively on Dorcas's shoulder and Joe had the clear impression that anyone offering a threat to the young mistress would quickly regret his rashness.

They exchanged a few pleasantries and commented on the weather and the condition of the horses. Impatiently, Dorcas peered through the windows of the car. 'No constable? No sergeant with you?'

'Sorry! No sergeant!' Joe laughed. 'Just boring old me but I have got something interesting in there for you.'

He produced the elegant box in its dark green wrappers. 'A thank you from the London CID for the help you rendered the other day.'

Dorcas, unusually, seemed to be speechless before the glamorous object and it was Yallop who broke through her social paralysis. 'Well, I reckon that's right kind of the police, don't you, miss? And I'm sure you'll be wanting to have a look inside. Why don't I take Dandy back to the stables and you go on and organize a cup of tea for the inspector? We can ride out later. Nothing spoiling.'

Could it be that easy? It seemed that luck and Yallop were on his side. Dorcas sat on the front seat, clutching the box on her knee, and they set off to drive the remaining distance to the house.

Next obstacle – Reid. Joe rehearsed his opening sentence.

'Just walk in, Joe,' said Dorcas. 'No good ringing. Reid's gone up to London for Aunt Bea's funeral. Granny and Orlando took him and Mrs Weston to represent the household.' She gave a wicked smile. 'I expect they're having a terrible time!'

Joe sat impatiently in the morning room waiting for Dorcas to bring the promised tea. She reappeared ten minutes later with a tray of alarming proportions. Joe hurried to take it from her and put it down on a table. 'Great heavens, Dorcas!' he said, overwhelmed. 'Are you feeding an army? . . . Just as well I'm absolutely ravenous,' he added, seeing her face fall. 'It must be the country air. Gives one such an appetite. Seedy cake? My favourite.'

'I gave the staff the day off,' said Dorcas grandly. 'Don't see why they shouldn't have some time off when there's no one here to wait on.'

They spent a companionable half-hour chatting and handing each other tea and cakes. Joe was not entirely comfortable. It would have been so easy to commit the solecism of slipping into the kind of nursery tea party games he was so often roped in for by his nieces. This was a game of a very different kind, a game in which he was being used by Dorcas in some way. She was anxious rather than playful and it seemed to be important to her that all went well and according to the rules. He went along with it, sparkling as he would have done for a duchess. This was not, of course, playtime but a rehearsal. Mistress of the house for a day and with every prospect of her father's taking it over and very soon, she was trying out her skills on an uncritical audience.

'Aren't you going to open the box?' he asked, seeing her eyes stray to it for the hundredth time.

'No. Not until you've left.'

'That's an unusual way of going on! I'd like to see you open it.'

'I don't care. I mightn't like what's in there and I wouldn't want you to see my disappointed face.'

'But you don't mind if I'm disappointed? Very well. Here's *my* disappointed face.'

She burst out laughing at the sight and Joe was happy to think that normal relations had been resumed.

'And now tell me what you've really come for, Joe,' said Dorcas as she tidied away the cups.

He told her. He didn't think that lies, concealment or flannel would get him far with this girl. She listened intently to what he had to say and was silent for a while before answering. 'I thought as much. I'm sure you oughtn't to be doing this and Granny would fly into one of her rages if she ever found out I'd let you in. But some-thing rather awful's come up. Something you ought to investigate, I think. So glad you're here, Joe! Come on. I'll take you up to Aunt Bea's rooms.'

Joe stood in the centre of what had been the Dame's sitting room and his jaw dropped in dismay. There were few pieces of furniture left and those that remained were shrouded in dust sheets. The shelves were bare, the drawers were empty. In the adjoining bedroom, the same scene. 'What on earth . . .? What's happened here, Dorcas?'

'They've taken her things away. All her things. They've been put on the bonfire or in the furnace. Granny's orders.'

Joe's shoulders slumped. He was confounded at every turn.

'Not quite all her things though,' said Dorcas. 'Audrey came in here on Sunday night – after you all left. I was putting Aunt Bea's dress away and I slipped into the wardrobe. She didn't see me. She seemed to know exactly what she wanted. It was a file. A big one the size of a large ledger. She took it away with her. Just that, nothing else.'

Joe shot out of the room and down the stairs to Audrey's apartment, Dorcas clattering after him. She watched from the doorway as he looked again at a sterile room, dust-sheeted and cleaned. The only remaining personal possession lay in the middle of the floor with a note on it: 'To be sent by rail to Miss Blount's sister' and the address in Wimbledon followed. Joe didn't hesitate. He forced open the lock using one of the house-breaking devices he'd brought with him, anticipating just such an emergency, and plunged his hands into the piles of clothes it contained. Nothing interesting came to the surface.

'You won't find it in there,' came an amused voice from the doorway. 'When we heard that Audrey had been drowned, I came in and took it away. Made it safe.'

Trying to keep his voice level, Joe asked, 'And where did you put it, Dorcas?'

'It's difficult when you haven't got a room of your own. But I thought of a place. Somewhere no one would ever dream of opening it!' she said proudly. 'Come to the kitchen.'

They went along to the family dining room and kitchen in the old part of the house. No stew was cooking today and no one was about.

'Mel's been left behind with the others,' said Dorcas. 'They're all over in the orchard.' She grinned. 'You call yourself a detective, Joe . . . go on – detect!'

Annoyed, he ran an eye over the room, remembering what had been there when he'd first seen it, looking for any changes and not seeing any. What should he do? Shake the child until she told him? Wring her neck? Swallowing his irritation he said, 'All detectives need a clue. Come on, Dorcas – give me one clue!'

'You hardly need one as it's in plain sight but let's say . . . um . . . The author of the Georgics would have been very surprised to see *these* contents!'

'Virgil? Latin poet? Georgics . . . agriculture . . . crops . . . trees . . . and . . .'

He walked to the one row of books the room contained. On a shelf high above the dresser lounged, shoulder to shoulder, a rank of dusty tomes, unread for years. He glanced at their titles. The inevitable *Mrs Beeton's Household Management*, one or two French ones by grand-sounding chefs, *How to Cook for a Family with Only One Maid*, *The Vegetable Garden* and, with a title printed in black ink running down the spine – *Beekeeping for Beginners*.

'Beekeeping – the fourth book of the Georgics. Am I getting warm?'

Joe took it down, put it on the table and eagerly opened it up.

He slammed it shut at once.

Blushing, he glanced sideways in confusion at Dorcas.

She was staring back at him, unruffled, amused even. 'Do you know the story of Zeus and the honey bee?' As he gargled something unintelligible, she carried on in conversational tone: 'A queen bee from Mount Hymettus (where the best honey comes from, did you know?) flew up to Mount Olympus and gave some honey fresh from her combs to Zeus. He liked it so much he offered the queen a gift – anything she cared to name. She asked for a weapon with which to guard her honey against men who might try to steal it.

'Zeus was a bit put out by this because he liked mankind really but he had to keep his promise. So – he gave the queen bee a sting. But it came with a warning: "Use this at the peril of your own life! Once you use the sting, it'll stay in the wound you make and you'll die from loss of it."

'Joe, do you think that's what happened to Aunt Beatrice?'

Chapter Twenty-Two

She was talking, he realized, to allow him time to pull himself together and he was grateful for that. 'Beatrice did something unforgivable,' he said at last, 'and it caught up with her, do you mean? Yes, I think it's entirely possible. Um, I wonder, Dorcas . . .'

'Have a proper look, Joe! I don't mind. And, yes, I have seen them.'

Tactfully she went to poke the fire and pile on a log or two while he sat down at the table and reopened the file. The contents were meagre. No notes. No printed pages. Secured with paper clips to the plain sheets inside were just five photographs, six inches by five inches, of different girls. He looked at the faces, trying to blank out the context. All young, all beautiful, all naked and in the arms of what appeared to be the same man in each photograph. He had no doubt that the man was Donovan. Five out of the eight members of the Hive? But who were the girls? Studying the similar haircuts and make-up, the kind you could see on any young flapper, he felt he was quivering on the point of recognizing one or two of them. His mind hesitated, stuttered almost, just failing to come up with a familiar name. With a sudden chill, he remembered that Tilly had been about to apply to join this sorry band. And Joanna, if she had answered the signal at the Ritz the other night? Was the intention to recruit her?

He turned the photographs over but found no clues to identity. The setting presented less of a difficulty. The silken divan, one corner of a Modigliani painting carelessly intruding into one of them, were telling enough.

Dorcas pulled up a chair and sat next to him. 'Now the question is, why? Why did Aunt Bea have these rude pictures? Shall I tell you what I've worked out?'

Joe muttered a faint protest but she continued. 'Was she collecting them? People do, you know. Well, I don't think that'll quite answer. Because, you see, they're not *very* rude. Not as rude as the ones Jacky's uncle brought back from Mespot. Anyway – I think they're rather arty. "Venus and Mars" perhaps? I've seen much worse on canvases in France. Look – the focus is on the face. They're meant to *identify* the girl. The man's got his back to the camera. You can't really identify him for certain. Except!' She ran to the dresser and from one of the drawers took a magnifying glass. 'Look – there. He's got a sticking plaster on his left arm. In *all* the photos! Now, I don't suppose these can all have been taken on the same day, do you?'

Joe swallowed and agreed that the logistical drawbacks to mounting such an operation would be insuperable.

'So they were probably taken over some time, and if they were – it can't have been a wound, can it? It would have healed. So it's something he's hiding from the camera. There's a man in the village who's in the Merchant Navy and he's got a tattoo in the same place. It's an anchor with hearts and . . .'

'Yes, Dorcas. I'm sure you're right.'

'She was blackmailing them, don't you think?'

'I'm afraid that's the most likely explanation.'

'But why would she bother? She had lots of money.'

'I think there must have been something else Beatrice wanted from them.'

'But who *are* these poor silly girls? They must be so worried, knowing their photographs are *somewhere* and the person who had them is dead.'

'I could ring a number and get hold of a man who could give me a list of eight possible candidates but I have a feeling that the information is no longer available to me –

or anyone. I'll have to find a different way of identifying them.'

'We could just burn these but have you thought, Joe . . .?'

'Yes, I have. The negatives.'

'I bet damned old Audrey had them.'

'Don't swear, Dorcas.'

'Bet she did, though!'

'And I bet she went to London to sell them to someone. She would have needed money. They never found her handbag. That's probably where they were. And now it's at the bottom of the Thames and the negatives will have been ruined. Good! These girls must be found and discreetly reassured that all is well.'

Dorcas gathered the photographs together. 'I'll put them on the fire.'

'No! Don't do that! I've just thought how I might get them identified. Scissors? Have you got a pair of scissors?'

Dorcas fetched two pairs of scissors from the dresser. Companionably, they sat side by side, cutting out each expressionless drugged face and consigning the rest of the photograph to the fire.

For a dislocated moment Joe was carried back to a winter's day of his childhood when he'd sat between his brother and sister at just such a kitchen table, clipping and sticking. The cook had made up a jar of flour paste for them and they'd mounted selected parts of that season's Christmas cards into albums. The sound and scent of Mrs Ross's drop scones being beaten in a bowl at the other end of the table and cooked on the griddle came back to him.

They'd been completely absorbed by their task. Georgie, the oldest, had chosen as his subject transport – cars and trains and sleighs – and Joe, the baby, had been told to collect toys. Lydia had laid claim to all the angels. As she snipped carefully around the haloes, she'd had much the same air of concentration, tongue sticking out of the corner of her mouth, as young Dorcas.

'You'll need to glue these to something if they're not to

bend. I'll get some of Granny's postcards.' She dashed off and returned with five plain cards and a pot of cow gum.

Minutes later she was pleased with their collection. 'That's better! I'll put them into an envelope. You could produce them in any company and no one would ever guess!'

Joe stowed his fallen angels safely away in his bag and was beginning to think about taking his leave when Dorcas exclaimed and went to the window.

'Another visitor! Oh, dear! It's that awful Barney Briggs! One of father's drinking set. Mel thinks he's a bad influence and ought to be discouraged. Come and help me discourage him, Joe.'

Joe glanced down the drive and saw a fine chestnut approaching with, he supposed, the despised Barney aboard.

They stood at the door with fixed smiles as Barney dismounted and hailed them.

'Halloo there! I was just passing and thought I ought to call by and see Orlando. Is he about . . . er . . .?'

'Dorcas,' she reminded him. 'No, he's in London at my aunt's funeral. They all are. There's just me and the other children and our Uncle Joe who's looking after us.'

Barney nodded vaguely at Joe and apologized for intruding at such an unfortunate time . . . he'd had no idea . . . how one lost track, continually commuting to London . . .

He made to remount then thought again and said, 'You *would* remember to give him a message if I were to leave one, would you, miss?'

'Of course.'

'Well, tell him to watch out because the police are checking up on him. No idea what the old fruit's thought to have been up to but a goodly number of his friends in London town have been subjected to harassment on his account. Interrogated! Turfed out of their beds at dawn for questioning, don't you know!

'I was able, however, to give him an alibi, I'm pleased to say. As luck would have it we travelled down from London on Sunday morning on the same train which corroborated what Orlando had been telling them all along.' His air of self-congratulation told Joe that this was the real reason for his turning up on the doorstep. He'd done Orlando a good turn and was looking forward to a gossip, joking with him about putting one over on the coppers.

'Jolly lucky either of us was able to remember the events! Both pi-eyed! Oh, I beg your pardon, miss! I'm not suggesting . . . Well, Orlando *would* be a bit the worse for wear after a family birthday party at the Ritz . . . you'd expect it . . .' He tried heavily to recover his faux pas.

Joe began to listen.

'Rather a boring do, I understand, compared with *my* evening.' He rolled his eyes at Joe. 'Goings on at the Cheval Bleu!' he confided. 'Ending in an unscheduled performance by an artiste Orlando particularly dislikes. When I told him the story, I thought he'd have apoplexy – he laughed so much! Made me tell it all over again!'

Joe gave a polite smile. 'Shame he wasn't there!' he said.

'Ah, here comes Yallop,' said Dorcas with relief, 'to summon me to my riding lesson. So good to see you again, Mr Briggs, and I'll be sure to pass on your message.'

Barney remounted his horse with nods all round and went lolloping back up the drive at a fast clip.

Judging by the glower cast at the retreating back from under Yallop's formidable black eyebrows, Barney was not universally popular in this household. In amusement Joe's eyes flitted from Yallop to Dorcas and back again as they stood side by side in profile, chins raised, faces set in disapproval, guard dogs on duty.

He hoped his gasp had not been audible. Physically shaken by the suddenness of his perception, he actually put out a hand and steadied himself against one of the door pillars. He struggled to suppress the mad thought.

When the unwelcome visitor had vanished between the gate piers, Yallop turned to Joe. Whatever he had been intending to say was left unsaid, swept away by the fresh awareness that Joe had not yet succeeded in wiping from his features.

For a moment the two men held each other's gaze, Joe questioning, Yallop calculating, then Yallop smiled slowly, nodded, and dropped a grandfatherly arm around Dorcas's shoulders.

Swallowing down his emotion, and knowing that there were no words he could ever use to express it, all Joe could do was take the groom's other hand and give it a manly squeeze.

Chapter Twenty-Three

'Joe, for a man whose unsavoury job takes him from the swamps of Seven Dials to the cocktail bar at the Savoy, you can be unbelievably naïf!' Lydia said on hearing his disjointed account of his day. 'Now we see from where Beatrice got her louche ways!'

'Lydia! Alicia Joliffe is a sixty-year-old widow who looks as though she's been expensively moulded in glass by René Lalique!'

'Doesn't mean she was always a saint. It wouldn't be the first, it wouldn't be the thousandth time it's happened! And the twentieth century doesn't have a patent on passion, you know. And you say this Yallop is a good-looking fellow?'

'Oh, yes. Undoubtedly. He must have been amazingly well set up when he was young,' said Joe. 'But he doesn't strike me as being the type who would . . .'

'All men are the type who would . . .!' said Lydia crisply. 'Particularly if they were young and impressionable and seduced, lured, commanded . . . who knows? . . . by an attractive employer.'

'She's certainly the kind of woman who would expect to get whatever or whomever she wanted.'

'But she found herself paying the bill for her indulgence? A slip-up she regretted? Danger of discovery always there to torment her? It might account for Mrs Joliffe's questionable attitude to her son? But can you have got this right, Joe? I mean, didn't you say that Orlando was bequeathed the house by his father Joliffe? Old Augustus can't have suspected anything. What does Orlando look like?'

'More like his mother than anything. But shortish and wiry. He doesn't look in the least like Yallop. Not at all. No, I must have been mistaken. And I made a fool of myself, gawping and shaking the chap's hand in an emotional way. He'll think I'm a very unsuitable uncle for Dorcas. Probably getting the horsewhip ready as we speak!'

'Oh, I don't know . . . these things *can* skip a generation. Think of Great Uncle Jack's nose!' Lydia smiled and Joe rubbed his own nose thoughtfully. 'Do you think Dorcas is aware?'

'No. I'm sure she isn't. She's deeply fond of the old chap, you can tell. There's a bond there but I don't think she realizes what that bond may be. She puts her dark looks – as do they all – down to her fleet-footed gypsy mother.'

'It's all coming down to inheritance, after all, don't you think? "Who benefits?" you always say is the most important question in a murder case. Well, it seems to me you can say – Orlando benefits. The old girl was bending the rules to leave everything to Beatrice who, in her eyes, was the rightful heir. On two counts: she was the oldest and she was legitimate. It wouldn't matter a jot to a feminist, which I understand she is, that Beatrice was female. Many of us cannot accept the laws governing male inheritance over female.'

'Perhaps she told Orlando. Perhaps she threatened to expose his dubious parentage if he didn't agree to the house being turned over to Beatrice? How would one ever find out? No one's going to tell me, even if I were allowed to ask.'

'Well! I never dreamed we had such lively neighbours! I shall be sure to pay a call. It does sound as though that unfortunate Mel could do with a bit of support . . . I'll let you know how I get on, shall I?'

'I'd be fascinated to hear. But, listen, Lyd, old gel – don't go sticking your nose into anything that might get you into trouble with people like me . . . no – people a good deal shadier than I am. Nameless men from nameless departments. It's been concluded that the Dame was killed by her employee and we have no option but to go along with that.'

'Yes, Joe,' said Lydia, meekly.

Passing Joe's room on her way to the bathroom at one in the morning and seeing his light was still on, Lydia tapped lightly on the door and, receiving no reply, pushed it open and went in. She'd been about to offer him some cocoa but she stood and smiled to see him fast asleep, his bed covered in sheets of notes and photographs, his open briefcase by the bed.

Silently she gathered them all together and replaced them, then, her face alight with mischief, she crept from the room carrying the briefcase away with her. In the deserted kitchen she put some milk on the stove, threw her old gardening coat around her shoulders and settled at the table to put everything in order again. Joe would thank her in the morning.

At two o'clock Lydia was still sitting by the stove holding in her hand four sheets of paper and wondering. She read for the third time through the evidence and failed to find what she was looking for. But it was the merest detail. She was being ridiculous and fussy. After all, her sharp-eyed brother had been right there on the spot. It was probably in the notes somewhere. He wouldn't have missed it.

Lydia yawned, drained her cocoa and packed up Joe's bag.

When he got back to his Lot's Road flat on Friday morning, Joe sorted through his post and picked out the brown envelope bearing a Home Office stamp. Larry had been as good as his word and completed the fingerprint testing he'd asked for. There was a handwritten note from his colleague accompanying several typed report sheets. It was unsigned, on plain paper and obviously meant to be destroyed at once:

'Sorry, old man – axe fell halfway through your commission. Managed to get it finished but I don't think you're supposed to have these. If anyone asks, I'll say it was fait accompli, irretrievably in the pipeline! All right?'

Joe scanned eagerly through the results of the testing and analyses he'd asked for. In dismay at what he saw, he started again at the beginning and read with care.

'Using the extension of the Henry System devised by Ch. Insp. Battley for the classification of single prints . . .' ran the foreword, '. . . all prints submitted have been photographed and enlarged reproductions would be available for presentation in court . . .'

Fat lot of use that would be! He skipped on to the conclusions, wading through reports of loops, whorls, bifurcations and islands. 'When the imprints of two fingers or – as in this case – thumbs are compared and it is found that there are twelve essential points of resemblance between the two, the degree of probability that they come from the same digit is so high as to amount to a certainty. We are able, in this case, to attest to no fewer than fifteen points of resemblance . . .'

On his third reading Larry's report was still sending him the same devastating message.

He went to the telephone and asked the operator for Whitehall 1212. 'Hello? Commander Sandilands here. Put me through to Inspector Cottingham, will you?'

The following Monday found him sitting in his office, papers neatly arranged in front of him, a half-drunk mug of tea on one side, when Big Ben struck one. He greeted a simultaneous rap on his open door with a cheerful, 'Come in, Bill!'

Armitage came in, evidently invigorated by his week's

leave. His expression was of eager anticipation and readiness.

'Inspector says you want to see me, sir.'

'Yes. Sit down. Glad you could come. I see the sea air's done you a power of good,' said Joe. 'Must try it myself sometime.'

'Go on, sir! Don't tell me you spent the time chained to your desk?' He waved a hand at the evidence of work in progress. 'Though it does rather look like it.'

'No. I went to the country. I stayed with my sister in Surrey. I called on some of her neighbours, Bill. You'll be interested to hear your absence was noted and regretted by Miss Dorcas.'

A smile broke out but was instantly suppressed. 'Not poking about still, sir? That's all done and dusted, isn't it?'

'I believe so. Yes. The Dame was buried for a second time last week and we can all exclaim, "Good Lord! What a shame! Such a loss to the service! Her maid did it? Well, we all knew the servant problem was getting out of hand." And by next week we'll all have forgotten about Dame Beatrice.'

'Dame who?' grinned Armitage.

'Except that *I* shan't have forgotten.'

'Still ferreting, sir?'

'Yes. As a matter of fact I got more than I bargained for down at King's Hanger.'

Joe outlined the evidence he'd discovered for the existence of the Hive. And Donovan's involvement.

'Bugger me!' said Armitage, round-eyed. 'Are you telling me that she stood there – the Dame, I mean – and took photos of the girls in flagrante delicto with that . . . that . . .'

'Lothario?' suggested Joe.

'Can't we get him for something?' said Armitage hopefully.

'I wouldn't like to have to specify the offence on the charge sheet,' said Joe. 'Are you curious, I wonder, Bill, as

235

to what's *really* behind all this? They obviously had black-mail of some kind in mind – or coercion. I don't believe money was involved so what on earth could this unholy pair have been extracting from these girls?'

Armitage shrugged. 'You don't need to be an expert at differential calculus to work it out. Come on, sir! It's sex and sadism! They've been reading some French books they shouldn't oughter. But anyway – it doesn't matter now. I was hoping you'd called me in to say we'd got fixed up with another job?'

Joe side-stepped the question. 'Power. That's what it was all about, I'd guess. With evidence like that hidden away and a threat to send copies to . . . parents perhaps? Rich, well-placed members of society with a good name to lose? "Dear Admiral X, You will be interested to see the enclosed art study of your daughter Amelia enjoying the company of a naval petty officer. Signed, A Wellwisher."

'Two girls from the Hive committed suicide, Bill, I do believe as a result of this pressure. And that also deserves to be properly investigated. They chose death rather than dishonour for their family but above all they were rejecting something else: whatever it was they would be required to say or do or give when the Dame pressed the button. And what I intend to find out is where precisely was that button and what was at the other end.'

Armitage was silent for a while. When he spoke his voice had taken on a firmness and even steeliness Joe had never heard before. 'God! You don't give up, do you? Listen, Captain! I'm telling you! You said to me the other day down in Surrey that you loved your country enough to fight a bloody war all over again if you had to. Well, there's no need for such a dramatic gesture. You can do your country a favour by doing nothing. Nothing! Is that so difficult? I shouldn't be saying this but you always were a pig-headed bastard.' He smiled when he delivered the insult. 'Tell me you understand, sir. Both our careers depend on it.'

So, the gloves had finally come off.

Joe's reply was polite, teasing even but deadly: 'Your career? Now which one are you thinking of, Bill? The career outlined in your doctored CID file? The file that omits to mention your physical impairment? We can forgive them that omission, I think, since there's nothing wrong with either leg. Nothing to stop you playing a nifty game of alley football with your young Russian pals. And all that clever reverse stepping through Soho on the night of the murder! Perhaps there's another file that reveals you're actually an understudy for Fred Astaire? Or is it John Barrymore whose talents you emulate? "Let me do the climb, sir!" All that tight-lipped, white-knuckled drama! I should have asked for an encore.

'Or have you in mind the file that will never be open to *my* eyes? What name is stamped on the cover? Foreign Office? Special Branch? MI5? Room 40 . . .'

'No name,' said Armitage, shaking his head almost regretfully. 'No name.'

'Thought probably not,' said Joe, heavily. His worst fears had been confirmed with those two words. He patted his pockets, feeling for his cigarettes and encountering the reassuring bulk of his Browning revolver in his left pocket.

'Cigarette, Bill? No? I think I'll have one . . . calm the old nerves . . .'

He lit a Players and was careful to hold it in his right hand as he always did.

'There have been whispers about a department that no one seems to be able to put a name to. One that no one wants to believe exists. Not in this country that we all love. After all, it's the sort of thing foreigners get up to, isn't it? Russians, Turkomen, Balkans . . . probably even the Frogs if we did but know it . . . they all go in for a little discreet . . . assassination. But not the British! No, no! Not the British! Remuneration good, is it? What did they pay you for killing the Dame, Bill?'

Chapter Twenty-Four

'This is rubbish! Dangerous rubbish! It's never going to get an airing outside these walls but even if you could get anyone to listen to this blather, you've got absolutely nothing.'

Pleased to have rattled him, Joe pressed on. 'Oh, but I have. I have evidence of the best sort. The sort that would convince any Old Bailey jury. A big bold thumbprint on the poker that killed her which corresponds with your right thumb, Bill. To say nothing of your right index finger on her throat. Not so clear, that one, but the thumb's a cracker!' He picked up his tea mug, saluted the sergeant and set it down again. 'Fifteen matching details, they tell me. I've got whorls and loops enough to hang you with.'

Bill was silent, pale and staring. If Joe had read it right, not even name, rank and number would be forthcoming from the tight lips but he decided to go on needling the sergeant anyway.

'Why the hell did you get involved with a bunch like this? You're doing well in the force, aren't you? What is it? Money? An urge to kill for which you've found a legitimate – or, at least, state-approved – outlet?'

He wasn't seriously expecting a response. Men in this line of work were, according to police folklore (and this was the only source of information), granite-jawed thugs who would go to the grave in silence, taking their secrets with them.

The sergeant shrugged the pressure away. Slowly, the

old Armitage smile appeared again and, to Joe's surprise, he seemed not just prepared but even anxious to communicate something. He considered for a moment or two then began slowly. 'I never stopped counting the minutes. You think, like most, that we've been through the war to end war. We're rebuilding ourselves . . . jazzing our lives away . . . lighting up London, trying to forget, but some of us know it didn't end there where we thought we'd buried it, there in the Flanders mud. We're under attack still from more than one direction. I used my skills to knock minutes off that war and if I have to use the same skills to buy time from the next one, I will.'

Was there the faintest sneer as he went on? 'Loving your country isn't the prerogative of the upper classes, Captain, though I know they think they own the title deeds to the finer feelings. I've got less reason than most to feel gratitude to bloody old Britannia – the old bag's never shown *me* any favours! But it's my country and I'll support it however I can. And that's not an unthinking, visceral reaction. I question everything, including patriotism.'

'And you think you've come up with the right answers?' Joe hardly needed to offer encouragement. Armitage seemed eager to unburden himself. The life of a government-paid assassin, Joe reflected, must be a lonely one.

'In fact, I'd say it's the lack of patriotism of the flag-waving sort that's the saving grace of this country. In my class, at least, we don't much admire the jingle of spurs and the parade of power. Did you notice in this last lot – when we marched, it wasn't the victories we sang about, it was more likely to be the disasters. It wasn't our glorious leaders – it was the rotten old sergeant-major we immortalized in bawdy verse.'

'So unmilitaristic are we, you'd wonder we ever managed to acquire an empire,' Joe commented mildly.

Armitage glowered, angry to be misinterpreted. 'Bloody old Kipling would have understood,' he said. 'You only have to look at those peaked Prussian helmets to see what

I mean. Mad! Try issuing those to the British Army and you'd be greeted with outright guffaws through all ranks. You can't get away with nonsense like that without breaking up on the British sense of humour.'

'Good God, man!' said Joe raising an eyebrow. 'If you launch into a eulogy on jellied eels I'll have you chucked into a cell to cool off.'

'Of course you will!' Armitage smiled. 'See what I mean? It's to keep blokes like you from having to get their hands bloodied again that blokes like me wield the occasional scalpel. You're not all worth the effort but – where else in Europe would inordinate appreciation of jellied eels be a criminal charge? I've thought it through. I have my own philosophy.'

'A killer with a conscience?'

'That's right. For your own good, Captain, we've never had this conversation. This goes so high it'd make your head spin. You risk annoying some forceful people. Can't imagine what the going rate is for making a Commander of the CID disappear but there's bound to be one.'

'But what possible danger could she be to the state?' Joe persisted. 'Playing Girl Guides with a bunch of silly debutantes and the lout Donovan?'

He was pleased to have provoked the response he wanted.

'Not silly girls at all! Clever, able, well-trained girls.' Armitage hesitated, weighing the knowledge that he was exceeding his brief against his understanding of his superior officer which was pushing him beyond his limits. He came to a decision. 'Girls who, though they were unaware of it,' he went on, 'had, in their charming little heads, the power to lose the next war for us.'

'*Lose* a war, Bill? But they were training to help *win* wars.'

'Tell you a story.' He leaned back and Joe had a clear impression that he was about to call up a brandy and soda. 'Know who I mean when I mention Admiral Sir John Fisher?'

240

'Of course. Father of the modern navy . . . innovator . . . brilliant man. Destroyers, submarines, torpedoes, guns – he was responsible for the state of readiness of the fleet when war broke out. It was Jack Fisher who said: "On the British fleet rests the Empire."'

'And he wasn't wrong. It was his protégé, Admiral Jellicoe, who actually led the fleet into battle. Now, the Germans were caught on the back foot on several occasions early in the war because Jellicoe always seemed to know where and when they were massing for attack. The reason he was able to give them a bloody nose was the SIGINT warnings to Room 40. Signals Intelligence. Wireless telegraphy, radio, whatever you like to call it. Their shipping movements were being monitored, the information collated and interpreted and handed to Jellicoe on a plate. He and Admiral Beatty were on their way while the German fleet was still in harbour. At the battle of Jutland, he had victory in his pocket and the German fleet trapped at night in open waters at the entrance to the Skaggarak. He was ready to blow them out of the water come dawn but – he faltered. He was given signals information and he ignored it. Let them get away. No one's quite sure why.'

Joe wondered why Armitage was imparting this information so freely and who was his source. He had remarked an unusual political slant which didn't quite chime with what he had understood to be Armitage's philosophy.

'Jellicoe decided to accept instead the inaccurate information from his scouting cruisers,' Armitage revealed, watching for Joe's reaction. 'Reverted in the middle of battle to the tried and tested old methods. If he'd acted in accordance with radio intelligence supplied, which was very clear as to the position of the High Seas Fleet, Jutland might have turned out really to be the victory Churchill told us afterwards it had been and not the uncomfortable and bloody draw it actually was.'

'Why was the intelligence not acted on? Do you – or your masters have a theory, Bill?'

'You fancy yourself as a psychologist – you tell me! There is a phrase they've invented to cover it: the Incredulity Factor. A sudden refusal to put your trust in modern technology.'

'I know it well,' said Joe. 'It affects me every time I change gear.'

He thought he would get the most out of Armitage by keeping their exchanges as light as possible and maintaining, as far as he could, their old relationship. 'But I do begin to see how a well-placed squad of Wrens could wreak havoc at sea,' he added carefully.

'Yes, there's no doubt that Jellicoe's hesitation was due to incredulity but – think! Suppose a wireless operator had been in a position to send him a further communication confirming his own doubts. "Ignore previous message . . . we got it wrong . . . HSF now reported sailing west . . ." Bound to have influenced his decision!'

'Certainly. We all like to have support for our own misjudgements.'

Armitage looked at him steadily for a moment then continued: 'The navy was pivotal. If the Germans had destroyed us at sea in 1916 and blockaded the country – no supplies coming in and no troops going out – we'd have been on our knees in six months.'

Joe knew Armitage was not exaggerating when he said, 'One duff message, Captain, that's all it would take.'

Joe's reply came haltingly, unwillingly. 'And if the sender has knowledge of the language, coding, wireless technology . . . and – perhaps most vital – an understanding of overall strategy . . . Oh, my God! But would a woman ever be given such an influential role?'

The full enormity of the scenario had hit Joe and he shuddered.

'It didn't take the navy long to discover the girl recruits were smarter than the men when it came to SIGINT and they're nothing if not innovators at the Admiralty – if it works, use it. If war were to break out again, I'd expect Queen Bea's girls or the like to be operating in the signals section. Wireless, signals, codes. The next lot will be won or lost in the airwaves not in the trenches. One bad communication from a trusted source at a critical moment, that's all you'll need!'

At last Joe was in possession of the awful truth.

'Are you saying the Dame was preparing to betray her country to the Bolsheviks?'

Armitage's laugh was derisory and triumphant. 'God no! I never thought I'd hear myself say it but – you're wrong on two counts there, Captain!

'For a start, *her* country, the one she really paid allegiance to, was not England. Given the chance, she was intending to foul up things for the British fleet and bring about a victory for the country she truly cared about – Germany.'

Joe felt suddenly awash with horror. Armitage must have been watching his every movement intently. He produced his brandy flask. 'Gulpers, I'd say, sir. Go on!'

Joe was thankful for the warmth searing its way down his throat. Too late he remembered who had offered the drink.

'It's all right,' said Armitage, amused. 'Only the best scotch in there. I'll have one myself.'

'What a headache she must have given the various departments once they found out! But how did they get to hear?'

'One of the girls who killed herself – no idea who . . . no need for me to know that – is understood to have written a letter to her highly placed father confessing all and warning him. Action was swiftly taken.'

'Ah! The sting!' Joe mused. 'The venomous shaft she placed killed the victim but brought her own death with it. I like a neat, classical ending! But I see the problem: difficult to charge her with anything because, technically, she'd done nothing wrong. Her crime was in the future. Conspiracy, perhaps?'

'You're forgetting the friends in high places.'

'Couldn't one of them have been primed to take her out

on to some terrace and hand her a brandy and a revolver, in the good old British tradition?'

'There'd still have been public interest aroused. And these days we have to consider the reactions of the bloody press at every turn. They don't just turn up and meekly take dictation from the Home Office any more. She was a colourful woman and very much in the public eye. There'd have been talk in any circumstances – but the tragic, though understandable, death at the hands of a burglar is a nine-day wonder. Cat burglars have become a national obsession – everyone was expecting something like this to happen. Just a question of time. She was unlucky. No one minds the press running with that story – let them enjoy it. But think, sir . . . if the truth came out about the Queen Bea . . . Remember the scandal of the trial of Sir Roger Casement after the war. We're still in the outfall of that seven years on.'

'And he was an Irishman! How much worse if a woman regarded by some as an English heroine were similarly exposed!'

'More or less the conclusion the department arrived at, sir. Thought you'd get there in the end.'

'So, they send in Armitage under cover – and what cover! A CID sergeant no less! He watches his subject go up to her room – noting that she's alone – sets off outdoors on patrol wearing a cape and, on his two good legs, shins up the building, breaks in, murders the Dame and spends some time laying confusing evidence that will send the Plod off in several wrong directions.'

Joe paused, deep in thought. 'No. You didn't break in, did you, Bill? No sound of glass smashing reported by anyone . . .' Then, seeing his way through, 'You let yourself in by means of an unlatched casement. You'd been on patrol throughout the building earlier that evening. What was to stop you getting into her room – pass key part of the security man's kit? Perhaps you borrowed one from a maid on her 9 p.m. rounds? And you unlatched the window while she was down below at the party? Then, when

244

the hour comes for your external patrol, you simply push the window open silently from outside. You kill the Dame, steal her necklace, mess up her clothing to make it look personal, bash in the glass, muffling the sound with a Ritz towel, and redistribute the glass from the window. There, that'll give someone a double headache! You probably put the jemmy and emeralds inside the pockets of the cape . . . I did wonder what that bulge was when you sat by me at the coffee stall . . . no, all right! I didn't! Any blood splashing would have been fended off by the waterproofing of the cape and would have been invisible outside in the dark on a wet night.

'So you go back out through the window, parting company with the poker halfway down . . .' Joe hesitated. 'Then you smarten up, with all the time in the world, in the staff cloakroom and rush about efficiently when called upon later on the discovery of the body. Of course, as it turned out, you didn't have all the time in the world. You hadn't bargained for Tilly Westhorpe taking it into her head to pay the Dame an impromptu visit. Very nearly wrecked everything for you, Bill. No wonder you wanted her off the job. Sharp-eyed, saucy young Tilly watching your every move! Playing detective! Nightmare!'

'You're doing well, sir,' said Armitage affably. 'There's only one thing wrong with it and I don't mind mentioning it as I see you've clocked it as well. Doesn't quite make sense, does it? I *didn't* kill Dame Beatrice. They've paid me for it all right but I had to confess that someone had already done the job for me. She was lying there dead when I went in. Just as you saw her later.'

'So what happens now, Bill?' Joe sighed.

For a moment he thought he might have overplayed his role. Indecision from his commanding officer was not what Armitage would have expected. But he seemed to think it a reasonable question in the circumstances and replied with a perceptible relaxation of his taut muscles. 'Only one thing that can happen, Captain. You say, "Case closed and let's look forward to working on the next one." Then I bugger off.'

Joe narrowed his eyes, flinched, exclaimed sharply and examined the end of his cigarette which, unregarded in his absorption with the story, was burning his fingers. Armitage's eyes followed it. A tap on the door divided his attention for a split second. It was long enough.

'Come in, Ralph!' Joe called.

The inspector entered to find Armitage still seated, staring, unbelieving, down the barrel of the Browning Joe was holding steadily in his left hand.

'Ralph, did you bring them? Good. Cuff him to the chair, will you, and remove his gun. It'll be on his inside left. Holstered. Try and stay out of range, Ralph – if he moves, I'll shoot him.'

A pale but defiant Armitage, hands locked behind his back and a further set of handcuffs fastening him to the chair, listened in silence as Inspector Cottingham produced a warrant for his arrest and began to read it out.

'This is a bloody farce!' he hissed, exasperated. 'There's nothing you'll be allowed to stick on me. Don't think it! And I told you,' he sneered, 'I didn't even bloody well do it.'

'I know you didn't. Just have a little patience, old chap, and hear the inspector out. He's about to do you for . . . what have we got, Ralph? . . . breaking and entering the premises of the Ritz, stealing an emerald necklace, interfering with evidence to a murder, pre- and post-commission obfuscation . . . Carry on, Ralph. You read it – I'll sign it.'

Cottingham, having completed his arrest manoeuvres with professional smoothness, now stood to one side, agitated and questioning. His eyes flicked nervously between the revolver which Joe still held at the ready and its target.

'He wasn't armed. Sir! It's Armitage! He's one of us!'

'*Was* one of us. Technically still is. He goes through the motions, draws the pay, uses the cover but his loyalties are with some other department. Probably under the same roof, though we'll never know it.'

'Special Branch?' asked Cottingham. 'One of McBrien's busy boys?'

'Special? No, I'd have said rather – Extra Special. We're not allowed even to think about it. A branch of a branch of the Branch, perhaps? A twiglet?' He composed his features. Mistake to descend to levity. In a voice of purring conspiracy he added, 'And if I guess rightly, there'll be several firewalls between the grandee who first murmured from the depths of his leather armchair in a St James's club that perhaps the Dame had gone too far and the time, sadly, had come . . . and, at the end of the line: the finger on the trigger, the hand on the poker.'

Cottingham was uncharacteristically nervous. 'Dangerous work perhaps, sir, to meddle in matters like this?'

'Oh, yes! Which is why I've taken certain precautions. I sent off this weekend a thick envelope for delivery to my lawyer. In the event of my unforeseen death, the letter will be copied to . . . and there follows a list of ten influential people. And, just to be sure, memos have gone to Sir Nevil, the Head of the Branch, the Foreign Secretary, the editor of the *Mirror* and, perhaps most importantly, to the Leader of His Majesty's Opposition, to inform them of my insurance policy. A mixed bag of heroes and villains there! Having this in common – none of them will want what I've said to become public knowledge. I'll be roundly cursed in some quarters but – what the hell! – this is England, not bloody Russia!'

He wondered if he'd been melodramatic but Cottingham seemed impressed by the speech.

'Should have included your resignation with that little lot,' Armitage growled.

'But what will happen to *him*?'

'Yes, Ralph. I share your concern. The situation is most dangerous for the sergeant. Broken tools get thrown away. If we let him loose on the streets we'd probably find that a passing hackney cab driver would accidentally lose his grip on the wheel with disastrous consequences for the sergeant within the week.'

'Harsh retribution, sir? Considering you seem to agree with him that his only crime was burglary and tampering with evidence. That's five years maximum.'

'It's just a holding charge, Ralph. He'll be out of our control – and protection – as soon as his papers reach a certain level. Get your coat and hat. We've some ground to cover before he gets released. We're going to pick up evidence of his other crime and then we'll have to think about a further warrant. Get on the phone, will you, and whistle up an escort down to the cells?'

Armitage had turned pale and was frustratedly tugging at his handcuffs. He glared in silence as Ralph asked, 'Other crime, sir? What have you in mind?'

'The murder of Miss Audrey Blount. Let's not forget Audrey.'

Chapter Twenty-Five

'Where are we going, sir?' Cottingham asked as Joe commandeered a police car and driver.

'We're going to pay a call on Armitage senior. According to the file, Bill's home address is Queen Adelaide Court, just off the Mile End Road beyond Whitechapel. Being unmarried, his next of kin is a Mr Harold Armitage, his father. Retired soldier. Nothing so helpful as a search warrant in our pockets, Ralph, so we'll just have to charm our way in. And while we go, I'll fill you in on the latest developments in the Hive you discovered.'

'What are we hoping to find *chez* Armitage, sir?'

'Audrey's handbag? The negatives? If Armitage is motivated by money he might have kept them back to do a little business on his own account. He claims to be motivated by patriotism but . . . I don't know, Ralph . . . I think perhaps financial reward might play a starring role in all this. And let's not lose sight of that necklace. No information from the usual sources?'

'None, sir. Usual fences claim no knowledge. Could have gone abroad by now.'

'Or been hidden until someone thinks we've taken our eye off the ball.'

'But what's the connection between Audrey and Armitage?'

'She was prowling the corridors well before the murder – we only have her word that she saw nothing untoward. Did she catch sight of Armitage doing something questionable? Like letting himself into the Dame's room with a pass key? She needed money in her changed circumstances and I think she was bold enough to attempt a spot of blackmail. She was certainly giving him a close inspection when we interviewed her down in Surrey. I put it down to the sergeant's charming exterior but I think she very probably recognized him. She'd only have to ring up the Yard and leave a message. He would ring her back and arrange a meeting. The whole murder scene on the bridge has a professional ring to it. The rendezvous was set for exactly the time of poorest visibility. The witness, Arthur, said she turned to greet someone when the beat bobby approached. Wrong chap in fact but she could have been expecting to see a man in uniform.

'Suppose, Ralph, our killer is waiting on the Embankment wearing, let's say, a river policeman's slicker and cap. No one would take any notice as their headquarters is right there by the bridge. They're coming and going all the time. So he waits until the beat bobby has done his job and gone on his way then he approaches Audrey, grabs her bag and throws her over. Bag goes into the inner pocket of the cape and he strolls off unnoticed. I got taken for a policeman by a tram conductor myself, leaving Waterloo Bridge in a borrowed cape.'

'Then perhaps I should be arresting you, sir? But, to answer my original question myself – we're looking for a police cape possibly still stained with Group III blood and this item will have, secreted in an inner pocket, a lady's bag containing photographic evidence of a dubious nature. If our luck holds, in the other pocket we'll find an emerald necklace and a jemmy. And it will, no doubt, be hanging handily on the back of the door. With a confession pinned to the collar.' Cottingham sighed.

'Ralph, go home!' said Joe on impulse. 'I shouldn't be involving you in this underhand operation. You've a wife and family to think about. I'm sorry! I was getting carried away. You're right. I haven't a clue what there may be to be found in Armitage's house. He's a careful type and has, of course, got rid of anything incriminating days ago. I just want to give it a try. Nosy, I suppose, but I wanted to get an impression of the man from his surroundings. He's many-layered and I'm sure I don't know all there is to know about Bill Armitage. Go back to the Yard. I'll go on by myself. Constable! Stop here!'

'Constable! Drive on!' Major Cottingham of the Coldstream's authoritative voice countermanded Joe's order.

'Ralph, you're not obliged –'

'I know that. But I'm not happy about closing down this case any more than you are. It's like looking at a suppurating wound and being ordered to slap a sticking plaster on it in the hope that it'll go away. No, this calls for the scalpel and if I can help you wield it, I will. You said it, sir – "This isn't bloody Russia!" We didn't give our all in that hell for four years to emerge into an autocratic state where faceless men decide for us what the Law should be.'

They were dropped off at the City end of the Mile End Road and the driver assured them that if they struck out to their right they'd find what they were looking for. He didn't risk taking his motor vehicle down into that warren – he was likely to emerge with bits missing and lucky if it was just the motor. He arranged to wait for them on the main highway.

They found the narrow entrance to Queen Adelaide Court. A grand-sounding title for a Victorian collection of slum dwellings erected for workers in the nearby docks. They stood, silently taking in the squalor and overcrowding of the terraced houses grouped around a central square. Joe spotted four outdoor lavatories and a central water pump. Washing lines crowded with drying linen filled most of the yard, reminding them that it was a Monday. Doors stood open on gloomy interiors; a few inhabitants were out on the doorsteps gossiping and casting an occasional eye on the bands of young children who played together in groups.

Springtime games were in full swing. Skipping ropes,

whips and tops and hoops were being used by groups of girls, the inevitable football game, much circumscribed by the washing lines, raged around the perimeter. Once his initial shock at the noise and obvious poverty of the court had subsided, Joe noticed that all the children seemed happy and busy. A gang of small girls were first to challenge the strangers. Arm in arm, they were strolling along chattering and one was pushing a cart made from an old wooden fish box mounted on two perambulator wheels. It was lined with a dirty blanket and contained a selection of rag dolls. Joe bent to admire them as a friendly overture and was alarmed to see one of them move. The girls shrieked with laughter at his startled reaction.

''Sawright, mister! That's just our Jimmy. 'E won't bite yer! Not 'less you was to put yer finger in 'is marf!'

Joe explained that they were friends of Bill Armitage and were looking for his house.

'Rozzers, are yer? That's all right then. I'd took yer for gennlemen – watch chain an' all,' said the oldest with a sharp look at Cottingham's waistcoat. 'Well, come on then. 'Is dad's in.'

Joe handed them a penny each and they set off, an unlikely cortège, to weave their way across the court, their every step followed by dozens of pairs of eyes.

'I say, sir,' said Cottingham quietly, 'bit odd, all this, isn't it?'

'Bill's a London lad. I expect he was born here.'

'And that's what's odd. Remuneration's not wonderful in the force, I'm sure we'd all agree, but he's drawing a sergeant's pay and he's a single man. He could afford to live in the leafy suburbs like most of the CID blokes. Why's he still here and what's he doing with his salary?'

The girls led them to the open door of a house at the end of a row. It seemed larger than the others and the proud Victorian builder had, according to tradition, immortalized his wife or his eldest daughter by fixing her name over the door: 'Violet Villa'.

'Knock! Knock!' sang out the girls in chorus. 'Mr Armitage, you're wanted! Visitors!' They moved away in response to a raucous call from the other side of the court to come in for their dinner.

The doorstep was freshly donkey-stoned, the windows clean and the over-sized brass knocker gleamed. An elderly man appeared in the doorway. He peered out, failing to focus on either of them until Joe spoke. He had noticed that the old man's eyes were both dimmed by the milky-white film of cataracts.

'Sir!' said Joe cheerfully. 'Two visitors. I am Commander Sandilands and this is Inspector Cottingham. We are both colleagues of your son Bill and we're all working on a case . . .'

'Oh, yes! I know who you are. Come in, come in! Bill's told me all about you. And if I've got it right, Commander, it's not the first time my lad's worked with you. His CO, weren't you, at one time?' Armitage reached for Joe's hand and shook it vigorously. 'Can't be often a man has the chance to say thank you to the officer who brought his son safely through all that. Makes me thankful I put him with the Royal Scots Fusiliers. His mother was a big strong Scotch lass – a fisher girl I met up with when the fleet was down at Southend . . . never did settle down here – and my Bill was up there with her family when war broke out. I wanted him with a regiment where the officers knew their trade so I said, "Go on, lad. Sign on."'

Joe wondered if the old man was lonely in spite of the hubbub outside in the court. He seemed to be pleased to have someone to chew the fat with.

'A soldier yourself, Mr Armitage?'

The back straightened and the right hand trembled with the effort not to salute. 'South African war. 2nd East Surreys. Clery's Division. Wounded and invalided out.'

Joe launched into a knowledgeable military man's appraisal of the campaign, agreeing with the old man that the best thing that had come out of that war was the lesson learned from the Boers in the matter of rapid fire. 'Served us well in the early months in France,' Joe commented.

'Always taught young Bill to fire fast and accurate. 'E don't mess about!'

'No indeed!' said Joe. His eyes, while he talked, had been scanning the appointments of the room, noting the table laid ready for a tea that Armitage would not be coming home for, the comfortable armchairs one on either side of the coal fire. The fire dogs shone in the hearth, the mahogany furniture gleamed, where the surfaces showed, under protective doilies and runners. The alcoves on each side of the chimney breast had been fitted with shelves and every inch was taken up with ranks of books. Joe saw, as well as battered volumes of Nuttall's Standard Dictionary, Meiklejohn's English Grammar and the works of Shakespeare, a collection of, it seemed, every published title in the Everyman Library. The shelf at hand's reach of the armchair was most revealing: a collection of French novels in their familiar yellow binding, one or two Russian works, Palgrave's *Golden Treasury*, Carlyle's *History of the French Revolution*, Tom Paine's *Rights of Man* and, sideways on, with a bus ticket marking his place, a dog-eared copy of Montaigne's essays. With a flash of distress, Joe realized that this was a distillation of his own collection.

The regret that he would never now exchange thoughts and opinions with the sergeant stopped the easy flow of his talk and he was relieved to hear the old man acknowledge his interest. 'Ah! You've spotted the lad's books, then? Quite a sight, in't they? Spends far too much money on them but then, he's lucky at the dog track and it's his cash to do what he likes with. Cup of tea? Would you like one? I can call someone to make it. Having a bit of trouble with the old eyes. Can't see very much any more but Bill's going to take me west to get an operation. Got an appointment. Twenty-fourth of May. Empire Day . . . shan't forget that. They can work wonders these days, 'e says. Been saving up for it. 'E's a good lad.'

Joe refused tea for both of them, saying they were under pressure . . . in the middle of a case. While the old man's attention was firmly being claimed by Joe, Cottingham began to move around the room, eyes darting. He arched an eyebrow at Joe on noticing the heavy police cape hanging exactly where they had predicted behind the door. Catching sight of a large ginger cat installed on a cushion in one of the fireside armchairs, Cottingham moved towards it making noises which just might have been interpreted as flirtatious by a cat, Joe supposed. Surprisingly, the suspicious glare disappeared and the animal allowed itself to be picked up by the inspector. Moustache to moustache, they appeared to be communicating with each other.

'You must excuse the inspector – he's a cat-fancier,' said Joe, reclaiming the old man's attention. He had realized that Cottingham had located something of interest on the mantelpiece. The green velvet, bobble-trimmed drapery along the shelf over the fireplace was held down by Staffordshire dogs at each end. Other ornaments were lined up with military precision between them but the object that had caught Cottingham's eye was a piece of white card pushed sideways between a toby jug and a crinoline lady. Under cover of romancing the cat, Cottingham tweaked it out, scanned it and pushed it back in place.

Joe was entertaining Armitage with a lively account of how his uncle had had the doubtful honour of being the first man to fall to the bullet of a machine gun at the storming of the summit of Spion Kop, spinning out the story until he was certain that Cottingham's survey was complete. 'But we must get on with the next phase,' he began to say. 'We seem to have lost contact with Bill who's been sent down to Surrey again.'

'Ah, yes,' said Armitage senior, tapping the side of his nose. 'Surrey!'

'And we urgently need a certain item in evidence. Forensic testing, you understand . . .' Joe just restrained himself from making the same gesture.

'Say no more! You've come for the package!'

'Yes. The package,' said Joe faintly.

'It's not here.'

'Not here?' Joe hoped he didn't sound too anxious.

'No. It's over the court at his aunty Bella's. Half a mo. I'll give her a yell and tell her you've come for it.'

A ritual exchange of hallooing and bellowing went on from the doorstep and their safe passage across no man's land was negotiated. With handshakes all round, they wound their way through the washing lines to a similar house opposite. Predictably this was 'Daisy Villa'.

'You've come for it, then?' said Bella, a buxom woman with frizzy hair, a gap-toothed smile and large red hands. 'Hang on, I'll get it.' She disappeared for a moment, leaving them on the doorstep.

'Not the nicest job I've ever had from Bill,' she said cheerfully, handing them a parcel done up in brown paper and tied with string. 'In fact, that were right nasty! "Wash it carefully," he said. "You sure that's what you want?" I says. "I mean, I don't want to go washing evidence down the plughole, do I? You can get into trouble that way." "Just you wash it," he says. "Careful, mind! None of your carbolic and pack it up neat for me. Keep safe till required." He often asks me to keep things for him. I splashed out on a box of Ivory Snow soap flakes. Cost me eightpence! Hope that was all right?'

'Quite all right. Quite all right,' said Joe. 'Well done, Bella. Now, here's half a crown for your trouble and we'll be off.'

They regained their car and settled in the back, Cottingham clutching the parcel on his knee.

'Well, we broke no rules at least,' said Joe. 'It was freely handed over to us, whatever it is!'

Cottingham squeezed it gently, held it to his ear and shook it. 'It's not a handbag. It's soft, squashy and soundless. When shall we open it?'

'As soon as we're unobserved. Lord knows what might come spilling out to embarrass us. But tell me, Ralph, what was that card you found on the mantelpiece? A pawn ticket? That would be useful!'

'No. Bit of a puzzle that. It was a steamship ticket. It was a booking for a passage from Southampton to New York on board the *Mauretania*. It's this Friday's sailing. Two passengers, sir. Travelling in one first class cabin.'

'Ah,' said Joe. 'Bill's going to be very upset to miss the boat.'

'Do you think this might be the reward for services rendered? No financial record to be traced and your instrument is shipped off out of the way. Perhaps this is how it happens nowadays? One shot and throw away, like razor blades. Disposable assassin? Seems a waste of a very particular talent. I wonder who else is going to be disappointed, sir?'

'Well, his father . . .'

'. . . is expecting to pay a visit to Harley Street at the end of May. Poor old sod! I wonder who Bill was intending to share his palatial accommodation with? And why he would draw attention to himself by booking first class. I'd have gone second.'

'It's not so special any more, Ralph. Since it was refitted they've got more first class cabins than second on that boat. Over five hundred. Easier to get one at short notice? I expect the second class get snapped up quickly. Be interesting to find out where the cash has come from. Must have been saving up his ill-gotten earnings for years, I'd guess. And now he's restarting his life in the style he means to adopt in the New World.'

'Perhaps his travelling companion is someone who insists on nothing but the best, sir?' suggested Cottingham. 'Oh, by the way, I managed to give the cape a frisking while you and the old man were shouting to Bella. Nothing in the pockets. Not so much as a cigarette paper. But there was something – I turned the pockets out and, not easy to see, the lining being navy, but there was a large dark stain in the right-hand one. No smell. I assume it had been scrubbed out, but you know what bloodstains are – the devil to get out completely.'

Asking Charlie to make sure they were not disturbed, they went into Joe's office and closed the door. They stood over his desk, the package in the centre between them. 'Will you do the honours?' said Joe, offering a penknife.

Swiftly Cottingham cut through the string and peeled back two layers of brown paper. He exclaimed in astonishment when he caught his first glimpse of the contents. Plunging both hands in, he took out and held up to the light a black lace evening dress. A faint trace of the scent of Ivory Snow soap flakes lingered in the delicate fabric. He shook it and two black satin gloves slithered to the ground.

Chapter Twenty-Six

'What's it say on the label, Ralph?' He had a memory of Tilly paying respectful attention to such details in the Dame's room.

'Lanvin. Paris.'

Joe fingered the flimsy fabric. 'Bloody old Bella! If this was caked in blood, and I think we can guess it was Group III, it's all been washed away. No use to Forensics at all.'

'What is Armitage doing with a bloodstained dress? Keeping it as evidence? But why, then, wash the best bit of the evidence away? Was he filing it away as insurance? Blackmailing someone? It still makes more sense to leave it caked with blood, surely?'

They were gazing in fascination at Armitage's secret when Joe's telephone rang. The duty sergeant was relieved to hear Joe pick up the receiver. 'She's been trying for the past two hours, sir,' he said in a pained voice. 'It's a Mrs Benton. Claims to be your sister. Says it's urgent.'

'Put her through.'

'Lydia? Joe here. Got a problem? Can you make it fast? I'm up to my ears here.'

'Only your ears? Well, lucky old you! I'm in over my head. I went to King's Hanger this morning as I promised and walked into the most appalling scene. Melisande's gone mad. Quite mad! She was, according to Dorcas, having a row with Orlando all weekend. He moved out of the house – or she threw him out – and he spent the night in the caravan. She went out early this morning and set the thing on fire. Not a bad move, I'd have thought, but

259

Orlando was in there at the time. He's all right. Shaken and furious of course but not much damage done – Yallop pulled him out in time . . . I see what you mean about Yallop, by the way! Oh my goodness!'

Joe groaned. 'Lyd, I really can't look at a domestic problem or even arson at the moment. Has Mrs Joliffe called the local police? That would be the thing to do.'

'Joe! She's had enough bad publicity for one week, don't you think? She's washed her hands of the whole thing and retreated into her room.'

'Where are you now, Lydia?'

'I'm at home. I loaded the children and Melisande into the car and brought them all back with me before worse occurred. Any chance you could come over here and calm them all down? That gallant little Dorcas is quite a trooper but she swears like one too and I'm having to keep my girls out of earshot in the nursery.'

'I can't get down before the weekend. Oh, Lydia, I'm sorry to have landed you with this! I'll do my best to get over the minute I can wrestle down a problem or two I've got on my desk. Look, Lyd, I'm going to impose further on you! Can you spare a minute to answer a question? . . . The dress label Lanvin . . . Expensive? And who would wear and for what occasion a . . .' He studied the dress Ralph was still holding, '. . . short, lace dress, black, straps at the shoulders, no sleeves and a pair of black satin gloves?'

'So – they've turned up, have they?'

'Eh? What do you mean, Lydia?'

'Ah! You hadn't noticed then? Well, aren't I clever? I looked at your files on Thursday night and, Joe, there was something missing. Probably something it would take a woman to see. That list of belongings so meticulously put together by your constable – it was quite obviously everything the Dame would need for a two-day stay at the Ritz, down to the last handkerchief. I was curious to know what she was planning to get up to on her second night so I cross-checked with her diary. You didn't correlate the two, did you?' Lydia was triumphant.

'She was booked in for a dinner at the Savoy with an admiral. But, Joe, where on the list was a suitable outfit for a glamorous evening like that? The long formal frock she was wearing for the Ritz party wouldn't have been quite right and I don't imagine she'd wear the same thing two nights in succession. There was no second dress, no second pair of gloves listed. But what you're describing sounds just perfect. Jeanne Lanvin, eh? Discreet but dressy. Quiet elegance. Perfect for the Savoy. Whoever the owner is – and I think I can guess! – she has jolly expensive taste!'

'Perfect for the Ritz too,' Joe added silently. 'God, Lydia! I wish you'd mentioned this earlier!'

'Ralph! Someone's been playing Blind Man's Buff with me all along!' he exclaimed as he replaced the receiver.

He sank into his chair, head in hands, lost in dark thoughts.

'You all right, sir?'

'No. I'm not. I've just shaken off the blindfold and got a clear look at the jokers who've been spinning me around, tripping me up and walloping me with a pig's bladder! Trouble is – I can't see *why*. Why would they do it? Listen, Ralph and tell me if you think I'm quite barmy . . .'

Ralph listened in growing horror and confusion while Joe outlined his theories as to how the murder had been committed.

'It all holds up, sir, even the poker halfway down the building and the bloodstained dress – balancing each other out, you might say – except for that very fundamental question, why the hell? I acknowledge the Dame could be a most irritating lady but what on earth had she done to bring down such a vicious attack? It does smack of a personal involvement – hatred, revenge, outrage, something of that sort. Which is what you've been saying all along. Where's the link between victim and murderer? Can't see one! And that story you got out of Armitage? So much misleading blather, I suppose? He never was up on the roof to break in and kill her.'

Cottingham looked sideways at Joe and his eyes widened. 'Great heavens, man! You never did believe all that Assassination Branch stuff, did you?'

Joe smiled. 'No, Ralph. Armitage is a good yarn spinner but he doesn't have the monopoly on blather.'

'And your "insurance policy" – all those letters to lawyers and various holders of exalted state office?'

'I was afraid I'd gone a little over the top. Can't be sure it deceived Armitage. Still, he's never heard me lie before, he may have been taken in.'

'I'd say he was, sir. I was. But how did you know he wasn't what he was implying – a state-paid killer, working alone?'

'In the later stages of the war I worked in Military Intelligence while I was recovering from a wound. Interrogation. Breaking up spy networks. You learn to be very suspicious of the ones who tell you a story. The genuine undercover men say nothing. They wouldn't tell you the time from your own watch if you asked nicely in six languages. Armitage could have given Scheherazade a run for her money! He still had something to gain by spinning us another yarn.'

'But why put his hands up to a crime like this if he didn't do it? Suicidal, surely?'

'No. We all know – and most importantly *he* knows – there's no way an articulate time-bomb like Armitage is going to be allowed to take centre stage on a very public platform in the witness box at the Old Bailey. His detailed knowledge of the Dame and her doings – and we can guess where he got that from! – and his readiness to share it with the Great British News Readership amounts to his immunity from prosecution. But there's something more. Two things. We know he's protecting, for whatever reason, the murderer's identity but he's also disguising his own particular crime or crimes.'

'What? This is a different crime we're talking about?' Cottingham was bemused.

'Yes. He's an intelligent man, largely self-educated, I'd say, but – educated. He's also an exceptional fighter. Distinguished record. Had he been born into a higher class of society, Armitage's talents would have been recognized and valued – he could have been running the British Army in a few years' time. And he knows that. A proud man. He would go to great lengths to avoid being identified by his commanding officer – and I think he's always had a grudging respect for me – as no more than a common thief.'

'A what!'

'A thief, Ralph. He was up on that roof that night to do exactly what he did – steal a jewel or two. What better cover for his activities? Sent in as uniformed security, if he's observed observing – well, good man, he's doing his job, isn't he? I don't believe he's the only nimble gent on the rooftops of London but he's one of them. I checked his work record. Several spells of duty at grand hotels. Overtime willingly undertaken. Far too bright to queer his pitch by nicking stuff on his own watch but he was able to do his reconnoitring at leisure. Robberies Section were able to provide me with some interesting dates on these. A carefully irregular pattern, but a pattern, of thefts following on Armitage's overtime stints. A week, a fortnight, sometimes a month later. No one would have spotted the connection.'

'But he was breaking his routine that night at the Ritz?'

'A last flourish? Couldn't resist those emeralds? Any thief knows the best moment to grab the goodies is when a single lady, travelling without her maid, retires to her room, tired, intoxicated even, chucks her jewellery on to the dressing table and heads for the bathroom. Just too tempting! Probably planning to do a runner by then anyway.

'If all had gone according to plan, he'd have unlocked the window while on patrol and later, when she went to her room, he would have climbed up intending to watch through the window for the moment when she went into the bathroom. He'd have let himself in quietly and, just as quietly, left. By the time she raised the alarm – which might well have been the next morning – it would have been put down to her own carelessness.

'Armitage would have been on hand to roundly declare that no burglar had gone to her room. He was on patrol outside after all. Inside job? Fake insurance claim perhaps?'

'Unluckily for our hero, he saw quite a different scene through the window!'

'Yes, Ralph. And I think young Armitage made the mistake of his life.' Joe smiled. 'His mistake was to react like the policeman he was. He intervened.'

'But, I tell you what, sir! Even I am beginning to think Sir Nevil – and bloody old Armitage too – has a point. Perhaps it's better the way the all-powerful have decreed it shall be? Closed, sealed, filed away.'

The telephone shrilled again. 'Leave it to me, sir,' said Cottingham. 'I'll fight a rearguard action if need be.

'Cottingham here. Ah, yes, sir. 'Fraid not. He's just popped out to Trumper's for a haircut. A theft in St John's Wood Park?' He listened intently, waggling his eyebrows at Joe. A hand over the mouthpiece, he hissed, 'I don't believe this!' Then he spoke again, picking up a memo pad and a pencil. 'Just a moment, sir, I'll take down the details. What was that again? Countess Zanuti-Lendi? Have I got that right? And the butler is thought to have gone missing at the same time as the silver? I'm sure the Commander will be delighted to put his mind to that, sir. He may even have the answer for you within the hour.'

Joe sighed.

'And Sergeant Armitage has been released from custody? He won't be so delighted to hear that. On whose authority, may one ask? The Commander will want to know . . . Oh, I see.' Ralph swallowed. 'Very well. Of course. Wouldn't dream of it, sir.

'Bad news, Joe. He's been released on the very highest authority.'

'Home Office?'

264

'Sir William Joynson-Hicks himself has taken time off from making his stirring anti-communist speeches in the House to ensure that Armitage is never accorded a starring part in a witness box. Serious stuff! Better back off, I think!

'This new case they've given you is a gentle hint. You might almost say somebody up there has a sense of humour. They're rapping your knuckles by sending you off to St John's Wood to feature in a musical comedy extravaganza. Give you a tip, shall I? The butler did it! Polish up your epaulettes, slip on your spurs and go and give this Countess Maritza a twirl around the floor this afternoon.'

Joe rewarded the inspector's valiant attempt at lightness with a grin. 'You're right, Ralph. And now we so nearly know the truth I won't embarrass you any further. But I'll tell you what – there are just two things I have to do before I draw a line under this sorry business. I don't know how long it will take to achieve both aims but I'm going to stick at it. I'm going to identify those members of the Hive we have on record and, if ever I can be certain that those negatives have been destroyed, reassure them as tactfully as possible that the danger has passed. And secondly, I'm going to look this murderer in the eye and say clearly, "I know you did it. I know why you did it. The highest authority in the land may, for understandable reasons, have exonerated you but the Home Secretary is not the Ultimate Authority." I shall wag a minatory finger.' He practised this. '"You will answer for your sins in a Far Higher Court," I might add if I'm feeling particularly sententious.'

Maisie looked up from her book and smiled a welcome. 'Well, look what the cat's brought in! If you're here for supper, you'd better tell Mrs Jameson.'

'I already have. We've got Irish stew. I've brought you a

265

bag of those Australian apples and a box of chocolates in a lover-ish sort of way.'

'Liverish, you mean, if it's of the same gross dimensions as the last one. Had to give half of them away. Help yourself to whisky if you like and tell me what you've been up to.'

'Tiring afternoon, Maisie,' Joe said, settling down on the sofa with her. 'I had to arrest a Transylvanian Countess for stealing her own silver and roguishly laying the blame on her innocent butler whom she'd had the forethought to sack a week previously. I advised her to retract the insurance claim she'd made and confess all.'

'Doesn't sound all *that* tiring.'

'Fending off the Countess's determined efforts to distract, suborn and seduce the instrument of the law took a bit of effort.'

Maisie gurgled. 'The risks you run, Joe, navigating the shoals of high society! And only just recovered from the last lot! Did you see yesterday's paper? No? Hang on – I kept it for you.'

She fished about underneath the sofa and produced a copy of the *London Weekend News*. 'Here we are. Society page. "Entertaining evening at the Kit-Cat Club. Cream of London society crowd in to dance to the music of world-famous jazz band under the baton of Paul Whiteman." There's a picture of the Prince of Wales doing what I suppose might be a rumba with Lady Mountbatten but here's the really interesting bit, look, under the headline "A Fair Cop? Dashing Detective Joe Sandilands, caught on camera. But who is the lissom lady he has in his grasp? A little bird tells us it's none other than Mayfair Maiden, Mathilda 'Tilly' Westhorpe (debut '22). As our same talkative bird would have it, Miss Westhorpe, when she is not locked in the arms of her governor, is, in fact, a woman policeman. We wonder who has put the emotional cuffs on whom?"'

'Oh, my God!' Joe groaned. 'How utterly appalling!'

'Oh, I don't know,' said Maisie. 'You make a rather arresting couple. At least she doesn't look boring.'

'We were working, Maisie!'

'Yes, I can see that. Another exhausting undercover job, no doubt. I just thought you ought to know that the press has got your number! Watch out. You're still a good-looking fellow and very distinctive. You'll find yourself being trailed all over London. Dazzled by photo flashes. Sir What's-it won't like that! Might even find you're being shipped out back to India to cool off.'

While Joe poured himself another whisky, Maisie straightened the paper and looked again at the photograph. 'Westhorpe? Name's familiar. Professionally familiar, I mean. Let me think . . . Is this girl's father an army man? A rather grand army man?'

'A general. I've met him.'

'Oh, you are making progress, then! Yes. He was a client. Got him! A month or two ago. I can check my records if you like but I can remember most of it . . . He came to make contact with his wife. She died, was it three years ago?'

'Ah, yes. Nice chap but he seemed to have an aura of unhappiness about him, I thought.'

'An aura, eh? Don't think you got that from the police training manual!'

'This is no time to be flippant, Maisie! There was something he said which gave me that impression . . . something sorrowful.' Joe frowned with the effort to remember words casually spoken. 'He told me to take care of Tilly because "she was all he'd got left" – something like that.'

'Yes, I suppose she would be. They always come with a question, you know, Joe. Sadly, no response was forthcoming that evening to his, but what he wanted from his wife was reassurance that their elder daughter had made it over safely and was with her mother in the spirit world. Some people still have doubts that you're welcome over the other side if you're a suicide. She killed herself, Joe '

Chapter Twenty-Seven

'Well, she's no Dorothy Wilding, is she?' said Cyril, examining the photograph Joe had reconstructed and placed on the table in front of him. 'A pint of bitter, please, if you're buying. And a ham sandwich with mustard.'

Joe made his way over to the bar at the Cock Tavern and placed an order. He carried the tankards back to the seclusion of the corner table they'd chosen and they took a grateful swallow. He decided on a general conversation topic while they were waiting for the sandwiches. 'Let's enjoy this while we can, eh, Cyril? No knowing how long it'll be before supplies dry up! Do I count myself lucky to have got you on a Tuesday morning – what they're calling the first real day of the strike? No tube. No trains. Violent speeches in the House, mayhem breaking loose in the streets – I'd have thought your editor would have had you stripped to the waist and chained to your typewriter, labouring to get it all down.'

Cyril made a disparaging noise in his throat. Evidently, his good humour had deserted him. 'Just the opposite. It's a bloody lock-out! Government orders. They closed down the *Daily Mail*, now us. The rest will follow. But don't concern yourself – there'll be news of a sort published: I heard from a mate at the *Morning Post* that they're taking over their offices as of today and pumping out a propaganda rag called the *British Gazette*. To be edited by the Chancellor of the Exchequer!'

'That fire-eater Churchill? He's rabidly anti-strike. Sees it as an attempt to overthrow the government.'

'Hardly makes for unbiased, objective reporting,' sniffed Cyril.

'Are you shocked, Cyril?' Joe said quietly. 'I'm shocked. Is this the freedom of the press we all value?'

'Oh, it gets worse!' said Cyril lugubriously. 'They're moving in on the wireless. Putting out government news bulletins five times a day, starting with Baldwin's fire and brimstone speech in the House. They're calling for the general public – that's anyone between seventeen and seventy – to volunteer for strike-breaking duties. Driving buses, working on the railways and in the power stations. It'll be murder! Can you imagine? Undergraduates in plus-fours at the wheel of a London omnibus! Schoolboys at the controls of an underground train! Grannies in the signal boxes!'

He took a fortifying swig of beer and ranted on. 'And have you driven past Hyde Park lately? Looks like an army camp. I was up there this morning. Food distribution centre, they're saying. It's bristling with titled ladies, all wearing identical pork-pie hats and military-style mackintoshes. Looks like they rang around and decided what one ought to wear for a General Strike! They've rallied to the call of Lady Astor to save their country from the filthy Bolshevik strikers and show the rest of us where our duty lies. I got a shot of them smiling smugly, pretending to peel potatoes – emergency rations for the volunteers. Some of those women have never seen a potato in its natural state before, let alone peeled one! It's wreaking havoc with their manicures, I'm pleased to say.'

'Watch it, Cyril, your allegiances are showing!'

'Haven't got any allegiances. I pride myself on being able to see all points of view and I suspect you do too, Commander. But – I'll tell you – we're in a minority. The rest of the country's divided itself along class lines and the two sides are determined to have a go at each other. Resentment of generations about to boil over.'

'I saw something really stomach-churning coming down the Mall this morning,' said Joe 'Mob of about thirty polo players, prancing about on their ponies, looking for trouble. I stopped one and asked if I could redirect him to Hurlingham. Told me they'd signed up – the whole bloody club! – for what he called the "Special Civil Constabulary" and were patrolling the streets of London to quell the troublemakers. I told him I was the "Regular and Rather Rude Constabulary" and I'd nick him for incitement to violence and spreading public disorder. He took my details! Threatened to horsewhip me and demanded to know which side I thought I was on . . . Do you know, Cyril, I was lost for an answer. I don't want there to *be* sides but I know I couldn't ride knee to knee with that arsehole! And I play polo! If I ever came across him on the field I'd cheerfully crack his skull.'

'What the hell's happening, Joe? This isn't what we fought for.'

Cyril's spirits lifted at the sight of the ham sandwiches being delivered to their table and Joe decided, when the waiter had left, that the time had come to get him back on track. 'Dorothy who?' he asked.

'Dorothy? Oh, yes. Sorry, Joe. Let's return to our little baa-lambs, eh? I forget you're not a photographer. Dorothy Wilding. She has a studio in Old Bond Street and if you were to stand on the pavement opposite, you'd see a procession of famous faces turning up for her attentions. Royal personages, to say nothing of the royalty of stage and silver screen. Noel Coward . . . Gladys Cooper . . . Tallulah Bankhead. She's good. At the sharp edge of the art. I model myself on her.'

'These aren't bad, considering the circumstances,' said Joe. He had produced his gallery of the Hive members and, to provide Cyril with the full picture, had fitted round one of the faces a frame he'd managed to hide from Dorcas as she fed them on to the flames.

'Practical rather than professional but, I agree, not bad. Indoor shots always difficult. She used artificial light, I'd say, looking at the shadows – two sources – but I think, not flash powder. That would be dangerous anyway in a tight

270

space with so much Eastern drapery to go up in flames. I wouldn't try it. Look at those tassels!'

'There were two large wall lights on the back wall,' Joe offered. 'Very large. Would have looked more at home in the Tivoli Cinema.'

'Ah. If you'd checked the bulbs you'd have found they were a thousand watts. That's what Wilding uses. And the camera? It would have had to be something small and unobtrusive for this sort of game. I'd say these girls were drugged or drunk and probably didn't know arse from elbow at the time, but I can't see her fitting out this little snuggery with cumbersome studio equipment. What sort of range are we talking about? Eight, ten feet? It'll turn out to be one of those new Leica 35 mm jobs. Neat.'

'It's the subjects I'm really interested in, Cyril.'

'Right. Tell you what – hand them to me one at a time and you can write their names on the back – if I know them. Oh, by the way – the bloke with the starring role in this little peep show I'd swear is Donovan. I expect you know that? Can't claim to have an intimate knowledge of the chap's rear elevation but there are clues that might help. Have you noticed the Elastoplast where a tattoo would be and the mole on his right shoulder blade?'

Joe handed him the first of the card-mounted photographs.

'Well! Who'd have thought it? Joan Dennison! I *am* surprised!'

'Just the names, thank you, Cyril.'

'Right. That one's Portia something . . . you know . . . daughter of that judge . . . hanging judge . . . "Blackcap" Blackman! That's it!

'This one? Sorry, no idea. Never encountered her before. Perhaps one of the others would be able to fill you in?

'This one looks familiar . . . Ah yes, well, she would, wouldn't she? This was the jumper. Leapt off Beachy Head. Lettice Benson.'

Joe passed him the one he'd reserved for last.

'And this is the other suicide girl. Took an overdose of

her dead mother's painkillers that'd never been cleared out of the bathroom cabinet. This is the one I told you about. The one who spilled the beans to her father. Brave lass! Lovely girl,' said Cyril thoughtfully. 'Marianne Westhorpe. She lived up in Mayfair somewhere.'

'I know where she lived,' said Joe.

'Can't help wondering why only five out of the eight were subjected to this,' said Cyril.

'Clever scheming,' said Joe. 'The psychology of the group. I expect each victim was given to understand that she was the only one involved. Some of the eight would be behaving naturally because for them there was no problem. Each of these poor girls would have been living in her own private hell, unable to confide in or question the others. She would be unsupported, totally alone, hugely vulnerable.'

'You'll tread carefully, Commander?'

'Of course. Kid gloves. Reassuring avuncular manner. But don't forget I haven't yet established the whereabouts of those negatives. Shan't rest easy until I have.'

'And Donovan? What have you got planned for him?'

'I'd like to say "police boot in the groin, swiftly followed by the clink of cuffs" but he's on someone else's shopping list. There are others more elevated than I am who will be taking a close interest in Donovan and his future career. Though if we were to meet head on in a dark alley, I'm not sure he'd ever come out at the other end. Another pint, Cyril?'

Returning to the Yard to write up his notes on the Zanuti-Lendi silver theft enquiry, Joe was not surprised to find on his desk a series of orders hastily handwritten, cancelling all but essential activities and directing him to strike-emergency duties. His roster apparently resumed the next day and was to send him to the Palace to oversee security arrangements against an insurrection by the mob.

He finished his notes, wrote up his diary, sighed and

came to a decision. He took up the telephone and was surprised to find that his hand was shaking. He asked the operator to connect him with a number in Mayfair.

At least the Westhorpe butler no longer affected not to know him. 'Miss Mathilda is indeed at home, sir, today being her day of leisure,' he intoned, unable to refrain from putting gentlemen callers on the wrong foot. 'If you will wait a moment, I will ascertain whether she is available to come to the telephone.'

A moment later a drumming of feet, a clatter as the earpiece was picked up and Tilly's eager voice: 'Joe! Sorry – Commander! How good to hear you again! Can I do anything? That Clubbing at Claridge's we spoke of – has it come about already?'

'Sorry, Tilly. No. Ordinary crime fizzles out when there's a war on or even a strike. Nothing more exciting to offer you, I'm afraid, but dinner. How about it? I'd like to see you again. On Friday. Would Friday be a good day? Will you be free?'

'Friday?' There was a pause then, regretfully, 'No, sorry, Joe, I've already got an engagement that day.'

'Then,' said Joe firmly, 'it will have to be tonight. And I'm making that an order, Constable! I'll pick you up at seven. Better warn your father.'

Chapter Twenty-Eight

'Where are we going?' Tilly asked excitedly, settling into the Oxford.

She was looking extraordinarily attractive, he noticed, and felt flattered that she had taken the trouble. Her outfit was of the very best, discreet but costly, he would have thought. A short, oyster-coloured silk dress, a row of pearls, a black cashmere wrap and an immaculately made-up face – did he deserve this?

'Somewhere special,' he said, threading his way through the streets of Mayfair.

Reaching their destination, he handed the keys to a commissionaire and held out an arm to Tilly.

'The Ritz?' she said wonderingly as she stepped out. He was pleased to hear the disappointment in her tone as she added, 'You didn't say we were still working, sir.'

'Well, it may not be unadulterated pleasure, having dinner with the guv'nor,' he smiled, 'but it's not work. I think I told you, and I say again, the Jagow-Joliffe case is closed. Done up in pink string and filed away from sight for the next seventy-five years. It seemed appropriate to wrap it all up here where it all started. And we'll get a jolly good dinner. We've deserved it!'

He glanced approvingly at the reflection in the many glittering mirrors which flanked their progress to their table. He almost wished Cyril were on hand to record the occasion but he remembered that no camera flash journalists ever breached the defences of the Ritz. Probably all

274

off in Hyde Park, anyway, busy snapping the militant aristocracy.

As they settled, he looked around, grateful that the management had been as good as its word and given him what he had asked for – a discreet table at some distance from the others.

In spite of Joe's agitation the evening seemed to be going well. Tilly was calm, attentive, responsive and amusing. The perfect partner. Joe thought she would undoubtedly be granted Maisie's seal of approval on this showing. Maisie's? His own, too. For a desolate moment he was aware of a void in his life, a loneliness, and played with the thought of returning from such an evening with such a girl on his arm and no need to say goodnight. 'Listening to too many popular songs,' he decided. 'Brace up, Sandilands!'

They chattered happily through three courses and Tilly looked relieved when Joe suggested to the waiter that they might like a pause before the desserts were presented. Now or never. Joe reached into his pocket and produced a white card. He watched Tilly's face as he put it down in front of her.

Her eyes widened slightly and she stared at the photograph of the dreaming face. The familiar face. The family face. Silently she trailed a forefinger around the cut-out line of the photograph.

'Thank you for your sensitivity, Joe. How like you to have censored the rest of the . . . unpleasantness. It must have been . . . unpleasant.'

'Can you confirm that this is Marianne? Your older sister?'

'Of course. But there were others. What have you done with them?'

'I have them safe and they've been doctored in the same way. I was going to reassure the subjects that all danger has passed from them but . . .' He paused and held her gaze. 'I can't do that until the negatives are in my possession or, at the very least, I am confident that they have been destroyed.'

'They have been destroyed, Joe.'

He waited, willing her to go on.

'They were handed over to me and I put the evil things on the fire,' she said finally. 'They made a fine blaze.'

'I'd be interested to know how they made their way into your hands?'

'I'm sure you would. "Still ferreting," Bill would say.' She smiled. 'When they give you a knighthood you can have it for your motto. You must let me devise your coat-of-arms.'

Joe grinned. 'What do you see? A ferret rampant gardant and above, a scroll saying *semper vigilans*?'

'Something like that. Well, Mr Ferret, the negatives were brought to London by that scheming Audrey. She was intent on raising money to finance an idle future by selling them to me for whatever she could get.'

'I think Audrey had something even more valuable to sell to you,' suggested Joe.

Tilly smiled as though acknowledging an opponent's clever chess move. 'My life or liberty, you mean? Yes, that. She recognized me the moment I took off my hat at King's Hanger. Though I didn't register her as anything other than a maid, she saw me going into the Dame's room. As she said, she was interested to catch a sight of Bea's latest conquest! She lurked about and watched me come out later . . . much later . . . and go down in the lift.'

'And your presence could perhaps have been explained away when she realized you were a policewoman . . . had it not been for one extraordinary fact.'

Tilly nodded and looked down at her plate.

'You went into the Dame's room wearing a black lace dress and black gloves and emerged in a silver-grey dress – a bit long for you and hitched up at the hips with a silver belt – and a pair of spanking clean white gloves. Perhaps Audrey even recognized the dress – it was one of her

276

mistress's best. She had been planning to wear it at the Savoy the next night.'

'When we interviewed Audrey she managed to make it quite clear that she understood what had gone on and I made the opportunity to speak to her alone.'

'Ah, yes. While I was dispatched to admire the tulips.'

'I agreed to whatever she suggested. I told Bill . . .'

'I conveniently sent you both off into the orchard to compare notes,' sighed Joe. 'You told him everything, didn't you? About the Dame and her treacherous intentions . . . the Hive . . . Donovan . . . the lot!'

'I confided in Bill, yes. I was very sure I could trust him.'

'Your trust was well founded. He protected you well. And I think you persuaded him to deal with Audrey?'

'Yes. He rang her when we got back. He . . .' she hesitated, 'dealt with everything and handed me the negatives afterwards.'

'Don't be so mealy-mouthed, Constable!' Joe's voice hardened. 'He lured her to Waterloo Bridge, grabbed her bag and threw her into a cold, dark, fast-flowing, filthy river where she drowned. You made use of Armitage.'

Tilly breathed deeply. 'You've worked it out, Joe. You know perfectly well we used each other. Had to! Had to!'

'It must have been quite a stand-off, the two of you facing each other over the Dame's dead body – or was she still in her death throes?'

'Death throes, I think,' said Tilly, unperturbed. 'I was determined to have it out with her. She'd killed my sister with her foul corruption and blackmail! We all thought Marianne was grieving still for our mother but she didn't get over it. She got worse in fact. Depression, flashes of temper, strained silences. We couldn't understand what was wrong with her. One day I found her dead in her bed. An overdose. Looking very much as she does here,' she said, gently touching the photograph on the table.

'She'd left a letter for us. Explaining all. Father was beside himself with rage and grief. I had to stop him from rushing out with his gun. No, there are better ways, I told him. More people involved than us: the other victims, the country itself. It needed our discretion. We decided to take it to the very top. And I think they listened to Father. But we waited and waited and nothing seemed to happen. I suppose they were investigating her. Then it became evident that they were taking the easy way out. The creature was going to be allowed to get away with a rap on the knuckles and an early, discreet retreat from public life.

'I hadn't intended to kill her. I'm sure I hadn't. I didn't take a gun or a knife or a dose of cyanide with me. I meant to confront her with her crimes. I'd seen her making eyes at Joanna and I thought, "Oh, Lord! She's not given up! It goes on!" I had a quiet word with Joanna in the powder room and advised her to leave there and then. She was bored out of her brains by that stage and very pleased to take my advice.'

'So, you went up in the lift after all – in your black dress, you did not, at that stage, answer the description the lift boy was given – if indeed Armitage bothered to ask him . . . I have long ago discounted any evidence provided by the sergeant. I expect the Dame was very surprised to see you instead of her chosen prey when you walked in through the open door a minute or two after she let herself in.'

'She was furious, in fact, with me for interfering! I told her who I was, which made her even angrier. I informed her that my sister had confided everything before she killed herself. I told her that she was under surveillance and her days were numbered. Any naval man she encountered was silently observing her, despising her for the traitor she was. I laid it on thick! An avenging angel, you'd have said. I wanted to see her squirm. She went quite mad. She's . . . was . . . a frightening woman when she was angry. You saw on her dead face the faintest echo of what she was capable of. Well, I'd over-steered. She picked up the poker and hit out at me. I dodged and she tried again. I dashed about the room, fearing for my life. She cornered me over by the fireplace. I was so desperate by then I wrenched the poker from her . . . I'm stronger than I look, sir, and I've got used to tackling reprobates.'

Joe nodded. 'Seen you in action, Westhorpe. And then?' Urging her on towards the hardest part of the confession.

'I hit her on the head. I thought I'd just stun her. But once wasn't enough! She wouldn't die! I had to keep hitting her. The blood splashed everywhere. I never heard Armitage climb in until he shouted in his police voice, "Put down that weapon, miss!" Well, I stood for a while pulling myself together. I was covered in blood by then and she was moaning and dying on the floor. But my senses were unbelievably sharp, sir,' she added wonderingly. 'At a moment like that, people in books – and in the dock! – say, "I was confused, mad, didn't know what I was doing, out of my senses." It's not like that. I was very much *in* my senses. Seeing everything with perfect clarity. I looked at Armitage. He had a nice face. Looked dreadfully concerned.' She smiled. 'But I did wonder what he was doing up on the roof at that time of night, climbing in through a window, and I guessed.

'He took off his glove and put a finger to her neck to check for life. "She's a gonner," he said. I solemnly surrendered my weapon. I handed him the poker, sticky end first, and he took it automatically, then, realizing what he'd done, he dropped it as though it were white hot. I grabbed it and threw it through the window. We heard it clanging down over two floors. Impossible to find it in the dark.

'Well, a face to face snarling match ensued! I told him I was a policewoman and a friend of the dead woman. I knew him to be a thief and I'd call the police and tell them I'd found him standing over the body in the act of stealing her emeralds when I'd come up to her room. I'd tell them he'd thrown the poker out of the window and there'd be bound to be a fingerprint on it to clinch my story.'

Joe's face was a stony mask of disgust.

'So, thief and murderer, you stood quarrelling over the body and plotted your way out of it.'

'Yes. He's very clever, you know, your sergeant. It was his idea that I should get out of my black dress and gloves, tidy up in the bathroom and slip into the Dame's reserve evening dress. He put my bloodstained things away in his pocket – a trade-off for the poker. I had something on him and he had something on me. Then we planned what we would say and do.'

'You laid a trail of utter confusion and misdirection for the wretched investigating officer they sent to clear up the mess.'

'We were unlucky it was you they sent. Father made a few calls and got it all diverted. I was allowed to stay on the case, close to you, to see what you were up to. Make sure you didn't arrest any unfortunate innocent party. Keep you spinning in circles. Pity you didn't obey orders. You exasperated some important people.'

'But you *were* lucky with your timing, Tilly – you and Armitage. With the strike looming, the merest whisper of the Dame's treachery would have been disastrous for the government. They could foresee the propaganda value to the opposition. Can you imagine what the socialists, to say nothing of the communists, could have made of such a scandal? A country that can be betrayed to a past and possibly future enemy by one of its ruling classes – its military aristocracy if you like – a woman honoured as a Dame of the British Empire, is a country that needs a radical overhaul. First Sir Roger and now Dame Beatrice. It seems our lords and masters aren't fit to rule over us, as we've long suspected. Time, surely, to sharpen the guillotine? Time for our own People's Revolution? First France, then Russia . . . now it's our turn. No wonder the rug was pulled out from under my feet.'

'The country's much better off without her, Joe.' She reached across and touched his hand. Joe tried not to flinch.

'Will you be able to cut that albatross loose now?'

'Two. There was Audrey as well,' he sullenly reminded her.

'What will you do now?'

'Carry on as though nothing happened, I suppose. A wiser man. A less trusting man. What will you do, Tilly?' he asked carefully, knowing she would not betray her last secret. And, after all, it was none of his business what she did with the rest of her life. He would forget her bright, deceitful face in time. He thought it might take his sergeant a little longer, his sergeant who had so carefully kept her dress, not, as he had at first supposed, as insurance against treachery, but as something much more intimate. Poor old Armitage! He could almost feel sorry for him.

'It's all been a bit of a strain, this last bit, Joe. Perhaps police work isn't for me, after all. I'm resigning my post. I'm going to spend some time away from London.'

'Going anywhere interesting?' he asked conversationally.

'Oh, yes. You'd be very surprised to hear!'

Inspector Cottingham wobbled into Queen Adelaide Court later that week on his bicycle. The streets were littered with burned-out buses and the carcases of strike-breaking vehicles of one sort or another and two wheels were the most reliable way of getting about the seething capital.

He knocked on the closed door of 'Violet Villa'. He'd come on an errand of mercy. If, as Joe and he supposed, Armitage was fleeing the country, even now checking into his first class cabin, the old man was going to be feeling somewhat let down. Cottingham was going to offer to escort him to his appointment up west in Harley Street, if indeed such an appointment existed. The twenty-fourth of May, he'd mentioned. The very least they could do was check that suitable arrangements had been made, Sandilands had said.

He banged again and called, 'Mr Armitage!'

'Yer won't get no answer terday,' said the pram-pushing

escort who'd crowded round him the moment he entered the court.

'No? Why not?'

''Aven't you 'eard? 'E's gorn orf. Both of 'em. They've gorn west. All the way to America!'

'West? Ah, yes,' mumbled Cottingham. 'Seems a long way to go for an eye operation but I suppose they have good surgeons in New York. Devious old devil! Like son, like father, I suppose!'

'Wot you on about, mister? 'Ere – you're the one as fancies cats, int yer?'

She delved into the mass of cushions and blankets in her box pram and produced a cat. The cat. 'Left 'im behind. Auntie Bella can't stand cats. Don't suppose you'd take 'im off our 'ands? Let yer 'ave 'im for a bob!'

Cottingham sighed. 'Well, I suppose we ginger-nuts must stick together . . .'

Rehearsing a speech for his wife, Cottingham tucked the cat into the basket of his bicycle and pedalled back up west.

Chapter Twenty-Nine

'Lydia's asked me to bring you a tea tray, Joe,' said Dorcas, waking him from a blessed snooze in the sunshine on the lawn. 'You've got Assam and scones and jam. We're finishing up last year's strawberry so you can have lots. And *I* made the Madeira cake. Oh, let me pour, you're still half asleep! Can it have been *that* exhausting, working at the Palace for two weeks? She's sent out the *Tatler* as well.'

'Thanks, but I don't read scandal magazines,' said Joe.

'That's very narrow-minded of a man in your questionable employment,' said Dorcas sententiously, using phrases he thought he'd heard his sister use more than once. 'You need to know what all these villains are getting up to . . . who's divorcing whom, who's lost all his money gambling and what that Duchess gets up to on the Riviera. I'll read it and tell you the interesting bits.'

Dorcas fell silent, all her attention on the much-treasured and pored-over society magazine. For a child who never went out in society, Joe had noticed that she knew a very great deal about the way it worked. He was still feeling guilty about his impetuous burdening of Lydia and her family with the refugees from King's Hanger. But at least now, most of the troops had returned to barracks. Orlando had arrived, to beg them to come back. Had even apologized to Joe for wasting police time with his stories. 'Couldn't resist, old man!' he'd had the effrontery to remark happily. 'Can't stand coppers. None of us can see the point of them. Thought I'd make life easier for myself and save you the fag of going around checking up on me.

If you'd just taken my word for it you'd have saved yourself hours of work.' Joe embarked on a defence and explanation of police procedure and gave up after three halting sentences, seeing Orlando's eyes glaze over.

Dorcas had stayed behind to 'go into training' as Lydia put it. 'Give me that girl for two years and I'll have her curtsying to the Queen, just you watch!'

Joe wasn't so sure. Still, he approved of the newly clean face and combed hair, the freshly ironed, red-striped dress.

'Oh, you'll want to see this, Joe!' Dorcas crowed. 'Friends of yours on page twenty. Isn't that the lady policeman you brought down to King's Hanger?' She thrust the magazine in front of him and pointed. 'It's on the "Forthcoming Marriages" page. Look!'

Unwillingly, Joe looked. And looked again. He snatched the magazine from Dorcas and peered at it closely. Tilly's shining face beamed exultantly out at him as she stood posing in a photograph that might have been taken by Dorothy Wilding, so smooth and professional was it. Her groom-to-be stood by her side, with slightly the air of a buffalo surprised at a water-hole, Joe thought unkindly.

'Great heavens!' was the only expletive he could allow himself in the presence of a child and he felt it didn't go far towards expressing his astonishment.

Excitedly, Dorcas took possession again. 'Bloody hell!' she said. 'Who on earth writes this nonsense? Just listen to this!' She read out: ' "In the turbulent wake of broken engagements, disaster and family loss on both sides, the happy couple announce they are putting the years of unhappiness behind them and, after a whirlwind romance, are to be married in the autumn. They will start their new life together in the groom's ancestral estates in Norfolk. On the death of his grandfather the Earl of Brancaster last week, Sir Montagu Mathurin inherited the title and much else. The ring . . ." Look, Joe, you can just make it out. ". . . is a rose diamond set in platinum and was bought for the bride-to-be at Asprey's." Asprey's! Huh! They'll need the "much else" if the bride has such expensive tastes. Will you be sending them a wedding present, Joe?'

'I don't think they'll be expecting one from *me*. But why not? Yes! I'll send them a barrel of oysters from Wheeler's. That should strike the right note. Wonder if she'll remember?'

'Oysters? Are you sure? Well! And there I was, thinking she was your *sergeant's* bit of fluff!'

'Not very ladylike language, Dorcas,' Joe said automatically. 'Good God! I mean – well, well! As you say! To tell the truth, I think my sergeant *was* fond of her, but I'll tell you something else, child. He's had a lucky escape. She wasn't the girl for *him*! Though, come to think of it – she may be *exactly* the girl for Mathurin.'